Night Warriors
Warriors, Book 2

Brenna

Lyons

Will of the
Stone

FIREBORN
PUBLISHING

Fireborn Publishing Copyright Statement

This book is written in US English.

PUBLISHER

FIREBORN
PUBLISHING

**PO Box 5216
Haverhill, MA 01835**

Dedicated to...

Sean and Lisa for badgering me with: "But what happens NEXT?"

Dawn and Beth, my first readers, who compared this series to David and Leigh Eddings' work.

Loves that are just meant to be, like the one in my life.

All the other vampire lovers out there, who run their tongue over their eyeteeth and eat blood-rare steak! You know why this series continues.

Glossary of Warrior Terms

Beast- Beasts are what humans erroneously refer to as vampires. The stories humans tell are obviously not correct, but you can't expect a human to get everything right.

Blutjagd- The "blood hunt." Warriors crave battle with the beasts, as the beasts crave blood. Warriors are tied to beasts in that they sense many of the beasts' special powers. A Warrior can feel the use of coercion, feeding, and other controls of humans. They also feel other Warriors engaged in *Blutjagd*, the death of beasts and Warriors in their range, and the presence of nearby beasts that are not fully ghosted. Rigorous battle training will quell the *Blutjagd* for short periods of time.

Elder- One of the original beasts, the Stone stealers who were damned for their crimes against the Stone and the Warriors. The elders are gifted with powers turned beasts are not, including the ability to reproduce with a *Blutjagdfrau*, the ability to turn other beasts, and the inability to be killed by anyone but a Warrior.

Endspiel- The point in printing when a Warrior must either seal printing or go insane. A Warrior who feels printing may not progress should break printing long before this point. Note that they are rarely smart enough to do so.

Fluch- The Warrior's curse, passed from father or cursed mother to son or daughter. The *Fluch* may be removed from a daughter but never a son. If the *Fluch* is not removed in the *Zeremonie der Freiheit* by the time the menses begin or the *Zeremonie des Schutzes* is performed before freeing, the daughter is cursed to become *Blutjagdfrau*, a female Warrior.

Because elders target *Blutjagdfrau* as mates, Warrior fathers will go to any lengths to free a daughter not marked by the Stone.

Ghosting- A talent that both beasts and Cursed Warriors learn to harness. Ghosting can hide the physical form of Cursed Warriors or beasts and all they hold or carry from each other and humans. In a lesser strength, it can "blur" the image of the user so that humans do not note the passage in particular but still see a person there, which avoids accidental collisions. Even a ghosted beast cannot hide uses of power that a Warrior can track. Warriors sometimes ghost in tandem to remain visible to each other but not other Warriors or beasts.

Krankheit- The "sealing sickness." In the final stage of the transformation between human and Cursed Warrior, at or about the sixteenth birthday in males and a year after the start of menses in females, the sickness strikes. The young Warrior will suffer nausea, vomiting, a high fever, disorientation, dizziness, and may become incoherent. It is usually the only time in a Warrior's life that he or she becomes ill, save morning sickness in a *Blutjagdfrau*.

Printing- Like imprinting, a Warrior becomes tied to his mate for life. He cannot choose another, if she's lost, cannot be unfaithful while she lives, and cannot ever divorce or otherwise dissolve the union. A printed Warrior is the most stable of men, unless his mate or children are endangered or lost. Then, he will suffer the printing madness and may have to be killed by his house. Likewise, a Warrior who breaks printing, even early printing, will suffer for it. A Warrior who breaks printing too close to *Endspiel* will face the madness.

Veriel- The Mad Elder. The Destroyer of Lives. The Mad Deceiver, who led the traitors and freed the elders from the Stone. The most hated and hunted of all the beasts. Fixated on one woman, he would destroy the world to own her. Or... At least, that's what the stories say of him.

Warriors- Also called Cursed Warriors, *Krieger der Nacht, Soldat der Nacht,* or Sons of the Stone. The Warriors were an ancient race of protectors who spawned the beasts and now are driven to hunt their former brothers to extinction.

Stealing Innocence

Prologue

March 15, 2021

Lorian panned his gaze over the packed nightclub, biting back the urge to laugh at the young pups playing at 'creatures of the night.' He supposed he should be thankful that humans found such a fascination with the occult that this garish display of that fascination had lasted for almost half a century.

Lorian hated the term "vampire." Overall, it was a foul, over-commercialized bastardization of his kind, but playing vampire had its uses. It was a simple way to find willing, young women without coercing them—or even hiding what he was.

Not that Lorian had problems attracting women. Quite the contrary. Even in his earliest days as a Cursed Warrior, the days when he was still known as Dado, Lorian had no difficulty having nearly any woman he wanted for the evening. Meeting a woman's eyes and smiling his wolfish smile was typically enough to send her tumbling into the closest bed with him. She would survey his six-feet-three-inch frame, muscular from his years of training, and mentally gauge his sexual prowess in thoughts so loud a first-turned couldn't miss them.

He started moving through the club, rejecting one possible female after another. The one who grasped his backside through the simulation of his jeans was tainted heavily with drugs. The one who murmured an invitation was with someone, and Lorian was in no mood to play at stealing another man's property tonight.

That one... He shuddered. Despite what he was, Lorian occasionally encountered a woman who was more bloodthirsty—he scowled at the pun—than he was. Sometimes, he took the time to educate them in true fear, but tonight was not the night for that.

Tonight, Lorian was restless. He wanted something different. But what? After fifteen hundred years, what hadn't Lorian encountered so many times that he was weary of it?

He paused, scowling deeper as he gave a wide berth to a female protected. One would think that she would avoid places like this, having been bitten once, by one of the remaining turned, but what had she to fear while the Cursed Warriors protected her? She was in more danger from a human pretender than from Lorian.

A woman laughed, and Lorian perked, turning eagerly to the sound. There was something pure in that laugh, something young and full of life, something Lorian hadn't tasted in a very long time. Yes. A touch of innocence was a rare find in this circle.

Lorian had grown complacent over the years. He'd fallen into the habit of taking what was easy to take, what threw itself on him like a bitch in heat instead of what he would have to entice to his bed. He'd forgotten how sweet the blood of a pure heart could be. It was time to change that.

She came into view, a beauty with strawberry blonde hair, pale green eyes, and a spray of freckles over her nose and cheeks. She was dressed in a pair of black jeans and a black satin, boned bustier, but she shifted uncomfortably, as if she was embarrassed to be seen in it.

He moved closer, searching her mind and chuckling at her train of thought. Lorian let his fangs extend just far enough to peek past his lips, his beast as pleased as Lorian was with the possibilities this woman represented.

{Why did I let Angela talk me into this? How is a man supposed to take me seriously in this getup?} She glanced at Lorian and swallowed hard, smoothing the front of her bustier nervously. *{Especially a man like that!}*

Lorian swallowed a laugh. Innocent or not, she was no more immune to him than dozens of other females he'd brushed away as he walked across the club, but this was the one that Lorian wanted. The thrill of the chase was with him, and there would be no settling for what was readily available tonight. That road led to pain and anguish, and Lorian had learned it well long ago.

He put his hand out to her. "Would you care to dance?" he asked in a voice rough in arousal and rich in his old-world roots. *Very old,* he thought without humor.

Her eyes widened, and a pretty, pink blush stained her cheeks. The woman beside her shot her an acid look as she placed her hand in his.

Lorian ignored the other woman studiously, refusing to meet her eyes when she made obvious overtures for exactly that. Her emotions were dark and twisted: disbelief, envy, hatred. She was Angela, the one who'd invited this lovely creature out tonight, certain that her diminutive stature and lack of sophistication would make...*{Haylie}* the perfect offset to her own allure. It galled Angela that Lorian preferred her plain—

He furrowed his brow. *Plain?* Angela found Haylie plain? She was anything but the typical fare this crowd offered him, and for that reason, she was anything but plain.

Lorian led Haylie onto the dance floor and pulled her close to his body, her face only reaching his mid-chest. Haylie hesitated, winding her arms around his neck and stretching her back uncomfortably to accomplish it. He guided her hands to his chest, pressing them to the heat of his body. Haylie gasped at the connection then again as Lorian wrapped his hands around her waist, brushing his thumbs over her hip bones.

He guided her through a sensuous brush of his body to hers. She licked her lip slowly, pressing her crotch to his thigh as he slid his knee between her thighs. Lorian had danced this dance many times, tens of thousands of willing women over the long centuries. The ones who were new to the dance gave him the greatest thrill—the ones like Haylie.

Her eyes were wide in wonder, her breathing edgy and uneven. Lorian heard the rush of blood in her veins and felt the pounding of her heart against his chest. *Yes. Her blood will be sweet in her innocence and wild in her—not fear—apprehension.* It had been well over a century since he'd tasted that combination, and his cock ached in need.

As a Cursed Warrior, he'd believed his drive would make him mad. The drive of a damned beast was easily ten times as uncontrolled. He forced his fangs back, denying his beast's demand to taste Haylie. A prize like this was not to be rushed.

"Do you honestly enjoy these things?" Haylie asked suddenly.

Lorian looked down at the mounds of her breasts, shelved in the bustier, and smiled. "What would those be, my dear?" he teased.

She followed his line of sight and blushed again. "Not— Oh, for pity's sake!"

"Forgive me. Do I like what, precisely?"

Haylie reached up and touched his lips, searching out the tips of his fangs. Lorian shivered, taking the opportunity to suck in her fingertip, savoring her unique flavor on his tongue as he caressed her.

"These," she whispered so low that Lorian would not have heard her over the low throb of music were it not for his superb hearing. Haylie raised her voice, believing him ignorant of her first statement. "Do you really enjoy this scene?"

Lorian nipped playfully at her finger and released it, sighing at the restraint he was showing. "It is a game," he admitted. "It *could* be a very exciting and erotic game," he offered.

"This?" she asked dubiously.

"This."

"How?"

"Let me show you."

Haylie glanced at Angela. The dark-haired woman practically bled and perspired thoughts of wrath. Lorian set his jaw in fury. He would have to educate Angela in fear another night.

He turned Haylie's face back to his gently. "Trust me," he mouthed.

Though she didn't verbally agree, Lorian felt her interest peak. He led her into the dark recesses of the club, corners that were all but unlit. In twenty years, this club hadn't changed much. The recesses were notorious for exhibitionists and voyeurs alike. Over the years, Lorian had taken at least three dozen women in this place, in these dark alcoves.

Haylie lost herself in the gyrations of his lengthening cock against her stomach, pressing herself against him in silent invitation. When the wall met her back, he pressed hard to her, smiling as she moaned. Her scent had the beast all but mad for her.

Lorian cupped Haylie's face, kissing her slowly, dragging his teeth over her tongue and lips. He moved to the line of her jaw and up to her ear. Haylie's hands fisted in the illusion of his black t-shirt and jacket.

"Pretend," he whispered, drawing her earlobe into his mouth. "A vampire wants you. He wants to taste all of you." Lorian trailed his tongue over the seam of her lips. "Your mouth."

She opened for him, sucking at his tongue as she pulled him closer, caressing his fangs with the tip of her tongue. Lorian pulled her into his arms, lifting Haylie until he pressed her to the wall as if he was locked inside her, her legs drawn up over his hips.

"The honey deep inside you," he offered. "He wants to taste that, too."

"And my blood?" she managed weakly.

Lorian kissed at her throat, tracing the tip of his tongue over her. He suckled at her, teasing her with more, marking her in the human way. Haylie pressed to him, grasping his hair and holding his head to her.

He eased away slowly. "Are love bites really so bad?" he asked.

"No," she admitted, panting.

Lorian teased her nipple through the black satin. "Let me teach you. Let me teach you what loving a vampire is."

She shivered. "Soulless. Heartless. Dead."

"No. Alive and warm. A vampire isn't cruel. He hungers. He needs, and he will give you as much pleasure as you give him."

That was a lie. Not even Haylie could give Lorian true pleasure. She could still the need for a night or two. She could ease the emptiness and longing for everything he'd lost when he went beast. He could live vicariously through her pleasure, tasting distracting shades of kind emotions while he fed from her.

Any strong emotion in feeding charged him beyond the taking of blood, but kind emotions were best. The faint touch of what Lorian couldn't feel alone anymore drew him to Haylie. He hadn't felt pure desire without design in a long time, only once that he could recall in his lifetime as a Cursed Warrior—and that had been a lie.

Lorian eased her breast out of the bustier, lowering his mouth to the peak. "He wants to taste all of you, Haylie. Can he?"

"Here?" she asked nervously. She looked around, gasping at the sight of the couple further down the wall. They were just barely visible in the near darkness for her, though they were fully on display for Lorian.

Haylie's reactions were a jumble of half-formed impressions that tickled his dark sense of humor. She was horrified and amazed, repulsed and aroused.

Lorian suckled at her breast more fervently. Haylie moaned, her fingers winding in his hair as the other woman dropped to her knees and took her lover in her mouth.

The fool. Never trust a woman who is that eager to pleasure you.

He freed her other breast, smiling as he licked at the hard bead of the nipple, ready for him before he touched it. She shivered, her gaze darting between Lorian's mouth and the length of the other man disappearing between the kneeling woman's lips. Haylie's inhibitions were being forgotten, her objections falling away. She stroked his cock distractedly, but her mind still rebelled at the woman on her knees in the dark corner of the club—*thank the gods.*

The other man pulled his woman to her feet and captured her in a bruising kiss. He whirled her around and pressed her hands to the wall, mounting her with a grunt of satisfaction. Haylie shied, shaking her head. The image was too much for her.

Lorian nodded. "I agree. Not here. Name a place," he offered. "I am not like that beast."

Liar. How many times have I taken pleasure like that—in the early years before I learned control of my beast...and even recently with a willing wanton? He was undeniably a damned beast, but Lorian hadn't taken a woman like Haylie with so little regard in a thousand years. Not since he had gotten over Riberta—

He winced. He wouldn't think about Riberta now. His only regret in how that particular woman had died was that Jörg hadn't known about her talents. Lorian would gladly have told his esteemed youngest brother all he knew just to watch her die in a way more fitting of her crimes.

Haylie met his eyes hopefully, her quaking fingers still laid over his rigid length. She was confused, afraid to believe him, though she ached to experience what he offered.

"Anywhere," he offered. "Anything you want, Haylie."

She nodded. "My place is close."

Lorian smiled, arranging her breasts carefully back into her bustier. He slid her down his body until she settled shakily on her strappy heels. He steadied her for their trek across the club.

Halfway to the door, a vision from Lorian's darkest nightmares appeared in the form of a Night Warrior—a young one. Lorian held his breath for one heart-stopping moment while he assured himself that it wasn't Hunter of *König*-Crossbearer. Hunter was the only Warrior alive who had a chance of killing Lorian.

He scowled, wishing he had paid more attention to his enemies in recent years. The boy was either one of Stephen or Colin's sons. There were so many *Jäger* boys, Lorian hadn't seen the point in identifying them all, and taking the time to ask one of his turned to identify the boy was worth even less of his time.

It wasn't unusual for a Warrior to show up here. The club was a perfect cover for beasts, and what better break for a roving Night Warrior than coming to this club? Lorian wondered, not for the first time, if the Warriors made use of the dark recesses to find release while they were here.

Lorian smiled. He could ghost them both fully and slip past the unsuspecting young Warrior, but there was a better option, a way to humiliate the pup and teach that vicious she-beast Angela a lesson at the same time.

He picked his two subjects carefully, sending a

powerful coercion over them. The pup raised his head, bloodlust swelling in an impressive *Blutjagd* for one so young. There was no searching. The Warrior tracked the coercion back to his location without difficulty. That not an issue, Lorian released the light ghosting he'd been maintaining all evening. Warriors would scramble to the location, but he was certain the pup was the only one close enough to be of concern.

The first of Lorian's puppets reached Angela, sweeping her up with offers of sex and more. The fool was flattered—until the second man reached her, doing the same. The duo pulled at her and punched at each other. Angela panicked at her inability to escape them.

The Warrior unsheathed his weapon and pushed his way through the crowd toward his 'prey.'

As if I am prey to the likes of you, infant. Lorian smiled, letting his fangs extend fully. He jerked his head toward the struggling trio as he sent another flurry of coercion to still the bouncers and management heading into the fray. The struggle grew from three to five to nine bodies in the blink of an eye.

The pup faltered, gleaning the challenge at last. He had a choice—his duty to end Lorian or his duty to protect the humans being injured by the elder's actions. Even if the Warrior killed Lorian, a bar fight like this wouldn't end with his death. Lorian had chosen his coercion well. The combatants became more numerous with every passing moment. Too soon, even the bouncers wouldn't be able to stop it, even without Lorian's push to continue fighting.

Lorian chuckled as the Warrior sheathed his weapon and turned into the fray with a series of curses, doing his best to end it without injuring the

11

humans further. *Good choice, Warrior. You have no idea how close you came to dying at my hand tonight.* Lorian was an elder, and he was fated to die by *König* hands. No mere *Jäger* pup could stand against him.

"Something wrong?" Haylie asked, struggling to peer over the shoulders of the crowd.

"Bar fight. We should go before the police get here."

She nodded. "Or before we get our heads broken open," she agreed.

Lorian cast one last mocking smile at the pup's back. He'd hold his coercion for a few more minutes before he let the humans come to their senses. In the end, the Warrior would suffer instruction at his lord's hand, and Angela would think twice about baiting men. Perhaps she wouldn't die as Riberta had.

* * * *

Haylie closed the door to her apartment, an attack of nerves making her hand tremble against the lock. Lorian cupped her waist and drew her to his body, his erection pulsing at the line of hooks down her back.

She shivered. "You're hungry." *{I hope he's as hungry as he seems.}*

Her internal musings brought a wry smile to his face. She had no clue how hungry he was; all of his appetites screamed at him for satiation, and Haylie could feed them well. "Yes. I am." He ran his fingers up the line of hooks, releasing the first two as he kissed the column of her neck. "Vampires live to taste a woman like you."

Haylie nodded, as he released more of the hooks. "Would a vampire take such care?" she asked.

"An elder would, though the urge to destroy this garment would be nearly maddening." *Nearly? It is maddening.*

"Why don't you?"

Lorian stilled. "You wouldn't mind it?" His cock ached at the game they were playing. Lorian hated the word "vampire," but he would gladly play vampire for Haylie for the rush of her excitement.

"I hate this outfit," she assured him. "It was Angela's idea."

He grasped the heavy material of the bustier between his hands and tore it in two, letting it fall away as he cupped her breasts. Haylie whimpered in a combination of arousal and apprehension.

"Turn for me," he requested, crowding her body to the door. Lorian knelt and suckled at her breast, steadying Haylie as he removed her heels.

"How old is my vampire?" she whispered.

Lorian shivered at the longing in her voice, nipping her breast with his fangs as he released her. "The one who wants you is the oldest alive by centuries, the elder Lorian. He is more than fifteen hundred years old, and his hungers are very strong."

She played her fingers in his hair. "How strong?"

He grasped the waistband of her jeans and ripped them to a point deep on her thigh. "Very strong."

Haylie watched, wide-eyed and barely breathing, as Lorian peeled the fabric away and tasted the skin he uncovered. He traced the edges of her little red panties—crushed silk, pushing the jeans down her legs and past her knees.

Lorian pulled her feet up one at a time to remove the jeans. He planted his lips as high as he could between her thighs. "Open for me," he instructed her.

She spread her feet wide, crying out as Lorian snaked his tongue past the silk and deep inside her without preamble. Haylie grasped at his dark curls, her legs trembling in the cascade of sensation that ripped through her.

"That's hungry," she noted breathlessly.

Lorian groaned into her body. He was more than hungry; he was ravenous. It seemed he'd wanted to play with an innocent forever. He pushed the silk aside, scraping his teeth over her engorged flesh. The blood pumped in her veins, calling to the beast howling inside him.

Haylie's fists tightened in his hair. "Please, Lorian," she begged.

He resolved to send her over in a style she'd never forget. It was a trick he hadn't used on a woman in decades. As Haylie's body reached for the elusive orgasm beating at her senses, he caused his tongue to thicken, stretching her body around him.

Had he done it earlier, she would have questioned it, been frightened by the unfamiliar sensation. Haylie screamed in pleasure, begging for more breathlessly.

Lorian lengthened his tongue, leaving the thick shaft rasping inside her, as he nipped at her clit, at the neglected center of her sensation. Haylie's muscles locked in surprise and the coming wash of orgasm. He suckled hard on her hooded nub and sent her over.

Her mind wouldn't be buried forever. Lorian wanted her awash in a pleasant confusion. He left her body and caught her as Haylie fell into his arms, trembling. He moved for the bed at a speed no being on Earth could match, not even one of the turned beasts, dispelling the illusion of clothing so that he was nude when he ripped away the soaked silk crotch of her panties and filled her in a single stroke.

Haylie's hands grasped at his shoulders as he thrust deeper within her, her muddled mind opining that she should push him away even as she dragged him closer, deeper into her. She moved under him, seeking all he had to give.

Lorian nodded, his fangs lengthening in anticipation. "Will you feed me in every way?" he asked. He knew she was willing, but asking would increase her pleasure and his by extension.

"Yes. Taste all of me."

He didn't hesitate, sinking his fangs deep in her neck and erasing the pain automatically. Lorian closed his eyes, basking in memories of emotions, in the tidal wave of her pleasure as he took her over again.

"Let me drink you," she whispered.

Lorian shuddered at her unintended double meaning. Drinking of him as he was drinking of her would be lethal for her. He'd learned that the hard way.

"Let me taste you," she asked again.

He groaned in need. Lorian avoided that pleasure as a rule, though it had once been his favorite way to climax.

Riberta danced behind his eyes. "Are you saying you don't want me, Dado?" *She chuckled as she stroked his aching cock.* "Your body says otherwise."

Oh, yes. He wanted her, but the laws would see him dead. Riberta knew he wanted her, and so she came to Dado again and again, trying to tempt him with her body. He guided her hand away, scowling down at her. "If I take your barrier, your brother will kill me."

She pressed her body to him. "You wouldn't be the only Warrior who hasn't lived the sanctions," she taunted. "We women talk."

"Who?" he growled, grasping her arms. His rational mind argued touching her, but he was near mad in fury. "How?" Who was breaking the sanctions while Dado was near mad in keeping them, and how did he hope to keep from being caught at it?

"How?" Riberta repeated. She pulled at the lacing on his leggings. "You are not the only man who likes a woman's mouth. It leaves no proof, Dado."

He stood, frozen in a surge of need, as she unlaced him. Dado knew he should stop her, but something dark and dangerous argued his right to a woman who threw herself at him so willingly. She was baiting him. Who could turn her away?

"What do you want from me?" he asked, shaking. Could he make this bargain—whatever it was?

"Choose me."

Dado hesitated, groaning as she took him in her hand and stroked him.

"Your cock is begging for me. Or—does it want someone else?" She pouted, her blue eyes glowing in implied knowledge.

"No," he admitted. "It wants you." Anything you want if you give me this.

"Choose me." Riberta went to her knees and slid most of his length into the hot, moist, welcoming depths of her mouth.

Dado pulled her deeper, thrusting into her hopelessly until he exploded for her. "Yes," he gasped. "I will choose you."

Lorian closed his feeding site. The memories of Riberta made him ache for what he'd denied himself for so long. He rolled to his back, pulling Haylie around him again.

His mind worked furiously as he pistoned in and out of her willing body. Haylie wasn't Riberta. She wasn't offering to serve every man around in hopes of her title. *In hopes of making men fight for her to satisfy her ego.*

Lorian had been damned for one reason. He'd been the only Warrior stupid enough to fall for Riberta's offer. Marclef demanded as many willing beasts as he could muster, and he'd ordered Tilbrand to use any means necessary to get his volunteers.

Dado had been a coward, afraid to die at Wil's hand and willing to be damned to live another night, while Riberta turned her whiles on Ger within a day of Dado's fall from grace. *A coward! At least Jörg chose death and had to be convinced another way.* He sobered. Jörg had loved his woman, while Dado had simply taken what was readily available. How he wished he'd waited for the one he loved.

Now I will never know love. But I can know other pleasures. "You want to taste me?" he panted, his resistance crumbling.

Haylie shot him a hungry look and ran her hand down his sweat-coated abdomen to their locked bodies. Gone was the innocent. This woman was lust unleashed.

His cock pulsed in acceptance. "Take me," he ordered.

She pushed off of him and buried her face in his

lap, his length disappearing between her lips. Haylie met his eyes as she worked him in and out. She drove him on ruthlessly.

Lorian felt every muscle tense. Yes. This was perfect. His formidable brothers were long dead. No one was waiting to use this moment against him. He cried out as he filled her throat with his seed. He shivered as she licked the head slowly. Not even Riberta had done that.

Haylie crawled up his body, brushing her breasts over his chest, attempting to entice him into her body again. Lorian took her mouth feverishly, tasting himself in her.

"Don't leave," she offered.

Lorian nipped at her chin. "A vampire always leaves after he's fed."

"Why?"

"He has enemies." Lorian felt the faint stirrings of the pup from the club, as he knew he soon would. He pushed from the bed and strode to the window, opening it a few inches.

Haylie sat up, watching him curiously. "Does he ever return?" she asked.

"Perhaps. Would you like me to return?"

Her arousal was instantaneous. "Yes."

"My enemy will offer you his protection. If you refuse it, I will come to you again."

She furrowed her brow. "Protection from what?" She looked to the pounding on the door in confusion.

"From me, Haylie."

Lorian waited until she looked back at him then dematerialized. She paled, and her fingers went to the faint marks at her throat.

The pup bypassed her locks and came to her. "Are you all right?" the Warrior asked urgently.

Lorian streamed away before she could answer. *The choice is yours, Haylie.*

* * * *

Lorian surveyed the scene in the clearing, squeezing his eyes to a slit behind the dark glasses. The morning sun didn't reach him deep in the recesses of the trees, but the glare of it shining on the grass and flowers made his eyes water and heart ache for the freedoms he could no longer have.

Three youngsters played in the clearing, two of them boys near—or perhaps just after—first night, armed even in play. They were *Schwertträger* and not *Jäger*; he'd traveled half the night to track the girl this time, but he'd travel much further to see her...and had many times.

Corwyn Lord *Jäger*, elder hunter and Stone lord, stood guard over the young ones in the ascending sun. Like Lorian, he wore dark glasses to protect his predator's eyes. Unlike the elder, he could walk the sun with impunity.

Lorian ignored them all and focused on the girl. She was the reason the others were armed and watchful. Erin was never alone. Warriors held position at her door and window every moment she slept and trailed in her wake every other moment of her life, serious Warriors who were ready to kill or die at a moment's notice.

He came to see her often, ghosting in to watch her sleep and accepting the pain of facing the sun to watch her at play. Erin was his, *Blutjagdfrau,* born to be his bride, the one who could give Lorian what he'd ached for since the night he went beast—companionship and children.

It shouldn't have surprised Lorian that Erin looked like Regana. Stone-Chosen were always of a type. He remembered what Regana looked like at the same age, and the resemblance almost sent him from her the first time. It was no wonder that Jörg was so intent, and the fear of Jörg's wrath was a hard thing to shake.

But, Jörg was dead. All his brethren lay dead, all for the stupidity of trying to possess or kill Erin's mother. Jayde had been fully trained when the others came for her. Lorian hadn't lived this long by making foolish moves like that, and he still wasn't stupid enough to start now.

He'd bide his time until Erin was loosely guarded and take her before she began her training, avoiding her older brother Hunter if he could. It was the only way that Lorian would live long enough to enjoy his bride and children.

He sucked in his breath in surprise as the Frisbee caught in a wind shear and flew his direction. Erin turned, chasing it. Her curls bounced and flew about her face, and her color was high. She laughed as the Frisbee landed at the edge of the woods.

She stopped little more than an arm's length away, close enough for Lorian to grab if the need arose. He watched her in awe, wrapped in the light streaming over the trees as he was bathed in shadow. Lorian scanned his gaze over her, not fully grown but already a woman in her own right. Her breasts were small mounds and her waist narrow over the lush hips that would support his sons...and perhaps daughters. Erin dropped to one knee and grasped the Frisbee.

Lorian stilled, taking in her scent on the wind. His fangs lengthened in response. Erin was clean and innocent. She smelled of sunshine and her woman's blood. He shivered in the knowledge that her body was ready for him. The mad urge to reach into the light to touch her assaulted him.

Erin shifted, rising to her feet slowly. Lorian locked on the bracer that held her parents' amulet to her wrist, fury rising in him. That was the first thing that had to go—and quickly. No bit of cursed metal was going to steal his bride from him. Erin would take her place as she had been born to.

She gasped, staring into the trees, her eyes going wide while she white-knuckled the Frisbee. Erin took a step back, her eyes darting this way and that, scanning over his position, as if she was tracking him. Lorian stiffened as an edge of *Blutjagd* burned under her skin, a trainee's level, still invisible to the Cursed Warriors who surrounded her. He nodded in understanding. Erin had begun the change that would make her his. It wouldn't be long until her parents and Corwyn realized it. Her training would start very soon.

The time had come. Lorian hadn't planned to take her this early, but he had to have her unprinted and untrained, fully innocent. That meant he had to take her soon, before she got more than a month or two into her training—at the height of her cycle, if he could arrange it.

Her eyes locked firmly on his position, and she took another step back into the light. Lorian watched the move curiously, meeting her eyes fully. Erin felt his presence. She looked at him instead of through him. No Warrior saw through his ghosting, not even a glimmer. Even Jörg couldn't match Lorian's prowess in ghosting, and Jörg had excelled at everything.

A movement over her shoulder caught his attention. Lorian watched Corwyn stride toward his granddaughter, the lord's brow furrowed and one hand resting on the hilt of his sacred weapon. The two young Warriors fell in behind him, sensing at last that something was wrong.

Lorian almost laughed at that. He could have taken his bride and been gone before the pups realized danger was near had it been night. He looked at the bracer in annoyance—*were it not for that!*

Erin didn't seem to note their approach. When Corwyn touched her shoulder, she jumped, dropping the Frisbee at his feet, and turned her wide-eyed, pale face to him. She fell into her grandfather's arms, shivering.

Lorian nodded grimly. She'd been trained to fear her place. They'd turned her against him already, as Lorian knew they would.

Corwyn scanned the trees, lit up for battle, his fury a living force worthy of his title of elder hunter. "What did you see?" he whispered to the girl.

The younger Warriors launched to his side, hands on their weapons.

"What did you feel?" he continued.

"I don't know." She faltered. "S-something. There's something there."

"Where?" one of the boys demanded.

She turned her gaze back to Lorian, meeting his eyes though she could not see him with her physical form. Erin motioned to him. "There. Close. Too close." She shuddered and pulled further away, straining against the lord's embrace, indicating that she didn't consider him protection enough.

And she shouldn't.

Corwyn nodded and pushed her into the quiet Warrior's hands. "Take her to the house—now," he ordered. "Tell the others we're leaving. They have half an hour to pack."

He nodded and took Erin by the arm. "Yes, my lord," he rumbled.

Lorian bit back a groan as she was swept away from him. Warriors had gathered to meet them before they made it to the top of the hillside, probably investigating the blaze of *Blutjagd* from the Warriors standing between Lorian and his chosen mate.

"Do you honestly believe that she felt something?" the young Warrior asked. "It's so bright...the height of the day."

Corwyn nodded. "I have no doubts. Pack. He'll go to ground before we find him. The best we can hope for is to leave him far behind."

"Yes, my lord." He sprinted for the Warriors who had closed ranks around Erin.

Lorian nodded. He'd have to take her soon, but he needed leverage. Erin had to give up her amulet willingly. He considered the knot of her family, leading her inside, and Lorian smiled. Which of them would be her weak spot? He'd have to watch them closely to know her mind.

He sighed, praying to gods who had forsaken him that Hunter wasn't her weak spot. Her older brother was the only member of her family who posed a danger to Lorian, which meant that the Stone, *in its amusement*, would set him as her weak link to thwart Lorian.

In the meantime, Lorian had training to engage in. His bride was an innocent. Lorian would have to practice his technique with the most innocent women he could draw to him in preparation for winning his mate. Once Erin was properly enthralled with him and printed willingly— He smiled. She could never be separated from him.

He played at Haylie's feed thread, smiling that she'd refused the amulet. Lorian would have his playmate, a playmate to give him his pleasures and keep him sane while he practiced at stealing innocence.

"Goodbye, Erin," he whispered, as the door closed behind her. Lorian laughed aloud at Corwyn's look of shock. "We will see each other again, my mate," he promised. "They cannot take you anywhere that I cannot follow." He dematerialized and streamed away, as the Lord *Jäger* launched toward him.

König Cursebreakers

Chapter One

April 17, 2021

Nineteen-year-old Hunter Jonas of Crossbearer, the *König* prince, stared at the book in his lap and sighed.

His grandfather raised an eyebrow over his own volume. "Problem, Hunter?"

Hunter panned his gaze over the old man. It wasn't hard to see Corwyn Lord Hunter, elder hunter and Stone lord, as every title he had. The man was strong—even into his seventies, bold, practically fearless, wise, and had seen more hurt than even a Cursed Warrior deserved in his lifetime.

"I'm just not sure I'm prepared for this. I always assumed that I'd live like the other *Königs* forever—traveling, seeing everything." He shrugged. "I never thought I'd be called to be a house lord of any house but *König*."

Then the Stone—the inconstant, self-serving Stone—had made the latest of many life-altering decrees. The mysterious plan to save *Haus Kreuzträger* revolved around the *König* prince taking his father's place as lord of the house while Talon remained head of *König*.

The reason was obvious. *König* was to be the women's house. The *Blutjagdfrau* were destined to be wanderers, to mate and drag their husbands into *König*. Hunter, as the prince, could be relegated to more mundane tasks. He was *Krieger der Nacht*, a Night Warrior, something the women would never be permitted to be. Hunter could—and should—hunt the night, which made him the perfect answer to Crossbearer's problems.

When Talon married his mother, Jayde Marie of Hunter-Crossbearer, elder killer and *Blutjagdfrau*, he was forced to relinquish his place in Crossbearer range to protect his wife. It looked as if the Cross family would die as its own house with that match. The last of his line, the family was willing to make the sacrifice of Talon in exchange for the birth of the true elder killers that would come from the mating between a *Blutjagdfrau* and Warrior, the foretold end to this seemingly endless war. But the Stone likes its puzzles, and this puzzle meant that the freedoms Hunter loved were about to be lost to him forever.

True elder killers— Hunter almost laughed at that. The *König* name was something hard to live up to. His grandfathers, Corwyn Hunter and Piers Cross, were both elder hunters. His mother had the distinction of being the only Warrior in history to kill the first elder she ever encountered. Talon almost died at the elder Veriel's hands before Jayde intervened, but that was his priming run. Since that time, Talon had killed three elders—one in single combat and two with the help of other Warriors. It was jokingly said that Hunter had the assist on the last of those kills, since his newborn screams had distracted the elder long enough for his mother to plant a blade in him from her birthing bed and his father to deal the killing blow.

Hunter shook his head hopelessly. "It's just..."

Corwyn nodded in understanding. "Frightening," he decided.

Hunter's eyes widened in surprise. "I wouldn't say," he began proudly.

"It's perfectly normal, Hunter. I was terrified when the seal passed to me. At least Piers will be actively grooming you for the job over the next few years. Jonas acted as if he would live forever. I was unprepared for the duty of house lord in the extreme."

Hunter nodded slowly. Unprepared— Yes, Corwyn still blamed his youth and inexperience for the loss of his wife and daughter. It took twenty-four years for the fickle Stone to bring Jayde back home to the Warriors...with no memory of the few hours she'd had in their midst at birth. Jayde's indoctrination into the life had been a hard one, but Talon had been there for her. In the end, that was enough for her.

"I just wish my father would take his place first. He's the next in line."

Corwyn set his book down and steepled his fingers in front of his face. "You know he can't. When he and Jayde married, Talon had to relinquish that life. He can never be Talon Cross without being Lord *König* now. Even if Jayde died, there's Erin to protect."

Ah, yes...Erin. The Stone threw them another loop, in the form of Erin. One *Blutjagdfrau* wasn't trouble enough. It marked Erin, too. She was the belle of the ball. Their princess was twelve now, and that was no easy age. Though Hunter loved his sister dearly, Erin could try the patience of the Stone. Not to mention, being the young princess meant Erin would have the life Hunter wanted and was being denied. She would never have the drudgery of running a range.

Hunter scowled. "Until Erin mates, and a Warrior relinquishes his range for her."

"You don't understand why she seems favored." His grandfather smiled crookedly.

"Seems, hell! Erin *is* favored. I'm capable of producing elder killers, too. I'm marked. I'm chosen."

"You aren't hunted—not like Erin will be. Remember why your mother named her Erin. Being hunted cost Jayde her life with us."

Hunter felt his cheeks heat at the rebuke. His mother had been born as Erin Allison Hunter, but Veriel's attempt to take her before she could be freed resulted in her complete loss by both sides for all those years. She came back as Jayde Marie Albright, the name her adoptive parents had given her, based on the *Jäger* seal on her amulet.

"I seem to remember that there was a war the day I was born," Hunter reminded his grandfather. "You were injured in the fight, as I recall."

"You won't be forced to serve as a sexual slave to a beast elder if you're defeated. You won't be pursued as a mate by every Warrior of marriageable age. You have no choice but to marry a human. Even if you meet the freed daughter of a house that you desire, she will still be human."

"Is that why you sneak in training for Erin?"

Corwyn darkened, and his eyes hardened. "It isn't formal training, Hunter. You know that. Your parents won't allow it yet. The first cursed were permitted to play at battle together from the time they could hold a wooden blade, and Regana was permitted to play with them. As Stone-Chosen, Sibold permitted it."

"She was Regana. She was Raga," Hunter countered. "That was different. Erin doesn't have the mark of Ani like our mother does. She isn't Raga."

"The Stone says it's no different. Erin is Stone-Chosen and marked, though the damned thing won't tell me what she's chosen for. It does insist that she should be treated as all Stone-Chosen women have been treated so far. Jayde's upbringing was orchestrated for her survival to mating. Erin's must be as well. So, I do what must be done."

More Stone secrets? Hunter shook his head in annoyance. The Stone had a love of puzzles. It would give riddles or remain silent to amuse Itself, until a Warrior figured out what was so damned funny this time. So, Erin needed training that the sanctions and her parents didn't approve of. What was so funny this time?

"What makes Erin's children so important?" Hunter asked suddenly. Hadn't Corwyn said that often enough? Hadn't he proclaimed how important *her* children would be?

"The Stone says they are, and I can't speak for the Stone, but I imagine that each generation of *Blutjagdfrau* that intermarries with the Warriors will produce a stronger stock. Your children will be superior, because they're yours, but Erin's will be more so."

Hunter nodded. "I suppose that makes sense."

Their heads swung around as Erin charged into the room, looking rather jittery. Hunter groaned, wondering what trouble she had gotten into this time.

"What is it, Erin?" Hunter asked in exasperation.

"Something's coming. Coming fast," she replied urgently. Erin looked over her shoulder and back quickly, swinging the fan of small braids she loved so dearly around her head in a wave.

Hunter groaned again. "Erin, please play Warrior somewhere else. The adults want to talk."

His sister narrowed her eyes and darkened in anger, looking very much like Corwyn had a few minutes earlier. She shook her head furiously, tossing the braids in a cloud around her face. "Are you dense?" she demanded. "Can't you feel it?"

"Erin! Just stop it. There are two Warriors sitting right here. If something was coming, we'd feel it, not you. Your curse isn't even due for another four years," he muttered. "Now, go away."

She stamped her bare foot in annoyance. "Fine. Ignore me. It's your skin, Warrior. I'm going to the training room. At least I'll have weapons available to me when they take you out." Erin turned on her heel and ducked his hand as Hunter reached for her.

"You're not allowed to handle sacred weapons yet," he bellowed after her. Despite what Corwyn was doing, the sanctions clearly stated that.

"Yeah? Well, tell me about it when you learn to sense like a normal person," she shot back sarcastically.

Erin started to storm away, but Corwyn vaulted across the room to her and snagged her arm. Hunter smiled at the thought that Erin was about to get a little well-deserved discipline, but his grandfather knelt to her level with earnest concern.

"What do you feel, Erin?" Corwyn asked. "Quickly now. Tell me. What do you feel?"

"Something   mean   is coming...something...dark...cold. The night is moving." Erin grimaced then shivered, shifting her weight from foot to foot nervously, bending her knees slightly and adopting a defensive stance seemingly without noticing that she had. "I don't like it. It's close."

"How close?" he demanded.

"I can't tell. Too close. Let's leave, Grandpa," she pleaded, pulling at his arm ineffectually. "Please, we have to leave. We have to leave, now!" Her eyes were wide and wild and her face pale. Her hand clutched at Corwyn's sleeve, tearing the black fabric at the shoulder seam, her arm muscles tensing, her breathing going ragged.

Hunter watched her, cataloging every move in confusion. "What the hell..." Erin didn't fear anything, but she was shaking in terror, nonetheless. This was panic. It was something primal, something he'd never seen or experienced before.

Corwyn touched her face, gently soothing her. "It's too late for that, Erin. Get your shoes and hide in the training room where the Stone will protect you. Stay in there, no matter what you hear. Unless I come for you...or Hunter does, stay there. We won't call for you. Do you understand me? We won't call; we will come for you."

She nodded sadly and bolted from the room.

Corwyn stood and unsheathed his weapon, taking a deep breath to center himself. "Get up, Hunter," he ordered gruffly. "We'll have an enemy to fight shortly."

"I don't sense anything," Hunter protested, taking to his feet nervously.

Corwyn nodded, his jaw tightening. "Anna— My wife did this more than once. The Stone had planned for her to bear Jayde for me. Though it never touched her directly, it protected Anna by announcing danger to her." He motioned to the doorway Erin left by with his blade. "Just like that, Hunter. Prepare yourself for a battle. They're coming," he asserted.

"No beast ghosts that perfectly. I always sense something. You know that."

It was a gift Hunter had, a gift that made him invaluable in battle. Despite the scene a month earlier in Armen range, there had been no indications that Erin could sense a beast. Hunter had never believed that Erin's reaction in the woods was more than her wild imagination. He sobered. Corwyn believed her. Their grandfather was the only one who'd believed her that day. Everyone else had acted, because they'd trusted Corwyn's instincts...not Erin's.

Corwyn shook his head. "You've never met an elder before. The last time you encountered one was the day you were born."

"Lorian?" Hunter breathed in shock. "Here?"

"Yes."

It was a quiet confirmation, too calm to be a comfort. Corwyn was ready to die. That unnerved Hunter worse than the older man's usual battle style.

"Why would Lorian come here now?"

"My guess is that he knows how unprotected Erin is. She has only us tonight."

"He intends to take her, doesn't he?"

Corwyn nodded.

"But, she hasn't reached change," Hunter noted with a sick certainty that he knew what was coming.

"Does Erin bleed? It's hard to miss her maturing body. Has she started her cycles?"

Hunter blushed and nodded. Erin had started cycling months earlier. He had been teasing her unmercifully about her attendant aches and pains of womanhood, including the bras she despised but Jayde insisted on.

"But, she's still human," he pleaded.

"All the better to pleasure and amuse him until she can bear his child. Lorian wants Erin defenseless. He doesn't want her able to fight him."

Hunter felt bile rising as a foul wave in his throat. "Never!" *Blutjagd* lit his blood up like a volcano. "Not Erin. He can't have her."

"She's your responsibility, Hunter. Even if Crossbearer dies in the exchange, Lorian must not take Erin."

"Only if I die." An image of Erin stamping her foot and shaking her braids assaulted him, fueling Hunter's rage. "Here they come," he commented coolly.

The first wave of beasts consisted of four high-level turned. Hunter fought in a haze, barely registering their names before taking the lives of three of them to Corwyn's one. By the time the next six arrived, his entire system was humming. Lorian was closing.

Hunter's muscles burned as he fought, but visions of Erin—newly-born and placed in his arms while their mother shielded them both with her body and her blades—stoked his bloodlust for more. It was him now. Hunter was placing his body and blades between the beasts and Erin. She should be safe in the training room. The Stone was there to protect her, as long as she stayed put.

He watched Corwyn out of the corner of his eye. The Lord Hunter was in his seventies now, and though honor demanded he never reveal it, he was flagging. A beast would take him soon, as one took Colin only a few years before. Hunter only hoped it wouldn't happen that night.

So far, Erin had been well-insulated against the

harsher realities—at least in practical experience. She read every volume she encountered ravenously, but Erin hadn't seen, with her own eyes, how the beasts killed and died.

Part of it was the fact that the *Königs* were hard to track, but even more was the fact that the beasts avoided their family like the plague. Unless forced to battle by an elder, no beast sought out the elder killers. Since Erin's birth, the *Königs* had only had a half dozen encounters with beasts that they hadn't specifically sought out.

A beast suddenly materialized behind his grandfather, and Hunter shouted Corwyn's name in warning. As Hunter took the heart of the beast in front of him and his grandfather did the same, the new beast—the elder Lorian—thrust his hand through Corwyn's back and ripped out his beating heart. Hunter tramped back his nausea painfully. He had never seen such a vicious, cold attack. Lorian smiled as he sank his fangs to drink from the still-leaking organ. Having drained it, he dropped it with a sickening splat next to Corwyn's fallen form.

"A barbaric way to kill that I picked up from Resten," Lorian informed the young Warrior. "It doesn't give the rush of truly feeding, but it is quick and effective."

"And doesn't allow your mind to wander," Hunter noted evenly.

"That does tend to leave one open to attack," he admitted.

"I should probably remind you that Resten died at Pauwel's hands for his barbaric ways," Hunter warned.

Lorian scowled. "A lie told for more than fifteen

centuries and no better a lie today. Jörg had all but killed Resten already. Only the fact that he was constrained from doing so stopped him from taking the killing blow himself. He gifted your great-sire Pauwel with the killing blow on a half-dead beast elder to avenge himself."

"Avenge? Why would Veriel want to kill Resten? You can't even tell plausible lies."

Lorian laughed bitterly. "For the loss of his woman, Jörg would kill anyone in his way. It was fitting that he should go beast. He always was a beast," he finished distastefully.

"What woman? Veriel went beast before the battle. He had no woman," Hunter countered.

"Oh, he did—taken deceitfully and in a beastly manner, but Jörg had her, again and again. Gawen would have killed him for it, but luckily for Jörg, he went beast before that could happen."

"You're saying Veriel went beast because he would have faced Gawen's blades for taking Regana?" Hunter asked in disbelief. Some part of him ached that Corwyn hadn't lived to uncover the knowledge he'd sought for so long, the secrets of Regana and Veriel.

"No, Jörg didn't care if he faced Gawen's blades. Such was his madness, but Resten and Marclef threatened him with Regana's death as well—for baiting him to madness. It was a lie, of course. Jörg was the source of his own madness."

"Why tell me this, now?" Hunter asked in confusion.

"Marclef made promises to get his beasts."

Hunter set his jaw angrily. "Your promised mates are long dead. You will not take my sister in the place of the one you were promised."

"She is Stone-Chosen to bear my children," he decided quietly.

"She is Stone-Chosen to bear children for whatever man she chooses," Hunter countered furiously. "Do you honestly believe she'll choose a beast that just slaughtered her grandfather?"

"With the proper incentive, I believe so."

"What? Lies like Veriel tried to offer my mother?" Hunter scoffed. "Erin knows better."

Lorian smiled rows of perfect, white teeth, his fangs retracted, looking charming in the illusion of a white mandarin shirt and dark gray suit that showcased his dark features, all traces of the blood that stained his face and hands moments before eradicated. "Call to her, Hunter of *Kreuzträger-König*."

A chill rushed through Hunter's gut. "Never. I will never betray Erin," he gasped, praying he was strong enough to take what punishment Lorian was about to dish out for his refusal. *For Erin. If Erin is safe, I can take whatever he does in stride.*

"As you wish. Fight me, then."

* * * *

Erin clapped her hands over her ears. The scream that ripped through the house had to be Hunter. She stifled a sob. Hunter could be an insufferable jerk sometimes, but he was still her big brother. He was still there to hold her when things got really bad.

She vaguely remembered two beast attacks. In one, Hunter hadn't even started his training yet. Still, he'd held her with her face buried in his strong chest, someone's spare weapon in his free hand, daring the beasts to try for her. Erin couldn't have been more than four at the time.

The other time, Hunter had been a proud first-nighted and blood-sealed young Warrior. Even so, he'd held Erin huddled to his side, in the circle of one arm, while both hands held his own weapons to defend her, as if the physical impossibility of defending Erin while she hung on him like that had never occurred to Hunter. She was nine that time.

Hunter cried out again, and she wiped away a tear. The house went silent, deadly still. Erin dragged down a set of training blades on a belt and strapped them on. She had an amulet to protect her, which was more than Hunter and her grandfather had.

She could admit that her hand-to-hand was almost non-existent, but Corwyn hadn't trained her for close-quarters combat. He'd trained Erin for distance, for throwing. Her grandfather had assured Erin that she was fast and accurate enough to kill all but the most skilled beasts silently. She only prayed that whatever was out there wasn't the most skilled.

Erin swallowed another sob. *If it took out both Hunter and Corwyn, it was highly skilled.*

No, she wouldn't think about that. She couldn't.

She shook her head and made sure her weapons were ready. Taking a deep breath, Erin slid from the training room. They used this house in Hunter range at least twice a year, so Erin knew very well which boards squeaked and where the best hiding places were. With her amulet to keep her off radar until she was seen physically— Well, she hoped she had a chance, anyway.

Erin made her way to the living room without incident. She stared at the carnage, feeling suddenly ill. The smell of beast blood turned her stomach, but the sight of her grandfather, crumpled like a yarn doll in a lake of his own blood, a gaping hole in his back, was decidedly worse.

Her stomach rebelled violently, and the force of controlling it left her shaky and cold. Erin couldn't puke. The sound would draw them, and the stench on her would ensure that Erin couldn't hide again.

She scanned the room, searching for Hunter, but aside from one of his discarded blades, she saw no sign of him. Erin furrowed her brow and headed across the hall. *There!*

Her brother sat on the floor, sagging against the sofa in the library. She could tell his injuries were serious. Hunter was bleeding from several wounds on his chest and arms. A purple bruise marred his face just below the temple, and blood trickled down his jaw from a cut at the corner of his mouth. He appeared unconscious, though his left hand still held a blade cradled in it. Erin doubted Hunter could raise his arm with it, though. The damage seemed designed to render him unable to battle.

Erin bit her lip painfully. Had Hunter driven the beast to ground, or was it carefully ghosted? If it was a trap, why didn't the beast strike? Surely, it could see her now.

But it can't touch me. Erin could argue where the beast was 'til the end of time and only cost Hunter his life, but it still couldn't touch her. Fury at herself for procrastinating while her brother bled steeled her resolve.

She crossed the room to him, looking around nervously and wiping her sweating palms on her jeans. Erin knelt to check his condition. Hunter was alive, and he should continue to live unless more damage was inflicted before help arrived. His eyes opened as she pressed her hand to the worst of the wounds, trying to slow the flow of blood.

Hunter's eyes widened and he swiveled his head, looking for his enemy. "No," he breathed. "Go back. He wants you."

Erin felt her blood chill, but that was hardly news. Of course, she was a target. Erin would always be a target. *The* target. She shivered at the thought then startled as a feeling like a cold wind passed by her back. "Stop that," she snapped at him. "I have my amulet. A beast can't—"

She screamed in pain and fear as she found herself dragged away from Hunter by her hair. Her head slammed into the back edge of the sofa and her lower back into the edge of the seat, and Erin scrambled for some purchase beneath her feet. Just as she found it, a long blade bit into her throat.

Erin flailed, trying to push it away, but it cut deep into her hand. She threw the hand out toward the hilt of the sword, trying to touch the beast's hand to force him away with her amulet, but her arms weren't long enough to reach him. The same proved true for the hand that held her hair behind the couch. Erin sobbed hopelessly as she realized that the beast had planned this so that she couldn't use her amulet offensively.

Weapons! Her father warned Erin that they had discovered the use of null weapons against the amulets, but this use of it was new as was using her hair to hold her. Hair was dead, she realized, like clothing was dead. Unless the beast touched her back or scalp in grabbing it, it was just another null weapon to him. Erin closed her eyes and promised herself a really short haircut if she survived.

"Your amulet," a male voice purred. "Take off your amulet."

Erin opened her eyes and tilted her head back to take in her attacker—and wished she hadn't. Somehow, the beautiful face with the flashing white smile and the sleek black hair, the familiar warm, brown eyes of a Warrior, and the pristine suit that fit him as if tailored to him seemed more threatening than any nightmare her mind had come up with. He looked about Hunter's age, and his entire aura spoke of friendship and safety.

While he has a sword to your throat?

Okay, that wasn't the most intelligent observation she could have made at that moment.

It's just that he looks like a Warrior. You trust Warriors not beast elders.

His gaze caught her, soft, inviting eyes that sent a wave of warmth through her. Erin's eyes suddenly seemed heavy, and her limbs were weighed down by exhaustion. Her grip on the sword hilt slipped, and her hand thumped to the sofa. She tried to fight her eyes open again, but the order never left her numbed mind, and they slid shut.

He was there, her friend, the one who would protect her. He was beautiful.

"Dade," the boy sighed, close to Erin's face.

He kissed her. His tongue was sweet and soft in her mouth, and she groaned as Dade pulled her to his body.

Erin's hands played over the strong muscles of his back. Was he wearing a shirt a minute ago?

"No," he breathed, capturing her mouth again.

Dade's lips trailed to her throat, and he licked at the blood mark there, sending shivers down Erin's spine. His hands cupped beneath her buttocks and drew Erin up until she felt the erect length of him. Dade anchored her against it, and an aching warmth pooled deep inside her in response.

"My Erin." His voice seemed to come from all around her.

His mouth continued its exploration of her blood mark, tracing it gently as Erin arched closer to that hard ridge pressing to her. She groaned her approval.

"No, Erin," Hunter thundered.

Erin snapped awake, snatching one of her blades from its sheath and reaching to do damage automatically. She froze in mid-swing as his blade pressed deeper, uttering a strangled cry as it scraped flesh.

"Now, now," the beast taunted. "It would be such a shame to sever that lovely head."

"Better dead than had by you," she panted.

"Really? I thought my little preview was better than that. You did enjoy it, didn't you?"

Erin blushed. The beast knew she had. The damp heat still pooled and swirled in her, and he could surely sense that it was there. His mocking smile set off a series of muttered curses from Erin, and she glanced at Hunter miserably.

Her brother maintained a stony exterior, though she could tell he was boiling inside, an explosive *Blutjagd* burning in his skin. Erin could have lost herself in that lovely little daydream, if Hunter hadn't helped her when he did.

Shame of how she had been tricked made her angrier. "It was a lie, beast," she spat, trying to avoid Hunter's eyes. "You can't expect me to believe you'd treat me that tenderly."

"You'd be surprised what I'd stoop to for the chance to have you for my own," he crooned.

"Nothing wonderful, I'm sure."

The beast sighed. "Perhaps not," he decided. "I could, however, maim you, mar your beauty just a bit. If I take your arm above the bracer, you'd be mine immediately—and completely unprotected."

Erin looked at him in shock, suddenly certain that the beast meant it. He meant to take her arm, if she left him no choice.

She tried to calm her breathing. He would hold that as a last resort. They had time. Someone could get to them. The beast would have to release her to fight...or run. *Oh gods, something!* He couldn't hold her hostage forever. The sun would rise. Maybe on Erin's dead body, but it would rise.

Hunter swore fluently, struggling toward them on uncertain and very damaged limbs, his wounds reopening. The beast's sword flashed to draw a deep cut on his shoulder. Her brother ground his teeth as he fell back, but Erin's scream was loud enough for both of them. She bucked the beast's grip on her hair, feeling the burn in her scalp as hair ripped away in small patches. The beast swung the blade back to her throat, scraping off more skin as he convinced her silently to still. The metal came to rest under her chin, pulling Erin's head up at an awkward angle.

"As I thought," he mused. "You're prepared for me to harm you. Your brother is your weakness. I'm glad I kept him alive."

"Erin knows better," Hunter groaned. "She'll let me die first."

"Is he right, Erin? Would you let him die for you?"

Erin felt tears escaping down her cheeks, and she bit her trembling lower lip. She looked at Hunter out of the corner of her eye, unable to turn her head far enough to face him. His eyes pleaded with her.

"Yes," she choked out. "It would be my duty."

Hunter nodded his approval, his shoulders relaxing. Erin tried to wash away the fact that he was preparing to die for her, making his final pacts and requests of the gods on his way.

The beast growled in frustration. He lunged the sword deep into Hunter's shoulder. "Can you watch him die, Erin?"

"No," she screamed, twisting, trying desperately to reach the beast with her blade, but he had her pinned effectively.

Hunter lost consciousness again.

The beast chuckled. "Yes? No? Which is it, Erin?"

Erin lunged for him again, but he dragged back on her braids, slamming her head into the wood frame hard enough to make showers of stars dance before her eyes.

Damn this long hair! Inspiration struck. She glanced at him, wondering if he could stop her. If he was distracted— "You've killed him," Erin wailed, making her voice as shrill and panicked as she could affect.

"He's not dead," the beast snapped.

His gaze flicked to Hunter, and she took the opportunity to spring into action. Erin yanked her head forward and sliced the razor-sharp training blade through her braids, as close to her scalp as she dared. Freed, Erin slid to the floor, the beast's roar of rage making her heart stutter.

He lunged at her, and she sliced wildly, tearing his face open with her blade. Erin grimaced at the splash of foul blood that ran over her hand and arm. She rolled away under the coffee table, as the beast drew back, then sliced off the three braids he had missed when he grabbed her for good measure before coming up again. As she came to her feet, the beast dragged his sword from her brother's shoulder and swung back.

"You want him dead, Erin?" His formerly-dark eyes glowed the yellow-red of embers, and his fangs extended. "I'll take his head and drink him dry for you, if you like. Will you yield?"

Erin looked from the beast to Hunter and back several times. Either option was unacceptable. He was obviously a very high-level. He'd touched her mind despite the amulet. There was no way her thrown weapon would suffice.

"Erin," the beast barked. "Make your choice. I warn you that you will be mine either way. Will your brother die for no reason?"

She shook her head slowly and stepped toward him, keeping her mind closed tight. Erin had to get close to pull this off, and she couldn't let him know what she planned. The beast watched her with cold eyes and a colder smile. She shuddered at the thought of actually having those lips on her throat as he had in that little vision of his. Her only hope of avoiding that was pulling off this one damned desperate scam.

Erin reached the couch and looked down at Hunter sadly. If this didn't work, they were both as good as dead. The beast would either kill her or take her arm off for the amulet. She hoped he'd kill her, but she doubted he'd be so kind.

"The amulet," he reminded her. "Mustn't forget the amulet."

She fumbled at the buckles. The tears on her cheeks weren't part of the act. Nor were her shaking hands. She watched him out of the corner of her eye. He was frowning at her progress. *Damn!* She needed his guard down.

Erin growled in genuine frustration. She took the weapon from her left hand and worked it beneath the highest strap on the bracer, sawing it slowly. If he didn't relax his stance by the time she reached the second strap, she and Hunter had real problems.

Her shaking intensified as the first strap broke free. Finally, she saw it. The beast set his sword tip-down on the floor and leaned on it. She met his eyes miserably as she extended the blade toward the second strap.

Locked on his eyes, Erin lunged at him, bracing her left hand behind the hilt to drive her weight into the blow. He had little time to react. The blade slid home inches from a killing blow. She dragged back on it as she moved away, opening a deep gash. It would bleed heavily. If she could get him to lose enough blood, he'd go to ground.

The blow he dealt her made him stagger back from the force of the amulet and threw her back over the coffee table. Erin landed hard, groaning at the pains shooting through her shoulder on impact.

The beast's sword came up again, and she flipped her blade and let it fly. Her aim was far off, but it planted solidly in his chest again. She pushed herself to her feet painfully, while he stared down at her blade in disbelief. He ripped it free with a snarl and threw it across the room, embedding it in the wall.

He was bleeding heavily from all three wounds, now. The sword was drawn back again, and she sobbed in exhaustion.

Just enough time to bleed him to ground. Am I asking too much, here?

Erin launched herself over the coffee table and onto the couch, bracing her arms out toward the beast. He stared at her in shock, as if attacking a beast empty-handed had never occurred to him. She bit back a peel of hysterical laughter. She had to be insane to be doing this, but some part of her couldn't stop. Erin needed the time to bleed him to ground. This was all she had left...her amulet and what she could do with it. She couldn't trust her arm for another throw.

The force sent him reeling back into the bookcases with a sickening thud and crack. His sword flew from his hand as he hit. Erin landed on the hardwood table and rolled off, gasping for breath.

She staggered back to her knees, praying she didn't have to attack again. She was too tired and too hurt to keep it up much longer. One more landing like that, and she wouldn't be able to get up.

The beast pulled his sword from the floor unsteadily and glared at her. His smile spread slowly. Erin forced herself to keep a poker face though she felt like crying.

"We'll see each other again, Erin," he promised. "I have all the time in the world to pay you back for this."

She nodded wearily and bit back more hysterical laughter. What could she say to that? Erin certainly wasn't looking forward to the rematch. She'd rather see him burn in hell...and herself as well than set eyes on him again.

"What? No words of love in parting for your future mate?" he taunted.

"No. Just leave."

He bowed a rather tipsy bow and faded away. Erin wished desperately that she had Hunter's ability to sense. She couldn't tell if the beast was truly gone.

She considered her options. He *might* not be gone, but Hunter *would* bleed to death, if she didn't do something about it. Erin cursed the choice she was faced with.

She unsheathed her remaining weapon and made her way to the closet. It hurt to heft the heavy medical kit, but Hunter couldn't wait. Erin cut his shirt away and groaned at the damage. She didn't think she was capable of stitches, so she packed the wounds that seemed to need it with surgical sponges and used butterfly tape on the others. She only hoped help would arrive soon. Someone had to have felt this.

Erin ran her hand through the jagged mess of her hair and grabbed the scissors from the medical kit. She grasped handfuls of hair and cut them close to the scalp. By the time she was done, her hair was little longer than a crew cut and most likely a jagged mess. She looked at the piles of black curls in a detached sense of loss. "Try grabbing that," she grumbled.

Chapter Two

Talon looked at Kord Maher in disbelief. "Calm down?" he bellowed. "Are you insane?"

The older man sighed. "Save the *Blutjagd*. You'll burn it off now if you're not careful."

"You're sensing it too. I know you are. Corwyn is dead, and both of my children are injured, Kord. I know that damn elder laid hands on my daughter, one way or the other."

"He's gone to ground," the Lord Maher soothed him.

"But, has he taken my daughter away with him?" he demanded.

Jayde ran a soothing hand over Talon's back. "How long, Kord?" she asked nervously.

"Five minutes," he assured her.

"Then, we'll know in six minutes," she decided quietly.

Talon grimaced at the hitch in her voice. This was her worst nightmare come true. If Erin was gone, or either of her children died, he wasn't sure Jayde would survive it.

Talon took her hand and kissed it. "We'll make it right," he promised.

Kord cleared his throat. "If Erin is still there, we leave for my range tonight. I don't want you anywhere near here when Lorian comes back up. Hunter must have driven him to ground. That damned elder is going to be bloodthirsty when he comes up for a kill."

Talon nodded. "Thank you, Kord. This is a bad position to be in. He won't be happy with anyone who helps us."

"Making beasts happy isn't in my job description," he joked. "Being brought to justice makes most of them more than a little pissy."

The rest of the trip passed in silence. Talon watched the miles slip by.

An hour! He ground his teeth at the memory of those first few moments, locked in an impotent *Blutjagd* while his son lit up brighter than Talon had ever seen him and stayed that way. Erin's fear had intensified with that step, and he could tell something bad was coming next. Suddenly, Corwyn and his son were under attack. Kord and Jayde had all but dragged him to the car with them.

He'd felt it when Lorian arrived on the scene. Corwyn was suddenly gone, and Talon had screamed in frustration for Hunter. The boy was good, but this was a fifteen-hundred-year-old elder, who took out Corwyn easily. His heart sank as he felt the first of Hunter's injuries, but the beast didn't kill him.

That fact only had confused him until he'd felt Erin's fear. What he got from his daughter via the amulet was maddeningly little: a rolling cycle of pain, anger, and fear he couldn't defend her from. The amulet had been tested several times. Overall, the experience had driven him to the brink of insanity.

From the fact that Hunter had continued to accrue new injuries, Talon could only assume that Lorian was attempting to use Hunter against Erin, as Veriel had tried to use Talon against Jayde. He prayed that this beast found it as useless, but Erin was only twelve and she loved her brother desperately.

When the house came into view, Talon was out of

the car before Kord managed to stop it. He hit the door at a run and surveyed the living room in amazement. In his panic, he hadn't kept track of the dying beasts, and nearly a dozen littered the room around Corwyn. He swept Jayde away as she launched through the door and motioned to Kord behind his back. Gods willing, Kord would cover Corwyn's body before Jayde saw what had been done to her father. He cringed at the knowledge that Erin probably saw it in gory detail.

He pushed the library door open and froze. Erin sat on the couch with a weapons belt on and a training blade in hand. The black cloud that surrounded her feet made no sense until his attention locked on her shorn head. Blade scrapes marked her throat, and a bruise marred her face, covering the right edge of her mouth. She had beast blood splattered over her, and her own—or Hunter's on her hands. *Possibly both.*

Erin looked at them with eyes that Talon would have classified as either unseeing or uncomprehending, until he moved. That she understood perfectly. Her gaze locked on her parents, and she launched unsteadily to her feet with the weapon raised in mute warning.

"Erin? Honey, it's Dad. You need to put the weapon down," Talon crooned. He could disarm Erin easily, but he had no wish to frighten her any worse than she was, and any sudden movement on his part would only accomplish that.

His daughter took a step closer to Hunter protectively. Her eyes were wary, her stance measured and rigid. She was trying to project an air of confidence in her position that she obviously didn't feel.

Jayde put a hand on his shoulder and drew one of

her weapons. She cut her palm wordlessly and showed Erin the line of blood.

Tears welled up in Erin's eyes, and she eased toward them, glancing back at Hunter suspiciously. As her outstretched hand touched Jayde's, Erin dropped her weapon to the floor. She touched Talon next. Shaking and crying, she fell into his arms.

Jayde nodded and sheathed her weapon. "I've got Hunter," she whispered.

Talon led her to an oversized chair and sat, drawing his daughter into his lap. He tried to comfort her, but his usual smoothing of Erin's hair brought him up against the soft fuzz on her head and caused her to cry harder. Finally, Talon rocked her with her cheek to his chest, murmuring to her about how he would never allow it again, the same thing he'd promised Jayde years earlier. He cursed himself for letting his guard down this far with Erin.

Jayde nodded to him across Hunter's body. "A week to ten days down time. He'll need some stitches on the stab wounds and antibiotics. Other than that, I'd say Erin did a pretty good job of patching him up. How about Erin? She's still human," she finished wryly.

Talon grimaced at that. *Still human.* Her injuries would take four times as long to heal as they would if she was a Warrior already. "Erin, where are your injuries?" he asked gently.

She looked at him miserably and opened her hand for his inspection.

"Knife cut. Maybe six or seven stitches," he called to Jayde.

"Sword," Erin corrected him.

He nodded despite the tension in his jaw. "What else? I see your face and neck. Anything I can't see?"

"My back," she whispered.

Talon peeled up the back of her shirt and swore fluently at the swelling and bruises that covered her from shoulder to waist. "X-rays," he called out.

Jayde's head snapped up in surprise. "For?"

"You'd have to see this bruising. It's..." He sighed and shook his head.

She crossed the room at a dead run. Jayde reached out to touch the blocks of bruises but stopped just short, doubtless realizing how bad it must feel already. She grabbed Erin's left wrist and ran her hand over the bracer, checking for the amulet, reassured to find it safely beneath the leather. Jayde flicked the severed buckle strap and met his eyes with a questioning look.

Erin looked down at it, her expression weary, and groaned. "Tactics," she grumbled, thumping the side of her face against his chest. "I hate tactics."

"Your hair?" Jayde asked gently.

"He had me trapped by it." Erin ran a hand over the thick crew cut she now sported and stifled a sob. "Try grabbing this, you bastard," she whispered. She buried her face Talon's chest, her body quaking.

"Did Hunter drive him to ground?" Talon asked suspiciously. Something was definitely off with this scene, and he hoped he was reading the signs wrong.

Erin shook her head. "No, Hunter was hurt—ou-out cold," she managed.

Jayde sucked in her breath at the implication. "Do you know who the beast was, Erin?"

She shook her head again, settling her cheek against him as if she intended to go to sleep on his lap.

"I know he was a high-level. Dade. He said his name was Dade." The last word came out with a wide yawn.

Talon furrowed his brow. *Dade?* "You're sure?" he asked.

"If that was a low-level, how did it take out Hunter and Grandpa?" Her voice went shrill then subdued. "No. It was too good to be anything else."

Talon's mind started working, seeking out possibilities to explain her experience. Veriel had called himself Jörg when he'd pursued Jayde's mother. "Could he have said Dado?" he asked urgently.

"Maybe. I was a little busy at the time." Erin seemed to pale at the memory. She rubbed her scalp and winced.

"Your head hurts?" Jayde asked, probably fearing a head injury.

"A little. I think he ripped some of the hair out before I cut it."

"Okay, let's get you in the SUV. Dad and Kord will bring Hunter out."

"Our stuff?" she asked weakly.

"Stephen will come out tomorrow." Jayde didn't add that he would also take care of his brother's remains and collect his lord's seal. Erin didn't need that reminder.

She nodded, levered herself off Talon's lap, and trudged toward the door. Erin stepped aside as Kord breezed in. The older man nodded to Talon, letting him know Corwyn had been taken care of before Erin or Jayde could see it—or see it again, as the case may be. Kord looked at Erin sadly and touched her cheek near the dark bruise, before she continued on.

He turned back to Talon. "Looks like it was ten

high-levels that our guys got and Lorian," Kord reported.

Erin stopped her forward motion and turned back to Kord, looking pitifully tiny and scared. "Lorian?" she managed in a shaky voice.

Kord stared at her in confusion, his brows lowering behind his shaggy mane of hair. "Yes, honey. The last beast, the one driven to ground."

Erin laughed nervously then wrapped her arms around her ribs and hitched in what might have been silent sobs. "Dado. Lorian. I have Lorian planning to get even with me. I think I'm going to be sick." She took two choppy steps toward the door then stopped, whirling to look at the bookcases behind Hunter with wild eyes. "Mate," she breathed as she collapsed into her mother's arms.

Jayde checked her over quickly. "It's all right. It was just a shock," she assured herself more than the men in the room. "Kord, I could use your help getting her into the vehicle. Be careful of her back. It's bad."

He nodded uncertainly as he reached for her. "Sure. Did I say something wrong?"

Talon stood and shook his head, feeling slightly shaky himself. "Hunter didn't send Lorian to ground, Kord. Erin did."

* * * *

Hunter came to a groggy half-sleep. The bed he was in was too soft, and his entire body ached. He had never been seriously ill before, save his sealing sickness. He didn't think that was possible for Warriors, so he couldn't imagine what was making him so sick now. Faces and voices danced through his mind as he searched for an answer.

Lorian's laughter haunted him. "Can you watch him die, Erin?"

Erin fighting him, screaming with every pain the beast caused Hunter in her name. "No!"

His eyes snapped open, and he assessed the room in the dim light. Bandages and stitches pulled at the move. It wasn't a dream. Erin really said she couldn't watch him die. He'd failed her.

Hunter screamed in anguish. Erin was gone. Lorian had her. Gods only knew what the elder had done to her. Had she surrendered her amulet to buy Hunter's life? Had the beast taken her arm? How badly did he fail her?

The door flew open, and his mother hovered over him. "Calm down, Hunter. What is it?"

He struggled to sit up, but pains tore through him, forcing him back down. Hunter cried out again. "He has Erin. I have to get her back," he pleaded as much to his unresponsive body as to his mother. How could she ask what was wrong? He had to make her understand. He needed Jayde's help. Every minute on his back was a minute Lorian had Erin.

"Hunter, calm down," she soothed him. "We have Erin. Lorian doesn't have her. Calm down."

He stopped struggling and panted in agony. "How?"

Hunter knew how far away help was when he surrendered consciousness. It had to be more than thirty minutes between when he went down and when help arrived for her. And Lorian would have felt them coming. The beast would have taken Erin's arm before he freed her to the Warriors. He'd made that much clear.

A motion over his mother's shoulder caught his attention. Dressed in a Warrior's shirt that came to her knees and rubbing her eyes, Erin curled onto the wide bed beside him.

Hunter looked at her in awe. He started to smooth hair that he thought was pulled back behind her head, but what he encountered was short and sweat-soaked. "You cut it to get away," he breathed. "Oh, Erin." Hunter choked back a sob. Her beautiful hair was her pride and joy—or had been until Lorian got hold of it.

"It'll grow again," Jayde soothed them both.

"No," Erin whispered. "I won't let it grow."

His father sauntered in. "Told you we should've let her sleep here. She was bound to end up here after the night they both had."

"How?" Hunter asked again.

"I drove him to ground," Erin replied quietly.

Hunter laughed heartily, wincing at the pain in his chest and shoulders as he did. "Ow, that hurts. That was a good one."

"I wasn't joking," she countered in a voice laced in misery.

Hunter's jaw tightened down at that pronouncement, and met his father's eyes.

Talon nodded. "If you didn't, she sure's hell did."

"She couldn't," he protested. "She couldn't even protect herself from his coercion."

Erin groaned. "Let's not talk about that, Hunter. Please. Not now."

"It's not your fault, Erin. He's an elder with fifteen hundred years of dirty tricks." He smoothed his hand over her bruised cheek to soothe her.

"And I'm just a human," she grumbled. "Drop it. I'm sick enough just thinking about it. Please, don't talk about it."

"What coercion?" Jayde demanded.

Erin buried her face in his ribs. Hunter noted a bandage on her hand as she wrapped herself around his body. He searched out the memory of the blood running down her hand from the sword cut with a grimace.

He placed his arm around her protectively. "I'm sorry, Erin. They need to know."

"No, they don't," she assured him, her voice muffled as she buried her face further into him.

"What?" Jayde demanded again.

Hunter sighed. "From what the beast said to her, I'd assume it was some sick sort of mind-fuck."

Erin stiffened. "It didn't get quite that far," she offered miserably, "barely."

Jayde started to rub her back, and Erin hissed in pain. Their mother moved her hand to Erin's arm to continue her soothing. "I'm sorry, baby. I forgot how sore you are."

Hunter looked to his father for confirmation, and Talon nodded. Fighting an elder is not a pretty thing. Hunter just hoped she had amulet-bruises and not more stitches from the sword blade. His stomach churned at the thought.

Erin is human. She decided to fight an elder as a human. Gods only know what he did to her.

His mind reeled at another thought. *She won—as a human.*

Jayde pulled him out of his reverie. "I was just going to tell you that I had something similar done to me when I was a trained Warrior. Elders aren't like other beasts. It's no sign of weakness that he tricked you."

Hunter knew what she was talking about. When he was training, he'd heard the story of the many things Veriel had done to try to get Jayde's amulet off. Sending one of his substantial dream-illusions of their father to convince her to remove it had been one of the worst for her.

"Great," Erin grumbled, no doubt unsettled by the idea still. "Tell me how to win Mom, because he's coming back someday, and he left pissed off and promising revenge."

Hunter groaned, half at the thought of it and half at the impossibility of her doing any more than she obviously had. "You sent him to ground, Erin. What more do you want?"

"Let's see. To survive in less pain next time and to kill him so he won't be coming back."

"Fine, but let me assure you that if you ever again balk an order a Warrior gives you in battle, I'll wring your neck myself. Beyond that, I'd say Corwyn was right. We have to train you. Nothing else will save you next time."

Chapter Three

April 18, 2021

Curt Maher watched as Erin made her way down to the summer training grounds. She looked like hell in his hand-me-down jeans—ill-fitting and so large that she had them cuffed up at least three times, one of his caps turned backward on her head, and one of Kord's shirts which reached her knees. He understood that her own clothing required major cleaning or disposal, and the rest of her things hadn't arrived. Still, it seemed a shame to batter so lovely a face and dress her this way.

He shook his head, trying desperately to dislodge his next discovery, but it wanted to stick with him. The battering and the clothes did little to mask Erin's body, unbelievable for her age. She had blossomed into a hot young woman in the ten months since Curt had seen her last.

Curt shook his head again. It was a completely inappropriate thought, he decided. Erin was a young girl, he reminded himself sternly. Worse, she didn't have autonomy. If Curt even showed interest in her, Talon and Hunter would take his head. His curse be damned! Curt knew better than to let his control slip that far.

"Hey. Get to work," Adam grumbled at him, cuffing Curt on the back of his head for his inattention. With Kord and Lewis busy relocating the *Königs* and cleaning up the mess left behind by last night's battle, his twenty-five year old brother was in charge of the day's training, and Adam was in a foul mood for his lack of sleep.

Adam had planned on a single night of sleep after a long track. When Lewis rolled them out of bed after midnight, he'd found himself pushed behind the wheel of a car with his two younger brothers half-asleep in the back and sent off to meet his grandfather and the *Königs* at the training house that housed the Stone room. That drive had taken him nearly all night, and there was still the training to see to.

Lewis was headed to Hunter range to retrieve the Stone. Corwyn was dead, which made him the new Stone lord, and the Stone had called for him to do his duty. Kord was seeing to whatever errands Lady *König* had requested of him, and the *Königs* themselves were doing whatever royalty saw fit to do. That left Adam in charge of training and facing hours more longing for a bed.

Bryant, his twenty-two-year-old brother, grinned. "Got a thing for the princess?" he teased. Bryant liked to insinuate that Curt had inherited Kord's drive to print.

Curt darkened despite his attempt to stay neutral on the subject. His need for release had always been more difficult to control than most men found it, he was assured by Kord. Still, if Kord could survive it to a decent age before printing, so could Curt.

At fifteen, Curt had just started his training, and already release was a difficulty at times. As if that wasn't problem enough, his brothers—seven and ten years older than he was—delighted in giving him a good pounding whenever an occasion arose they thought they could hide it with. Adam wasn't called 'Conan' for no reason, and the last thing Curt wanted to do was take another beating from him—for any reason.

He scowled at Bryant. "She's a child," Curt dismissed the idea. "I take release with women." Luckily for Warriors, they had the size and appearance of full grown human men at fifteen. Otherwise, release would be even more difficult for them.

"She doesn't have the body of a child," Bryant mused with a predatory smile that made Curt want to deck him.

"Go print or go dunk your head. Talon and Hunter would kill you."

Erin ducked under the fence stiffly, and Adam scowled at the weapons belt she wore, half buried in the folds of the shirt and the billow of the rolled sleeves she had pushed past her elbows.

"This is a training ground," Adam told Erin, dismissing her.

She met his eyes coldly. "I know. That's why I'm here. I need to practice."

"You're trained?" he asked in disbelief.

"Training," she corrected him.

"So, get out there. You're pitted with Curt."

Curt's eyes widened. *No way!* There was no way Adam could pit him against her. If Curt hurt her, Talon would kill them all. Worse, he would rather die than raise a blade or hand to her. Erin was still a human girl. Pitting Curt against her went against every rule about protecting humans there was.

"No, I'm not," Erin answered Adam calmly. "I'm not here for hand-to-hand."

"Why not?" Adam's lip curled into a sneer.

"Until I heal, I'm not allowed. Ask my father."

"Then what do you intend to do? We're not wasting time here."

"Move," she ordered as she unsheathed one of her weapons—the right one since her left hand was wrapped in a thick bandage. Erin balanced it on her wrist as if to test it and eyed it critically, marking the slight imperfections that would affect its flight like a pro.

"What did you say to me?"

Curt noted the gleam in his brother's eyes warily. Adam was in a bad mood, and Erin was pushing buttons Curt had learned not to push when he was less than ten.

"I said 'move.' Did I stutter?"

Erin knew she was pushing him. Curt had no doubts about that. Adam was being overbearing, and Erin had a reputation for not accepting that attitude from anyone but her father. Not even other house lords would talk to her the way Adam was.

"Why should I?" he challenged.

She sighed. "Your choice. If I have to, I'll work around you." It was a dismissal, clear and to the point.

Adam glared at her, taking in the bandage on her hand and the bruising on her face. "I want to know by whose authority you've been given weapons so early. It's against tradition."

"The Stone's," Erin replied patiently, pushing her collar aside with her injured hand to bare her blood mark.

Curt cleared his throat. This whole thing was getting out of hand. The Stone was on her side, and if Corwyn said the Stone wanted her trained, there was no higher word. "Adam, this is a bad idea. I think you should back down," he suggested quietly.

"I don't think so," he snapped. "Even if what she says is true, she's training under me in my range. It's not like our young princess has killed a beast before."

Okay, trying to talk him down is going to have the opposite effect.

Erin laughed harshly, and Adam's jaw tightened. "No, you are right there," she admitted as if not being blood sealed made not a bit of difference to her.

"In fact, it looks like you took a pretty beating for your trouble," Adam continued angrily. "Maybe you should let the real Warriors protect you and give it up."

Erin's eyes hardened. "Not an option."

"Why not? That's what we're here for."

"Tell that to Corwyn Lord Hunter," she growled.

"He was an old man—nothing more."

"If you believe that, you're a fool."

Curt watched the escalation in shock. Corwyn just an old man? Adam wasn't thinking. Corwyn was the first Warrior to survive Veriel, the first Warrior to best him in battle and drive him to ground. He was an elder hunter at least six times over. He had been Stone lord and the youngest house lord in two centuries. To top it off, no one had a better grasp of the hidden secrets the Stone wouldn't tell than Corwyn had. His theories were revolutionary.

"Then, show me something he taught you. Impress me."

Erin regarded him warily and started to turn away, sheathing her blade. Curt let out a breath he hadn't realized he was holding. It was over. Adam would take his punishment for turning her from her assigned training later, but Erin would be out of his brother's line of fire until after the chips fell.

"Good," Adam taunted her. "I don't have time for spoiled little girls."

Erin moved so fast that even Curt barely tracked it. Her blade flipped back out of her sheath. Her shoulder turned, and the weapon flew. Adam stared at the grip brushing the tops of his thighs, just shy of his sac, his breathing harsh in shock.

She smiled crookedly. "And I don't have time for self-important fools. Don't worry, Adam. I rarely miss my mark. Impressed?" When he didn't respond, she shrugged.

Curt swallowed a hysterical laugh, too shocked to find the look on Adam's face truly humorous, but needing the release of the laughter all the same.

Erin turned to leave. "You can return the blade to my father. I'm sure you have a lot to say to each other. Good day to you, gentlemen," she added with obvious rancor.

Adam locked on her retreating back in a full fury. His *Blutjagd* was the worst Curt had seen on him since his senses kicked in at the onset of the curse. Granted, that had only been three months, but it was still a frightening sight.

Erin turned suddenly, as Adam started to move, her eyes wide and her body adopting a fighter's crouch awkwardly. A bellow of animal rage ripped from Adam's lips.

Curt didn't try to analyze how she knew Adam was coming for her. He didn't think at all. He reacted. He plowed the larger man off his feet and placed his body between them, prepared to fight Adam if he had to.

"I don't need you to protect me," she whispered,

sounding peeved at Curt's interference in her fight.

"Relax. It's no reflection on you. I can't allow a Maher to attack you in Maher range. It's my duty. Let me do it."

"Can you win?" she breathed, the anger leaving her voice.

"No," he admitted. "I'm not even fully trained yet, but I have to do this."

Erin groaned. "I'm sorry, Curt."

"My honor," he told her. "Not my pleasure by the time he's done with me, but my honor."

"Thanks."

Curt moved forward to give himself space to fight, as Adam wiped the dirt from his face.

Adam pointed a finger at his youngest brother with a dangerous gleam in his eye. "You will pay for that, Curtis," he promised. "Stand aside."

"No. You're sworn to protect the *Königs*. You can't do this."

"I'm sworn to obey the Lord and Lady *König*," he countered. "Move or pay the price for it. I will take you to trial for ignoring my orders."

He shook his head, and Adam closed on him. Curt glanced at Bryant, but the middle brother seemed intent on staying out of Conan's way. Curt squared his shoulders. This was going to be a hard beating, but if Erin ran for it while Adam was busy with him—

Erin moved up behind him.

"Move back," he grumbled. "I need space. Be ready to run when I take him on."

"Follow my lead." Her voice caressed his ear as she moved away.

Curt's heart pounded. He couldn't let her do this.

Adam was beyond caring about his duty to protect and do no harm. If Adam got his hands on Erin, he'd hurt her for the stunt with the blade. Adam's favorite line was that no Warrior should make a move he couldn't back up. Curt had to stop her, but he couldn't stop both of them at the same time.

"Bryant," Curt bellowed. He needed help. He needed Bryant to either help him with Adam or take on Adam while he got Erin out of there. Curt would damn well carry her if he had to.

"Not me. I'm staying out of Conan's way on this one," Bryant replied evenly.

"Smart move," Adam growled.

Erin dragged herself onto the top fence rail, holding onto the upright to steady herself as she stood on it. Curt sighed in relief. She was out of the way, at least.

He threw himself to the ground as something flew at his head.

"Legs," Erin yelled out as she braced her legs for the blow to Adam's chest.

Curt swept Adam's feet from under him, while his brother stood frozen in shock. Between that and Erin's blow, Adam landed hard, but it wasn't enough.

Adam had her before she was away. As Erin stumbled off his chest, Adam grabbed her by the arms and flipped her onto her back roughly, eliciting a sharp cry of pain from her as he landed over her.

"You have to be tougher than that, princess," he spat, crushing her into the hard-packed earth.

She ground her teeth, refusing to cry out again. "I'm already injured. You have an unfair advantage," she reminded him through clenched teeth. "I'm not allowed to fight hand-to-hand yet."

Adam ignored her warning. Curt had no doubt that what she said was true, and Talon would have his brother's hide for this.

"Sure you're injured," Adam chided her. "You're just a sassy little girl." He pulled the cap from her head and looked at the remains of her hair in confusion. It took a moment to recover his wits. "It takes more than a boy's haircut to make a Warrior." He tossed the cap away, leaving her barely-there hair exposed.

Curt's heart twisted, as Erin shifted her eyes away and swallowed what looked like a painful lump. "Let her go, Adam," he pleaded.

"Not until the princess learns her lesson. She shouldn't make threats she can't back up."

"She's learned it. Let her go, and I'll take her back to the house. You've overstepped your bounds." He made a move to reach down to Erin, but Adam released her long enough to land a punch to Curt's face, sending him stumbling two steps back with the force.

Adam clamped down on Erin's arms again, stopping her move to throw him off. Erin yelped at his weight pinning her down.

"No, she has. No Warrior should make a move he—she can't back up, and no Warrior training under me throws a blade at me without proving she's the better Warrior eventually."

"Get off," a new voice thundered.

Curt jumped back as Talon unghosted beside him, skidding to a halt from a dead run with his hand on his weapon and lit up brighter than Adam was. The Lord *König's* face burned in fury and the exertion of coming at a run when he felt Erin's need of him.

That was a gift of the *Königs*. They felt more than beasts where their children were concerned, as if the Stone considered *König* children too important to risk to any danger.

Adam startled and pushed off Erin, jerking to his feet beside her. Not satisfied with that, Talon grabbed him by the throat and shoved him five yards farther away. Adam stared at the older Warrior in pure terror. Corwyn had been an elder hunter, but Talon was an elder killer three times over.

"She attacked me," Adam explained weakly. "She attacked me twice."

Curt skirted behind Talon and dropped to one knee next to Erin. He reached down to give her a hand as she struggled to her knees. "Can you stand?" he asked gently.

"Just sore," she groaned as she made it to her feet.

Curt stood beside her for lack of any better idea. *Better with her than next to either of Talon's probable targets.*

Her father returned to her and glared at Curt. "Back off," he growled.

Curt took a hasty step back.

Erin reached for his arm, stopping his retreat. "No, Dad. Curt helped me," she informed him.

The Lord *König* surveyed him with a calculated look then nodded. He turned Curt's face to view the rising red mark where Adam had struck him. "Good. You have my thanks. That means you're the only young buck who won't face me—after I secure Kord's permission, of course." His smile was cold and his voice gruff.

Adam paled at that look, and Talon nodded in

satisfaction at his response. He took his daughter's hand and motioned for Curt to join them.

When they were out of earshot, Curt sighed in relief. "Thank you, Lord *König*."

"For helping my daughter?" he asked in confusion.

Erin smiled. "That too, I'm sure, but I think he meant for not allowing Adam to beat him to a pulp for protecting me."

"He would have," Curt admitted. "Adam doesn't like being told he's wrong. If you wouldn't have made your request for my presence clear..." He shrugged.

"That body check you dealt him was pretty sweet," she noted.

"He'd've run you down like a Mack truck otherwise. I couldn't allow that. Besides, I've wanted to do that for years."

Erin laughed, the first honest laugh he'd heard from her this trip. "If he's always like that, I can believe it." She ran a hand over her head, and her smile disappeared into some indefinable sadness.

Her hair... All her beautiful hair was gone. The braids—or curls when it was unbound—that reached to the middle of her back were no more. It still hurt to look at.

Curt pulled off his cap and settled it on her head. "Here. I have a hundred of them."

She nodded gratefully. "Thanks, Curt."

Talon wrapped an arm around her, but she stiffened and scooted away.

"Dammit," Curt cursed softly. "Adam really did hurt you."

She shook her head. "He just aggravated what was already there."

Talon drew her to a stop. "I'm sure my cell is ringing off the hook. Your mother is in town getting some supplies. Let me see it now, so I can calm her as soon as I open the connection."

Erin nodded and dragged the back of her shirt up to her shoulders. Curt knew he should look away. He was accustomed to evaluating wounds, but it was impossible to be clinical with Erin, he decided. The sight of the deep purple bruises covering her back touched a chord in him, and he couldn't look away.

She shouldn't be training. Erin shouldn't even be out of bed. She was human, after all. Her injuries had to be hell.

And, Adam ignored her and made it worse. Curt turned and started to stalk back to challenge his oldest brother. He might get beaten to a pulp, but he could not, in good conscience, do less.

"Curt?" Erin called. "What are you going to do?"

"Kill him," he muttered, forcing his jaw to move by iron will alone.

"Curtis," Talon ordered. "Stand down. If you want to get even with Adam, I have a better plan. Are you interested?"

"What plan?"

Talon smiled that same cold smile he had in the training area. "Let's go see Hunter," he invited. "It will be a week before Adam gets his pummeling, but it will be a week of torture for Adam, and he won't be able to take it out on you in the meantime. You have my vow on that."

"How?" he asked suspiciously.

"I'm going to make your brother a deal that he'll jump at. You get to fill in some key information he'll be missing when he accepts that deal."

"What information?"

"The truth about what happened last night."

Erin turned a deep crimson and looked at her stained tennis shoes. "Not everything, Dad. Please, not everything," she whispered.

Talon nodded in seeming understanding and kissed her forehead. "No, not everything," he agreed.

Curt felt a stab of unease. They knew nothing about what happened the night before but that Hunter was now an elder hunter, but the young Warrior had paid dearly for taking on the elder. "I'm in," he decided.

* * * *

Curt was reading an early Maher history, when Adam strode into the room. Curt scowled behind the volume. His brother looked far too cocky for his own good. The plan couldn't have worked. He sighed. Even if it had failed, Curt would make Adam feel like the jerk he was before he was through, beating or no beating in response for it.

He considered his opening gambit carefully. Curt didn't even crack a smile as he did it. His fury over Erin's injuries kept him firmly in a mild form of bloodlust.

Adam crossed to Bryant's empty bed and kicked back on it. "So, you're going to spend a few weeks training with Lord *König* near the lake?" he drawled. "It won't save you, you know. You'll be back training with me in no time."

Curt closed the book over his finger to save his place and regarded his brother, feigning concern. "Yes, but I'll be back with a whole host of new tricks from the elder killers. That edge might just save me. When's your battle?"

Adam smiled smugly. "We'll get to it," he decided.

"You actually accepted Hunter's challenge, didn't you?" he asked in disbelief. Despite their assurances that Adam would swallow the bait, Curt had been secretly convinced that the plan would fail. Of course, that still meant his older brother facing Talon—

"What if I did?" he shot back. "That barely-trained pup has only battled beasts a half dozen times in the last three years."

Curt threw his head back and laughed. "Oh, that's rich. They are *good*." They were damn good at what they did to Adam. Of course, the fact that the young *Königs* rarely trained with anyone but house lords, a few lucky *Jäger*s, and older *Königs* worked in their favor. It was unlikely that Adam had ever been pitted against Hunter or even seen him train.

"You're saying they lied?" Adam asked archly.

"Oh no. I'm saying you've been royally had without a single lie."

"How?"

"They didn't happen to mention that he took down seven high-levels last night, did they?"

"With Corwyn's help," he scoffed.

"No. Actually, Corwyn took down the other three while he was busy with those seven."

Adam stared at him, clearly working at that information and how it changed his perceptions. "Still better than facing Talon, elder killer," he decided.

Curt opened the book again. It was time to start his gambit. "If you say so," he agreed in a voice that spoke volumes of his disagreement.

"I do," he affirmed, moving for the door. "He certainly didn't come away unscathed from those seven. Not to mention, he's not an elder killer."

Curt snorted in suppressed laughter, and Adam looked at him curiously. Adam's eyes narrowed and he turned to face him fully while Curt feigned interest in the book.

"It is better to face Hunter, isn't it?" Adam asked quietly, finally scenting danger in the wind.

Curt closed the book again and adopted a look of deep consideration. "I'd rather face Talon," he decided, whipping the book open.

Adam crossed the room in two long strides, wrenched the book from his hands, and threw it against the wall. His eyes burned and his arms tensed in warning as he loomed over Curt. "Why?" he demanded. "What do you know?"

"That was a protected book, Adam. Kord will turn you inside out if it's damaged," he complained, pretending not to hear the question posed.

"You'll need protection from me in just a minute if you don't answer me. Talk, dammit!" Adam locked his hands on Curt's shoulders, scowling.

"Fine. No, Hunter isn't an elder killer, but he is an elder hunter, and he's a son of Raga. That means he's more than capable of it. Keep in mind that even Talon and Pauwel didn't kill the first elders they encountered, and they weren't sons of Raga. Still, they succeeded the next time around, didn't they? Talon fared little better than Hunter did, and Talon was ten years older and had been a roving Night Warrior that whole time. He also had Jayde saving his skin."

Adam released his grip and uttered several curses. Curt could see his mind working through the possibilities he had missed earlier. Being younger and a son of Raga made Hunter even more dangerous than his father was.

"Oh, and those seven high-levels Hunter killed never laid a claw on him. He was completely unscathed...until Lorian took him on."

"I'm a dead man," Adam decided.

"Entirely possible. Corwyn gave Hunter the Stone's duty to protect Erin with his life. Once he's back on his feet—"

"And now he's primed. He's faced his first elder and survived."

"By the way, I'd stay away from Erin," he counseled his brother.

"Between two elder killers and an elder hunter as her protectors? You are kidding, right? Jayde killed her first elder, didn't she?"

"Yes. She's the only Warrior in history who has." Curt paused to let Adam begin digesting that fact before hitting him solidly with the rest. "I mean, even Erin only drove hers to ground, but I'm not sure that this encounter with Lorian really counts. After all, she's still human. Once Erin faces the change, the Stone only knows what she'll be capable of."

Adam paled. "No way," he breathed in disbelief.

"Yes way. Our little princess is an elder hunter, and she's not even cursed yet. Hunter was unconscious when Erin drove Lorian to ground, just like Talon was unconscious when Jayde killed Veriel. Believe it, Adam.

"Only the effects of the beast all but crippling her

in her frail human state saved you from Erin's full force today. She couldn't go hand-to-hand because she's simply not capable of it until she heals. Talon might permit you to see the damage, if you care to, or maybe I'll convince her to go for a swim. Most of her damage should be visible in a suit."

"She really wasn't lying, was she?"

Curt felt his temper burn at that. "I'm surprised she can walk," he confirmed. *And you made it worse.* "I'm not sure I would be if it were me."

Adam nodded and rose slowly, his hands in his pockets. He wandered across the room, tossed the book back to Curt, and headed for the door.

"Adam?" he called out, deciding his brother needed one last push for good measure.

He didn't look back, but he stilled. "What is it, Curt?"

"Lay off about her hair. It takes a lot of courage for a woman to do that to herself. Lorian had a handle on her, and it was Erin's only means of escape. Don't make it worse for her."

Adam's shoulders dropped in defeat. "Yeah. I think I understand now."

Chapter Four

Talon met Kord and Lewis at the door, looking grim and determined.

Kord's smile disappeared. "Is there a problem, Talon?" he asked, knowing there was.

Talon was typically easy-going and relaxed. He was tense and skirting the edges of fury now. "I need to speak to you. Both of you," he replied evenly.

"Sure. Let's go to my office. Boys," he bellowed.

Bryant's face appeared at the top of the stairs, looking—terrified. Kord's eyes narrowed, taking in the glance the young Warrior shot Talon. Kord glanced back at Talon's tense jaw and felt his blood heat in anger.

"Get your brothers and unload the truck," he instructed coolly. "The bags are fairly self-explanatory. Make sure they find the proper rooms."

"Adam's gone to town, but I'll get Curt to help."

"No," Talon ordered him. "Curt is talking to Erin right now. Leave. Them. Alone." There was more than an order in that last part. There was a blatant warning involved.

"Yes, Lord *König*. As you wish." Bryant rushed down the stairs and ducked outside, avoiding Talon's glare and the nervous looks Kord and Lewis threw each other.

"What did Bryant do?" Lewis asked.

Talon looked at the door, closing behind the young man's back. "The office," he decided.

Kord took a deep breath and led the way. "This doesn't bode well," he commented.

Lewis grunted his agreement. "My son better have a damned good explanation for this, or he's going to be very sorry."

Talon flopped into one of the overstuffed chairs and waited for the other two men to sit. "I want permission to deal with your boys harshly," he told them.

"Boys?" Lewis parroted. "All of the boys?"

"Actually, Curtis is a very honorable young man. I'd like permission to train him in my usual style with Erin and Hunter for the next few weeks."

"We'd be honored. He'll learn a lot from your family."

Kord cleared his throat. "Talon, I've known you for a long time. You don't believe in harsh lessons," he reminded the younger lord.

"Until now. Some lessons should be as painful as I can make them. This is one of them."

Lewis groaned. "What did my boys do?"

"I have your permission to train Curtis?" he asked distractedly.

"Yes, of course you do. I can see the advantage of it."

"The advantage you perceive is only half the reason. Training with me means Curtis will be safe from his brothers until they're taught their own lessons. I think it's safe to say that Adam would have taken Curtis apart piece by piece today without my intervention."

Kord shook his head in confusion. "That sounds like an internal Maher problem. I'll take care of this," he decided. "After all, we're supposed to be fighting the beasts, not each other."

Talon's jaw tightened another notch. "When

Curtis's crime is protecting my daughter from Adam, it is no longer internal to Maher. Deal with Bryant for his cowardice if you like, but I must insist that Adam face Hunter as he agreed—when Hunter's healed, of course."

"Cowardice?" Lewis asked in shock.

"That's what I call a Warrior who ignores a trainee's call for help in a hopeless situation, especially when the enemy plans to plow right through the trainee to teach an injured, human girl 'a lesson.' Yes, before you ask, Erin told Adam she was injured, and he all but called her a liar."

Kord took a deep breath. "I think we should hear the whole story," he decided.

The Mahers listened to the story, and Kord felt a sick certainty that every word of it was true. Adam had picked up many of Calvin's training techniques, more than Kord cared for. He had also exhibited problems with his judgment in training and battle. Adam was a fantastic Night Warrior. He simply had too many problems dealing with other Warriors.

In the end, only one question remained for him— one that Kord was fighting with himself not to ask. "By all means, Talon. Adam will face Hunter as agreed, with my blessing and support. But, I will handle Bryant personally, unless you think Jayde would prefer the honors."

"I'll check with her and let you know within the hour. Thank you, Kord."

The question still burned at him. On inspection, it wasn't a question that could be left unasked. "Talon? We've never dealt with a *Blutjagdfrau* at this stage of development before. Are you sure their curse develops as the boys' do? Could they develop in conjunction with the onset of menses as protection?"

"I don't know. She's as fast as many Warriors already. She's strong, but Erin doesn't seem to heal any faster. There's no manual for this, and the Stone wasn't giving me answers the last time I checked."

Kord nodded, thinking uneasily about her driving Lorian to ground and her attacks on Adam. "Then, maybe it's better that you're training her."

* * * *

Curt had little trouble convincing Erin to take a swim with him before dinner. The idea of the cool lake water sounded very soothing to her. He made a point of making sure Adam knew they were going, knowing his drive to see the damage for himself would be overpowering. Some dark place in Curt hoped it would make his brother feel worse to see it.

The difficulty came in convincing her to remove the oversized shirt she was wearing over her suit. She steadfastly refused at first.

"Come on, Erin. You can't swim in that thing. Besides, I've seen the bruises already. Everyone has, really."

"Not your Dad and brothers—and not Hunter," she managed miserably.

"None of whom will be headed this way," he assured her. "You know the wet fabric will hurt. If we see anyone, I promise I'll get your shirt and drag it into the water for you."

She blushed. "Okay, Curt. It's a deal." She pulled the shirt off over her head, peeling the ball cap with it.

Erin pushed her hand over the remains of her hair and smiled ruefully. "Guess I can't swim in that either."

"It'll grow. You'll see. It will be as beautiful as ever in no time."

"No." She headed for the lake. "I can't let it get long enough to use against me again."

"I'm sure there's a middle ground. Long enough to let you feel feminine but too short for a beast to use?"

"He'd have to touch scalp for the amulet to work."

"You have curls. It can be much longer and accomplish that," he assured her.

"We'll see."

It was more of a concession than Curt had hoped for when he'd broached the subject.

They swam for half an hour before relaxing in some trees along the far shoreline. Curt never saw Adam, but he was sure his brother stayed long enough to see the bruises on Erin's back and legs.

Curt found that he was very comfortable with Erin. They had always gotten along well. They were close in age, much closer than either of them was with his or her brothers, but there seemed to be a new closeness this time. Whether it was because he'd protected her from Adam or his damned curse making him want anything female and appealing, he couldn't tell. Either way, she was still a child—and *Blutjagdfrau*, which automatically meant hands off.

* * * *

Kord looked around the table, taking a mental head count. "Where are the others?" he asked.

Jayde smiled. "I gave Erin and Curtis permission to

eat with Hunter. If it's a problem, I can call them down."

"No. That's fine with me. I imagine Erin isn't keen on some of the company she'd be keeping down here, anyway."

Adam rubbed his forehead roughly, and Bryant winced and looked away. Neither of them, Kord noticed, offered either apology or explanation.

He scowled at his grandsons before smiling at Jayde. "How are Hunter and Erin feeling?" he asked. "I haven't had a chance to see them today."

"Good. Hunter's stitches can come out tomorrow. I imagine he'll be able to join us for dinner tomorrow evening or maybe the following morning. It will take several more days for the deeper wounds to heal and his strength to return."

"And Erin?"

His grandsons pushed their food around their plates without looking up.

"Sore. I think we've established that her healing is as slow as it always was. It's going to take three weeks or more for her to heal completely. At least her stitches will come out in another four or five days. I know they're bothering her."

Adam met Jayde's eyes miserably. "I got something for Erin, but I don't think she'll accept it from me. Will you pass it along for me? If it's from you..." He shook his head.

"What is it?" she asked.

He dropped his fork and went to the sideboard for a large Wal-Mart bag. Adam handed it to her and dropped back into his chair. "It's not much, but there's not much I can do to make things right at this point. I can take my punishment and not make such an ass of myself again. Anyway, check it out. It might help. I hope it helps."

Jayde pulled the bag into her lap and looked into it. She sucked in her breath and nodded in obvious awe. "Thank you, Adam. This was very thoughtful of you."

Talon looked around at her in surprise. "What is it?"

"Bandanas, scarves, and hats...all in eyelet, lace, ribbons, pretty colors. All very feminine."

Adam nodded. "I didn't know what would appeal to her, and I couldn't exactly ask. I hope she finds something she likes, and you can return what she doesn't to buy her more of what she does." He shrugged.

Talon favored him with an appraising look. "Well done, Adam. You might want to add an apology, though."

"I didn't think she'd let me offer it," he admitted.

"That's between the two of you. You still owe satisfaction to Hunter, though."

Adam ground his teeth and nodded grimly. "My hide is his to destroy as he will. I have no doubt that my best will not be nearly enough."

Kord stared at him. "Why the change, boy? Be honest with me."

"I'll admit that I realized my hide was in deep shit early on." He moved his neck as if it was stiff from Talon's shove at the training area. "As for being a world-class jerk? Probably about the time Curt told me what Lorian did to her. Until then, I was just too damn sure..."

"Sure of what?" Jayde demanded.

"That she was nothing but a spoiled little girl that always got her own way and did whatever she wanted to do with no reprisals." Adam shook his head in embarrassment.

Kord dropped his fork forcefully. "What would give you that idea? I've known Erin a long time, and spoiled is not a word I would use for her. If anything, Erin had less freedom than any Warrior-born daughter ever born. She had to. Her life depended on it."

Adam darkened. "I'm used to a certain level of respect being paid me. My brothers—"

"Fear you, I'm sure," Talon inserted acidly.

He nodded. "I won't deny that. A twelve-year-old with an attitude who thinks nothing of ordering me to move out of her way, calling me a self-important fool, planting a blade so close it brushed my cock, flat out attacking me and ordering Curt to help her—"

Bryant cleared his throat. "As I recall, she attacked you to save Curt's skin. Erin didn't raise a hand against you when her own butt was on the line."

Lewis glared at him. "Which wouldn't have been necessary, if you had given them help when Curtis asked for it. Together, you could have defeated Adam, but you refused. It wouldn't have been easy, but it would have been impossible for Curtis to do it alone, and Erin's assistance only put her in further danger. Why did you allow it to go on when you could have stopped it?"

Bryant pushed his plate away and flicked an uneasy glance at Adam. "Because the next time I faced him, it would be alone," he admitted.

"You fight beasts and you're afraid of your

brother?" Kord demanded.

"Beasts are easier to defeat and a lot less threatening. Beasts can only attack you after dark. I've never met a beast that equaled Adam in full *Blutjagd*. Only a fool takes him on then, and he was lit up hard."

Talon set his jaw. "Only a fool or a better trained Warrior. Or maybe all it takes is a trainee and a little girl who have nothing left to lose. Hope you never meet an elder, Bryant. Your brother will cease to impress very quickly."

Kord caught his younger grandson's attention and glared at him. "Well, Bryant. I can see we have been remiss in your education. We considered letting Jayde, elder killer, instruct you in what to truly fear, but she graciously allowed that your problem was a failure in Maher training that thankfully has been rectified since you trained. You will face all the older Warriors of Maher except Adam. After we've finished with you, you'll face Curtis. You have wronged him as surely as you wronged Erin by refusing them both aid.

"Adam, you know your fate already. I can't stand in Talon's way on this. I wouldn't even if I could. Your offense was directly to his house. It was the choice of *König* and of you to allow you to face Hunter rather than the Lord and Lady *König*." He noted Adam's grimace and guessed that he knew he wasn't getting off easy in the deal, now.

"I had considered giving what was left of you to Curtis, but I don't imagine there will be much left of you, and your brother has already proven he can blindside you. I think you require extra training for that. Erin is an elder hunter. Her getting the drop on you is understandable, but *Blutjagd* or no, you should have seen Curtis coming."

"Yes, Grandfather," he breathed in a tense voice. Adam had never cared for correction.

"Good. Eat up. You'll need your strength. Bryant, you face us day after tomorrow. Adam, you are at Hunter's leisure."

Bryant worked at that in seeming confusion. "Why the delay on me?"

"I want Hunter well enough to see how Maher will deal with you, so he'll see the least I expect him to deal your brother."

Chapter Five

April 19, 2021

Hunter was glad to see the stitches go, though the intense itching of his rapidly healing body was threatening to drive him insane. Despite lingering pain that he was taking Tylox for, he managed to pull on a pair of jeans and join the others for dinner. He gave up on the idea of a shirt because of the agony of trying to drag one on, but the thought of his adversary staring at his wounds and getting more nervous cinched it for him. Hunter pulled on his boots and headed for the stairs gingerly, feeling every step as if glass was being driven through his healing tissues.

Kord smiled widely as he entered the large dining room. "It's good to see you up, Hunter. Take a seat and eat with us."

He nodded and crossed to a chair next to Erin, controlling his urge to wince as he moved. Hunter tugged at the black eyelet bandana and smiled at her as he sank into his chair. "Looks good. Matches that Warrior's shirt nicely. Is that one of mine?" he teased.

"Maybe." Her smile was crooked and strained because of the bruise on her face. "You're not wearing it."

Hunter laughed at that observation. "Just clean and return it when you're done."

"I always do." Erin stabbed a forkful of spinach from her plate. "Red meat, spinach, rolls, OJ, and milk. Healing food. Eat it," she ordered.

"You, too." He raised an eyebrow, until she stuffed the vegetable into her mouth and started chewing.

Hunter smiled indulgently as he watched her taking in the healing foods. Gods knew she needed it more than he did. His curse would take care of his healing, even if he neglected himself. Her body wouldn't.

His smile disappeared and he glared at Adam, issuing a silent warning. The other man nodded his acknowledgement and looked to Erin sadly. The interaction wasn't lost on Erin, and she started pushing her food around her plate.

"Eat, squirt," Hunter commanded her.

She stabbed a mouthful of meat and started working at it.

"That's better," he decided.

Jayde shook her head in wonder. "You two haven't gotten along this well in years," she noted.

Hunter nodded as he swallowed a mouthful of milk. "Leave it to an elder to remind you what's important in life."

"So, do you think you'll be up to a walk down to the training area tomorrow?" Kord asked.

"Certainly. Another night's rest and good food like this, and I can pull that off."

"Good. Then Bryant will face his punishment tomorrow."

Hunter raised an eyebrow at the second of Lewis's sons. "I wouldn't miss it, Kord."

Bryant stared at his plate miserably.

"Nothing to say, Bryant?"

The other man raised his head and flicked a glance at Erin, who was trying to ignore the exchange. "I was wrong, but I don't think anyone would buy that I'm sorry at this point. It'll be a hell of a show, I suppose." Bryant shrugged.

Erin gaped at him, her fork wavering, halfway to her mouth with another dollop of spinach on board. Her color dipped several shades toward a pasty gray.

"What's wrong, Erin?" Talon asked.

"I don't want to watch this," she managed.

"It's an internal matter to Maher, though you felt the fallout from it. We were invited, but you're not required to attend."

"Thank you. I don't want to attend."

"You should attend when Hunter fights Adam, though," their father cautioned.

Erin met Adam's gaze head on and nodded. "I can do that," she decided.

The rest of the meal passed in relative silence. When Erin finally pushed away from the table, Adam nodded to Talon and followed her from the room.

Hunter watched him warily. "What's this?" he asked, tense, a hair off *Blutjagd*.

His father smiled. "Adam is trying to offer an apology—if your sister will accept it."

"Now? Why?"

"Better now than after he takes his beating. It will sound more honest now."

"Even if she accepts it, I'm taking him apart," Hunter warned. "He's not talking his way out of this one. He was way over the line."

"He knows that. This is between him and Erin. It has no bearing on what goes on when you heal."

"Erin! Stop," Adam thundered.

Hunter pushed to his feet painfully. "Unless I kill him now," he growled.

Adam raced into the room and snatched up his weapons belt from the back of his chair. Hunter snagged him by the throat, stopping his headlong dash back to the doorway.

"Hunter, I need," he rasped, gasping for breath.

Hunter shook him, wincing at the lance of pain in his shoulder. "What did you say to her?" he demanded.

"Nothing. I apologized," he managed hotly through the grip Hunter had on him.

"Then, why—"

"Later, Hunter. She took off, and it's getting dark out there. Let me go after her."

The room was suddenly in motion. Hunter's blood ran cold, and he released Adam slowly. Too much time... He'd wasted too much time fighting Adam, while Erin was heading away at top speed. She could be anywhere by now.

"Find her," he whispered. "Find her or it's your life, Adam."

Bryant was already strapping on his belt. "Where's Curt?" he asked in confusion.

Adam groaned. "Hopefully, bringing her back. Let's get flashlights and radios before we go."

* * * *

Erin startled as Adam's hand settled on her shoulder.

He pulled back with his hands up in surrender. "I won't touch you," he soothed her.

She took another step away, watching him warily. "What do you want?"

Adam was a big man, a good three inches taller than her father and Hunter, making him over six and a half feet, and just as broad. She had been afraid of his sheer size when she jumped at him, and it terrified her now.

As if reading her mind, he shoved his hands in his pockets and took yet another step back. "Look, I wanted to apologize."

"Apologize?"

"I overreacted. I didn't know."

"Didn't know what?"

"I heard about Lorian—all the things he did to you. Once I asked some questions, I understood."

Erin felt her stomach turn a lazy circle. "What did you hear?" she asked, just to be sure. She hadn't stayed in the room with Curt and her family. Worse, only her father promised not to share everything. She couldn't even be sure Adam got his information from Curt. He asked around, he said. If her parents told Kord and Lewis— Her stomach rebelled at the thought of Adam knowing all her secrets.

Adam sighed and averted his eyes. "Look, I know what he did to you. Having him touch you like that— I'm sorry. I'm sorry he hurt you, and I'm sorry I made it worse. You didn't deserve any of it, but taking your dignity was probably even worse for you than the physical abuses. I could see that in your eyes the other day, but I didn't understand what it was then."

She backed away, looking at the floor through a haze of tears. This was her worst nightmare come true. Of all the people she'd rather not share this with, Adam was just about lowest on her list.

Adam took a step closer. "You're safe now, Erin. I know you don't believe me, but I'll make sure he never touches you again...in any way. I promise even the emotional scars will heal in time. I'm offering a blood oath of—"

Erin had heard enough. She launched out the door and into the woods, feeling the tears coursing down her face. She ignored Adam, when he ordered her to stop. He was the last person she wanted to set eyes on.

By the time she reached the lake, her leg muscles burned and her lungs hurt. Erin launched in without removing her shoes and socks, letting the cold water wash over her. The shock to her system helped clear her mind.

Why the hell would they tell Adam that? She supposed Kord might not know how much it upset her, but how could it not upset her?

Erin groaned and dunked her head again, trying to stay warm. The water was cold, but she could deal with that. The cold wind blowing over her skin when she rose above the waterline was almost more than she could bear.

She startled at a noise from the shoreline. Panting and shaking in exhaustion, Curt stood with his hands on his hips, watching her.

"What do you want?" she asked miserably. And, why couldn't anyone just leave her alone?

"Come on out and talk, Erin," he invited.

"No. I can't trust any of you." *And, I'd freeze my ass off if I came out,* she added silently.

"You can trust me. You know you can trust me."

Erin shook her head stubbornly. She thought about sending him away, but Curt would either ignore her or go back for her parents, and that was not an option for her.

"If you don't come out, I'll have to come in after you and drag you out," he reasoned in a voice that brooked no other options.

"You wouldn't dare," she growled, her anger at that idea almost overwhelming the rest put together.

Curt sighed and dragged off his boots and socks, while she watched with wide eyes. He waded in after her, before she could stop him.

He grimaced, shooting her a look of pure pain. "Damn, this is cold! Sure you won't come out?"

Erin closed her eyes in resignation. Curt would just keep coming until he was as soaked as she was, and it would be her fault. "You're really going to drag me in, aren't you?"

"You'd rather be a Popsicle?"

"Not particularly," she admitted. More important, she'd rather he wasn't a Popsicle because of her. He would drag her out, even if it meant coming away as wet as she was. Curt would see that as his duty.

"Then, come out and talk to me."

She nodded and swam back. "All right. Since you're so determined."

He held his ground until she passed him on her way to the shore. Erin curled into a ball with her back to a boulder, shivering, trying to make as little of her body accessible to the cold wind off the higher peaks as she could.

Curt sank down next to her and wrapped an arm around Erin for warmth. "So, what stupid thing did Conan say this time?" he asked quietly.

"Nothing," she stormed. *I was wrong*, she decided. Erin wanted to discuss this with Curt even less than she wanted to discuss it with Adam.

"Bullshit! You take off like a bat out of hell and come throw yourself in a frigid lake when it's fifty degrees outside without even removing your shoes. What set you off?"

Erin shook her head miserably. "I really don't want to discuss this, Curt."

"Just tell me what he said. I know you don't have any reason to save Adam's life. Well, neither do I, but Hunter will kill him, if you don't come up with something that isn't entirely Adam's fault."

"He just— Dammit! Can't everyone just drop it?"

"What is it?" Curt asked in frustration. "I can't help if you don't tell me."

"You can't help anyway. Not unless you can erase Adam's memory."

He furrowed his brow. "I don't get it."

"Adam knows something I'd rather he didn't. Whether he got it from you or my father or Kord— I don't care really, but he has no right knowing it. I wouldn't have told him."

"Told him what?"

"Lorian used some sort of coercion on me, like a directed daydream but very real. Hunter pulled me out. I couldn't fight him. That beast would have won, if it wasn't for Hunter."

"What's so bad about that? Beasts win, even against seasoned Warriors. It happens."

Erin felt her cheeks burn. She didn't question why the thought of telling him hurt so badly. A cursory examination told her that Curt was her friend, and losing his respect would kill her. She couldn't seem to stop the tears when they started.

Curt pulled her to his chest and held her. "Tell me, Erin. I can't help, if you won't talk to me."

She shook her head into his shoulder.

"Please. Nothing can be that bad. There is nothing you cannot tell me."

Erin ached to believe him. She needed to believe him, so she launched out the words before she could talk herself out of it. "He was seducing me—more or less. It was so real. It hurts to think about." She held her breath and waited for his response.

"It was brutal," he guessed.

"No. He was tender, too tender. He'd never really be like that." She sighed.

"Is that it?" he asked in surprise.

"Don't you get it? I was enjoying it. Until Hunter broke me free—" She shuddered. "He could have— Well, Lorian could have done just about anything, and I wouldn't have had the common sense to stop him."

"No! It was a coercion. It was—like a rape in some ways. The emotional part was just part of the package for Lorian. You *weren't* enjoying it. He added that."

"How can you be sure? I can't," Erin admitted, ashamed at the truth of it.

"When you first laid eyes on Lorian, what was your first impression of him?"

"He frightened me, and it wasn't just being trapped with a sword to my throat. His looks frightened me. I can't explain it," she moaned.

"Were his fangs extended? Was he bloody? Was he grimacing? What frightened you?"

"No, he...he looked like a Warrior. That's dumb. Of course, he looked like a Warrior. All the elders were originally Warriors. He was handsome, smiling." Erin shivered. "But, there was something frightening in that just the same."

"Would you have kissed him? Let him touch you

and have sex with you?"

"No," she responded in horror.

"After Hunter freed you, did you still want him? Did you want Lorian's hands and his lips on you? Did you want him to take you?"

"No!" Erin tried to push away, but Curt cradled her closer to his chest and started to rock her. "The thought makes me sick, Curt," she whispered into his chest.

"Then, he added your enjoyment to his coercion," he concluded gently, running his fingers over her cheek to punctuate the words. "Never doubt that. You didn't want him before, and you didn't want him after. The rest was nothing but a trick."

Erin pushed away slowly and met his eyes in the dim light. Curt was being honest. There was only concern written in the depths of his dark eyes. She hugged him tightly, needing to know he was still there for her. "Thank you, Curt," she breathed, when he didn't pull away from her.

"Anytime. Now, I need to get you back before we both freeze. It's getting dark."

She snapped her head up. A nameless panic settled in her chest. No, not nameless. *Lorian.* "What have I done?" After dark, Erin was a sitting duck. They were five minutes from the house at a dead run, and it was too dark to travel that way.

"Hand me my boots. It will be okay," he soothed her. "We're close enough."

* * * *

Hunter looked at his mother angrily from his perch

on the wide staircase. "For the last time, I'm not going back up until Erin is back."

Being unable to join in the search was maddening. The Mahers had left the entire *König* household behind with the excuse that they didn't know the terrain, but Hunter suspected that his parents were left to keep him from following them out.

So far, the men had split up to head for all the lower grounds: the rock face that fell away from the house, the meadow where the training area was, and the thick stand of trees due west. They doubted Erin would head uphill if she was running, and those places held more danger for her. If she headed up, Erin would eventually have to cross water to go further. In the cold evening air, they assumed she wouldn't try to cross water for fear of hypothermia.

His head snapped up as the door opened.

Erin slipped in followed closely by Curt. She was drenched head to toe and dripping large droplets of water on the front hall floor. Curt was solidly wet to his thighs—except for his boots, which were simply splattered—and had wet imprints on his lap and chest that seemed to indicate he had either grabbed or hugged Erin to himself. Both were shivering and pale.

Hunter calmed himself to wait for the explanation. Talon trusted the boy, and nothing Hunter had seen so far belied that initial sense of duty and friendship the young man had for Erin.

"What the hell happened?" Talon demanded, less patient for an answer.

"She decided to soak her head," Curt chattered, wrapping his arms around his ribs.

"Can I get dried off?" Erin pleaded. "I'm freezing."

Jayde moved toward Erin and guided her to the stairs without a hint of censure. "Come on before you end up with pneumonia," she invited. "Are you coming, Hunter?" There was the censure.

"After I hear the explanation."

His mother nodded and led Erin away.

Hunter met Curt's eyes. "Do you need to dry off or can you talk?" he asked evenly.

"I can manage."

"Good. Dad, call the Mahers in before they get any further."

"Wait for me," Talon ordered as he scooped up the radio and arranged for the other men to meet up at the training area and come back in as a group. That settled, he nodded to Hunter to continue.

"Now, what happened?"

"She went for a swim to clear her head," Curt offered, pulling his boots off and revealing the soaked material beneath.

"Why? What did your brother say to her?"

The boy darkened. "He—um—mentioned something she didn't want him to know. I didn't tell him. I swear, I didn't even know," he finished miserably.

"Know what?" Hunter demanded.

"About Lorian playing that little game of seduction with her via coercion."

"She told you about that?" Talon asked in surprise.

Curt nodded. "Yeah. She didn't want to, but I think she needed to talk it out. She's better with it now—I think. She seemed to be, anyway."

"Better with what?" Hunter asked suspiciously.

Curt shuffled from foot to foot and avoided their

eyes. "You should discuss this with Erin," he decided quietly.

"Erin won't discuss it with us. She discussed it with you. Talk, Curt."

He nodded and blushed deeper. "I had to explain that the..." He met Talon's eyes for a moment, sighed, then averted his gaze again. "The pleasure she experienced wasn't her own. It had to be planted. She saw through his beautiful act first thing. Erin wouldn't have touched him willingly—ever. She wanted Lorian touching her even less after the fact. The thought of it makes her physically ill. A simple illusion wouldn't have changed that.

"Erin...wasn't...sure about... She thought..." Curt shifted his weight again. "If the pleasure had been her own... I can't do this," he grumbled. "I'm sorry, but I can't discuss this with you."

Talon nodded grimly. "You did just fine, Curtis. She understands now?"

"I think so. She seemed—not even relieved but overjoyed when I explained the difference to her."

Hunter smiled. "Good. I owe you some lessons that will knock Adam on his ass for years to come."

Talon furrowed his brow. "But, how would Adam know anything about it?"

Curt cleared his throat. "Erin thought maybe you told Kord, and he let it slip."

"No. This one stayed in-family until Erin told you."

"It won't go any further from me," he promised.

"See that it doesn't," Hunter counseled.

The door opened again, and the rest of the Mahers tramped in, wiping mud off of their boots as they came. Bryant howled in laughter at the sight of his younger brother.

Curt scowled at him. "Go soak your head, Bryant. Preferably until you drown," he added.

"What'd you do? Jump in the lake?" the young man inquired, poking at the dripping jeans in amusement.

Curt batted his hand away. "Yes. As a matter of fact, I did jump in the lake," he growled.

Bryant sobered slightly. "Why?"

"Don't ask. Hunter, Lord *König*—if you're finished with me, I need to dry off before I freeze."

"Go on," Talon told him. "Jayde will not be amused if you get pneumonia for your trouble. That was good work tonight. We may have to give you an extra week's worth of training in gratitude."

"Thanks, but at this moment, I'd settle for hot coffee and dry clothes." Curt nodded to Hunter and sprinted up the steps.

Kord watched him go in concern. Whether for Curt or for Erin was uncertain, but he was concerned. "How's Erin?"

Talon shook his head. "Much calmer, but she's freezing."

"Did she go wading, too?" He raised an eyebrow in surprise.

"No, she opted for a swim. I think Curtis was pulling her out. Notice his boots aren't doused? Her shoes were, along with the rest of her."

"Why?" Adam asked nervously. "All I did was apologize and offer my protection. I'm not lying. Honest."

Hunter and Talon exchanged a weary look. "Tell us exactly what you did say," Hunter decided.

Adam repeated it in halting tones, and the other men listened intently.

Talon nodded when he finished. "She misunderstood." He sighed in relief. "She'll be glad to hear that."

Hunter pushed to his feet to climb the stairs, giving in to the need to grimace. "You're off the hook on this one, Adam."

"But, I don't understand," Adam complained. "What did I say wrong? I don't want to do it again."

Hunter looked back at him and smiled sadly. "She's not ready to discuss Lorian with you. Leave the subject alone."

Kord furrowed his brow. "She's been talking about him for days," he noted.

"With me. With Curt. Leave it alone. I'll explain the mistake to her. Just—don't try to apologize to her again, okay?"

"Sure," Adam replied half-heartedly.

Chapter Six

April 25, 2021

Erin sat outside the fenced area, watching Hunter warm up and casting nervous glances at Adam.

She wasn't worried about Adam hurting Hunter. At only eight days since Lorian's attack, her brother wasn't at top form yet, but his joke that he hardly needed top form for Adam was dead-on accurate, and none of the *Königs* questioned it. If anything, it would be even more embarrassing for Adam to lose to a barely-healed opponent. No, Adam would be lucky to land a single punch on Hunter. In all honesty, she was worried about Adam's state at the end of it all.

Erin was glad she hadn't watched Bryant's pummeling. She understood that Kord left him largely intact for Lewis. Lewis left him standing for Curt. Erin still couldn't picture Curt taking his turn, but he had, just as he was ordered to and did it well. Bryant had to be carried out of the training area to his bed.

She'd overheard Hunter musing to their parents that Curt's words to his brother as he took the field were: "This isn't for me. This is for Erin."

Knowing that Bryant had been bedridden for two days and knowing that his broken bones were still knitting, Erin hadn't been particularly happy with the idea of his injuries being inflicted in her name.

Now Adam was facing Hunter, and her brother would do as much to Adam as the others did to Bryant—*or more*—in her name. Worse, this time she couldn't beg off. Like it or not, Erin had to watch while the man was taken apart.

This was what it would be like for any Warrior who crossed her, who pressured Erin or took pleasure with her before she earned her autonomy...or who went mad in printing. *This or something worse.* Corwyn had warned Erin that she would be sought after until she felt she might go mad. Would her entire life be a parade of Warriors being beaten to a pulp or killed in her name while she was forced to watch?

She shivered at the thought. Erin decided one thing right then and there. Once she had her autonomy, she'd be fighting her own battles. At least then, she could decide when enough was enough.

Curt sank down beside her. "Are you ready for this?" he asked.

"No," she admitted.

"I thought not."

"Think if I puke they'll let me go back to the house and not watch?" she asked hopefully.

"Nope."

Erin groaned, fighting the urge to puke anyway.

"Don't worry. I'll figure something out."

"I hope so."

Hunter stripped off his shirt and his weapons belt and tossed them over the fence. Erin grimaced at the sight of the ragged pink lines of his healing scar tissue. Still, her brother was a good-looking man. She wondered if his scars would be a hindrance in finding a wife. She hoped not, especially since he got them in her defense.

Adam followed suit, stripping to his waist. He was taller, but he seemed to have less of a presence. He paled next to Hunter somehow. Erin was sure it wasn't simply the fact that she liked Hunter better. It was more than that. It was something indefinable that Adam lacked. But, Hunter had it.

Erin looked at Curt out of the corner of her eye. Curt had it, whatever *it* was. She wondered for a moment what he would look like prepared to battle this way. She had seen Curt in a swimsuit, but there was something intense and—male about the Warriors in their boots and jeans, letting *Blutjagd* sweep them away for a challenge match or trial. Erin considered that she would know what Curt looked like if she had come to Bryant's trial. She shifted her gaze back to the match, uncomfortable with the idea of just how male Curt would be out on the field.

Stripped to the waist and unarmed, the two Warriors circled each other. Far from being a comfort, the fact that they were unarmed meant that they could inflict much more pain on each other with the almost sure knowledge that they wouldn't kill each other. However, they could do so much damage that one man—or both might wish to die before it was over or in the days after it was over.

Not surprisingly, Hunter landed the first blow. The solid punch to his ribs lifted Adam and dropped him to the dirt with a sickening thud that made Erin cringe.

Curt squeezed her hand. "He'll be fine. Watch. He's getting up."

She nodded as Adam pushed to his feet. He was wincing already and slightly breathless. Hunter stood back and allowed him back to fighting readiness before he landed his next blow, adding insult to the very real injuries he was dealing out. He took Adam's ribs again, this time with a roundhouse that threw the older man half the distance of the training circle.

Adam took longer to pick himself up that time. He staggered to his knees and looked at Hunter wearily as he pushed back to his feet.

Erin sighed. "I've been there before."

Curt shot a startled look at her. "You mean in the condition Adam's in, don't you?"

"Yes. After the last time I attacked Lorian. I forced myself up, determined to take him again if I had to and praying every second that I wouldn't have to. I was done in, but I had to keep him from killing Hunter long enough to bleed him to ground. The first time I saw him stagger, I swear I almost cried."

"You took him on with training weight weapons and still won," Curt noted in awe as he turned back to the action.

Erin felt her face darken, and she looked back in time to see Adam go down again—a face shot this time. "Most of the time," she admitted.

"What else did you fight him with?" he asked in interest, not taking his eyes off of the fight.

"My bare hands, for the last run I made."

Curt's head snapped around, and something resembling fury burned in his eyes. "Are you insane? What kind of a brainless—"

"I asked myself that same question. He certainly didn't expect it."

"I'll bet! What could you possibly do with your bare hands?" he demanded, trying to keep his voice low despite his anger.

"Bounce him off the wall hard enough to hear the crack of some bone somewhere."

"How? How could you, even with all your weight, pull that off?"

Erin flicked his amulet. "It's an old trick my mother used on Veriel when he wanted to feed on my father."

Curt shivered and swallowed hard at the thought.

She traced his amulet slowly then drew her hand away, realizing what she was doing. Erin looked away from his chest abruptly and tried to sound matter of fact. "Your amulet is a powerful weapon. Use it as long as you have it. Your body becomes a battering ram. Of course, you get thrown, too. Try to land softly."

"You didn't," he guessed.

Erin shook her head. "No, I didn't. Not when he hit me and not when I hit him."

"So, what was your offense when he hit you?" he asked comically.

"That would be the time I planted my blade just a few inches east of his heart and dragged it out to bleed him."

"Dragged?" Curt barked then lowered his voice again. "You stabbed instead of threw? Why?"

"Tactics. I had to get him at an unguarded moment. I couldn't risk missing at that point. As it was, the one throw I made was way off. It bled him, but it was about as far from the heart as you can strike a blow and still hit the chest cavity," she commented in annoyance. "Of course, I had just landed on my shoulder and—"

"Tactics?" he spat in disbelief, cutting her off. "What was your plan? How do you get a beast elder to drop his guard?"

She felt her cheeks burn and looked back at the battle. Adam was almost through. He wouldn't be capable of standing much longer, she noted. From the looks of it, Adam hadn't laid a single blow on Hunter.

"You don't want to know."

"No way. You started this. Tell me what your plan was. Now, Erin." Curt was furious, shaking in his restraint—probably to keep from shaking her bodily.

For just a moment, the sunlight seemed to shimmer around him, causing a halo of subtle color. Before she could question the effect, it was gone.

Erin sighed and avoided meeting his eyes. "I made him think he'd won."

"How?" His jaw was set tight, and he ground his teeth, growling out his words.

"I walked up to him and said I'd surrender my amulet."

Curt sputtered and looked back at the battle. His hands fisted, and he seemed to have trouble breathing.

Adam was recovering from another blow, and blood ran freely from his split lip, streaming down his chest. One eye was swelling shut, but still he pushed to his feet and lunged for Hunter. *Honor demands that he fight, until Hunter calls a halt or he can't fight anymore.* One glance at her brother confirmed that Hunter would choose the latter. The three punches that took Adam down again confirmed that for her.

"Told you that you didn't want to know," she managed quietly.

"Do your parents know you did that?"

"They never asked. All they know is what Hunter was conscious for—in other words, not a damn thing except his coercion and him having me trapped. I think it's probably better if they don't know the rest. They haven't asked, and I haven't offered the information."

"Why haven't you told them?"

"Are you crazy? They'll kill me."

"Okay, so you walk up to an uninjured elder—"

"He was injured. I had already sliced his face open."

"Do I want to know?" he asked in exhaustion.

"He lunged at me, and I hit the first thing that came my way and rolled away."

"I didn't want to know that. I know why Talon is going gray now." Curt rubbed his eyes. "I may be gray before the end of this conversation. Okay, you walked up to a barely-injured elder and offered yourself up... I assume you did this to save Hunter."

"I never intended on keeping that promise," she countered hotly. "You know I didn't."

"Then why make it? To save Hunter? Do you have any idea what Lorian could have done to you for lying to him that way?"

"Do you have any idea what he was going to do, if I didn't lie to him that way? If I held firm or if I failed, the penalty was the same for Hunter and for me. Our only chance was what I did succeeding." Erin looked at him miserably. "Boy, did I get lucky."

"What could he do to you?" Curt shot at her. "You had your amulet."

"Not if he took that sword to my arm above the bracer. That was *his* plan, and I didn't happen to care for that plan. Neither did Hunter, actually."

Curt looked at her in shock. "How did you get his guard down? How did you get a blade in him without him seeing it coming?"

"I—well, pretended is the wrong word. I *was* shaking so badly that I couldn't undo the buckles, but I damn well would have faked it if I hadn't been. I fumbled for awhile on purpose. That had his interest, but he was still guarded, and he was getting annoyed. So, I took out one of my weapons and started sawing through the first strap. I had no intention of going farther than that first one. If he was still guarded, I had a major problem on my hands. I made it—barely. He put his guard down when the strap snapped."

"I think you're right. I think your parents would kill you," he managed, looking pale.

She snuggled her chin onto her knees. "I know it."

"Oh, I don't know about that," her father's voice came from just over her shoulder.

Erin groaned.

Curt skittered further away as if he expected to take a blow for his part in the discussion. His eyes widened, and he looked back and forth between Erin and where her father had obviously unghosted behind her shoulder.

"Why?" she asked simply.

"Well, when you two were so engrossed you missed most of the battle, including the fact that it was over... Your argument caught my attention, so I decided to find out what the problem was. Imagine my surprise."

Erin glanced at him and found his face stony. "Are you furious?" she asked.

"I think furious would be a little harsh. You're as devious as your mother and you have skills, but we really need to work on your tactics."

"Well, I doubt that move would work a second time," she admitted.

"I'm surprised it worked the first time."

"What else was I supposed to do? What tactics would you have used?" she asked miserably.

Her father motioned for her to follow him. "I don't

know. But we have to talk about this."

* * * *

Erin looked around at the room full of Warriors nervously. She was human and injured, so she wouldn't face fist or blade, but this firing squad effect wasn't any better on her nerves. She laced her fingers together tightly and locked most of her muscles to hide the worst of her shaking.

After Adam had been taken to bed and tended to medically, her father had called all of the other Warriors to the training room. Knowing instinctively that it was about to go badly for her, Erin sat at the far end of the room and awaited her father's judgment.

Her mother tried to go to her, but Talon pulled her back.

"Not this time," he growled dangerously.

Jayde flicked an uneasy glance between her husband and daughter before nodding to him and taking a seat next to Hunter. Erin's heart sank. She would have no allies.

Talon trained cold eyes on her, and Erin shivered before she could stop herself. He nodded grimly then faced the other Warriors. "We've been walking on eggshells around Erin. That will stop now. From what I just overheard between her and Curtis, I would guess her pure gall would see her through any interrogation we make of her."

Erin swallowed a sick swirl. "As you wish," she managed weakly.

"In this matter, you are absolutely correct. Now, I heard very little of their conversation, so I will admit to both interest in and apprehension about the rest."

Erin groaned, and he shot her a venomous look.

"I'll make this as painless as I can. Tell us everything that happened after your brother lost consciousness. Don't try to play it down or sugar coat it. Don't make me drag it out of you like Curt had to. I want the brutal, honest truth about every single move you made with that beast. After you finish, we will question what we will. Do you understand me?"

Erin nodded slowly. "I understand."

"Good. Then you may begin."

She waited for him to sit with the other Warriors, but Talon stayed where he was, an intimidating shadow over her. Erin shifted her attention to Curt, hoping for one friendly face in the crowd, but he looked as scared as she was.

There was no reaction from the crowd when she told them about her fake hysterics, cutting her hair, or slicing his cheek to get away. Erin told them everything, every thought and every move. When she outlined her plan to save them both, the Warriors exhibited a mixture of shock and anger that made her distinctly nervous. Erin pressed on, desperate to finish her story and allow them their questioning so she could escape to her room.

She watched, frozen for a moment in time, as Hunter lunged for her. She had been describing how she sawed through the buckle, when her brother bellowed in rage and threw himself toward her. Erin covered her head with her arms, sure that he would forget himself and strike her. When no blow fell, she looked up shakily.

Hunter was flat on his back beneath both of their

parents and Kord, fighting their restraint with all his strength while his eyes burned in bloodlust. He locked his gaze with Erin's and roared at her as he tried to wrench free again.

"Release it, Hunter," Jayde ordered. "Release the *Blutjagd*. This is inappropriate. She is not your enemy."

Hunter's eyes closed, and his muscles tensed. He shuddered and lay very still, no longer straining against their grip, though he panted and a tear ran down his face. Erin wondered if the tear was in pain, sadness, or some other emotion even he couldn't name. His breathing slowed, his muscles unclenched, and he turned his head and regarded her miserably.

"I'm sorry," he whispered.

Erin nodded and blinked away her own tears. She hadn't wanted this. She hadn't wanted to hurt Hunter. She'd only wanted to save him. "I understand," Erin assured him, dropping her gaze to the floor and wrapping her arms around her stomach. She felt nauseated and shaky, and she wanted it to be over.

"I relieve you, Hunter," Talon informed him. "You don't have to stay here for this."

Erin heard the rustling as everyone moved off of her brother and he pulled himself up.

"No. I want to hear the rest. I'll control myself. You have my word."

She wanted to scream. Hunter should leave now. Erin couldn't face him and say the rest. She couldn't hurt him worse than she already had.

"It gets worse," Talon warned him. "Right, Erin?" he asked pointedly.

Erin met her brother's eyes, and he sucked in his breath at the sight of her. "Yes. It does," she admitted.

"I'm sorry, Hunter. I couldn't let him kill you."

His eyes narrowed. "Answer me one question. Did he take you?"

"No," she replied in horror, her stomach rebelling at the idea. "I'd rather turn that blade on myself first."

Jayde nodded her approval.

Hunter sighed in relief. "Then, I can stay," he decided. "I can control myself for anything else."

He sat next to Kord, and Jayde took her place, pinning him between them. Talon took up a stance in front of and slightly off center of her position, a clear warning to her brother to keep it under control or face him. The other Warriors moved closer to the center and tensed to stop Hunter if he moved again, and Curt gave her a nod that told her he'd be first in line to land on the dog pile.

Hunter smiled viciously at her description of Lorian relaxing his guard and her driving the blade home and ripping it free. His face darkened at the news of the beast's answering blow. She admitted that her next blow came while she was still felled, bleary-eyed and grunting at the pain shooting through her shoulder as she brought the blade up. Hunter considered that blow grimly and nodded at her to continue.

Erin pressed her back into the wall as she described her final run at Lorian. Hunter's eyes narrowed dangerously, and his jaw tightened. She watched his hands as he fisted them, and the other Warriors closed on his position. She finished as quickly as she could, trying to avoid an outburst. Erin flicked a glance at his eyes then looked away before he could lock on her. Even if Hunter didn't do it, he wanted to hit her—or worse.

"Is that it?" Hunter asked in a strained voice. "Is that all of it?"

"Yes. He left with a warning that he had all the time in the world to get even with me. I swear that's all."

"Good. I'm not sure I could take much more," he informed her.

"Neither could I. I was shot. I'm not sure I could have attacked again. I would have. I mean...I think I would have, but I don't know how. I could barely stand up, but I would have, Hunter." *Stop now. You're rambling.*

"Do you have any concept how close you came to dying?" Hunter asked calmly, raising his eyes to meet hers.

He was angry, but there was more than that. He was scared. That gave her pause.

"Yes," she admitted. "But, if it came to death or him taking me— You know what his plan was."

Hunter nodded. "I do. I hate to admit it, but it would have worked."

Lewis caught her attention next. "You really think Lorian would have taken your arm and risked losing you to the blood loss?"

"You didn't see his eyes. He was only holding off on the slim possibility of forcing my compliance some other way. Lorian fully planned to follow through if he had to. You don't need your hand to have a baby," she reasoned.

Erin bit it off and closed her eyes as an oppressive wave of nausea assaulted her. She felt chilled, and the sweat beading on her brow only made her feel worse. The air seemed thick and hard to draw into her lungs.

"Erin?" Kord called in a way that made her wonder if he had called before and was repeating himself.

She forced her eyes open slowly. "What is it?" she asked, her voice foreign in her own ears.

"When you were attacking, did you feel *Blutjagd*?"

Erin furrowed her brow. "I don't know what *Blutjagd* feels like. How would I know?"

"Was it a choice to act or a compulsion? Could you stop yourself?"

"When I went at him bare handed, I knew it was insane. I wanted to laugh hysterically and cry at the same time. Some rational part of me wanted to run the other direction as fast as I could."

"But, you didn't. It wasn't a conscious choice on your part, was it?"

"Only as far as the thought that he couldn't be allowed to kill Hunter or to take me. Beyond that..." She shrugged in exhaustion.

"You couldn't stop fighting until he went to ground or died. You knew that was true. It was your driving force and nothing—not pain or rational thought—could stand in the way of that. You couldn't stop fighting, could you?"

"No, I couldn't," she admitted. "I have no idea why, but I couldn't."

Kord's jaw tightened, and Erin was afraid that she had said the wrong thing though her mind couldn't seem to work out what the wrong thing was. He looked at Talon, and Erin shook her head in confusion at the way Kord's outline seemed to fuzz, at the glow that encased his body. A quick assessment of the room showed that the only window was shaded; there was no sunlight to cause the effect. If there was no light, her eyes were playing tricks on her.

Her stomach clenched hard enough to make tears pool in her eyes. How sick was she? Was she sick? Erin rubbed the sweat from her brow, trying to make sense of this feeling.

"I was afraid of this," Kord grumbled. "She's changing. A trainee's first *Blutjagd* are weak, almost impossible to sense, but they are absolutely uncontrolled. The trainee hasn't learned the control he needs to make it work with his mind."

"You can't know that for sure," her father exploded. "Her healing—"

"Would be the last thing to change. It is with the boys. Why wouldn't it be that way with her? She's fast, strong, easily enraged, and showing signs of *Blutjagd*. Consider the possibility, Talon."

"Not 'til sixteen," Hunter thundered. "The curse doesn't manifest until sixteen."

Erin pushed a shaky hand through her hair. She was sweating heavily, and she felt feverish. If she could have stripped off her clothes and jumped in the lake, she would have. She wished she knew why she felt so damned sick. It couldn't just be stress, she realized.

Lewis waved a hand for quiet. "It makes sense. Girls develop younger than boys in many ways. They mature emotionally, intellectually..." He sucked in his breath as he met her eyes.

"Sexually," she added for him. Erin pushed to her feet unsteadily. "If he had taken me?" She let the question hang between them.

Lewis cleared his throat. "I don't know where in your change that would fall. Boys are just—able. It might have been too late," he admitted.

The dizziness assaulted Erin full force. Arms encircled her as her knees buckled, and her rescuer fell with her to their knees, cradling Erin to a broad chest.

"It's all right, Erin," Hunter soothed her. "We won't let that happen." His hand brushed her cheek then over her wet hair. He murmured something that sounded of confusion, but she was too busy biting back the urge to vomit to note what it was.

The debate continued in the dark fuzz that surrounded her. "She's too young for her autonomy," Jayde noted.

"So, don't give her autonomy until she's sixteen," Kord reasoned. "Precocious or not, human children can't drive a car until they are sixteen, vote or buy cigarettes until they're eighteen. I don't see a difference."

"How can we be sure of what we're seeing?" Talon questioned.

Lewis called for a moment of peace. "The Stone confirms it. She is changing," he told them.

Erin pushed weakly at her brother's chest.

"What is it?" he asked. "What do you need?"

"To throw up. Please. I can't do it here."

Hunter nodded and cradled her to his chest as he got to his feet.

"How far into the change is she?" Jayde asked as Hunter swept her away.

"The Stone doesn't see the change in stages as we do," Lewis replied. "To it, there is only human or cursed. Anyone who has begun the change is cursed."

Hunter left the discussion behind. He lowered her to the floor in the downstairs bathroom. "Do you want me to leave?" he offered.

"No. I don't want to pass out. Keep me up." Erin white-knuckled the edge of the toilet as she let her stomach win the silent rebellion it had been staging. After flushing, she stayed with her head on the seat, feeling weak and spent.

Hunter started to rub her back but drew his hand away abruptly, mumbling his apologies.

Erin groaned. "No, rub it. It's the best I've felt in over an hour," she pleaded.

"It isn't too sore?"

"No. Feels better today," she managed.

"Can I check it?" he asked urgently.

"Sure. Why?"

Hunter didn't answer. He pulled the back of her button-down shirt from her jeans and dragged it up. His hand ran lightly over her lower back. "How's that feel?" he asked.

"Good. Your hands are cool," she murmured, wondering if she was really feverish or just imagining that.

He pulled her shirt back down. "Can you walk?"

"Do I have to?" Erin complained.

"We have to go back to the training room. If you can't walk, I'll carry you."

She nodded at the air of decision in his voice. "Help me up. I need to wash my face."

Erin surveyed her face in the mirror: pale with high patches of color, shadowed beneath the eyes, the eyes themselves too bright, and—no longer human? She closed her eyes and splashed cool water on her face. After she rinsed her mouth, Erin braced her arms on the sink and bowed her head. She wasn't prepared for this. She'd lost four years of her humanity, and impossible as it was, she wanted them back.

"Do you need to be sick again?" Hunter asked gently.

"No. I'm done with that, I hope. Let's go."

The other Warriors were still debating the various permutations of her change and what it meant in general, when Erin made her way unsteadily back into the room with Hunter's guiding hand on her lower back. Jayde smiled at her warmly as Talon started speaking.

"Obviously, Corwyn had the right idea. We need to begin real training. I just wish we knew how far into the change she is."

Hunter cleared his throat. "I think I can answer that, but you won't like the answer."

Every head turned to him, including Erin's.

"What are you talking about?" she asked him nervously.

"Turn around and show them the bruises on your back," he told her.

"Hunter, Mom checked it last night," she protested. "She knows what it looks like."

He met Jayde's eyes. "And?"

"It was sickly purple and green. Her back was much worse than her face," she confirmed for everyone.

"That's what I thought you'd say. Show them, Erin."

She edged away from him. "How much better are we talking, Hunter?"

He sighed. "It's healed, Erin. It's completely gone. You're sick. You feel sick right now. It's *Krankheit*.

You'll feel better in a day or two."

Her mind whirled, as Hunter started describing her fever and sweating to the assembled Warriors. *Krankheit.* It sealed the change. It was too late now. Erin sat down heavily, staring at her hands, lying on her bent knees...boneless, shivering.

Her mother was suddenly at her side, and Erin felt them pull up the back of her shirt to look at the bruises that were no longer there. "It will be all right," Jayde told her.

"No, I don't think it will, Mom. I don't think it will ever be all right again." A cold certainty that her life was effectively over stole into her heart. "I want my life back," Erin whispered. "I was supposed to have four more years. I want them back."

"It's the fever talking," Jayde assured her. "Hunter will take you to bed until it passes."

The voices rose, pressing in on Erin until the blackness gave her peace.

Chapter Seven

January 6, 2025

Sarah Kaufmann strolled along the dark street, fingering the amulet beneath her bracer nervously. The beasts were everywhere. It seemed they were congregating in this place. She seethed. Kohl knew it. She was sure he knew it, because she could read it in his shimmer. Still, he brought her here.

"Why, Kohl?" she growled at the man next to her, her house lord and adoptive father.

"We're searching for someone," the old man replied absently.

"A Warrior? Alone here?" Sarah's mind whirled at the thought. Even if most of the beasts were ghosted— and her power wouldn't tell her that, many were of low enough level that they couldn't be ghosted. The Warrior had to sense them, at least. Whoever he was, he was sorely outnumbered. "Who would do so foolhardy a thing?" she demanded.

"Our *König* prince," he informed her.

Sarah sucked in her breath and her eyes widened. "Hunter? We've come to see Hunter?"

His almost imperceptible nod sent a spike of pure pleasure through her. Sarah had heard such stories about the *Königs*! They were bold and practically invincible. Each of them had survived—some even killed elders.

"How many do you sense?" Kohl asked suddenly, reminding her of her job.

She furrowed her brow, completing a new sweep. "Seven yellow and ten red," she reported, indicating the number of low-level and high-level beasts respectively. Sarah poked her gloved hands into her coat pockets and watched her breath curl before her mouth.

Kohl grunted. "Can you see *König* yet?"

Sarah searched her mind shimmers again, annoyed that he hadn't asked her to check on her last sweep. Kohl had never truly appreciated how her power worked. The shimmers came again at her bidding: the seven yellow, the ten red, no black elder. Sarah had seen black elder once, and she hoped never to see it again. She returned to her examination of the shimmers. There were two green human forms—*food*, she thought wryly. *Entertainment.* No blue sensitives. She hadn't really expected to see another sensitive. They were rare. Kohl was his usual silver. She started to say she didn't see the young prince when his shimmer hit her, white hot and brighter than any she'd ever seen. It hurt to concentrate on it.

"Yes," she whispered. "Down this alley about half a block."

As if confirming her determination, the prince took on an enclave of the beasts, three reds at once. Sarah gasped, her mind tracking his fluid motions, noting numbly that the first fell within seconds of engagement.

Kohl grabbed her hand and dragged her along. Sarah held her breath, anticipating the moment when she would enter the active range of the beasts. She hated that part. Going into the midst of the beasts was always nerve wracking for her. In close quarters, the shimmers were with her always, unable to be shut down by anything but her medication. It was painful and draining after a time.

Sarah knew the moment the beasts circled them. Most of the shimmers were yellow. Two were red.

Kohl motioned her back so he could battle. At sixty-two, he was still as fit as most young Warriors were. In battle, she always obeyed Kohl. Not so much at other times, but at least in battle.

As he took the heart of the first beast she directed him to—a yellow, the young prince turned their direction, abandoning his own prey abruptly to make a run for them. One level of her mind continued its direction of Kohl, ordering him to kill three low-levels before switching strategy to order him to an edgy red getting ready to move on them. The movement of the shimmers told Sarah unerringly which beasts would be most easily taken, and the codes to set Kohl in motion flowed from her lips smoothly.

Another level of her mind reached out to touch the prince. He was swarmed in and making his way to them by way of an unearthly slaughter the likes of which she had never seen. He was locked in a fierce *Blutjagd*, but his mind raged at more than the beasts. He raged that any Warrior would hunt Cross land without leave from the Crossbearer house, would interfere with his hunt, and would drag a protected woman into battle.

Sarah smiled at that. Hunter of *König*-Crossbearer, elder hunter and prince, worried for her. It sent a thrill through her. Battle was one issue where few worried about her, Sarah decided.

She ducked, as a red shimmer lunged at her. Her scream was more pain than terror. The slightest touch of a beast sent knife points of agony through her brain. Though the hand that skated her shoulder barely triggered her amulet, crushing Sarah to the ground, her mind exploded, fragmented like glass thrown against a brick wall.

Kohl took the beast's heart and scowled at her. "Get up, Sarah. The battle isn't over yet."

She cursed at him under her breath and directed Kohl to another red that started closing when it perceived him as distracted. Her mind screamed in pain as she pushed to her feet. All her shimmers came through a fog. Her directions left her lips in gasps. Once, Sarah even slipped into an older code, earning a scathing glance from Kohl.

"Couldn't you see him coming?" he demanded, annoyed at her flagging strength and wandering mind.

"Shut up, old man! I don't have your speed. You know that." She may listen to him, but Sarah didn't have to take his criticism. Kohl knew she wasn't up to this after traveling all day. He did this to her, over and over.

She directed him to two yellows to his left quietly, trying to train her mind on the correct code. Sarah panted, pressing her hands to her temples for the illusion of relief it brought her. "Kohl, I can't do this much longer."

"It will be done soon," he replied absently.

Sarah gritted her teeth in fury. "It better. I have no intentions of spending days in bed for you."

But Kohl would expect that of her. She had no doubt that he would rationalize it as one more repayment for his saving her—or for Darrien. Sarah wanted to quit. She'd asked to quit, but Kohl kept demanding one more hunt, one more night. Some angry kernel in her wondered how much more of this torment she could take without snapping on her house lord.

The shimmers shifted, and her heart thundered in her chest. "The remaining have all gone for the prince," Sarah informed him in a thick voice. "You must help him."

Kohl grunted and grabbed her hand to drag her along. Together, the two Warriors made short work of the remaining beasts. Hunter didn't seem to register anything else until the beasts were dispatched. Then, he turned on Kohl with a fierce rage building in his shimmer, worse even than he'd expended on the beasts.

"Kaufmann," he bellowed. "How dare you upset my hunting this way."

The old man smiled coldly. "Even you must admit that your battle would have taken three times as long alone."

"That isn't the point. You dragged a protected woman into a battle and allowed her to be injured. Are you insane?"

"She's a fighting sensitive. She chooses this life, and she's not injured. She is...fatigued."

Sarah started to protest then groaned. "Kohl, we have to go. There are three more reds misting in."

"Reds?" Hunter asked in confusion.

"High-level beasts," she explained, trying to focus on his face through the fuzzy shimmer.

Kohl dragged her between the two Warriors, and she bit back a scream at the shimmer burn that radiated over her arm from his grip. Tears pooled in her eyes, and Sarah hit his shoulder, not caring how much it hurt anymore. Kohl released her in guilty realization she'd passed the point of no return. His emotions and thoughts coursed through her mind unbidden. At this point, she couldn't block them out any more than she could the shimmers that carried them.

He turned his back on her, bringing his weapon up in preparation.

"Damn you, old man! I told you I'm wiped out. I can't battle again."

"Stay there. Three won't take long. Besides, you were sloppy enough to allow that beast to touch you. The pain is your own fault."

Sarah gasped, as Hunter sheathed one of his weapons and scooped her to his body, but the burn didn't come as she expected. His body felt cool and hard next to hers.

Hunter took off at a run. "We're leaving," he ordered. "Come with us or face them alone, Kaufmann."

She nestled into his embrace, closing her eyes against the shooting pains in her skull, slightly more bearable now. Was she further from the beasts?

Sarah stiffened as a beast closed on them. "Release me. There's one here," she breathed, knowing the beast could hear her too and unable to use the protective code foreign to the prince.

Hunter sensed his surroundings carefully. She could feel the wave of energy wash over her. "Where?"

Ghosting. He can't see it. "Back right quadrant. He's about to attack. Put me down, please. You can't fight this way," she pleaded.

Hunter wheeled around, finding a weak disturbance—*I would like to investigate further when*

I'm well—and took the ghosted beast's heart in a single blow.

He turned before it even hit the ground and bolted again. "I have practice at fighting this way," he joked. A crooked smile lit his face.

Erin. He's talking about fighting while he protected Erin as a baby.

At his truck, Hunter wrenched the passenger door open and slid Sarah in. His eyes were wide in concern and he touched her face fondly. She wanted to thank him, but all her remaining concentration was focused on controlling the sudden wash of pain that engulfed her when she was alone on the seat.

"We'll get you to safety," he promised.

Kohl caught up with them and labored the cold air in and out from the run. "I had to take out another on the way," he explained. "I don't know where the last one is."

"Bringing friends," she breathed.

Hunter's eyes burned. He threw a ring of keys at the old man violently. She could read the thought from him that if he hadn't forced them to leave, she would have been trapped for far longer than those three.

"You drive," Hunter growled. "I'll care for her."

Kohl scowled. "She requires no coddling, *König.*"

"You'll answer for that in good time," he promised. "Drive."

The cab was crowded, and the prince drew her into his lap to conserve space as they left the small New Hampshire town behind. The pain crested, threatening to swamp her, and Sarah groaned at the knowledge that she would be paying for this battle for days.

Hunter brushed his knuckles over her cheek and

pulled her further into the cooling shelter of his body. "What is it?" he asked. "What do you need?" His voice soothed back the wave of pain slightly.

Sarah forced her eyes open, seeing his dark good looks through an aura of his shimmer: white shot through with gold and other swirling colors she had yet to identify after she locked on the gold. She'd never seen metallic gold before. "Hunter," she mused, identifying his shimmer to her battered mind. It was beautiful. He was beautiful.

"Yes, I'm Hunter. What's your name?" There was no amusement in his eyes when he said it. He seemed sad. Yes, his shimmer showed that, the intricate swirl over his heart speaking of sadness and concern.

Sarah furrowed her brow, trying to make sense of the question. Name? Her mind was mired in agony, and trying to retrieve whatever information he was seeking hurt too much. One clear thought emerged. "Medicine," she croaked.

"It's not safe yet," Kohl snapped at her.

She sobbed and turned her face into Hunter's chest. Her eyes closed as she drank in his scent. He smelled of mint and pine and *Blutjagd* unleashed.

"What is the medication? What does it do?" Hunter demanded.

Kohl sighed. "It suppresses the center of her brain that senses the beasts and renders her unable to function normally. If we encounter some danger after we administer it, she'll be helpless, unable to move and protect herself."

"She's unable now," he stormed.

"She is not," Kohl asserted. "I've battled with her by my side many times. She can still function."

"Does it relieve her pain?"

"Yes. I imagine it relieves some of her pain," Kohl admitted.

Sarah considered kicking him. Some? It made her life bearable again, and he knew it. He simply didn't want to give her the medication while there was any chance that she still might need to defend herself.

"Give it to me," the young prince demanded.

"But, if we encounter another battle," Kohl started to protest.

"She is a protected woman. You cannot treat her this way, whether she battles or not. Her life must come before your own, and I can battle carrying dead weight, even if you can't." His voice was low and dangerous. It brooked no argument. "Give me the medication, Kaufmann."

Kohl sighed raggedly and pulled the pre-filled metal medicine pen from his coat. "It's IM. I usually administer in her upper arm," he informed Hunter.

"Will one dose be enough?" he asked as he peeled off Sarah's coat and pulled her arm from her sweatshirt.

Some part of her mind screamed that she should be embarrassed by a strange man taking off her clothes, but his touch was tender and calming.

"No," Kohl admitted. "She'll need it every twelve hours or so, probably for a few days. Being touched is bad for her. She usually doesn't allow it."

"Do you have more?" Hunter asked as he rubbed the alcohol swab over her arm and readied the pen.

"In the car," he ground out as Hunter injected the first dose.

"You left it behind?" he thundered. Hunter made a

soothing noise, as Sarah winced, mumbling his apologies for shouting so near her aching head.

"I hadn't planned on leaving any other way, and if she's not touched, one dose is sufficient for any after-effects she experiences."

Hunter swore fluently in several languages, a trait she found most Warriors shared. He pulled a cell phone from his jacket pocket and flipped it open. "Piers cell," he commanded the phone. His jaw was set angrily, and his eyes burned in barely controlled *Blutjagd.*

Sarah watched him through a drugged haze, her head already wrapped in layers of wet cotton batting. His shimmer caught her, and she started her examination again, touching the gold flecks that danced before her eyes. His shimmer swirled with more color than she had ever seen in one. It was like a fiery opal. Blues, purples, and golds warred with a wide streak of crimson that announced his fury in the brilliant white.

As the medication worked its magic, his shimmer faded away, stolen from her by the drug. Sarah cried out harshly in protest, and tears pooled in her eyes. Kohl startled at the unusual occurrence, but she didn't have the words to express how painful loosing that shimmer was to her. It was the most beautiful thing she had ever seen.

Hunter's face softened. He brushed a hand through her hair. "It's all right," he soothed her. "I'll care for you."

Sarah let the tears fall, touched by his kindness and tortured by the loss of his shimmer. Purple and gold. She had never seen purple and gold before. She wanted to know what the new colors meant. She closed her eyes with a sigh as her warm muscles seemed to melt into him.

* * * *

Hunter echoed her sigh of relief, as the young woman relaxed into his arms, oblivious to the pain that had wracked her mind only minutes before. Healing sleep. He could almost feel it seeping into her, easing the damage in her mind. He nestled her into his chest as the phone rang on Piers' end, enjoying the warmth of her against his chest and lap.

"Yes, Hunter?" Piers answered. "Who is with you?"

"Your old friend Kaufmann," he managed evenly.

"What's the problem?"

"Apparently, he was dangerously short-sighted. The protected woman in his care requires medication that he left in his car when we fled. We'll need some by ten o'clock in the morning. What is the name of her medication?" he demanded of Kohl.

The old man darkened. "It's specially made for her in our range. It takes weeks to formulate—or more than a day to send."

"You bastard," he growled. "Change of plans. We'll need the stash from his car, even if we have to break in to get it. Where is it?"

"In the trunk, packed in our luggage."

"I caught that," Piers assured him. "Where is the vehicle and what is it?"

Hunter got the information and relayed it to Piers automatically. He seethed at the situation. He couldn't even send Kaufmann back to do it himself. Until sunrise, it wouldn't be safe to return to the battle site, and they would be too far away to go back at that point without making her dose much later than was wise.

"How dire is her need?" his grandfather asked, breaking him out of his reverie.

"Dire. She's a human sensitive. The beast that touched her left her in agony. Kaufmann had only one dose on his person to hold her over."

Piers sucked in his breath. "He brought Sarah into our range without warning us?"

"Sarah? Is this Sarah?" he asked Kohl, his mind working at the possibility that he was really holding the legend in his arms.

He nodded in response. "Yes, that's Sarah."

Hunter felt his blood boil. He'd heard of Sarah of Kaufmann. Who hadn't? She was a true legend, the finest sensitive encountered in all of the second beast war. Why hadn't he realized? Surely, Kohl Lord Kaufmann couldn't have two sensitives under his personal protection.

"Hunter?" Piers called suddenly. "You're lit up. What is it?"

"I'll get back to you," he promised, his eyes boring holes in the older man in the cab with him. "We're going to the training house."

"Your family is there."

"I know. I need to see them. Goodbye, Piers." Hunter hung up before his grandfather could question him further and fisted the phone is his hand, trying desperately to release the fury that gripped him.

"You don't understand," Kohl said softly, nervously.

"You're damned right I don't understand! How dare

you risk one of our greatest treasures this way."

Kohl sighed. "It's necessary."

"You raised her as your own. Have you no compassion for her needs? For her pain?"

"I had to be ruthless...for her own good. It's necessary."

"Why?" Hunter thundered, shielding her deeper within his body. If she was his, Sarah would never have to face what she did tonight. He vowed it without wondering why he would think such a thing.

"Lorian has come up with a mad idea that human sensitives are descended from the Cursed Warriors and that they retain a portion of their curse—perhaps enough to allow them to carry beast children. I have made my own inquiries. Two of our sensitives are descended from Cursed Warriors. Sarah is five generations removed from *Haus Landwirt*. The others may be, but their connection would be further removed than I can easily trace."

"Then, you should keep her close and heavily guarded. All of the sensitives should be. You shouldn't be dragging her into battles. Erin isn't permitted to hunt, and she's a Warrior born and Stone-Chosen."

"None of Kaufmann's other sensitives are in danger. Two are beyond childbearing age. The last is too weak to be of any interest to Lorian. He wants Sarah. She's the youngest and the most powerful. He believes her curse runs the strongest. He wants her to be his mate."

Hunter shivered involuntarily at the idea. "But...if he touches her?" His stomach clenched. If tonight was any indication, if Lorian touched her, it would spell disaster for her.

"Yes, he'll destroy her beautiful mind," Kaufmann confirmed. "I cannot allow that to happen. I won't allow it."

"Then, why drag her into battle? Protect her."

"I wanted to teach her and to build up her resistance, but it hasn't worked. If anything, every touch leaves her more sensitive, more susceptible."

"Does she know? Does Sarah know what Lorian plans for her?"

He nodded. "Sarah thinks he's mad, but she knows. He—approached her. It took all of Kaufmann to drive him off, all working at Sarah's direction. The event traumatized her, but she started to battle. I don't know if she saw it as a way to learn to protect herself or as revenge. I didn't care. I thought it was a good idea at the time. She has never quite recovered from Lorian. To her mind, looking at the elder is akin to looking into the gates of hell." His expression crumpled into some indefinable misery.

Hunter watched her face, while Kohl talked. It was hard to imagine Sarah battling for revenge, but Lorian had a way of changing people. Erin all but cut herself off from people her own age after her encounter.

No, she had cut herself off completely now. She wasn't even talking to Curt anymore. The only people she interacted with were her own family—including the Hunters and Crossbearers—and a few older, printed Warriors and their wives.

"Why bring her here?" he asked suspiciously. "Why drag her all the way to Cross?"

"We can no longer ensure her safety. *König* is already committed to protecting *Blutjagdfrau*. It's the house of elder killers. There's no other safe place for her."

Hunter sucked in his breath in surprise. "You're relinquishing Sarah's care?"

"I have no choice." The house lord sounded tortured by the admission. "Every parent must release his child when the time is right. I may have waited too long. I vowed to protect her with my own hands. Instead, I must beg this favor and send her away to keep my vow. Don't think this is easy for me. The gods blessed me with this beautiful mind to protect, a girl after my wife gave me four sons. Sarah is my life, but I must do this or risk losing her to Lorian."

"She has my personal protection," he assured the old lord.

Kaufmann raised an eyebrow in surprise. "I thank you, but being with you would be not much safer than being in my range. I want you to speak with your parents. Sarah will be safer with the *Blutjagdfrau* and their company."

Hunter felt his jaw tighten, and his eyes narrowed in near *Blutjagd*. "The choice is hers," he decided.

"I am still her lord," Kaufmann reminded him. "Though not born of my house, she is my daughter in every other sense of the word. Sarah has autonomy, but I control her movements."

"Not if I terminate your claim on her," he warned.

"You can't."

"Try me. The council of lords will listen when *König* speaks, and all of *König* will speak for Sarah."

Kaufmann paled at the threat. "Why? Why would you do this?"

Hunter considered that carefully, afraid of the automatic answer that sprang to mind. He wanted

Sarah to choose to stay with him. He wanted it desperately. "I want her to have a choice," he managed.

* * * *

Erin watched the truck pull up through the front window of the Crossbearer training house. She'd recognize Hunter's midnight blue Dodge anywhere. "He's here," she shouted, racing to the door. Ever since Piers called and told them Hunter was coming and why he was, she had been waiting for him impatiently.

Hunter reached the door just after she threw it wide, hurrying in with Sarah of Kaufmann cradled to his chest. *Blutjagd* lit his eyes, and Erin stepped back at the unusual sight of it in this setting.

"Erin," he ordered, "I'll need your help."

She looked at him in surprise. "Of course," she replied quickly, following her brother and the bounce of ebony hair that cascaded over Hunter's arm to his hip. Erin barely noticed the angry Warrior that stormed in after them, but her parents shot to the door.

"Don't try it, Kaufmann," Hunter warned. "There will be no discussion of Sarah until I come back to join in it."

"You're not caring for her," the old lord thundered.

"I promised her I would. Erin will take care of her personal needs. I have no wish to take advantage."

Erin glanced back at the furious man and shook her head as she followed Hunter up the stairs. To her surprise, he turned right instead of left at the top. "The guest room," she reminded him.

"Is for Lord Kaufmann," he finished bitterly, as if he loathed saying the man's name. "Sarah will occupy the room I typically use. It shares a bathroom with you, and I'll sleep on your floor, in case she needs me—if you don't mind, that is."

"I don't mind."

Hunter was confusing her, but he seemed set on his course.

He swept the young woman into his room and laid her gently on the bed. Hunter dragged one of his button-down shirts from the closet and handed it to Erin with a pained expression. "Dress her for bed, please. I'll be in the hall...if she needs anything." He left with one last, longing look at the woman on the bed.

Erin took a deep breath and stripped off Sarah's shoes and coat before pulling off the jeans and sweatshirt beneath.

Sarah's arms were halfway into the sleeves of Hunter's shirt when she groaned. Her green eyes fluttered open. She looked at Erin blearily in something between fear and confusion.

"It's all right, Sarah," she soothed the older woman. "I'm Erin, and I'm just dressing you for bed."

She squeezed her eyes shut as if she was in pain. "Erin... Too bright," she breathed.

Erin nodded, crossing to switch off the overhead light. She tucked Sarah into the oversized shirt and buttoned it up. "The lights are off, Sarah. Do you need anything? The bathroom, maybe?"

Sarah groaned and nodded her fevered head. "Yes, please." She leaned heavily on Erin and fumbled to complete her bathroom routine with her eyes squeezed shut.

"The lights are out," Erin reminded her gently.

"The lights aren't too bright," she panted, heaving herself unsteadily back to her feet and almost falling against Erin. "You are."

Erin nodded. It was what Sarah sensed that was overpowering. "I understand. Let's get you into bed again, and you can sleep it off."

Sarah hung her head as if it was too heavy to lift. She collapsed on the bed in a heap, and Erin lifted her lightly into the center. She covered the tortured psychic with a heavy quilt and left the room with the armload of her clothes.

Hunter leapt at her as soon as she closed the door. "Is she all right?" he asked urgently.

Erin smirked at him. "Sarah's fine—or she will be. She was hurting, but she was making sense. She's sleeping again."

He relaxed visibly and nodded, making her wonder what he had seen to elicit this response. "Good. Then, I have to go deal with Kaufmann. I owe him a few for tonight."

"Deal with what?"

"Tag along. You're about to see fireworks."

Erin raised an eyebrow at him. It had been a long time since she had seen Hunter so fired up about anything, right about the time he had started training to be house lord of Crossbearer. She nodded and followed him back downstairs, dropping the clothing to be washed on the table in the front hall.

In the library, Hunter glared at Lord Kaufmann.

The man was complaining to their parents loudly. "I tell you Hunter overstepped his bounds. This is not his concern."

"And I told you," Jayde assured him, "we will not

discuss this until Hunter is present to tell his side."

"Hunter is present," he growled, "and I warned you not to try to get them to decide against me before I tell my side."

"Sit down, Hunter," Talon ordered. "We'll discuss this."

"Send the child away," Kaufmann dismissed Erin.

Hunter placed a restraining hand on her shoulder, before Erin could retaliate. "This affects all of *König*. Even though Erin won't have her autonomy for another few weeks, she has been fully cursed for well over three years and drove Lorian to ground unassisted before that. I want her here, and I want her input."

"I agree," Talon added. "If the discussion affects *König*, Erin will have her say in it."

Kaufmann looked put out, but he dropped into a chair and grumbled his acceptance.

Hunter settled into the couch and drew Erin down beside him. "I want you to be brutally honest," her brother warned her.

Kaufmann scowled. "If we're quite through, I'd like to discuss this matter."

"Go on," Jayde invited as if there was no tension involved.

"Sarah is my child," he began.

"Not Kaufmann born," Hunter countered.

"Hunter," Talon warned. "You'll get your turn."

Hunter nodded his agreement and leaned back into the rich upholstery behind him, brown velvet that tantalized the senses.

"She is my daughter. She is of Kaufmann, no matter how she came to me. Sarah was only five when she was gifted to me, and she barely remembers her birth family. I gave her autonomy, because I felt she deserved as much for the risks she takes, but like any Warrior, I control her movements.

"I need to know she's as safe as she can be. That is my duty to her, and I couldn't live with myself as a father if I did less for her. Though Hunter has offered his personal protection, he is not as capable of protecting Sarah long term as the system already in place to safeguard the young princess."

"I hate that term," Erin grumbled.

Jayde hid a smile behind her hand. "All right. Hunter, what is your side of this argument?"

"Sarah is not Kaufmann born. She deserves more than simple autonomy. It was kind of Kohl to raise her, but she isn't of his blood. He hasn't sealed her curse back onto himself, because she wasn't a cursed daughter to be freed. Sarah is a protected woman, but she isn't Warrior born. He has no right to order an adult human woman to live by his whims.

"Sarah is accustomed to being of a range. She may not want to accept the wandering life of a *König*." He paused, and Erin could hear the edited part of the statement. Hunter hadn't wanted to leave the wandering life of their family to be of a range, but he'd had no choice.

"I'm not demanding she stay with me. I'm offering her an option. If Sarah chooses that option, she will have my personal protection."

Kaufmann shook his head and groaned. "Lorian is after her. I told you that."

Erin stiffened. "So what?" she demanded. "Hunter has been solely responsible for me many times. Lorian is after me, too."

"But, the one time Lorian attacked, he failed you. Trusting Hunter again is foolhardy."

Erin launched at him in a rage, and Hunter dragged her back to his chest. He wrapped his arms around her.

"Release it," he breathed. "It's not worth it. He's right."

She shuddered as she forced the bloodlust back. "He's wrong," she decided. "Let go of me."

Hunter released her slowly, and Erin sank to the couch beside him.

"He's right, but that was almost four years ago. I wasn't a true Night Warrior yet. Even my father almost died the first time he faced an elder. He was an elder killer less than six months later. I'd like to think I'm capable of the same."

"You'd like to think it, but you can't be sure," Kohl countered.

Jayde's jaw tightened. "I was already an elder killer, and I failed to kill Draden. When Carstol attacked, neither Talon nor I could kill him alone. My point is, you will never have a guarantee. If Lorian attacked tonight, I couldn't say for certain that I would kill him. Talon can't make that promise. We might. Erin might. Hunter might. Both of them are already stronger than we are despite having less experience than Talon. I dare say Hunter has more practical experience than I do already."

"So, you're trying to convince me that Sarah may be safer with Hunter than with you?" Kaufmann asked archly.

Talon shook his head. "What she's saying is that every elder is different. Every encounter is different.

There are no guarantees for Sarah either way. We can't even guarantee Erin."

"You think I should allow this choice," he exploded.

"Absolutely," Erin replied hotly.

Kaufmann looked at her in a rage, and Hunter bit back his amusement. He *had* said he wanted her brutal honesty, and damned if Erin wasn't going to give it with both blades!

Jayde cleared her throat but didn't quite clear the tension in the air. "Maybe you should explain your reasons," she suggested.

"Fine. I will. I'm not given the choice of where I'll be. All my life, I've been told I have no choice, because I was born to it. The Stone chose me," she spat sarcastically. "Sarah wasn't born to a Warrior. The Stone didn't choose her.

"She has a tremendous gift that I wish I had sometimes, though not after seeing the price she pays for it," Erin admitted. "That power allowed her to evade the beast that took her parents. It saved her, and you took her in.

"Maybe Sarah was lucky a Warrior took her in. You obviously realized her inherent power. But realize this. You were lucky to be gifted with her. Sarah could just as easily have been found by humans and raised by humans. Humans would have given her every freedom society allows. I don't think she should be deprived of that freedom. Hunter is right. You're making her suffer for your whims."

Talon nodded. "Corwyn hated what Jayde had to give up when she returned to us. What you're dealing with here is the opposite question. Jayde surrendered many of her freedoms because she was born to it.

Should Sarah surrender hers because a Warrior chose to offer his personal attention in addition to his protection?"

"Sarah isn't asking for freedom," Kaufmann stormed.

"Isn't she?" Hunter countered in a cold voice.

The two men regarded each other warily for several long seconds.

"Explain, Hunter," Jayde requested.

"I heard her asking for the freedom over her own gifts and Kaufmann denying her that freedom. I heard Sarah beg him to leave before she was forced through another battle cycle she was too tired and mentally bruised to endure. He refused her that too.

"He called her sloppy for allowing the beast to touch her. What was the line Gunther used, Dad? Pain is an excellent teacher? He told Sarah that her pain was her own fault, because as a human, she simply wasn't fast enough.

"He ordered me not to coddle her. He claimed she wasn't injured and required no aid then admitted later that this night will leave her bedridden for several days. He denied Sarah the medication that would allow her peace and relieve her pain, because in a battle, she would be dead weight. I had to threaten him to allow her that simple courtesy. I had to threaten him, while Sarah cried for relief.

"I won't even go into all the short-sighted, uncaring things he did—all supposedly for her own good. He dragged her into battle, knowing each touch is worse for her."

"She usually doesn't get touched," Kaufmann argued.

"He left her medication behind and only carried one dose on him."

"There's a reason for that. If she's ever captured, Sarah would rather die or go insane than live with being taken by a beast. If they have medication, they can hold off the inevitable and torture her for much longer."

Hunter paused. "I think that's the first intelligent thing you've said tonight. Let me guess. It was Sarah's idea?"

Kaufmann turned deep crimson, but he didn't deny the charge.

"Thought so."

Talon put up a hand for silence. "I'll make you a deal, Kohl. We just got here. Barring an outright siege, we'll remain on Cross land for between two and four months. Sarah will remain with *König* for that long. When we leave, she'll have the choice of continuing on with *König* or remaining in Cross. Her only two choices will be *König* or Cross. If she weds, Sarah's husband will join her in one of those two places. She will not be permitted to live in any other range. Is that acceptable to you?"

Kaufmann looked at Hunter suspiciously. "I'll agree on one condition. Sarah is not to be influenced in her decision. Do I have your word, Talon?"

"You do. No one will influence her decision. Right, Erin?"

She smiled sweetly. "As you wish, mi'lord."

Kaufmann sighed and shot Hunter a look that said he was worried more about her brother's interference than hers. Erin found herself strangely offended. If any of the *Königs* were known for being a pain in the butt, it was her.

Chapter Eight

Sarah felt the evil coming. She tried to warn her Mum about the red mist streaming through the trees, but Mum told her it was just her imagination and tried to send her back to her cot in the tent. Sarah watched as the mist took shape into the figure of a man without color. He was all red fire shot through with black floaters...like dust motes on a ray of sunlight, filtered through stained glass.

"Look, Daddy," she cried, pointing to the new arrival. "Who is he?"

Her father—*Charles was his name,* she recalled—glanced around in confusion then looked at her Mum in concern. "Is she sleepwalking, Eleanor?" he asked.

"I don't think so. She seems lucid."

Sarah turned to watch the man move closer to her Daddy. No one could see him. Why couldn't anyone see him?

"Is she ill?" Daddy continued.

Her Mum's hand touched her forehead. Sarah pushed it away. It blocked her view of the figure.

"No fever. Sarah, talk to me," she pleaded, trying to draw the child from her examination of the man by waving her hand in front of her face.

The red man turned his eyes toward her. Black, fathomless pits burned where normal eyes should be. His laughter sounded in her mind, intended for only her to hear.

"Ghost," Sarah breathed. "He's a ghost."

Her Daddy leaned toward her. "Sarah?"

She screamed, as the ghost raised something that

looked like a knife and struck at her Daddy. Warm droplets of blood sprayed Sarah's face and outstretched hands. The red ghost dropped his face to the gush of blood and—ate. Her stomach rebelled at the sight.

Sarah ran to her Mum and grabbed her hand, pleading with her to help, to take them both away. Mum's eyes remained empty and cold, but Sarah's mind could hear the silent screaming from within her, the plea for Sarah to run before it was too late and the unseen enemy came for her.

{She is mine, little one. You will be mine, too.} His voice sounded in her mind, dark and amused.

Sarah turned and ran, his laughter following her into the night. Tears streamed down her face as her legs pushed her small body up the mountainside. Rocks cut into her feet through her thick, wet socks, and branches whipped at her face. At some point, Sarah realized that she'd lost one of her socks. A snag that tripped her had pulled it off, but she kept moving. Taking time for that was out of the question.

Behind her, her Mum screamed in terror and loss. Sarah tried to push the image out of her mind, but it was burned there for her to see. The red ghost came at her, and Mum's scream was cut off. Her stomach turned as Sarah pictured the thing eating Mum, too.

{You're next, little one. Will you lead me a merry chase?}

Sarah sobbed at the spike of pain that sliced through the block she tried to use against him, the block she used when her parents were fighting in their room at night.

{Is that the extent of your strength, little one?} He

was taunting her, and he was coming!

Her lungs burned and her body ached when she finally caught sight of the crevice. It was just a crack in the rock face, but it was big enough for her to squeeze into. Sarah pushed all the way back into the blackness, a good four meters and all of it too narrow for a man to follow. But he was a ghost.

It wasn't long before she heard sounds outside the hole. A long, red arm snaked in, but it couldn't reach her. She heard his grumbling of displeasure.

{Come out here, and it will be painless for you.}

You lie!

{Laughter. Very good, precious. Come out now, or I will make it very painful for you indeed. You will beg me to die.}

No.

Sarah shook in the darkness, while the monster raged. The arm reached for her then turned into the ghostly fog. She screamed at the mist, but Sarah soon learned that he could only cover her in his cold hate that way without actually touching her. It seemed he needed space to act, and he lacked that in the hole. His frustrated scream made her cover her aching ears. A sound like a trowel dragging on rock disturbed her sobbing. He wanted to find a way in to her desperately.

"Come for me, beast," a new voice demanded. "Or can't you handle a fair fight?"

"Ah, Kohl of Kaufmann. You think yourself a match for Braden?"

"More than whatever pitiful creature you have trapped in the rock," he countered confidently.

"A child. A precious baby girl, but more threat than you are, Warrior."

"Is she really? Must be a child of the *König* elder killers." He laughed heartily. "Do you have our toddler princess trapped in the rock? Have you lost her?" His voice was mocking. "Has she injured you with her mother's blades and danced away like Jayde?"

"I have no interest in your precious princess. This babe is far more interesting to me."

"Really? Why would a human child be of interest to you? Do you have trouble finding sustenance?"

"She's one of your revered sensitives. You haven't found one in over twenty-five years, have you? You will lose this one, Kaufmann. Her blood will run rich in my veins before the sun rises."

There was a moment of silence, and the air seemed to grow thick in tension.

"Then fight me for her," the one called Kohl demanded.

Sarah held her breath. She wanted to see the man that was trying to protect her, but she didn't dare go close to the opening. She closed her eyes, trying to imagine him, but all she saw was a silver knight with a baldric of crimson velvet draped across him. The red monster fought with him, and she saw the red flicker into a spot of black at his shoulder. Sarah wondered if he was injured.

She watched in confusion as the red monster turned into mist again and sped around the silver knight. "Behind you," she screeched as his form started to take shape.

The knight seemed to shimmer before her eyes, and the red monster flickered and faded.

Sarah opened her eyes to the absolute darkness, wondering what had just happened.

"Come out, child," a voice called—the friendly voice, the one called Kohl.

"No," she whispered. "What if you're the red monster? What if this is a trick?"

"Tell me how to convince you. For the love of all that's holy, you must trust me." His voice was desperate, on the edges of some nameless madness. "I didn't know whether to believe him, but he was telling the truth. Please, you must come to me."

"Let me see your hand."

Dutifully, a beautiful silver hand reached into the cave for her. Sarah crept forward. When she touched the hand, it grasped her and she screamed, sure it would turn red around her wrist. The hand released her immediately, and she scurried back, weeping in fright.

"I'm sorry. I thought you were asking for my help. Forgive me, child. Please, forgive me. If I pull my hand back, will you come out for me?"

Sarah didn't answer. She crept forward, still shaking. She touched the hand again. This time, it didn't grab her. It pulled back slightly. She followed the silver glow out, the arm retreating with each touch of her small hand.

When she finally stuck her head out and squeezed her shoulders and chest through the narrow crack, she met the man's dark eyes. Kohl's relief washed over her. His hair was dark but beginning to gray. Sarah guessed that he was a little younger than her grandfather was. The shimmer over him was still silver, but now she could see that it was shot through with green flecks and the crimson was more of a thin, decorative braid than a baldric. He was kneeling with his hands on his thighs and made no move to grab her as she worked her way out of the crevice and stood before him.

Kohl smiled and put his arms out to her. "Come, child. We must leave here now."

"Sarah," she whispered. "My name is Sarah."

"Sarah."

His smile widened, and she stepped into his arms. Kohl removed his warm coat and wrapped it around her shivering body. He regarded her scraped hands and feet sadly, trying to rub the numbness away, warming them with his body. He lifted her with him and walked away quickly.

Kohl didn't stop at the campsite but continued to carry her to a car parked on a dark, dirt road, shielding her face from the horrors she'd seen as if he knew she couldn't bear to see them again.

A young man in his late teens stepped forward with a look of concern on his face. His shimmer was clear and just off-white, like home-squeezed lemonade. It was a warm shimmer with that same braid of red.

"Father?" he asked uncertainly.

"This is your sister, Sarah," Kohl announced. "The gods have blessed this child with the finest gift of sensitivity I have ever encountered. They have brought her to me, Damien. She's mine now, a precious girl of my own to raise."

The young man nodded. "Yes, Father. I understand. Welcome, Sarah," he whispered, executing a smooth bow to her with something between fear and awe written on his face.

Sarah's head started to ache. She couldn't read what Damien was feeling like she usually could. The shimmers flared up white-hot around her, and Sarah closed her eyes to escape the suddenly painful glare of them. A wave of sickness pushed down on her, and she groaned deep in her chest.

"Sarah? What's wrong?" Kohl asked, seemingly panicked.

Her skin started to heat as if by an instant fever, and she grew restless in his arms. "The shimmers hurt," she whimpered. "Shut them off. Please, shut them off."

"Call your grandfather," Kohl thundered. "He must have the closest sensitive come to us immediately to train her. I cannot lose her this way."

* * * *

Jan 7, 2025

Sarah groaned as she opened her eyes to the darkness. No shimmers. She thanked whatever gods gave her this damned curse that the medicine was working now. The vague sense of her power was an itch in her skin, but nothing more.

The moment when Erin touched her had been agony. Sarah shouldn't have been able to see her shimmer or feel its burn, but she did. She wondered at that. Were *König* shimmers stronger than her medicine, or was the experience some sort of fluke?

She pulled herself off the bed unsteadily. Her head felt like it was packed with glass splinters, but Sarah had to go to the bathroom. She weaved across the floor, her eyes blurring.

After she relieved herself, Sarah tried to make her

way back to the bed. She was halfway there when a sound behind her intruded on her consciousness. She turned toward it slowly, trying to work out who would be in her room. Everyone knew not to disturb her solitude when she was like this, unless it was time for her dose or to give her an IV.

Erin was entering the bathroom from the other side. Sarah barely had time to see the younger woman's face before her shimmer fired to life, branding Sarah's mind with the swift fury of the burn she shouldn't be able to experience. Even beasts couldn't make her see shimmers when the medication was working. Why was Erin different?

Sarah crumpled to the floor with a whimper, clamping her eyes shut against the brilliant assault. She cradled her head in her hands and curled in on herself as the afterimage of the sunshone gold of Erin's shimmer scorched through her mind. She sobbed, the air like smoke in her unresponsive lungs. Her skin heated, and sweat beaded in response.

Hands touched her, searing her flesh. Sarah bit back a scream and tried to shake off the intruder. The hands left her, and the floor rumbled beneath her ribs as Erin sped away. A moment of blessed stillness followed where the pressure she applied to her temples with the flats of her palms actually seemed to give her relief Sarah knew was impossible.

Hands touched her again, but these hands were cooling. She relaxed her palms away from her head, feeling the boneless release of pain the drugs brought her but knowing that no one had given her any.

"Sarah," a man's voice breathed next to her ear. It wasn't Kohl. Hunter.

She remembered his beautiful, mesmerizing shimmer and forced her eyes open. It was there. The fire opal of him soothed her aching head, and Sarah reached out a hand to touch the swirl of purple that undulated before her eyes.

"Sarah, please say something."

She looked at his eyes, warm and worried, through the veil of his shimmer. Sarah closed her eyes again as a fresh pain lanced through, but as quickly as it came, it was gone again. "Hunter," she managed. Sarah wanted to say more, but any conscious thought— anything beyond that lovely shimmer was pure torture. Even his name was difficult to force past her stubborn lips.

He gathered her into his arms and lifted her to the bed. Hunter eased his hands away, and she moaned as the fire under her skin returned.

"Hunter," she pleaded, her head threatening to split in two.

His hands touched her again, and the fire receded.

"What is it? What can I do?" His voice was low and urgent.

Sarah touched his chin, unable even to ask him to hold her. His name— All she could say was his name, over and over.

"Sarah, do you need me to stay with you?"

She made an inarticulate sound that she hoped he would understand as agreement.

"I have to do one thing. I'll be right back. I promise you. I can send Erin to you if you would like."

She moaned and thrashed her head side to side, incapable of putting her refusal into words but needing him to understand how much Erin's shimmer would hurt her now. The movement sent fresh spikes of pain through her, but Sarah needed to make the point clearly. Not Erin. No one but Hunter. Anyone else would be agony for her.

"All right," he soothed her, running the backs of his fingers over her cheek. "Two minutes."

Hunter's hands left her, and Sarah sobbed as the burn started in on her again. She curled into her personal cocoon to wait for him.

From far away, she could hear water running. His morning needs, she supposed.

Sarah stifled another sob, determined to control herself. She was being selfish. This was a Warrior prince, a *König*, and an elder hunter. He would think her weak and foolish to demand this childish thing of him. Still, his touch was the only safe haven in the firestorm that was engulfing her.

She heard footsteps and reached a hand out for him, but it wasn't Hunter's cooling shimmer she encountered. Silver pain shot up her arm and ran like mercury through her mind. Sarah screamed and pulled her hands back to her head, trying desperately to keep her stomach from rebelling.

A scuffle ensued.

"You can't touch her," Kohl thundered. "Can't you see what it does to her?"

"I don't hurt her. She asked me to stay," Hunter replied, keeping a calm, low voice that held just a hint of warning.

"Impossible! No one can touch her when Sarah is like this. Don't you think we've tried? Leave, *König*."

Sarah moaned in protest. He couldn't leave. She didn't know how Hunter took the pain away, but he did, and she wasn't about to lose whatever magic he held.

"I'm not leaving. She's asked me to stay."

"If you don't remove yourself—"

The door crashed open, and another man's voice boomed over Kohl's. "What the hell are you two arguing about?" he demanded.

Sarah squinted her eyes to try and see the man. Lord *König*! His shimmer was silver and gold twisted shot through with red flecks and a controlled band of *Blutjagd*. It danced in her mind, burning a new trail there. Sarah screamed at the torture of it. Why were *Königs* so hard to look at? Except Hunter.

Kohl hissed in annoyance. "The medicine has worn off early. Sarah is in the worst stages of her pain. Our auras—our shimmers and our touch are torture to her. Until the medication arrives, we must leave her alone. Only complete solitude will be bearable to her. I know my child," he informed the great Lord *König*.

"He's wrong," Hunter interjected coldly. "I can touch her. She asked me to stay. I won't leave her while she needs me."

"Needs you? You flatter yourself. No one, not even humans or human sensitives, can touch her like this. I cannot comfort her. You cannot comfort her. No one can."

"Hunter," his father replied quietly, "perhaps we should discuss this away from here. If our presence hurts her..."

Sarah forced her eyes open, slitting them against the bright shimmers until she locked on the opal. The blurred outline of Hunter's hand was her target. She threw herself at it, grasping it in her hand while she closed her eyes tight to the pain the sudden motion set off. Sarah sank her cheek to the fabric of his jeans in relief as his healing touch washed over her.

Kohl sucked in his breath. "I'll be damned," he mused. "How are you doing that?"

Hunter turned, wrapping his fingers around her hand, and crouched until his breath warmed the now-cool skin of her cheek. The fingers of his free hand pushed her damp hair back gently. "Do you want me to stay, Sarah?"

"Hunter," she managed again, tightening her grip on his hand in response.

"It's all right. I promised I'd stay." His voice was tender, and he brushed at her hair again with his magic touch. "Do you need anything? Food or drink?" he offered.

"She doesn't eat or drink like this," Kohl explained. "An intensive siege means IVs while she's sedated. You may want to call your doctor before she dehydrates, now that the sun is up. Sarah can lose ten pounds easily, and this is a bad one. The medication doesn't usually wear off early."

Sarah grimaced at the thought of an IV. Hunter calmed her system. "Juice," she requested weakly, hoping he calmed it enough. She marveled that even thinking was easier for her with Hunter lending his strength. And, he was lending it. She could feel it coursing through her.

"Dad," Hunter commanded.

"Right away," the other man answered. "I'll bring you something while I'm at it."

"Thank you." His fingers traced lightly over her cheek. "Juice is on the way," he assured her.

"Whatever you need, Sarah. Ask and it will be provided for you."

* * * *

Hunter smoothed his hand over Sarah's hair. She slept, her cheek pressed to his bare chest and her slight body curled into his lap.

Kohl had stayed, watching him in awe while Sarah sipped apple juice and even swallowed bits of the muffin brought up for Hunter. He had pinched off pieces and fed them to her between drinks, and she had managed to eat almost a quarter of it before she fell into an exhausted sleep again.

Finally, the old man pushed to his feet. "I don't know how you're doing that, but I do thank you. Even with the medication, Sarah rarely sleeps this soundly."

Hunter nodded slowly. "I'm glad to be of service."

"This isn't just a service to you, is it?" Kohl's smile was strained. "If it's printing, I approve. Don't use her," he said calmly, in more of a conversational tone than a warning.

Hunter darkened. "I don't know what I'm feeling," he admitted. "At first, I just wanted to protect her, but every time I touch Sarah, it gets more confused. I won't pressure her to stay with me. I gave my word on that. I won't use her or take advantage of her, either. You don't need to worry about that."

"When you figure out what you feel, make sure you tell her."

"You wouldn't object to her staying in Cross? I can't join the *Königs*. You know that," Hunter reminded him.

Kohl shook his head slowly. "This ability of yours to touch her is worth its weight in gold. It must mean something."

Talon's voice came from the doorway, sounding strained. "It better be worth its weight. It's all we've got."

Kohl looked at him in shock. "What do you mean?" he demanded.

"Piers called me when he didn't get an answer on Hunter's cell. The beasts traced your scent back to your vehicle. It's destroyed."

"The medicine?" Hunter managed.

"Twenty-three metal pens, all crushed. Is that count right, Kohl?"

"Yes. Counting the one from my coat, that was the whole two dozen." He swore fluently. "I need to call my sons."

"I took the liberty. Damien assures me he'll bring a new stock to you immediately, but that also means we won't have them until at least noon tomorrow."

Hunter ground his teeth, but he kept his anger leashed. There was nothing to be gained in arguing with Kohl again. "I'll do what I can. I won't leave her while she needs me."

"I'd appreciate that," Kohl stated honestly. "Call if you need me. You have my leave. Care for her—whatever Sarah requires."

* * * *

In the hours after, that tempting phrase tortured Hunter. He learned quickly that his effect on Sarah only lasted as long as he touched her, and it was cumulative. The longer he held her and the more Hunter moved his hands over her, the more relief she got from his handling. Contenting himself with chaste stroking of her hair, face, arms, and back while his body screamed for release and hardened as she snuggled into him—while visions of stroking her in a much more satisfying fashion streamed through his mind—was maddening.

If anyone else could touch her, he would have released her. Well, Hunter would have tried to—forced himself to. If the alternative for Sarah wasn't so dire, he would have walked away. Some part of him craved her until even the thought of walking away seemed painful, all the more when she touched him in return.

At first, Sarah's movements were almost non-existent. She rubbed her cheek against the curls covering his chest and lay her hand against the muscles of his arm. When he fed her bits of lunch, she sucked at his fingertips, removing the honey butter on them and starting a fire in his blood that was impossible to ignore and almost impossible to resist.

Hunter tried to feed her dinner from a fork, but Sarah turned from it as if she was in pain. In desperation, he tried feeding her by hand again. She ate. Whatever his affect on her, it had to be Hunter and not simply his care.

Relieving themselves posed a more formidable problem. Hunter had to leave her to do it. Not only could he not hope to find a way to excuse it, despite the setbacks releasing her caused, but the very idea of touching Sarah while he was unclothed, even in that context, made him hard. Relieving himself would be physically impossible. Hunter cursed his lack of control.

Thankfully, Sarah didn't need to go often. She padded to the bathroom with his hands on her waist to steady her. She'd set the stage the first time in, and it worked well. Sarah had him turn his back to both her and the mirror—for which his libido was eternally grateful. Her arm brushed the backs of his thighs while she worked. It was the barest of contact, but it was enough to sustain her.

Her toileting wasn't nearly as disconcerting as the washing she'd accomplished after dinner. Hunter had steadied her, while Sarah splashed warm water on her face and neck and dried herself with a soft towel. His gaze had followed several water droplets in the mirror as they slid from her neck to the swell of her breast beneath his shirt.

Hunter closed his eyes, reliving the memory greedily.

Her nightshirt, he corrected himself sternly. It had to be simply her nightshirt, because the thought of her in his shirt was too appealing. He tore his gaze away, embarrassed at the direction his mind was taking.

"I wish there was a way to shower," Sarah mused in her recovering whisper of a voice.

Hunter closed his eyes, reining in his tortured mind. "I don't think I could justify that one to Kohl," he growled in a rougher voice than he'd intended to use with her.

"I have autonomy," she replied simply.

His eyes flew open and he looked at the teasing glint in her emerald green eyes in the mirror. "I have half a mind," he began dangerously.

Her eyes widened in something akin to fear. "I'm

sorry, Hunter. If you go—"

His anger and frustration dissolved into regret at the fear in her eyes. *Fear of what I'll do. Hunter didn't want her to fear him. "I won't. As long as you need me, I'll stay,"* he promised.

Sarah lowered her face, her hair shielding it from his gaze. *"If I've offended you, please go. I have four brothers, Hunter. I'm afraid I don't have much practice in discretion. Any barb is fair with them."*

"You sound a lot like Erin. I prefer it when people are direct. It saves a lot of trouble. You haven't offended me. Now let me get you back to bed. You're shaking like a leaf."

She nodded quietly and allowed him to lead her back and scoop her onto the bed. Hunter could feel her exhaustion. Sarah shook in it as much as in dizziness and her lack of food. He couldn't imagine how she managed this when she was sedated, on IVs, and not eating at all.

He had started to lift her back into his lap, when she spoke. *"Would it—would it be too much for you to lay with me instead? It would be more comfortable."*

"If it will help you sleep. I'll have an easier time relaxing that way." Hunter positioned them in the middle of the bed and pulled her body into the shelter of his own.

Kohl had checked on them before he retired for the night, nodding grimly at the sight of his daughter wrapped in Hunter's arms before turning away without comment.

Hunter didn't sleep for a long time after Kohl left. He watched Sarah sleeping, touching her in the same ways he had all day and aching for more.

One kiss. One caress, his mind taunted him. Hunter bit back a groan. Then what? He wasn't stupid enough to think he could stop at that. He surrendered to sleep—and to dreams of Sarah surrendering to him.

* * * *

Her mouth was mind-altering. Even as he emerged from his dream, Hunter knew he would give anything to feel Sarah's mouth on him like that.

Like this! He opened his eyes to confirm what his mind was telling him. Her fingers ran trails through the black curls over his heart and traced his blood mark while her lips followed each of his scars slowly, torturously retracing them with the tip of her incredibly soft, inviting tongue.

Hunter panted, running his two-day growth of beard through her hair and inhaling the musk on her skin, feeling himself at the edges of control. He trailed the fingers of one hand through her thick, silky hair, cradling her head to him and encouraging her to discover all of him she cared to. With his other, he reached beneath the edge of the shirt she wore, cupping her bottom and sliding her against the rigid length of his cock, giving her every chance to protest...to stop him.

Sarah arched to him. Far from stopping Hunter, she moved her mouth to his throat and groaned into his skin, her hands raking the curls down to the waistband of his jeans. They gasped together, Hunter as she nipped gently at his jawline and Sarah as he crushed her to his still-thickening member.

He turned his face, brushing his lips over her cheek until he encountered the edge of her mouth. His hips moved against her restlessly, seeking the response her body was giving without pause.

"If I kiss you, I won't be able to stop. I won't be able to let you go," Hunter warned softly. "If you want me to stop, tell me now."

Sarah panted hot trails against his cheek. "Hunter, can you—" She bit back a groan as he ground himself into her.

"Tell me," he breathed. "Anything in my power to give is yours."

She stilled. Her breathing came in gasps as her eyes widened and she started to distance herself from his body. "No, you can't do this," she decided miserably. "I shouldn't have started this."

"Why?" He tried to keep the hurt out of his voice, but his body and emotions were raw.

Sarah shook her head and pulled out of his arms. Hunter was sure she closed her eyes more out of pain than an emotional response, but she tried to wrench out of his arms when he reached for her.

Hunter dragged her to his chest. "Stop it," he ordered quietly. "I won't force you, Sarah. I won't kiss you or touch you other than this. I'll even go back to cradling you, if you feel safer that way, but I won't let you hurt yourself because of me.

"Like it or not, you don't have your medication, and something about me brings you relief. Until you have a choice, you're stuck with me—for this and nothing else. You have my word on that.

"You don't want more. I got it. I won't ask you to explain it. Right now, it might be better if you don't try to explain it." Hunter sighed, realizing he had stopped acting on reason long before. "Never mind. I don't know what's wrong with me. Just get better."

Sarah looked at him through tears. "It's not your fault, Hunter. I knew better than to start something. I let myself get carried away, and that's unforgivable. You should go."

"Why? Are you planning on baiting me again?" His anger deflated in light of her stricken expression. "I'm sorry. That wasn't called for. I think I've lost my mind." That almost seemed a certainty all of the sudden. Hunter was insane, and he had no idea how and when it happened.

"I didn't mean to," she moaned.

"I know. Go to sleep." Hunter didn't know what had just happened, but he wanted to know. No, he wanted to know, but he wanted to finish what she'd started more than that.

* * * *

Sarah handed Elani Kaufmann the brush and sat back to allow her adoptive mother to brush her long, black hair as she had every night for the last seven years. "Tell me about the *Königs*, Mama Elani," she sighed.

Elani started brushing her hair, brushing away her worries with the tangles that she removed. "The *Königs*," she said in her heavily accented English, her voice laced with amusement. "Every night it is the *Königs* or the Hunters. The Warriors have many stories. Let me tell you them."

"I've heard them, Mama. I like the stories about the

Königs and the Hunters."

Kohl laughed from the doorway. He leaned across the bed to kiss Sarah's forehead and smiled indulgently. "Tell her about the *Königs*, Elani. After all, a princess like ours should hear about kings. If it makes her happy, tell her."

The woman sighed and scowled at her husband, leaving the thoughts of how he spoiled their daughter unsaid. They each spoiled Sarah in their own ways, so it was silly for one to chastise the other for indulging her whims when they did.

Elani ran the brush through her hair. "The *Königs* are our kings, the Stone-Chosen elder killers that will end the curse. Corwyn Lord Hunter, master trainer, Stone lord, and elder hunter—and Anna, the human elder hunter, were the parents of Erin Jayde, the first *Blutjagdfrau*. Jayde survived twenty-four years with only an amulet and no lord's blessing or Warriors to guard her. Talon of Crossbearer slew a red named Grelden who dared lay hands on Lord Hunter's daughter and brought her home to the Warriors. He gave her his blessing, trained her as a Warrior, and gave her his love."

Sarah closed her eyes and imagined the Warrior woman that was Stone-Chosen as Raga.

"Jayde killed Veriel to save Talon, to save herself, and to save the child she carried."

"Hunter," Sarah breathed, letting Elani's shimmer wash over her—green shot through with silver and just a trace of blue. "He'll have his autonomy soon."

"Yes. In just a few months."

Elani slid the brush through her hair again, enticing her to sleep. As Sarah's mind relaxed, it went seeking Elani's, gathering information—a river of stories that were shelved there.

"Tell me about their women," she mumbled.

"All their women are bold and fierce. Anna fought Veriel three times. She, as a human, even drew his blood while she stood over her husband's fallen form.

"Jayde was a Warrior born and Stone-Chosen to give birth to the true elder killers, the princes of the Cursed Warriors, and she is their queen. It is said that in all the world, only Talon has been capable of defeating her in battle since she killed Veriel. At Hunter's birth, Jayde planted a blade in Cerran while she nursed her son. At Erin's birth, she handed her babe to her son and battled for her children's lives while she still bled from the birth.

"Erin, they say, fears nothing. She is every bit the Warrior princess she was born to be. Someday, she will choose a Warrior, as Jayde chose Talon, and give birth to more princes."

"And Hunter?" Sarah asked, half asleep already. She tried to picture his shimmer, but no color would come. It was blank to her, a pure white aura the likes of which an angel might have.

"Hunter is the prince, the next Lord *König*. He will find a human as special and bold as Anna was and make her the mother of his young princes. His bride shall be a human Warrior, and he will know her immediately, as Corwyn knew Anna and Talon knew Jayde. She will provide him with fine, strong sons to ensure the end to the curse and battle for them as a true Warrior woman should.

"Already, Hunter rivals his father, and it will take an exceptional woman to be worthy of his seed..."

As usual, Sarah was falling asleep to thoughts of the Cursebreakers, surrounded by the stories hidden in Elani's mind, spoken and unspoken.

* * * *

Sarah let a single tear fall as she opened her eyes. She surveyed Hunter's face in the lamplight. She would have done anything to let him finish what she'd started, but she couldn't risk the future that way—or him. Not only would Lorian kill any man that touched her, but Hunter was destined to marry a Warrior woman. His wife would be human but equal to Anna in strength and skill.

That definition hardly represented Sarah. Hunter needed a woman that could stick a blade in an elder for him, not one who would be weak as a baby and helpless for days after an encounter. Hunter needed a wife that could be depended on in battle, not one who would become dead weight at a moment's notice—with one slip that let a beast touch her.

No, as much as she wanted Hunter, as much as she had wanted him ever since she'd read his concern for her in his mind in battle, Sarah couldn't risk fouling his destiny. No. She realized she had wanted Hunter for even longer than that. Sarah had wanted him all her life, or maybe what she wanted was to be the bold Warrior woman he sought instead of the five-year-old sobbing in the rock crevice.

Chapter Nine

January 8, 2025

Erin answered the light knock at the door. It was barely sunrise, and she was the only Warrior awake in the house to answer it. She recognized Damien Kaufmann from the book of current houses that each house kept.

Damien looked at her in surprise then bowed his head, earning Erin's annoyance. "Erin of *König*, may I enter?" he asked in the formal manner of the old-world Warriors she'd met over the years.

She pulled the door wide for him. "Come in, Damien. We weren't expecting you for another four or five hours."

His gaze slid over her, and her heart sank. Yet again, Erin was being sized up as a brood mare and plaything for some Warrior. Damien met her eyes again and smiled the predatory, male smile she had come to despise. It never ceased to amaze her that the men always thought they were so sly and underhanded when they gave her that look and smile. It reeked of their hopes to bed Erin for her position, and she hated it.

"I got lucky making connections," he explained. "Noon was my worst case scenario."

"I understand. Would you like breakfast? You look exhausted."

"No. Sarah needs her medicine. I should take care of that first."

Erin pulled herself up onto the edge of the mahogany table in the entryway. "Well, she's asleep right now. Is it necessary to wake her?"

Damien raised an eyebrow in surprise. "Asleep? I guess there was no real rush after all. Your father made it sound like an emergency. Sarah must be feeling much better if she's asleep without her medication."

"Right. Like she can't eat or drink or talk or accept a touch... I'm starting to think you people don't know much about Sarah," Erin shot at him, annoyed at the second blatantly sexual look he gave her.

"Touch? I can touch her? Now?"

"Probably not," she admitted. No, touch was definitely Hunter's thing.

"You're not making much sense. I need to see Sarah and give her a dose of her medicine."

"Fine with me, but I think you're wrong." She slid off the table and headed for the stairs, well aware that Damien was watching every sway of her hips despite the fact that he was almost twice her age and she still didn't have her autonomy.

At Hunter's door, Erin knocked lightly. She heard her brother's mumbled reply and entered quietly with Damien close at her heels.

She smiled at the sight of Sarah wrapped in Hunter's arms. The young woman's cheek was nestled to his chest, and his arm was wrapped around her waist, his thigh tucked between her legs.

Erin turned abruptly as the malevolence built behind her. Damien's blade was drawn, and his eyes burned in *Blutjagd*. He moved as if to launch himself toward the couple on the bed. With a muttered curse, Erin locked her left hand around Damien's wrist, swept his feet from beneath him and landed astride him with her right blade to his throat.

"Stupid move, Warrior," she growled at him. "Attacking my brother for helping Sarah is about as brainless as attacking a Cross in Crossbearer range with a *König* in the room. Oh...wait. You did that, too."

"Erin, stand down," Hunter ordered.

"When he drops his weapon," she reminded him patiently.

"Now, Erin. This is my range."

"You are temporarily incapacitated. You are my responsibility, for the duration."

"I gave you an order in battle."

"I'm not human anymore, and my training demands that I never release an armed foe. Just drop the blade, Damien. Drop it, and I will gladly release you."

He glared at her and let his blade fall to the carpet.

Erin snatched it up and launched off him. She sheathed her own blade and twirled his lazily, testing the balance and finding it perfect for a throwing blade. You could learn a lot about a Warrior by the balance of his blade, she'd discovered. Damien cared for his blade. Too bad he didn't show as much concern for other areas of his training.

Damien pushed to his feet uncomfortably and put his hand out to her. "My weapon," he demanded.

"I don't think so. I'll hold onto it for awhile. Until you learn when it's appropriate to draw it, maybe?"

Damien darkened, but he didn't refute her charge in any way.

"Erin," Hunter warned.

"Keep it, Erin," Sarah groaned. "He needs taught a lesson."

"Give it back, Erin," Talon chimed in from the doorway.

"You have to be kidding, Dad," she complained.

"Is that all the better she's trained?" Kohl demanded.

Erin sighed and shoved the weapon back into Damien's hand. "Here. Oh, yeah. You're well trained," she drawled. "No wonder your father wants better for Sarah."

Damien sheathed his weapon and shot her a scathing look. "I don't suppose you'd consider a fair fight?" he growled at her.

Erin raised an eyebrow at him. "More fair than a Warrior half your size and half your age taking you down and disarming you, when you were already in motion with your weapon drawn?" she asked cynically. "Out of curiosity, what did you have in mind? Binding me or hobbling me?"

"A challenge match."

"After breakfast...with my father's permission, of course." It couldn't hurt to remind him that she didn't have autonomy. Maybe Damien wouldn't make a nuisance of himself in the sex-chase if he remembered that.

"You have it," Talon granted.

"After breakfast," Damien agreed.

Hunter laughed heartily. "Call that doctor, Kohl. Your son is going to need it."

"That's his problem," the old man decided.

Erin smiled coldly and wrapped her arms around her chest. No, he'd only need the doctor if he forgot his place and got too friendly during their match. If Damien fought her fair, she'd just defeat him. That was

Erin's personal rule on the subject.

* * * *

Hunter sat on the edge of the bed with a tray of dinner on his lap. Even under the influence of her drugs, Sarah still responded favorably to his touch alone. As long as it made the difference between getting a modicum of nourishment down her or hooking up an IV, he was at her service.

Sarah didn't wake immediately. Like the first dose, her medication wore off earlier than expected, and she was just a few hours into the oblivion of the next dose. Hunter set the tray aside and touched her arm.

She smiled lazily as she opened her eyes. "How do you do that?" she slurred.

"Do what?" he asked in confusion.

"The longer I spend with you, the clearer your shimmer gets," she mused.

"Is the medication not working? I thought it suppressed your ability to see them."

"It does, but *König* shimmers are very strong—yours most of all. I can't even see Erin's right now, though it would make itself known if she touched me again." Sarah grimaced.

Even drugged, she complained that touching Erin was dangerous work. Kohl explained that her personal safeguards were impossible to engage when Sarah was overloaded. In short, she couldn't shut it down...ever.

Hunter nodded and helped her sit up. "Here. I'll feed you and let you get your rest."

Sarah nodded, but she averted her eyes. "That's probably best," she decided.

"Do you need something?" Hunter wasn't sure what gave him that idea, but he was sure it was true.

"No," she denied. "You do too much already."

"Just because no one has ever pampered you doesn't mean you're unworthy of it," he ground out despite his attempt to control his annoyance.

She laughed weakly. "On the contrary, everyone pampers me. Haven't you heard? I'm fragile, and I'm too important to lose." Sarah was being sarcastic, but she seemed hurt by what she was saying.

"Don't give me that. I've seen the way Kohl treats you."

"He's a bear in battle," she admitted with a yawn, her eyes half shut. "If the beasts thought we were less than professional, less than detached, they would try to use us against each other."

"How is he otherwise?"

"Solicitous, overprotective...bossy. He gets everything his own way, even when his own way is making me happy. I've only heard him beg once."

"Kohl?" Hunter asked in surprise, trying to imagine the man stooping to begging for anything. "When was that?"

"The night he saved me. Kohl wanted so desperately for me to come to him and trust him...and for me to survive."

"You were injured?" Hunter realized it hurt to think of the beast hurting her, especially so young.

"Not physically. Oh, I had cuts and bruises, but I wasn't badly injured. The beast kicked in my senses, but I didn't know how to turn them off again."

Hunter nodded. "I understand. Well, you should eat while it's hot."

He started feeding her the meal: chicken, mashed potatoes, and salad. Hunter sighed. Obviously, no forethought had gone into the fact that he had to feed her by hand. He watched as Sarah ate, his body tightening as she took the food from his fingertips.

Sarah looked at him in a detached sort of understanding. "Maybe we should stop now," she whispered.

Hunter regarded her suspiciously. "You feel sick or you're full?"

She squirmed and looked away, blushing lightly.

"Then eat," he ordered.

"This isn't right. It affects you too much."

"I can handle myself," he growled.

"You're deluding yourself."

"So, you're saying you feel nothing?" he asked archly.

Sarah didn't answer that.

"What are you so afraid of?"

"You printing on me," she admitted.

"Would that be so horrible?"

"Yes. Don't you see? I'm not..."

"Not what? You were obviously affected when you invited my attentions. You were ready and willing. What changed? Why did you change your mind?"

She met his eyes miserably and seemed to have trouble making herself answer. "I'm not the wife for you, Hunter. I realized that. Remembered that," she corrected herself.

"Really? I knew you read minds and saw your shimmers. Are you telling me you see the future as well?"

Sarah darkened to crimson and found something

extremely interesting across the room to feign preoccupation with, hooking her hair behind her ear. "Everyone knows what your wife will be," she decided. "Substituting me before you find her would foul up everything."

"You're pushing me away because of a bunch of half-assed stories someone told you?"

She flinched. "You're supposed to have a wife like Anna and Jayde, a strong wife to give you strong sons," she mumbled.

"You don't think you're strong?" he asked in disbelief. "You're a human who walks into battles."

"Not willingly, and I don't fight. I'm a glorified traffic cop that ducks a lot. Look at me, Hunter! Do you want sons who have my frailty? Do you want children who shatter when a beast touches them?"

"You can't know that would happen," he countered.

"You can't take that chance. I can't let you. I'd only screw up the master plan."

Hunter clenched his teeth and forced down his rage. "I think... I think you're too exhausted to have this discussion. You're obviously not able to separate fact from fiction."

She glared at him, and he bit back a smile. Sarah couldn't even focus on him, but her look promised pain and suffering. She must have honed that look on her four older brothers over years.

"You're a fighter, all right. I'll leave you with two thoughts, Sarah. The first is that the Warriors' history is full of bullshit stories, fabrications, and re-written facts. We've discovered that, over and over. Never believe what even the house histories say—especially your own."

"And the other?" she whispered.

Hunter smiled a tight smile as he collected up the tray. "The Stone doesn't let anyone interfere with its plans. If it didn't want this, we wouldn't feel it. The Stone always gets what it wants eventually, even if it has to take the long way around. Think about it."

He left without waiting for her reaction. Hunter wound his way to the kitchen and set the tray next to the sink.

"Did she eat?" Kohl asked from the table.

"Some. Enough."

"Too tired?" he guessed.

"You know your daughter very well, Lord Kaufmann."

Hunter grabbed his coat from the hook by the door, black leather lined with fleece for the winter months. He shouldered it on, studiously avoiding looking at his adversary. He could feel the other Warriors tense from across the room.

"Where are you going?" Talon asked.

"Out. You are not my house lord anymore," Hunter reminded him.

"What if Sarah needs you?" Damien asked quietly.

"She won't," he snapped. "But you knew that. Your house stacked the deck, after all."

"Hunter?" Jayde cut in. "What's wrong?"

"Not a damn thing I wasn't born to." Hunter pulled on his gloves then stilled when he realized Erin was suiting up beside him. "Don't," he warned her.

"Hey, this is my kind of party."

"No, Erin," Talon ordered. "I *am* still your house lord."

"Mom?" she asked simply, not slowing in pulling

on her knit cap and gloves.

"Go on, Erin. No, Talon! Trust me on this one," she replied brusquely.

Hunter glared at her. "I can't hunt with Erin," he reminded her.

"You're right. Figure it out."

Cursing fluently, he stormed out with Erin jogging to keep up with him. "If I'm not hunting, I'm training," he warned her.

"Is that a threat?" she teased. "You think I can't handle you?"

"I'm not playing around, Erin."

"Neither am I. I need a good workout."

"If you end up bedridden—"

"I'll heal," she finished for him. Erin sobered slightly. "I'm actually counting on talking you down a little on the way."

"I don't want to discuss it."

"Too bad. Being upset with what you were born to is my thing. You're poaching on my range without my leave, and you need to explain yourself to me as lady of this range."

She said it so seriously that Hunter couldn't help but to laugh. Erin didn't join him. She didn't look at him. She kept walking with her jaw set angrily and her eyes faraway and sad. Erin had been sad a lot since she came to Cross this trip. Her fists were shoved in her pockets, and she kicked at the frozen ground with her steel-toed hiking boots.

Hunter sighed. "I want Sarah. Not just for release. I don't want to ever let her go."

"She doesn't want you?"

"Oh, she wants me but she refuses me anyway," he

spat. "I mean, she refuses me adamantly and absolutely."

"Why?"

"Because I'm the *König* prince," he growled in frustration.

Erin laughed bitterly. "What I wouldn't give to have men avoid me for that reason." She glanced at him, a wan smile twitching her lips up. "Yours is worse," she admitted, "but only because you want her. Wanting something you can never have isn't a good thing."

Hunter nodded. "What a pair we are. You have every Warrior at your feet, and you hate it. I want one woman desperately, and I can't have her." He stopped walking. "I don't want to fight you. I want to beat the Kaufmanns to a pulp for filling her head with this crap," he decided wearily.

"Don't bother. Damien's not much of a challenge. I doubt Kohl is much better."

"Then, why didn't you destroy him?"

Erin shrugged, changed direction, and started walking again.

Hunter loped after her and matched her pace. "No. I'm serious. Why didn't you? He expected it. You know that. You certainly have the reputation for it. Why did you hold back like that?"

"He had the common sense to treat me like a Warrior in battle," she offered.

"Versus what? I mean, you're facing him down with a blade. What choice does he have?"

"Plenty. I don't like destroying them."

"Could've fooled me," he decided acidly.

"Don't talk about things you have no knowledge of! I don't like destroying them. I never did."

"Then, why do you do it?"

"I'm tired of being baited, Hunter. I'm tired of Warriors treating me like a protected woman or child— or worse, like a damn piece of meat to be won and used. I'm not here to be leered at. It doesn't do anything for me. Honestly... Never mind," she grumbled.

"Have you explained this to Mom and Dad?"

"That makes the Warriors think of me as a protected child. I'm a Warrior, Hunter. I've been a better Warrior than most of them since I was thirteen. I need to reinforce that personally. That's the only way I get respect."

Hunter looked around, taking stock of their surroundings. "Where are we going?" he asked suspiciously.

"Ice cream. My treat," she offered. "I need something sweet."

"Oh no. You're looking for a fight, and you think I'll let you find it."

Her eyes glittered over a wide smile. "No, Hunter. I want ice cream," she countered in mock innocence. "If a beast or two are stupid enough to interrupt that..."

He smiled against his better judgment. Erin was damned devious, and she always had been. He wrapped an arm around her shoulders. "You just want your blood seal," he accused.

"I've driven an elder to ground, and no one will let me fight another beast, even a low-level. How can I build skills that way?"

"Mom and Dad will kill me," he mused.

"For buying your baby sister ice cream?" she teased.

"I thought you were buying?" Hunter bit back laughter.

"I have money. You have keys?"

Hunter released her and pulled open the garage door. "Get in the damn car before I change my mind."

Erin kissed his cheek and bolted for the passenger door. "Thanks, Hunter."

"For what? You're buying the ice cream, remember? I'm just driving. Unless you want to get in some driving practice?"

She slid into the seat, shaking her head. "Had plenty. It's the only useful practice they let me get."

The beasts didn't decide to attack until after they'd retired to a park off the main road to eat their ice cream. Erin smiled as she set her Blizzard on the picnic table. She surveyed the five approaching beasts with an almost feral glee.

"This won't take long," she decided. "My ice cream won't even melt."

"Don't get cocky," Hunter chided her, pulling off his gloves for a better grip on his blades.

"Never."

"Name yourselves," he demanded as he unsheathed his weapons.

One stepped forward, identifying itself as the highest ranked among them. He leered at Erin. "Good evening, *Blutjagdfrau*," he purred. "My name is Sharpe, and my associates are DeCarlo, Lambert, Piccosi, and Beale. We are your escorts to your mate, lady."

She smiled. "Your master sends you to die—or maybe to test me? Is he afraid I'll plant my blades in him again?"

"Lorian fears nothing, and our reward for delivering

you," he scanned his gaze up and down her body, licking his lips in sexual excitement, "will be most enjoyable."

Hunter felt his bloodlust burn, while Erin faced the beast cold.

"He's mine," she informed him.

"He's the high-level," Hunter protested.

"Which means two things. He'll come for me himself, and you can handle the other four easily while I take him on."

"Erin, you're not even lit," he argued.

"If I need it, I will be," she assured him.

"I'm not comfortable with this."

"Too late. They're circling. Get to my back and let them."

"Guess I don't have a choice."

"Nope. Let's go."

Hunter had two down, while Erin was still toying with her high-level. She was toying. She trained harder than she was fighting him.

"Finish him," Hunter ordered.

"When I'm ready."

Hunter took out the beast to his right, noting motion on the last low-level behind him. Erin lit, a quick snap of *Blutjagd,* as if someone had flipped a switch. He wheeled around and gasped. The high-level had been taken down by two blows in quick succession, heart and throat with her left blade. At the same time, she took the last low-level that had been charging at Hunter's back through the heart with a perfectly aimed throw. Before he could finish his assessment, her *Blutjagd* was gone without a trace.

Erin nodded and retrieved her blade from the low-level, wiping both blades on the grass and sheathing them. Hunter watched as she grabbed her ice cream. "See? Not even melted."

"Well, it is below freezing out here," he noted. "Get over here."

Erin took a bite of her Blizzard and knelt next to him. Hunter painted her blood seals in the high-level's blood reverently and smiled at her. "No one can claim you're not a Warrior now."

"Thanks, Hunter." She got back to her feet and swallowed another mouthful of her ice cream. "We should get back. I lit. Mom and Dad are probably worried sick."

"That concerns you?" he asked in surprise.

"Their worry? Of course, it does. Their coddling? You know the answer to that one."

The drive back took only a few minutes, but the older Warriors were pacing at the garage, waiting for them. Hunter pulled in with a groan.

"Don't worry, Hunter," she breathed, staring into the Blizzard. "Just follow my lead."

"That sounds dangerous."

"Trust me. I had this part planned."

"Good. I'm glad you planned something."

Talon practically dragged Hunter out, when he opened the door. "Are you out of your mind?" he demanded, slamming his son onto the hood of the car.

"Give him a break, Dad," Erin shot back before Hunter could reply. "He was doing a great job of keeping me out of it, until those two came at his back. I ignored Hunter's orders and took them out, while he finished the last of the three he handled."

Hunter turned his head and gaped at her. "Erin..."

It was warning, a plea. She had to stop. If she lied to them, the penalty was much worse.

She took a bite of her ice cream and furrowed her brow. "What? You expected me to let you take the rap for me? It was my idea to go for ice cream. It was my idea to stop somewhere and talk rather than coming straight back here," Erin looked at Talon in challenge, "so we couldn't be ghosted on. They could see when I let bloodlust take over. I figured they'd understand what happened. You can't really lie about a thing like that, you know.

"I didn't follow your orders, Hunter. You have the right to take me to trial. All my house Warriors do. I accept your judgment. I deserve that much."

He shook his head in disbelief. She *let* it take over? Erin stifled it to give him this cover. "No. You disobeyed, but you did it to help me...because you thought I needed it. If you hadn't, you might—just might have had to face them alone. Unlikely, but it was a possibility. I won't take you to trial for it."

Jayde crossed her arms over her chest. "Are you injured?" she demanded. "Are either of you?"

"Not a claw," Hunter breathed as Talon released his grip and pulled him back to his feet. "They never got a chance. It was four low-levels and a high. You felt how fast it was over, and we bagged pretty quick, before reinforcements could be sent."

"You're saying Erin took out two low-levels on her first night?" Kohl asked in awe.

Erin laughed. "No, I drove an elder to ground first night, if you really want to get technical about it."

"You disobeyed that night, too," Talon noted.

Hunter looked at his father in dismay. The decision

was going against Erin. He had the sinking suspicion that she knew it would and was letting it slide on purpose.

"Actually, she took out the high-level and a low tonight," Hunter interjected, hoping to sway the vote a little.

Erin shrugged and took the last bite of her ice cream. There was a slight tremor in her hand, and he realized she was using the ice cream as something to keep her focus.

"Those were the two that came at his back," she mumbled, staring at the empty cup.

"Did you at least throw your blades?" Jayde asked.

"One of them—the right one. The high-level— It was just more expedient to jump in and take him out before he saw it coming."

Hunter rolled his eyes. She wasn't helping herself with that admission. Erin could accurately throw both hands at the same time, and her parents knew it.

"She was flawless. Perfect shots. Every one was perfect."

Jayde sighed. "Did you learn anything?" she asked.

"Don't pass up on any help you can get?" Erin replied sheepishly. "I imagine I'll learn to follow orders when it's beaten into me. Sorry, Mom. I didn't mean to scare you."

"That's the one! Don't scare your mother. Okay, I'll accept that as a lesson learned."

Talon shook his head in disbelief. "I won't. You will face me tomorrow. Hunter, escort your sister back to her room. I expect you to clean your blades and yourself before bed, Erin."

She nodded. "It's your right," she decided. "In the

morning."

Hunter felt his heart sink. "Dad, if you need satisfaction, take it from me."

"She disobeyed your orders. She makes a habit of it," his father countered. "Do you deny it?"

"I should have known better than to stop somewhere isolated to talk. Erin wouldn't have been in a position to disobey, if I hadn't stopped. The error was mine. Make me pay for it."

"You're right, but I know something about you, Hunter. You allow Erin to run rule over you until she endangers herself. That ends tonight. Your own pain means nothing to you, but hers will be agony for you. No matter how this happened, no matter how she talked you into it, my decision stands. And you will attend to witness it. As Lord *König*, I'm ordering it."

Hunter felt Erin tug at his arm, and he yanked back against it. He wasn't done; this wasn't over. Not yet. Face to face with their father, he searched for the words to voice his protest.

"Come on, Hunter. Give it up. He's passed judgment. You can't claim I don't deserve it. I'll survive. They don't kill *Blutjagdfrau*. You know that. You can bring me soup and ice cream in bed, if it makes you feel better."

He let Erin lead him away, shooting a cold look at his father as he left. Hunter had believed Talon was above the brutality of the older lords, but he wasn't so sure about that anymore. Halfway back to the house, he finally found his voice. Hunter swallowed painfully and sensed the area before he opened his mouth. "Okay, they're not ghosting us."

"Are you sure? Let's—"

"Absolutely. I've got three at the garage, moving this way slowly, and one in the house. Damien guarding Sarah, I'd guess. Now... How the hell could you do this? Do you have any concept what he'll do to you tomorrow?"

"Of course, I know what Dad intends to do. How can you look me in the eye and tell me you didn't know this would be the outcome?" she asked calmly.

"I thought he'd take it out on me," Hunter protested.

"You haven't spent much time around Dad, lately. The closer I get to autonomy, the more erratic he gets— and the more predictable in other ways. He treats me like I'm made of glass. He never would have allowed me to first night."

"Mom never did," he muttered.

"Mom had so much of Veriel's blood on her, you wouldn't have been able to see the seal if they painted it," Erin countered. "And Mom wasn't raised a Warrior. She just wanted to give Dad babies. That was her job."

"Still, he's going to destroy you. Why did you lie to him?"

"Either way, he was going to hurt me. This way, the right person gets the blame," she reasoned. "Me and only me."

"How do you figure that? I knew what I was doing was wrong."

"You did me a favor, something you never would have done if I hadn't suggested it at a moment when I knew you needed to do something crazy. I needed my seal, Hunter. Those overbearing men would never see me as an equal until I had it, no matter how many of them I destroyed and how many times I sent Lorian to ground."

"So, it's worth getting destroyed yourself? Maybe if we come clean—"

"First of all, it wouldn't matter if we came clean now. However I talked you into it, remember? Second, I have no intention of being destroyed. I won't end up like Adam after he fought you."

"How can you be so sure? I've never seen Dad so pissed at one of us. How can you know what he'll do?" he demanded.

"I spar with Dad almost every day."

Hunter growled in frustration. "Dad doesn't give you his best. He holds back on you."

Erin smiled and raised an eyebrow at him. "I know that. I'm not stupid or sloppy. I know exactly what he's really capable of."

"Then, why are you so damned happy?"

"I hold back on him, too, and he doesn't know it. If he did, he'd demand I use it." Her smile widened. "I know what he's capable of, and he comes up short, Hunter."

Erin sauntered into the house, leaving Hunter staring after her, frozen in shock.

"She's insane," he decided.

Chapter Ten

January 9, 2025

Talon stripped off his shirt and weapons belt and tossed them over the gate in the direction of Hunter and Jayde. He was gratified to see Hunter looking so uncomfortable. Talon just wished Erin looked as worried. He might actually believe he was getting somewhere with teaching her proper respect, if she did.

Erin reached for her own belt, but he held a hand up. "Keep them," he told her.

Her hands went to her hips, and she furrowed her brow suspiciously. "We haven't trained like that for years. Blade on blade or skin on skin. What are you up to?"

"This isn't training. This is trial. You'll need them."

She nodded. "All right. I have enough control not to cut you."

"If you have a shot, take it," he ordered her. "I'll take not an ounce less. If you give less, you'll pay for it."

Erin smiled widely. "Okay. I'll meet you as hard as you like," she offered with a courtly bow.

Talon's eyes narrowed. "What does that mean?"

"That means when you give me your best, you'll get mine. Until then, I'll match you evenly on any level you care to fight."

He nodded. It was a bluff. If Erin had more, he'd have seen it in four years. "Deal," he decided. He watched in amusement as his daughter backed off. She had balls, making a promise like that. This trial was going to be an education for her.

Talon motioned for her to come to him, but she laughed easily.

"Your trial. You lead the dance," she told him.

He smiled widely in spite of himself. "All right, then."

They started to circle, and Erin adopted the cold, serious look she reserved for her challenge matches. Gone was the smiling, easy-going young Warrior from training in the snap of a finger.

He went at her at her training level, and she deflected everything he threw at her easily. Talon stepped up his attack a few notches without warning, and Erin retaliated and danced away to a crouch, awaiting his next attack.

Talon looked down in confusion at the thin line of blood rolling down his chest. Erin spilled his blood so quickly and smoothly that he hadn't registered it until it started to sting. He met his daughter's gaze, trying desperately to fathom where that speed and stealth had come from. It was nothing like what he'd seen of her in training or challenge.

Erin shrugged uncomfortably. "Want me to put away the weapons?" she offered.

"You could have made that count, couldn't you?" he asked seriously.

She nodded. "Not a killing blow. The angle was wrong for that, but you would have bled out if you continued battling."

"Keep your blades," he decided.

Erin nodded and adjusted her crouch to prepare for his next attack.

Talon psyched himself up. He had to treat Erin like he had Jayde when his life depended on her proficiency. He came at her hard and fast. She surprised him. Erin was faster and stronger than Jayde had been at twenty-four. She matched him easily, stepping up her pace without a hint of *Blutjagd.*

He felt himself slip over as the fight intensified, but Erin still fought him in the cold, calculated manner she'd started the fight with. For the first time, Talon found himself afraid of the possibilities she represented. Erin wasn't bluffing. He wasn't at his best, but she still wasn't trying. How much power did she really have? Even Hunter, who Talon had assumed was the most powerful young Warrior born to date, wasn't capable of what Erin was doing.

Talon fell on her in a full rage, and Erin snapped. In a lightening fast move, she swept him down, and her blade hovered, brushing the skin over his heart while her hands shook in her restraint. She closed her eyes and screamed through her clenched teeth as she released her bloodlust, a *Blutjagd* that would light up the entire range easily, eclipsing everything else of note.

Erin opened her eyes and sheathed her blades before dropping to her back on the grass with her leg still extended over his hip. Her breathing came in ragged gasps, and her entire body shivered convulsively as she tried to release the last tenuous strands of the fury that had gripped her moments before.

She looked up at him miserably. "Sorry, Dad. Almost lost it. I know," she panted while sweat beaded on her body in the frigid air. "Guess my best isn't so hot, huh?"

He laughed weakly. "We'll take care of that. That's

the level we train at now. You have to be able to control that reaction."

Erin groaned as Jayde and Hunter appeared, hovering over them anxiously. "Go away," she begged.

"Are you two all right?" Jayde asked.

Talon touched his wife's face gently, as she examined the cut on his chest. She was still a vision to him after all these years. "We're fine," he assured her. "Our little girl has just been lying to us about what she's capable of."

"I tried to warn you," Erin offered.

"Yes, you did, and I thought you were bluffing."

"I don't bluff."

"I noticed." He turned his attention to Hunter. "Did you know she could do that?" he demanded.

His son blushed. "No, I didn't. If I had... How could she hide that reaction? Erin lit last night, but this was nuclear grade lit. Never seen it before in my life."

"Automatic response," she apologized. "The beasts last night were a joke compared to you, Dad. I've never allowed myself to go full throttle before."

"Allowed?" Talon questioned. "You choose when and how far you light?"

"Usually. I allow myself temperate outbursts to accomplish what I need. This one hit me harder than usual."

"That means you can battle and kill off the scopes. With beasts."

Erin darkened. "Yeah, I can," she admitted.

Talon looked from his daughter to his son suspiciously. Hunter sat back, rubbing his jaw with his hand, a tremor of nervous energy belying the calm he was pretending to possess.

Talon pushed up to sitting. "Spill it, Hunter. You've seen her do it, haven't you?"

He nodded. "Yeah, I have. She was playing with the high-level the whole time I was battling last night. Erin could have killed him easily before I made my first kill without lighting, but she was out for practical knowledge of how a beast fights. She didn't light until the other one moved at my back. I swear, when Erin lit, she was so fast and deadly accurate that both of them were dead before I turned my head to look. She lit, killed, and snuffed out as easy as you please, but she didn't light for herself. That was reserved for when she thought I needed her to do it."

"This was information I could have used," Talon growled at him.

Hunter nodded. "Once Erin started talking, I realized she wanted to get me out of it, and I couldn't set the record straight without getting her in even more trouble for the lie." He shrugged. "So, I let her story stand...like she knew I would."

"Why the hell did you go along with it in the first place?" Jayde demanded.

Hunter slouched his shoulders and shook his head with a lost expression. It was always like this. Hunter never really understood why he went along with Erin's crazy plans, but they worked well.

Erin sighed. "My fault on that one. We were drowning our sorrows and having a fraternal moment. I didn't suggest we go hunting...exactly. I sort of suggested going for ice cream and seeing if any of the local color was stupid enough to take the bait. Sure enough, they were."

"That was an incredible risk, Erin," Jayde shot at

her.

"My whole life is a risk," she countered, "and no one ever lets me forget it. I'm obviously not made of glass. I train endlessly, but for what? Every time a beast attacks, I get shoved out of the way so someone else can fight it. I'm not allowed to go hunting them. I'm the Warrior I was born to be, and I'm never allowed to be what I am. It's too dangerous."

Talon met his wife's eyes with a sheepish grin. "She has a good point. You never wanted more. You battled only when other options failed and you were forced to, so we've always treated Erin the same way. She's not you. Erin was raised to be what she is. You were raised fight or flight."

"Are you suggesting we let her hunt?" Jayde demanded.

"No. That's far too dangerous, but beasts will still come for her. I think we should let Erin help hold them off. Someday, we'll be gone, and she'll have to do it. She should start helping."

Jayde nodded her agreement. It was, after all, a point she could not argue. "First things first. She has to learn to control that ten-megaton reaction of hers. It was too difficult for her to channel. Brush up, my dear. Our little girl is going to have to be pushed nuclear on a daily basis until she learns that control."

Chapter Eleven

January 11, 2025

Sarah stretched luxuriously and headed to the bathroom for a hot shower and her morning routine. She thanked several of Kohl's gods that there was a boxed toothbrush—obviously for her use, since she couldn't see her suitcase. One of the hazards of her drugged state was that Sarah didn't care much about more than the most basic hygiene. After a shower, washing and brushing her hair, and brushing her teeth, she felt roughly human again.

The clothes she wore in had been washed and placed on the top of the dresser. The rest of the clothes stacked with them appeared to be for her, but they weren't clothes she had ever owned. They couldn't be Erin's or Jayde's, she decided. What little she saw of the two women confirmed for Sarah that they were each about five inches shy of Sarah's five-foot-ten height. It still amazed her that, while the Warriors were all well over six feet, the female Warriors were so tiny.

She sighed and pulled on the clothes she was sure of, determined to ask what happened to her own things later.

In the kitchen, Kohl rose from the table with a smile. "Ah. I told them when you slept through the dose it would be over soon. Safe for a hug?" His tone was so hopeful that she found herself grinning at the childlike need he had to hold her.

Sarah nodded gratefully and wrapped her arms around his broad chest. "How much time did I lose?"

"The battle was four nights ago."

"Four? For that little touch? What kind of a powerhouse was that beast?" she demanded, her analytical mind taking over. Sarah did research that stunned the Warriors, both with her senses and with pure logic and science.

"Actually, it wouldn't have taken as long if we'd had your medication sooner."

She looked at him in confusion.

"The beasts destroyed our supply, and Damien had to bring more."

Sarah put a hand to her head, trying to make sense of some of the darker moments of the first two days. "That explains a lot. I knew Hunter was caring for me, because there was no medication, but I couldn't seem to hold onto why that was." She smiled at Hunter. "Thank you, by the way. I don't know if I ever said that."

"Repeatedly," he assured her. "Feeling better?"

"Much. I'm just starving."

A young woman with black curls cropped close to her scalp stood. Sarah gathered that it was Erin. "What can I get you?" she offered. "I'm a fairly decent cook. Better than most of these guys, anyway."

"Please, don't put yourself out. I'll just make myself a bowl of whatever cereal is handy and a glass of juice."

Erin nodded and grabbed down a bowl, spoon, and glass. She moved to another cabinet. "Total Raisin Bran, Boo Berry, or Fruity Pebbles?" she asked in a voice that declared she'd like to throw the Fruity Pebbles out the window, personally.

"Raisin Bran, thanks."

Erin handed the box to her and left Sarah to make

her food as she'd asked.

Kohl assessed her as she carried her food back to the table. "How much? Eight pounds?" he asked.

"Not that much, I think. The solid food helped a lot." Sarah avoided Hunter's eyes, remembering vividly how arousing taking food from his fingertips had been—and how arousing it had been when she'd baited him. Her dreams had been full of nothing but his hands on her for days.

"Well, let me introduce you to our hosts while you eat. You know Hunter."

She nodded with a mouthful of cereal and felt her cheeks heat. Yes, Sarah knew Hunter. Not as well as she'd like to know Hunter, but she couldn't deny that she knew him. She knew what it felt like to be cradled in his arms, to be anchored against his rigid cock, what his lips felt like on her cheek and his skin felt like beneath her lips and hands. She swallowed and took another bite, willing her mind to safer subjects.

"This young lady is Erin. Her father, Talon, and her mother, Jayde."

Sarah opened her mind to them and started cataloging their shimmers while she ate ravenously. Talon's was familiar. She must have seen him earlier but not cataloged him when she did. She made note of the silver and gold swirl with red flecks for later identification. Jayde was burnished gold shot through with green and white flecks. Sarah identified her quickly and moved onto Erin since she knew she'd cataloged Hunter the first night.

Erin, she remembered. Sarah must have identified her already. She stared at the startling gold with flecks of red and white in awe, her breakfast forgotten. The shimmers told her so much; Erin's was a riot of conflicting emotions and hidden agendas.

And fear that she keeps carefully hidden.

"Are you all right?" Jayde asked gently.

Sarah shook her head and pushed the shimmers away. "Yes. Sorry. Staring is rude, I know. I was just admiring your shimmers. They're unlike anything I've ever seen before. They're so—vibrant."

Erin smiled. "You told me I was too bright to look at while you were sick."

"You almost are now," she admitted. "I just wanted to catalog you, but I got caught up. I do apologize. I thought I had outgrown staring like that."

"Catalog?" Talon asked.

"Shimmers are individual, like fingerprints. When I encounter one, I can identify it in my mind, like using an address book. After that, I can identify the shimmer as being a particular person even in total darkness...or blindfolded."

"Or in a cave ten meters away, with no direct line of sight," Kohl teased.

"You should be glad of that," she shot back, taking another bite.

"Oh, I am. Every day of my life, I am."

"What do I look like?" Erin asked earnestly.

"Like polished gold set in the sunlight with red and white floating specks swirling through and your red braid of *Blutjagd* not in use. The braid becomes a thick band when it's in use. The more fiery the bloodlust, the wider the band becomes."

"Gold?" Kohl asked. "You've never seen gold before."

"All the *Königs* have it to some extent or another. It

must be a *König* trait," she dismissed.

"Appropriate," he decided, taking another sip of his coffee.

"What about me?" Hunter asked.

"Yours is the most unique shimmer I've ever seen," she answered clinically. "It's brilliant white with swirling specks of blues, golds, and purples. It's like looking at a living, breathing opal."

He smiled. "Wow. I wish I could see it."

"It's very—soothing," she admitted. "I think that's what makes your touch healing."

"Purple?" Kohl asked again. "I thought there was no purple."

"I've never encountered it in anyone before, but I'd never encountered gold before either. Face it. *König* shimmers will never be mistaken for anyone else."

"What does your shimmer look like?" Hunter asked.

Sarah darkened. "I've never seen it," she admitted. "They don't reflect in mirrors, and I can't see it on my own hand. Every sensitive sees something different, and it doesn't translate, so their impressions of my shimmer mean nothing to me. By my own standards, I know my base color would be blue, but I can't even guess at my identifiers."

"How do you know it would be blue?" he persisted.

"There are classes for me. I can tell what I'm looking at without identifying the person by the base color."

"Red is high-level beast," Hunter mused.

Sarah nodded as she swallowed another bite of her cereal. "Yes. Yellow is low-level beast, and black—" she shuddered, "is an elder. Green is a human, and blue is a human sensitive. All the other colors I've encountered are Warriors—silver, gold, tan, peach, orange, and off-white."

"So, you would be blue, because you're a human sensitive."

"That's my guess. It's disconcerting to talk to other sensitives. Tricia sees everyone as brushstrokes like portraits. Watercolor means one thing, color block another. Regina sees gemstones in the place of a chest and every stone means something different. Bernice sees shimmers like I do, but her color scheme is nothing like mine, and her perceptions are very weak.

"I've often wondered if when the ability manifests has anything to do with what you see—and what you know as well. Bernice was discovered young, maybe ten or so. Tricia and Regina weren't discovered until they were adult women in their own fields. Tricia was—is an artist. Regina was a bookkeeper, but her hobby is rare stones."

"I see what you mean about no translation," Erin noted. The young woman smiled. "Do you feel up to watching some training? No offense, but you need some sun."

Sarah nodded gratefully. "Normal routine is something I could use right now."

Half an hour later, Kohl, Jayde, and Hunter joined Sarah on a thick blanket laid on the ground for her. Though Sarah was wrapped in her ski jacket and gloves, the Warriors seated around her wore just their lined leather jackets, and the combatants were in shirt sleeves. It always amazed her that the Warriors didn't seem to mind the elements—and that they could fight so soon after eating, when she was looking for a cozy hole to hide in.

She watched them draw their weapons. "Blade on blade? Where's their armor?" she asked nervously.

Jayde smiled. "We don't use armor once we're fully trained. We have no use for it."

Sarah raised an eyebrow at the older woman. "Then how did Talon get injured?" she countered.

Her smile disappeared. "How do you know he was injured recently?"

"I can see the black line knitting in his shimmer." She ran her hand over her ribs. "Here. It's minor and new. Now answer my question, please."

Hunter laughed heartily. "Can't put one over on you. My sister has an aggressive *Blutjagd* we're trying to train. She typically doesn't light at all. She doesn't need to. When she does light, she chooses what she feels is a safe level to release at once. We want her to learn to release her full potential and utilize it when she does."

"So, you were unaware of Erin's potential until she loosed it on Talon, and she injured him in her lack of control?" She shuddered at the thought. By the rules of sanction, they could have killed her for that lapse.

Hunter darkened. "Actually, she injured him before she lit, because he ordered her to do so if she could. When Erin lit, she didn't hurt him, though it was almost impossible to leash herself. We want her to master that, so we're pushing her to a nuclear grade *Blutjagd* every training session. Blade on blade is more effective for that than hand to hand. Watch her shimmer. I'd be interested in what you see as she battles."

Sarah nodded. "I'd be glad to be of service."

Kohl laughed lightly. "Don't let her fool you. She loves something new to study."

She focused on the two Warriors as they started circling. Their braids of *Blutjagd* were steady for the first few minutes, though Talon attacked fast and hard. They had high thresholds, much higher than she was accustomed to seeing. When the tide turned, she sucked in her breath.

"What is it?" Jayde asked.

"Talon's braid is widening steadily, but Erin's..."

"It's not even touched yet," Hunter stated.

Sarah shook her head. "No. It's not expanding at all. How does she do that?" She bit her lower lip and moved forward onto her knees to examine their shimmers closer. Erin's swirls were expressive, showing patience and concentration, but her braid was silent and still.

"How long are we staying, Kohl? I'd like to study this, if there's time," Sarah noted distractedly, her mind doing extensive computations on the swirls in the girl's shimmer.

At the edges of her vision, Jayde's face turned an angry crimson, and her braid widened a bit. "You haven't told her?" she demanded.

Sarah scowled at the disturbance in her study. "Told me what?" she asked in annoyance.

Kohl cleared his throat. "You need more protection than I can offer, Sarah. After Darrien... You're staying with the *Königs* when I return."

She snapped her head around to glare at him. Kohl was trying to appear cool and assured, but his shimmer spoke of uncertainty and unhappiness. At least, there was no blame, Sarah noted. There never had been blame.

"No, I'm not. I'm going home," she assured him quietly.

"Yes, you are. It is necessary for your safety that you remain here."

"You don't want me to—not in your heart, and I don't want to. You can't just dump me with strangers. I won't stand for it."

"I'm not dumping you! I'll stay as long as you need me to feel comfortable, but you will stay when I go. You're still my daughter. I won't abandon you. I'll visit, but I must see to your safety before all other considerations."

"I don't want a wandering life. I don't want to live out of a suitcase without my treasures, moving from place to place every few months. I'd hate it. I've always had a range."

"You have a choice in that," her father managed.

"Then I choose to go home."

"That's not your choice."

"What is my choice?" she asked suspiciously.

"You may either travel with the *Königs* or stay in Crossbearer range under the personal protection of Hunter. You would have the solace of a constant range, and Hunter does possess a certain calming touch when you overload..."

Her cheeks burned. Sarah looked at Hunter and seethed that he was staring at the training as if the discussion wasn't happening around him. His face was impassive, though his shimmer revealed a mixture of nervous energy and fear.

"You," she spat. "This was your idea."

He didn't look at her. "Yes, I suggested it—before it

was necessary to care for you and only the choice of staying here. Your father wanted you to follow the *Königs* with no choice. Somehow, I knew you wouldn't appreciate that."

"I don't appreciate any of this."

Hunter nodded his understanding.

"You're still intent on your course? You still think this is a good idea?" she asked archly.

"Yes and yes. The offer stands."

"That'll change," she warned. Sarah had years of practice annoying men. By the time she was done, none of the *Königs* would want her with them.

Hunter's mouth quirked up as if in answer to her challenge. "Oh, look. Erin is just lighting up," he mused.

Kohl sucked in his breath. "Gods alive. It's stronger than yesterday."

Sarah swiveled her head back to the action. Her mind locked in shock for a long moment, and her mouth went dry. She wasn't staying here. No way! She skittered backward reflexively and screamed her protest.

* * * *

Talon smiled as the whole ten megatons landed at once. Erin was less choppy at entrance, at least. She attacked with a vengeance, driving him back effortlessly despite the fact that he outweighed her by a hundred pounds and was almost a foot taller.

"No," Sarah screamed in terror.

Talon avoided looking at her, needing to concentrate on Erin or risk losing his head.

His daughter stilled, and her eyes widened in shock. Her *Blutjagd* evaporated, and her weapons fell from boneless fingers and thumped to the frozen ground. Erin dropped to her knees, shaking and sweating, looking at him in confusion, looking like she had in the worst of her *Krankheit*.

He looked from his daughter to Sarah. The young sensitive was screaming piercing, heart-wrenching screams, while Kohl tried to hold her and Jayde and Hunter tried to talk her down. In the end, he saw Hunter wrench one of the medicated pens from Kohl's pocket and inject her with it through her jeans. Sarah sobbed and pleaded with Kohl, while the drugs dragged her down into oblivion.

He looked back to Erin, stunned to see that she was lying unconscious in a semi-fetal position. Talon sheathed his weapons and dropped to his knees beside her. Her breathing was shallow but even, and her pulse was rapid and erratic. She continued to shake and sweat. Her skin was hot to the touch, as if she really had slipped back into the sealing sickness.

Talon scooped her into his arms. "Jayde," he thundered. "Call Sylvia. Tell her to call in whatever favors she has to. We'll be there in an hour or less." He bolted for the garage with his wife close behind.

"What is it?" she asked as she punched the doctor's private number.

"If I knew that, I wouldn't be doing this."

"What do I tell Sylvia?"

"She lit. Sarah screamed. Erin seemed to go into shock. *Blutjagd* died. She's shaking, sweating, feverish— She collapsed and lost consciousness. Damned if I know."

"How's her condition? Hang on Sylvia. We're on our way to you."

"Pulse fast and choppy, breathing shallow, unresponsive." Talon turned the corner to the garage doors, vaguely noting Jayde's discussion with Sylvia.

"You got that? Good.

"We're not sure. She hit *Blutjagd* hard and got shocked out even harder. It was over in seconds.

"She couldn't tell us anything, Sylvia!

"Right. We're at the car, now. We'll keep her warm."

She hung up as Talon eased Erin into the back seat and followed her in. Hunter stormed in, handing Jayde their coats and reaching for the passenger door.

"No," Talon told his son. "I need you here. I need you to protect Sarah, and get me answers when she's able to answer. I need to know what she sensed that set her off like that, what she did, and why she's so scared."

Hunter looked at him in disbelief. "I have to go," he breathed.

"No, you need to field this. This is not going to go unnoticed. Already, her ten-megaton reaction has drawn calls from outside Cross. You know Hunter range saw that—maybe beyond Hunter. If Piers hasn't called you in less than an hour, I'll be amazed. They'll all want answers, and you can get them from Sarah and pass them on. Try to keep them calm, or it will be a circus here by morning."

Hunter nodded solemnly and reached in to smooth Erin's sweat-soaked hair before closing the back door and stepping away from the car. He walked away, looking dejected.

Jayde slid into the driver's seat and started out.

Talon looked at Hunter as they passed him. His hands were shoved in his pockets, his face stony. As he turned away, Hunter drew his cell phone and closed his eyes in a pained expression.

Talon sighed raggedly. Rumor control would be impossible, and the war had just begun. Piers would only be the first of many calls.

* * * *

Erin shifted uncomfortably. Of all the beds she'd slept in over all the ranges she'd traveled, this one had to be the worst. Her head hurt. Her entire body hurt, and she had no idea why.

The last thing she remembered clearly was lighting up in training. Did she black out or make some mistake and get knocked out? Either way, it wasn't something Erin wanted to repeat. She was sure of that much. And, pain was only an effective teacher if you remembered what the hell you did wrong in the first place!

Erin rolled off the bed with every intention of landing on her feet and going to the bathroom, but several sensations assaulted her at once. The cold tile beneath her feet jarred her. None of the houses she'd stayed in had tile in a bedroom. Warriors preferred wood and carpets.

Before she had a chance to examine that fact too carefully, her knees buckled and her head started to spin. Erin white knuckled the edge of the bed and forced her eyes open. She sucked in her breath in disbelief. She had never been inpatient before, but this was undoubtedly a hospital. Who would be crazy enough to put her inpatient? She launched to the window unsteadily and looked out. Dark! She'd lost the whole day. *Or worse.*

A bag on the chair held her clothes. Erin dropped into the chair and started dragging them on. She was fully dressed and tucking her shirt in, cursing the lack of weapons in her sheaths quietly, when the door opened behind her. She whipped around, prepared to battle hand to hand, but Piers filled the doorway.

"What are you doing?" he demanded softly, letting the door swing shut behind him.

"Getting out of here," she managed. "I can't stay here. I'm not even armed, and all these—people. This is nuts. Someone will get killed."

"You're not going, until Sylvia is done with you. Get back in that bed."

"And get caught unprepared? No way." Erin glanced at the Band-Aid in the crook of her elbow and ripped it off in annoyance. "I take it she's run her tests?"

"Yes. A whole battery."

"Good. She can mail me the results." Erin shook her head and headed for the door.

Piers grasped her by the arm. "In bed," he ordered.

"You're crazy. I *can't* stay here. Don't you get it? Every ounce of training—"

"Fine. Defeat me, and you can leave."

She furrowed her brow and rubbed her forehead to relieve the ache making her eyesight fuzz. Erin felt like her entire body was encased in lead. She was sweating, and her knees were still rubbery. She wasn't sure she could beat a kitten, let alone a Warrior.

"You can't, can you?" he growled. "You look like

hell, Erin. Get in bed."

Erin met his eyes wearily. "Get Sylvia in here. I'll answer her questions, and she's sending me home. Agreed?"

"If she doesn't release you, you shut up and get in bed," he qualified.

She shifted from foot to foot nervously. "I can't stay here," she repeated. Years of training backed that up. Erin couldn't pose a threat to humans. Her presence was a threat; surely, Piers could see that. "The risk—"

"Your parents and I are here. If necessary, I can have half the North American Warriors here before morning. You will do what is in your best interests. Understood?"

"Understood, but let's make an honest effort to spring me." She said it hopefully, and Piers nodded his agreement. "You call them while I hit the bathroom. I really want to get this over with."

He released her arm and watched while she headed to the bathroom then picked up the bedside phone. Erin heard the door open again before she was finished. She splashed water on her sweaty face, hoping she looked halfway competent. No time like the present. Erin made her way out, forcing a smile to her face.

"Hi Sylvia," she greeted the gray-haired woman in the lab coat.

"Well, you know me. That's good. Come sit down. I take it you know who you are and how old you are as well?"

"Erin Anne Cross, and I'll be sixteen next week." She sank into the chair. "Who do I have to thank for beating me upside the head?" she joked, looking at her parents over the doctor's shoulder and raising an eyebrow.

"Headache?" Sylvia inquired.

"My whole body aches, but no bruises. Any idea why it hurts?"

"Adrenaline overload."

"Ah. That's what got me," she decided.

"No, that was the result of what got you. You don't remember what happened?"

"I remember laying on steam. After that, I've got a regular black hole, Doc."

"Well, your tests came back with no brain damage, no heart damage, whacked blood chemistry even for you—"

"Can I do anything but sleep it off?" Erin asked pointedly.

"Not really," Sylvia admitted.

"Then, release me before someone gets hurt," she pleaded.

"Erin," Talon warned.

Sylvia considered it carefully. "Ibuprofen for the pain. I'll give you a vitamin supplement. Drink lots of fluids to help flush the toxins. No training for three days. Light duty for a few days after that."

Erin sighed in relief. "Agreed. Anything, just let me out of here."

The old woman laughed lightly and her blue eyes glittered in her wrinkled face. "I don't know why Warriors bother to come see me. There's not much I can do. Your systems are just too damned efficient."

"Wasn't my idea," she commented weakly.

Piers cleared his throat. "Not to be indelicate, Sylvia— Is it in Erin's best interests to let her go?"

"I wouldn't let her go if I thought she was in danger. She can relax at home, and that's what she needs. She won't do that here. She's already like a caged tiger. If she's not up to par in three days, or if she has a relapse, she's coming in for a few days."

Erin groaned at the thought of it. "I promise doctor's orders are law."

* * * *

Hunter paced the front room. They were on their way back, and he was fuming that Erin had talked her way out of medical care. Despite the risk to the humans at the hospital, she had to come first, but she'd refused to endanger them.

He heard the car coming and bolted out to meet it. The fact that Jayde pulled up to the door instead of going to the garage told him all he needed to know. Hunter pulled the rear door open and gathered Erin into his arms. "She's unconscious again," he noted bitterly.

"Asleep," Talon corrected him. "Sylvia says all she can do is sleep it off. She's weak, but you know Erin. That can't hold her down for long."

Hunter nodded and carried her in out of the cold night. Erin was practically too easy to lift, and he sighed at the thought that, for the third time in less than a week, he was carrying a woman he cared for into this house and praying she would recover from some strange malady. Hunter glanced at the door to his room sadly as he passed by. It was going to be nerve-wracking having both Sarah and Erin incapacitated at the same time.

He settled Erin on her bed and pulled her boots off. She curled to her side, dragging the blanket with her to cocoon herself. Hunter smiled as he brushed at her damp, black curls. He stood to leave, as Jayde sheathed the weapons Hunter had rescued from the training area into Erin's empty belt and hung them over the headboard where Erin would expect to find them when she woke.

Talon was waiting in the doorway, watching the scene with grim resolve. He waved for his wife and son to follow him to the living room where Piers was waiting for them.

"How is she?" the old lord asked.

Hunter smiled at that. How much could her condition have changed in the hour since he saw Erin to Jayde's car at the hospital before getting in his own to rush here?

"Asleep," Talon assured him. "How is rumor control faring?"

Hunter winced. Piers had insisted on taking over after the first three hours, when it became obvious that Hunter—speaking for either *König* or Crossbearer—would not be sufficient. Piers, as lord of Cross range, carried much more clout.

Piers started his report with a sigh. "About as well as you can expect. Lewis is sending one of his. He's convinced the beasts will see this as an opportunity. Being Stone lord entitles him to leeway I don't extend to anyone else. I've convinced the others to hold off, unless Erin has another collapse and/or goes inpatient."

Hunter nodded. "He's sending Curt?" he guessed, looking forward to spending time with the younger man again.

"No, he's sending Adam," Piers informed him with a scowl.

"Adam? I thought she was supposed to relax?" Hunter countered sarcastically.

"Better than Bryant," Talon noted. "At least Adam is printed."

"That's true," he conceded grudgingly. "So, Sylvia couldn't give you any idea of what happened?"

Jayde shook her head solemnly. "No. She had no idea what started the cascade. Could Sarah offer any more help?"

Hunter groaned. "I wish. She was awake a few hours ago, hysterical still. She wants to leave. She swears she saw a beast walking in broad daylight."

Talon shook his head in exhaustion. "Well, that's not possible, so where does that leave us?"

"Hallucinations?" Jayde offered. "Maybe she's not recovered."

Hunter shook his head. "I think I know what she saw. What I don't understand is what she did to Erin when she saw it."

"You think Sarah is responsible for what happened?" Talon asked. "If that's true, we can't keep our word to Kohl. I can't risk that type of attack again."

Hunter grimaced. "I don't think it was done consciously. I think what happened was a trauma to each of them in their own ways."

Jayde leaned toward him. "Explain what you think happened," she requested wearily.

"Remember what Sarah said at breakfast? She sees *Blutjagd* as a red braid when it's dormant. The more pressing the bloodlust, the wider the band becomes."

"Yes. Go on."

"She sees high-level beasts as a solid red shimmer—a red aura."

Jayde's eyes widened in understanding.

"I think Erin's entire shimmer lights up red when she goes nuclear. If I'm right, I'm not surprised Sarah went ballistic when she saw it. Look at it from her point of view."

"The stronger the Warrior, the stronger the curse," Piers mused. "How do we test this theory without hurting either of them again?"

"If it involves lighting Erin again, it's going to wait the three days of rest the doctor ordered," Talon reminded them.

Hunter nodded. "It does. I intend to explain what happened to Sarah and lead her through the experience of watching Erin blaze up through a normal *Blutjagd* all the way to nuclear grade. We know Erin can do a simple progression like that. We've seen it. Now, if we lead Sarah through and keep her calm, it should shield Erin from whatever fallout hit her last time. The only question is— Has Sarah discovered an offensive weapon in her arsenal and doesn't know it?"

"Offensive?" Piers repeated. "There's never been such a thing."

Jayde smiled wearily. "Perhaps for humans, the stronger the curse, the stronger the power."

Chapter Twelve

January 12, 2025

Hunter watched Sarah eat, tensed to stop her if she took off for the door, as she'd threatened several times. She was brooding and miserable.

"I am leaving," she assured Kohl for the third time that morning. "If I have to remove my amulet and run like hell, I'm leaving."

Kohl's face darkened, and he started to sputter.

Hunter waved him off. "Sarah," he began gently.

She turned on him in a fury. "Don't try your tricks on me," she spat. "You sedated me. I could have been long gone by now."

"As a raving lunatic," he qualified. "Look. I know what you saw. I expected it, and it's my fault for not preparing you."

"Preparing me? Tell me the truth. Is she really *Blutjagdfrau* or half-beast?" she accused.

Jayde sucked in her breath in shock. "How dare you! I would die before I'd lie with a beast or carry its child."

Hunter blanched. "Erin is a Warrior. There's not a drop of beast in her. Unfortunately, your senses perceive both the bloodlust of the Warriors and the state of high-level beasts as red. It's not hard to see how that could get confusing in the right circumstances."

"Don't give me that. It's not the same. A band! You have a band of red, tempered by the rest of your shimmer. Only beasts are all red."

"And there's no such thing as purple and gold,"

Jayde quipped. "There's a first time for everything."

"Bear with me," Hunter interrupted, before Sarah could retort. "My sister has a unique ability. She can slip into what you consider a normal *Blutjagd.* We've all seen her do it, even your father. We want her to learn to control a sudden burst of her worst, so we requested that she hold it in check until she could expend an explosive attack. I want to show it to you when she recovers. I want you to see her rise slowly, like any other Warrior, without stopping herself until she goes full throttle. Will you give us the benefit of doubt that long?"

Sarah looked from face to face expectantly, and Hunter followed her gaze. Everyone waited patiently for her answer. No one was going to force her compliance.

Finally, she met his eyes again and nodded. "All right," she conceded, "but if I believe for one second that she isn't in complete control, I'm leaving. Life is too short to mix with an unstable Warrior. Understood?"

Hunter darkened. "That's not my choice. You know that."

Kohl shifted uncomfortably. "If I think Erin is out of control, I'll allow you to leave," he grumbled unhappily. "Against my better judgment," he added.

Hunter snapped a fierce look at Adam as the older Warrior started chuckling over his coffee mug.

"What is your problem?" he demanded. "And, make it good."

"The idea of Erin out of control," Adam admitted. "If that woman lacked control, I dare say half of our younger Warriors would be dead right now. Me, first and foremost."

Hunter grunted his agreement. "If anyone posed the danger of killing you, it was me the night she ran away to the lake."

Adam stretched his neck, as if he could still feel the imprint of Hunter's hand, and his smile melted away. "I remember," he replied solemnly.

"So do I," Erin answered from the doorway. "I thought I got rid of you. Don't you have a mate to go drive nuts?" she grumbled.

"Yes I do, but Lewis ordered me here until you're recovered."

She leaned against the doorframe, looking pale but decidedly dangerous. "Why you?"

"Lewis stays close to the Stone, and Bryant seems to annoy you. Kord thinks Curt is too young for this responsibility. Plus, Lewis said he couldn't send Curt because of some four-year plan of the Stone's for him. You wouldn't know anything about that, would you?"

Erin shook her head, though she rubbed her temples in a way that told Hunter she knew more than she was saying.

"Figures. Neither does Lewis, actually. He's sort of annoyed at the whole Stone puzzle thing. I take it Corwyn never liked that either."

"That's the understatement of the century," she decided.

"Anyway, that leaves me. Besides, whether you like it or not, I made a vow to protect you four years ago. Face it. You're stuck with me."

She nodded, a smile curving her lips. "Closed that hole when you lunge yet?" she inquired.

"Try me when you recover and find out," he replied simply, picking up his coffee cup.

Erin's smile spread, no doubt in anticipation of knocking Adam on his butt for the hundredth time in the last four years. She started to cross to the table. Her eyes locked with Sarah's, and she winced, grasping the back of Hunter's chair roughly. Adam and Hunter vaulted to her, but Erin pushed them away.

"Ease off, Sarah," she growled. "You're too loud."

The sensitive looked at her in shock. "I'm not doing anything."

"Bullshit! Get out of my head. I have enough problems with my own thoughts. I don't need yours."

"I can't project. It's not one of my gifts."

"You tried with Tricia, but it didn't work. She thought it might, because she reads minds like you do, but it didn't mesh somehow. Interference...like static. Now, do you believe me?" Erin finished painfully, rubbing the heel of her hand into her forehead and tightening the grip of her other hand.

"You read minds," Sarah accused.

"I wish," she shot back. "I'm not the one doing this. If I were, I'd hear everyone, right? The only one broadcasting is you. Turn it off."

"I can't. If you're hearing it, you have to learn to shut it down. It's not my fault." Sarah set her jaw angrily.

"Fine. I'll try anything, if it will shut you up. Tell me how."

Erin squeezed her eyes shut as Sarah got a faraway look. The tension crackling in the room between them seemed to evaporate slowly. Erin relaxed her death grip on the chair and allowed Hunter to ease her into it, while the other Warriors watched the interaction warily.

Sarah trained her eyes on Erin. "Told you," she commented acidly.

Erin was angry and shaking in exhaustion when she opened her eyes. "What did you do to me?" she demanded.

"Nothing. If you've got it, you always had it. Mind reading isn't a virus. I can't—infect you."

"If I had it, don't you think I would have noticed it by now?"

"Not necessarily. I never saw shimmers until I saw my first beast. The shock of it set me off. It unlocked what I already had, and I had to learn to lock it."

"So, you set me off? Great. Remind me to thank you properly someday. Like in three days," she grumbled.

"How do you figure that?" Sarah demanded.

"You're the only one I hear, and I never did this until you came. You figure it out."

"You sat with me at breakfast yesterday without a problem. I think that blows your theory out of the water."

Erin furrowed her brow. "What else could it be? You're the only new thing in my life."

"Seems to me your problems all started when you went—" she ground her teeth, "nuclear."

Erin scowled at her. "No dice. I went nuclear at least twice a day for three days with no real problems."

"Trying to plant a blade in your father isn't a problem?" Sarah inquired, a cool edge to her tone.

"I controlled that," she protested. "Besides, what if you never projected until you saw me go nuclear? Maybe my relief came when you concentrated on the process of shutting it down."

Sarah darkened. "Impossible."

"Tell me why."

"Because I haven't shut anything down. I've opened mine, since you shut down yours. I'm reading your shimmer right now. There's no reason to be scared of this. You just have to learn to live with it."

Erin started to snap back at her, but Hunter dropped a hand on her shoulder to still her. "Okay. There is no way to settle this."

Sarah shot him an angry look, and he sent her a warning in response.

"What I suggest is the two of you experimenting with it. Learn to control the flow between you. There is every possibility that you are affecting each other exclusively."

"Meaning what?" Kohl asked.

"Meaning Erin's nuclear light-up shocked something in Sarah, and her hysterical response—with or without a psychic push—shocked something in Erin. I think they're linked, and that means they can learn to use it."

"Use it in what way?" Kohl continued.

"When you battle with Sarah, she feeds you information that you use to attack. The beasts ever respond to what she's telling you?"

He grimaced. "Sometimes. We've had to revert to an earlier code and hope for the best or even clear out entirely at times. Some beasts catch on too quick."

"What if Sarah could feed the information without talking? Even if it was only Erin that could hear her, with Erin's speed and skill and Sarah's abilities, they would be an unstoppable team."

Adam made a sound akin to a snort. "You're

suggesting we let our *Blutjagdfrau* and our most powerful sensitive waltz off to hunt together? You're insane."

"Not on your life, Maher," he growled. "What I am saying is that we have these two women—both of whom Lorian wants as mates, I might add—in one place. Now, that makes it easier to protect them, but it also makes a very tempting target. Eventually, beasts will come. The two of them can work as a team to stay safe, if I'm right."

Sarah raised an eyebrow at him. "Does that mean you've changed your mind about me staying in Cross?" she asked pointedly.

Hunter stamped down his instant arousal and managed an impassive face. "The offer stands. It's your choice. Kohl will only release you from your choice, if Erin is uncontrollable." He smiled. "Don't hope for that reprieve.

"Of course, if you can't work with Erin—if the two of you can't get along together, Crossbearer range may be the lesser of two evils."

Sarah's jaw tightened, and her eyes narrowed. "I can read your mind," she reminded him.

"Then, you know I told the truth," he countered.

"Yeah. Lesser and greater evils, only which is which is still my call."

He shrugged calmly. "As you wish."

Talon cleared his throat. "This little experiment really should wait until Erin is recovered from her first shock."

Erin met his eyes in a fury. "Who said I agreed to this training? The last thing I want is her in my head."

"Afraid?" Sarah taunted.

"Of you? You've got to be kidding. I'm just afraid I won't be able to control my gut reaction next time. I wouldn't want Kohl carrying a corpse back to his range."

"Reaction to what?" There was a challenge in that.

"Calling a sealed Warrior, an elder hunter no less, a beast is about as dangerous as you can get. I can read *your* mind, Sarah. 'Demon-spawn beast bitch' almost got your throat slit." Her smile seemed to drop the room's temperature by a dozen degrees. "With Maher's blade, just in case you're about to point out the lack of weapons on my hip...and you are."

Adam grimaced. "Not funny, Erin."

"Wasn't meant to be."

The older woman paled considerably. "I didn't—"

"Not much fun when the shoe is on the other foot, is it? Welcome to our world, Sarah. Nothing is private anymore. Nothing is secret. As you can steal it from us, I can steal it from you. It might be good for you to learn to live on a level playing field." Erin pushed to her feet and started to storm away.

"Erin," Jayde demanded. "Come back here and eat your breakfast."

She paused momentarily but didn't look back. "No thanks. I've lost my appetite." Erin started forward then stopped abruptly and faced Sarah with wide eyes. "You can't exist on even ground. You have to see yourself as superior to live, don't you?"

"If you don't like it, turn it off, princess. You don't have to listen just because it's there."

"You wish." Erin smiled wickedly. "You'll wish I'd turned it off by the time I'm through," she promised.

Sarah's face paled. "You wouldn't," she exploded.

"There are no rules of engagement in battle, and I always win in the end. Keep that in mind before you threaten me again. You have too many secrets to throw that first stone." She turned on her heel and glided away with a predatory look, while Sarah seethed at her retreating back.

Hunter looked at her barely-controlled fury in amazement. "What was she thinking?" he asked.

Sarah's face turned pure crimson. She hurled her napkin at him and stormed away. "Stay away from me," she ordered.

Hunter raised an eyebrow at his parents and sighed. "Well, it works," he mused unhappily.

"It works all right," Adam agreed. "Now the question is whether or not they can learn to use it to do anything constructive."

Chapter Thirteen

January 17, 2025

Erin growled at the disturbance in her sleep. Sarah was doing it on purpose; she was sure of it. The five days since Sarah's challenge at the breakfast table had been a mixture of torture and the thrill of battle.

So far, the two had managed to keep the other Warriors out of their skirmish, except for the occasional snippish backlash to a spoken statement. Most of Sarah's backlash was directed at Hunter, while most of Erin's were directed at Adam and her father. They circled each other dangerously, two angry Warriors in a whole new type of battle.

By the fourth day, Erin had been aching for a different, more satisfying type of battle. She'd demanded her training and was granted permission to resume.

She'd carefully closed her mind to Sarah before each match, determined not to allow a cocky psychic to distract her from her task—or injure her to make her go inpatient again. For some reason, the extra layer of self-control required to leash her inner link to Sarah also bottled her nuclear *Blutjagd* into a razor-sharp edge with exquisite control.

She'd smiled at Sarah's fury when Kohl rescinded his offer of letting her leave, as Erin was nothing if not controlled in her bloodlust. She'd sent taunting laughter after the other woman as Sarah had stalked away.

Under other circumstances, had they not been locked in battle as they were, Erin might have let herself slip just to give the woman the freedom she wanted, but there were other considerations. Not only would she thwart whatever Sarah wanted, but also Erin's own plans depended on Sarah staying right where she was.

For Erin's plans to succeed, Hunter had to mate and produce children. Hunter wanted Sarah, and he believed Sarah wanted him. The fact that she was simply too obstinate to accept Hunter was completely true, according to the thoughts rushing through Sarah's head. And it was completely unacceptable. Sarah would make her choice, and she would choose Hunter.

Sarah's answer to that particular victory had been a threat to tell Adam Erin's deepest secrets, all three of the topics she decidedly detested the idea of having laid bare to the eldest Maher brother. At Adam's insistence that he wasn't leaving, Erin had made the demand that his continued presence be contingent on the outcome of a challenge match. Unaccustomed to Erin in full *Blutjagd* and thinking himself immune for correcting his earlier hole, Adam had been unprepared for his crushing defeat. It had taken Erin exactly one and a half minutes and two blows to send the stunned Warrior packing—once he regained consciousness.

The battle was, at times, petty and childish, but neither was willing to back down. It was easy to tell when one was blocking the other for down time. That was one thing they were never childish about. By unspoken agreement, one never shut the other out in the midst of a heated argument.

From Sarah's reaction, Erin guessed the older woman was receiving an education in the eloquence of baser speech at times. She surmised that Sarah's brothers had rigid orders to regard her as a young lady in that respect—both in their minds and in spoken communication, something the Warriors around Erin had never worried about, knowing Jayde was akin to a sailor on leave when she was pissed off. Erin had laughed at Sarah's rather grudging and fuming agreement with that assessment.

Earlier that evening, they had celebrated Erin's sixteenth birthday, crowned by her grant of autonomy. Considering her internal plan—the four-year plan the had Stone let slip to Lewis, *damn the interfering piece of rock*—her autonomy was essentially a joke, but it did mean she had the absolute right to fight her own battles rather than allowing her parents that power.

Sarah had smiled secretively. *{Gee, autonomy?}* Her voice drawled inside Erin's head, sounding smug. *{Guess that means you can head to town tomorrow and find a warm body to take away your aches and needs.}*

Sigh. I don't require the rutting the males find so essential to life. She'd kept her thoughts as neutral as possible on the subject.

{Of course, you could always call Adam's little brother. As long as you picked a Warrior, I'm sure the whole world would rejoice in you getting a good fuck in.} Sarah was getting almost too comfortable with baser speech.

Coming from a person who's afraid of intimacy with one of my class, I'll take that with a grain of salt.

{Then again, you could always call Adam's other brother. He'd be glad to take care of your needs with no

annoying complications. Wouldn't that be divine revenge on him?}

Erin had laughed out loud at that one, stifling it as her parents looked at the two women curiously and rolled their eyes almost in unison.

{You do have one more choice. You could always take your amulet off and go find out if Lorian is as good in person as he is in your mind. After all, being so close to beast yourself—}

Right after you, dear. After all, you seem to be as cold and dead inside as he is. I think he chose well when he left me and went to you. You're more his type than Hunter's anyway. You're right, you know. You don't have the balls to live as a König.

Sarah had looked at her miserably as Erin swallowed the last mouthful of her cake and bussed her dishes to the sink. The other Warriors had looked from one woman to the other suspiciously but wisely kept their mouths shut.

"Good night, everyone," she'd called sweetly. "I have a few letters to write tonight, so I'll see you in the morning." *Sweet dreams, Sarah.*

Sarah had remained strangely silent after that except for the deep sadness she was trying to hide.

Erin cursed her luck. She'd hoped for anger. She'd hoped Sarah would go to Hunter simply to tick her off, not realizing the one fact Erin kept safely tucked away at all times. Erin wanted exactly that.

Erin felt the stirring in her mind again, a formless nudging. This was Sarah's revenge for Erin's victory. Sarah had discovered quickly that Erin lacked the practiced control to shut her out while she was sleeping, and the more experienced psychic was exploiting the advantage mercilessly, waking Erin and fading away behind her shield before the argument could begin.

Stop it!

Erin issued the command, as the disturbance came again, hoping Sarah would hear it before she closed herself off. With no answer forthcoming, Erin sighed in relief and snuggled down into her pillow. She growled her displeasure as the dark disturbance swirled in her mind again.

Goddamn it, Sarah! I will beat you senseless, if you make me come in there.

The warning was laced with as much venom as Erin could manage. Still, the vibrations were circling in her mind, formless and now threatening.

Erin swung her legs off the bed and grabbed her weapons belt, wishing she could use the blades on Sarah to ensure unbroken sleep in the future. She wouldn't kill her, just a scar to remind her to leave these games out of their struggle.

She kicked the thick carpet in annoyance as she walked, some irrational part of her mind wishing she could share the grief with Hunter. Plan or no plan, he really needed to wise up and get away from Sarah before he did something stupid and printed on her.

But, Hunter had taken the easy road and removed himself to the couch and out of the line of fire three days ago. He'd made it clear that until the two women either came to an equitable agreement or fought to the death, he was not going to be a part of the game they were playing.

She snorted at the fact that he was center stage, even sleeping soundly on the couch.

Erin stormed through the bathroom and into the other bedroom. "Sarah," she growled, stilling and looking at the other woman in confusion. *Asleep?*

She sank into the chair next to the bed, cursing this ability to read Sarah yet again. Erin was reading Sarah's dreams, and there was no way to control that. Wasn't being *Blutjagdfrau* curse enough?

She noted the troubled expression that crossed Sarah's face and sighed, opening her mind fully. The least she could do was look at what Sarah found so disturbing. Maybe it would prove useful. She closed her eyes to allow the impressions free reign without interference of what her eyes actually saw.

Erin sucked in her breath as Lorian leaned close, his breath tickling Sarah's cheek. At least the young woman had enough sense to fear him, though she seemed to lack in sense at other times.

Sarah sank back to the wall, as the black void that represented the elder approached her. The eyes, if one could call them that, were a deeper shade, a darker color than even the fathomless black of the shimmer. His entire being seemed like a black hole, a vacuum dragging her into its depths.

"Back off beast," a young man demanded.

Sarah's terror-locked brain dimly identified him as one of her older brothers, Kohl's youngest son, who was only five years older than Sarah.

Her voice wavered. "Darrien, you have to go. This is an elder—the last elder. You can't fight him."

Darrien looked at Lorian uncertainly before he squared his shoulders. "I can't leave you to him," he decided. "You know I can't."

Lorian's laugher was piercing, menacing, alive and horrible. Sarah shrank from that laughter.

"You? A mere boy? You think to take my mate from me?"

"Mate? Sarah isn't a Warrior."

"She is still cursed, descended from your kind and still cursed. Aren't you little one?" Those fathomless black eyes crinkled in amusement, and she could see the stunning smile hidden behind the black veil of pure death.

Sarah shook her head, and tears ran down her cheeks in a steady stream.

"Ah, Sarah," he crooned. "What is that so-called gift that gives you such pain if not a curse? You've called it such yourself many times. Be honest." Lorian moved closer until his breath was hot and sweet on her lips.

Sarah pressed her head back into the wall, unwilling to risk a shattering reaction worse than a high-level red caused her. She waved at Darrien to make him halt his rush at the beast. He would be dead if he tried that type of assault. She could read it in the black on black swirls in the shimmer. Lorian wanted Darrien to attack like that.

"Go away. I'm not a blood Warrior. I can't be what you want."

"You're wrong, Sarah. You can and will be exactly what I need."

"I'll die from the pain first. Even if you take my amulet, you can't touch me."

"You don't think I have the power to control that reaction?" he replied in a sensuous invitation.

"I don't want you to." She managed a slow, strong voice and enunciated each word carefully.

"Another woman that believes the old tales and thinks death would be better. What I wouldn't give to find just one of you before you were poisoned by those lies. I tire of this refrain. You have no idea the pleasure I could give you."

"You can't love me," she countered. Yes, love was an important thing. Sarah would never have a man she didn't love.

"That doesn't mean I can't treat you like a queen. You wouldn't even have to know."

She shuddered in revulsion at that thought. *"No. I don't want that."*

Lorian moved away with a look of disgust. *"I have tried honesty. I've tried reasoning."* He started to pace the room in anger, waving his hands to punctuate what he was saying. *"I've put myself out with promises of all I would do for one of you women. I am so tired of it all."*

Darrien glided toward her silently, as the beast conducted his private tirade. When he reached her side, he swept her behind him smoothly, shielding Sarah with his larger body as he eased her back toward the door.

Lorian turned abruptly, and Darrien froze. Sarah could smell the mixture of Blutjagd and sweat on the back of his shirt. Her hand closed on the fabric, and she pressed her forehead to his shoulder blade, shaking at the thought of what the elder would do next. It was sure to be horrible, she knew.

"I will be direct with you, Sarah."

She could hear his footsteps coming closer and peeked around Darrien's chest. Lorian snapped Darrien's arm with his left hand, as the Warrior attacked, then ripped the young man's heart from his chest with his right.

Sarah screamed and tried to cradle her brother's body as it fell. She knew Darrien was already gone. Coated in his blood, she sobbed hopelessly as she kissed his shocked, dying face and surveyed the empty hole in his chest.

Lorian dropped the heart back into the ragged pit with a sickening splat, and Sarah recoiled in horror. The beast squatted to her eye-level across her brother's body.

"I will not plead with you, Sarah. You will be mine. Either you give yourself to me, or I will take you after wading through every Warrior...just like I did this one. The choice is yours." He shrugged as if it made not a damn bit of difference to him which choice she made and moved away to await her decision, while she rocked her brother's cooling head in her arms.

Erin snapped her eyes open, as Sarah started whimpering and throwing her head back and forth. She cursed herself soundly. She knew what the nightmares were like, but Erin had let Sarah live hers so she could see it. Cursing herself again, she reached out and shook the other woman gently.

Sarah reacted violently, flailing and striking out a formidable blow that Erin deflected easily. She pressed her back to the headboard in shock and fear.

Erin met her gaze calmly...steadily and put her hands up to call a halt. "Read my mind," she ordered in a torn voice, knowing she was giving Sarah more ammunition than she was comfortable with, even as she knew that turnabout was fair play.

Erin closed her eyes and let the night Lorian came for her flood her mind in startling detail, much more detail than she had allowed herself to experience since the day the Warriors questioned her. She opened her eyes at Sarah's muted cry of alarm.

"Why did you show me that?" she asked quietly.

"Because you're not alone. I thought it might help to know that."

"I thought what he did to me was bad," she mused bitterly.

"I came away with my brother," Erin countered sadly. "I'm sorry for Darrien's loss."

"And Corwyn's. I know you loved him." She looked at Erin suspiciously. "So, where do we go from here? Are we okay or—or are we still tearing each other apart?"

"Let's kill the bastards," Erin offered with a wicked smile. "Are you hungry?"

"A little. Why?"

"Let's bring a couple of big slabs of that cake up here and talk. I'm not really tired, and I've always wanted another woman I could talk to, one whose major interest in me isn't my training as a Warrior." She ran a hand through her curls to fluff them.

Sarah raked her own hand through her long, straight hair nervously and bit her lower lip, probably picturing Lorian using her hair against her.

"There are hairstyles you can use at night," she offered quietly. "We can use a tight bun on you or pin braids to your scalp. You don't have to cut it."

"Then, why haven't you let yours grow?"

Erin shrugged. "There's always that in-between stage where it's too short to do anything with but too long. I never wanted to take any chances. I wanted to be sure."

Sarah nodded. "Let's get that cake. I'm hungrier than I thought."

Chapter Fourteen

January 18, 2025

Sarah giggled. "Won't we get into trouble?" she whispered. "What if someone wakes up and finds us gone?"

"So what? The sun's coming up. Any beasts around are headed to ground. Besides, you'd be able to see them if they're close, and I can fight them."

"I guess that's all true enough."

They slipped out into the gray of the morning and sped across the grounds to the old tire swing close to the frozen stream. Laughing like children, they took turns on the swing until the sun was rising behind the clouds. Sarah sat in the tire, swinging herself idly, while Erin leaned against a tree trunk, smiling a more relaxed smile than Sarah had ever seen on her.

"I haven't had this much fun in years," the younger woman decided.

"Even when Hunter took you to first night?" Sarah teased, knowing Erin had felt truly alive that night.

Erin sobered. "Yeah, I did," she admitted. *{Hunter. He was so upset. We both needed the hunt so badly.}*

"He needed it because of me, didn't he?" Sarah whispered.

She sighed and rubbed her forehead roughly. Erin's smile became strained. "I guess it wouldn't do any good to lie about it. You can see it for yourself."

Sarah groaned and settled her cheek against the cold rubber, wrapping her arms around the tire while her feet kicked lightly at the hilltop, keeping the swing rocking gently. "What am I going to do?" she asked the universe in general. "He won't ever give up, will he?"

"Nope, but you don't want him to. Be honest with me, at least. I think your worries are baseless. Do you really think the Stone would allow a *König* child to be so fragile? Any Warrior child, really? Cursed genes seem to supersede any weakness. We don't get sick. We don't miscarry. We didn't even die in times of high infant mortality. If anything, you'd have a capable, strong Warrior who was able to see shimmers. That would be incredible. Besides, you know Hunter couldn't care less whether or not he had children as long as he had you."

Sarah grimaced at that. Children were Hunter's duty. That wasn't an option. She smiled. "Like you could have a baby with midnight blue eyes?" she asked pointedly, wagging her eyebrows for effect.

Erin blushed and shook her head slowly. "Never going to happen," she assured Sarah.

"You know, Hunter told me that the Stone doesn't let people ruin its plans."

"So? This isn't the kind of thing the Stone can control. I mean, unless it wants to arrange a virgin birth, I have a little say in the whole thing."

"Why are you so sure he wouldn't be willing?" Sarah picked that thought from Erin's mind, as it flitted through. "Curt, I mean."

"I know what you mean. We're friends. We've always been friends. There's nothing more there for me. If there was... Let's just say he's had more than ample opportunity to express it."

"There are rules of sanction, you know. Maybe he wasn't expressing it because of that? You didn't have autonomy, after all."

Erin shook her head. "No. Things like that never existed between Curt and me. If there was something there, he would have let me know. I know he would."

"The one man who has a chance isn't interested? The Stone isn't that sloppy."

"Maybe it's getting old and worn out," she replied acidly. "Anyway, it doesn't matter. I'm too much a Warrior. I don't think I'd make a good mother, but Hunter would make a great father. I know. He should be the one to have children."

"Don't give up. Some men are just dense. Maybe some time away from him will make him wise up."

Erin sighed. "That's the plan, anyway. Well, not the wising up part. I know better. I just can't stay around him. It hurts." She winced and closed her eyes. It did hurt, more than Erin would ever admit openly.

"Is that why you told him you'd never print and asked to leave his range? Because it would give you an excuse to cut yourself off from him, along with all the other men?"

"Pretty pathetic, huh? The mighty *Blutjagdfrau* is scared to death of one man. I ran away, because I was afraid 'Sweet sixteen and never been kissed' would be too much for me. Can you imagine my father giving me my autonomy and me throwing myself into a disinterested man's arms to exercise it?" She laid her head back on the tree trunk. "So, I left before I could make a fool of myself," she finished miserably. "Pathetic."

"No. It's not pathetic at all. I'm terrified of Hunter— and for Hunter," she admitted. "I don't want him to end up like Darrien and Corwyn did."

"I'm not worried about that. Hunter is much

stronger now. Besides, eventually I'll bait that beast back to me and finish the job myself," Erin said bitterly.

Sarah shuddered at the young woman's resolve. "You want to face him?"

"Not particularly. I'm not planning on hunting him, if that's what you mean. I just want to be free of him, and doing it myself seems to be the most expedient way. After all, the Stone gave me this ten-megaton reaction for a reason."

Sarah stilled, a disturbing thought rushing through her that her mind refused to look at too closely.

Erin opened her eyes and furrowed her brow. "What's wrong? Your mind is a riot, and I can't sort it out."

"I was just wondering if our link means I'm supposed to help you." She shivered involuntarily as something chilled her...not the thought but something else.

"Not a fun idea," she agreed.

"That isn't the problem." Sarah opened her senses fully, looking for the source of her unease.

Erin's eyes narrowed, and she stood and moved closer, taking a defensive position in front of Sarah. "What is?" she growled under her breath.

Sarah sighed in relief. *Your father is ghosting up on us.*

Erin's eyes glittered, and she smiled a predatory smile. {*Laughter, harsh and playful at the same time. Want some training, Sarah? Teasing. Hopeful.*}

Her eyes widened. *Against Talon? Why?*

{*I'm tired of him spying on me. I want to teach him a*

lesson. *You in?}*

Sarah bit back a wide smile. *You bet! Close your eyes and concentrate on the shimmers in my mind.*

{Got them. Good, he's closing on me. Talk about something to keep him off guard. Not Curt, okay? Nervousness. Anticipation.}

I'd never. "I just think we should consider it. Working together has to be better than tearing each other apart."

"You'd trust me to guard you in battle?" Erin countered, not masking her cinicism. *{My shimmer really is pretty. Cool.}*

"Actually, I'd trust the other Warriors to stop without hurting me," she shot back. *Yeah, it is. Wait until you see Hunter's.*

"People die that way. If a beast moves suddenly, Warriors have made the mistake of following through into the victim." *{Can't wait!}*

"Wonderful. Maybe, I could do it from another position." *Like I am now. He's almost on top of you.*

Erin shook her head. "Bad idea. At least at the Warrior's back, she knows where you are at all times. You go elsewhere in the enclosure, and there're blades everywhere." *{I see him. Calm. Peace.}*

"Great," she grumbled. "I knew you were more dangerous than a—"

Sarah cut off the fake conversation as Erin went nuclear.

The young Warrior swept Talon down, using his shimmer for relative placement. Before his *Blutjagd* had response time, his daughter was planted on his hips with her thighs blocking his weapons, one blade to his ghosted heart and the other tucked under his chin. "Unghost," she demanded.

Talon did as she'd ordered, staring at her in shock and dismay. "How?" he asked.

Sarah laughed hysterically, flopping to the hard ground. "That was great," she whooped, as Erin pulled back her bloodlust and joined in her mirth.

"Don't sneak up on me, Dad. I told you how much I hate it," Erin replied, and edge of warning tainting the amusement.

"So, Hunter's idea works," he mused. "Do you mind?" he asked pointedly.

"How far are the others, Sarah?" she called sweetly, ignoring his plea for freedom.

"Closing fast. Kohl and Jayde are up front, but Hunter's not far behind."

"Excellent. I'm hooking in again." She furrowed her brow in concentration. "You're right. Hunter's shimmer is gorgeous."

"Erin," Talon reminded her impatiently.

She smiled crookedly. "Aw... You do want everyone to know what a success we were, don't you?"

"Erin," he growled in warning.

"Don't sweat it. Here they come." Erin smiled up at the crowd skidding to a halt around them. "Good morning, folks. Since Dad has already had his workout, who wants to try after breakfast?"

"Erin, get off your father," Jayde ordered in annoyance.

"Do you promise not to spy on me anymore?" she asked hopefully.

"Of course not," he shot back.

Erin sighed and sheathed her weapons. "Thought not. So much for autonomy." She slid off him and shrugged at Sarah. "Told you he was impossible."

Sarah nodded in understanding. "Leave a scar next time," she suggested. "Warriors seem to respect that."

"Yeah, they do at that," she mused as if she was seriously considering it.

"Sarah," Kohl thundered.

"What? You think I would have put up with that shit?"

Her father cringed at her choice of words.

Erin bit back a laugh. "Taught you well, I see."

"Damn straight."

That time, they both laughed.

Kohl turned a vivid red. "Well, no, but—"

"Just because you couldn't get away with it doesn't mean Talon should be able to because he can—or could."

Talon paused in the task of dusting the frost and dirt off his clothes and stared at her angrily for the implied alliance against him. "You've never had to try and raise this hotheaded hellcat," he countered, waving his hand at his daughter hopelessly. "You have no idea how nerve wracking she's been."

Sarah laughed heartily. "I think it's safe to say that I know better than you do. I know things you never will."

He snapped a startled look at Erin's raised eyebrows.

Erin chuckled and clapped Sarah on the back. {*Nice move! Let him wonder for a while.*} "It's a deal. You don't tell my family. I don't tell yours. Nobody tells the damn beasts. I'll even make it a blood oath."

Sarah blanched. *Thanks for the return favor. Kohl's already wondering.* "That's not necessary. My word is as good as a blood oath."

"I'll accept that." *{Yep. Oh, he's funny.}*

Of course, I never said I wouldn't tell Curt...

Erin smiled at her, releasing a razor flash of *Blutjagd* as a warning. "I like you, Sarah, but don't push it too far."

"I'm kidding," she protested.

"You better be. I have secrets to tell, too."

Sarah glanced at the milling crowd and locked on Hunter as he turned away. *The Stone doesn't let anyone escape his or her fate, does it?*

{Not according to what I've heard.}

* * * *

Sarah startled at the sight of Hunter in her room. She knew he left the breakfast table before her, but she hadn't expected to see him here. She replayed her discussion with Erin in her mind and wondered how she could open a conversation after the way she'd hurt him.

Mistaking her silence, he sighed. "Relax. I'm just getting some clothes," he assured her. "I'm not here to ambush you."

She examined his shimmer and felt a stab of regret. He was hurting, and he was angry. The red braid of *Blutjagd* was expanded into a barely-controlled band. Hunter grabbed a handful of clothing from the drawers of the dresser he kept for himself. He was hurting because of her.

Sarah touched his shoulder gently, letting his shimmer flow over her. She watched, mesmerized, as the *Blutjagd* shrank almost back to the non-existent braid. The purples became dominant, swirling in a hypnotic pattern before her eyes, dancing with her fingertips on his shoulder. "Hunter," she whispered, identifying the beautiful new development to her mind.

Hunter shuddered under her hand. "Don't," he pleaded. "If you do this, I can't promise I'll be able to stop this time." *{Please, mean this if you start it.}*

"You still want me." She said it in disbelief, but the knowledge sent a spike a pure pleasure through her. She hadn't lost him after all. Sarah kissed the spot on his back where the purple swirls seemed centered, shivering at the pulse of pleasure that arced from him to her at the slight touch. Suddenly, conversation didn't feel so necessary.

"Sarah, please tell me. Yes or no? I want forever. If I can't have that, I have to go before it's too late." *{It will already be more than I can bear.}* His breathing hitched, as she traced the expressive purple with her fingertips. "Sarah, please tell me."

She could see the desperate longing in him, in the swirls that played at her fingers. Her body responded in a flood of warmth that took her breath away. Sarah circled him slowly, tracing her hand through his shimmer and drawing the swirling colors with her as if she was a magnet affecting filings. More purple appeared with each passing second.

Her mind worked slowly as the sensations washed over her. How could she have doubted this? Every touch intensified the longing in her. "Forever," she whispered.

"Tell me," his voice was rough in his restraint. The drain on him was massive, but he wouldn't touch her without her vow. He couldn't.

Sarah took the clothing from his hands, dropped them without a clue where they'd land, and drew his palm up to her lips. "Touch me," she pleaded with him, laying a kiss in his palm.

"If I do, I can't ever walk away," he warned her, nuzzling his face to hers, rough in his morning stubble. *{Don't make me walk away.}*

Sarah turned her face to brush her lips through the now-purple shimmer to the sensuous lips that held her in thrall. She wanted to feel his mouth again, not tentative this time, but hot and demanding on hers. "Take me, Hunter. Make me a part of you."

"You're not afraid?" he asked with infinite patience.

She laid an enticing kiss on the edge of his lips and smiled at the tremor that raced through him. "With this much self-control, how can I think you'll be anything but gentle."

"Then, say it," he whispered, his hand moving to cup her head, pulling her lips to within millimeters of his own. *{Please, let this be real.}*

"I want you, Hunter. I want to stay with you forever. I want you to take me to your bed as your wife and give me your sons to carry." Sarah thought over it. She was pretty sure she'd covered all the things he had to know to seal printing.

"Say it." He brushed his lips over hers lightly, and she was at a loss to remember what he could be looking for.

{I love you, Sarah. I'll be lost without you. Please, say it.}

"I love you, too," she replied.

Hunter groaned as he pulled her mouth to his own, his tongue pleading mutely for entry that she granted.

The wildfire scorching her nerves made her dizzy; she dug her fingertips into his shirt, her eyes sliding shut. In her mind, Sarah could see his shimmer: all purple, bathing her, enflaming her, sensitizing her as his hand touched her with care.

He lifted her to his chest and carried Sarah to the bed, following her down onto the thick quilt. "Are you sure about what you said?" he breathed.

"How can you ask that?" she inquired, having difficulty believing he couldn't feel her arousal in that searing kiss.

"Not this." He brushed his lips down her neck to the vee of fabric between her breasts. "Do you want children? Are you sure? I have protection. I can see if we need it. I'll use it as long as you want to use it," he offered.

Sarah smiled. "Don't check. Don't get anything. Love me and leave every time alive with the possibility."

The purple intensified as his hand started working at the buttons of her shirt, his mouth following behind, tracing fiery lines down her chest and stomach to the waistband of her jeans. She arched to him, and Hunter smiled a lazy smile.

"Soon," he promised.

He pushed her shirt from her shoulders and peeled it down her arms slowly then pulled off his own and pressed her down into the bed, skin to skin, his mouth capturing hers again. Her breasts swelled against his chest, and she gasped into his mouth.

Hunter's eyes flashed with pure need as he dropped his mouth to her chest, laving her nipples in slow, torturous movements that had her arching her body closer to his. Sarah groaned deep in her throat, cradling his head to her. He responded to her encouragement by sucking her breast into the heat of his mouth and teasing the sensitized nipple with his tongue until she was rolling her hips against him, begging with her body for more.

"So impatient," he teased, moving to the other breast to continue his exquisite torture.

"Hunter, I have to feel you," she breathed. "I need every inch of your body close to mine. Please." She wound her hands in his hair and arched to him again.

Hunter pulled himself over her, pressing the hard ridge of his arousal into the sensitive core of her through their jeans. His eyes closed and he half-swallowed a deep groan. "This?" he panted. "Is this what you want?"

Sarah squirmed against him, straining to the intimate sensation and still needing more. It wasn't enough. "No. All of you," she decided. "Not your jeans. Skin to skin."

That time, he did groan. "I want to take you slowly." Hunter nipped at her ear as he poured the words into her mind. "Every time you demand more of me, that gets harder to do."

Already, Sarah could feel the tension in him. Holding back was difficult for him.

"Roll off of me," she suggested.

Hunter looked at her in dismay, and she kissed him.

"I'm not stopping you," Sarah assured him. "Trust me."

He nodded his agreement and rolled to his back. "Now what?" His eyes were wide and earnest.

"Stay there."

She stood next to the bed, slowly unbuttoning her jeans and pushing them over her hips. Hunter's breath caught as he watched her undressing for him. Heartened by his reaction, she kicked her jeans away and reached for the lace waistband of her silk panties.

"Let me," he requested simply.

Sarah smiled and eased her hands away. "Get rid of your jeans, and I'll come to you," she invited.

Hunter smiled a predatory smile as he panned his gaze over her near-naked body. "What if I come after you?" he asked.

"When I get what I want, you'll get what you want."

"Sooner than you realize, if you insist on this teasing," he growled.

She folded her arms under her breasts, shelving them on her crossed forearms. "You'll be gentle," she decided.

Hunter pulled open his buttons with a single tug and eased his jeans down his legs without taking his eyes from hers for a moment. They were a deep, smoky black in his excitement, and she was lost in their depths. He rose to sitting as he tugged the stubborn material from his bare feet. Sarah held her breath as he tossed his jeans away. Hunter moved slowly, with animal grace, his muscles rippling as he lay back down, just as she'd suggested.

"Your turn," he crooned, satisfaction etched on his face.

She looked at the length of him jutting rigidly off the surface of his stomach. Sarah moved slowly, crawling up the foot of the bed until she knelt next to his hips, drawing her hand over the silk-wrapped steel of him. Hunter pushed into her hand, reacting with a guttural sound to her touch and hardening further in her grasp.

She smiled as she opened her mind to him fully, grasping at the erotic impressions in his mind. Latching onto one, she sank her mouth around the shaft, sucking gently as she moved over him, teasing the sensitive underside with her tongue.

Hunter arched beneath her, every muscle taut as she fulfilled the vision dancing behind his eyes. He bunched his hand in her hair, gently guiding her movements, while more erotic images coursed through his mind. Sarah gave herself up to pleasure—his and her own as her body responded to his arousal.

She knew Hunter was at his limits, even before he released her hair and drew her up to latch his mouth onto hers. His kisses were hot and demanding, drugging her with his urgent need. Sarah cried out into his mouth as he rolled her beneath him, pinning her with his body like he had earlier, his cock rocking gently against her while his hands anchored her hips to him.

"We're still not naked," she teased breathlessly as his mouth traveled over her face and neck, coming back to explore her mouth avidly, over and over.

"If you were, I wouldn't be capable of stopping myself. After what you just did, I think you deserve some special treatment."

"Like what?" Sarah asked.

Hunter didn't answer. He continued his exploration of Sarah's body, easing off of her as he trailed his hands and mouth past her chest to the flat plane of her stomach. He smiled as he met her eyes. His fingers brushed by the silk panel between her thighs, and

Sarah jumped at the sensation. His fingers glided over the sopping fabric again and gauged her response.

"Now," he crooned, "tell me how an innocent like you knew how to torture me the way you just did." His fingers brushed by again, teasing her with the contact she wanted so desperately.

"I read it in your mind." Sarah smiled wickedly. "You have a lot of interesting fantasies, Hunter. Finding things that make you happy is going to be an easy task."

"Really? What would you like me to act out with you now?" he offered.

"Pick one. We'll get to them all eventually."

His smile widened as he slipped two fingers past the silk and dipped them gently inside her. Sarah gripped his arms in surprise as a wash of desire assaulted her. His fingers moved slowly, twisting and dipping in and out. His breathing quickened as he watched her reactions unfolding, as she moved against him, straining toward a release that she craved even as she feared she would shatter when she reached it.

Hunter guided his fingers away slowly, and she tightened her grip on his arm, trying to hold him to her. She was so close, it was maddening. Her eyes widened, as he met them and placed the two fingers in his mouth to suck them clean. Hunter pulled her panties off and tossed them away. Curling his fingers in the nest of dark curls between her thighs, he bent to rub his face in them.

"You smell so good," he whispered in a hoarse voice. Hunter bent to run his tongue over the folds so recently vacated by his fingers and held her hips to the bed when she would have pushed away in shock. "You taste wonderful," he soothed her. "Read my mind, Sarah. I want you, but I want to give you pleasure to make taking you as painless as I can. Let me do this," he pleaded with her. "Read my mind."

Sarah nodded and opened her mind to him. Hunter was focused on only one thing. She could feel his hunger and his overwhelming urge to do that which he believed would give her intense pleasure. He wanted to feel that pleasure, to taste it. Hunter waited, his gaze locked with hers and his breath warm on the moist heat of her while he teased her with his impressions of her enjoyment. Sarah arched to him, helpless to resist and seeking what his mind offered.

"Keep reading," he breathed as he sank to tease her with his mouth in earnest.

She threw her head back and forth, groaning at the unbelievable intensity of what he was doing to her. His mouth demanded a response from her unschooled body that she was obviously providing. Sarah felt his groan of satisfaction vibrate through her body as his tongue continued to seek out every intimate crevice of her.

A sharp knock on the door intruded on her daydreams, her weaving of Hunter's images with her own.

"Sarah, are you all right?" Kohl demanded.

Her head snapped up, and she blushed, realizing her position: Hunter poised between her legs and her ankles resting on his shoulders. Sarah wasn't even sure when that had happened. He replaced his mouth with his fingers, driving her crazy with the loss of his tongue as much as with his taunting smile.

"I'm fine, Kohl," she called out calmly, mouthing a

curse at Hunter which expressed her frustration. "Please, go away."

Hunter licked her sensitive nub, while his fingers continued to move inside her, and she tried rather unsuccessfully to stifle her cry.

"Sarah! Are you sure? May I come in?" Kohl continued.

Hunter looked up at her shocked expression with a playful smile. "Go away, Kohl," he ordered, his fingers continuing their erotic invasion. "My wife and I wish to honeymoon in peace."

Her father blustered for a moment before he started laughing. "By all means," he declared as he moved away. "It's about time," he added over his shoulder.

Sarah felt her face burn, and Hunter chuckled at her response. "What's wrong? You agreed to marry me," he teased.

"We're not married, yet," she reminded him.

"For all intents and purposes, we are. Kohl knows that. It's too late for me to change course. Once I claim you, my printing will be complete. Would you really ask me to stop now?" He licked her again, his eyes at once taunting and uncertain.

She groaned and threw her head back, lifting herself to him in invitation. "No. Don't stop. Please."

"Do you know what I'm thinking, Sarah?"

She locked on his thoughts, just as his mouth returned to his insistent and maddening plunder. Sarah bowed up to him with a cry of pleasure and need. She could feel the bolt of pure joy that raced through him at her inability or unwillingness to stifle that cry.

His intimate invasion continued until she lost contact with his mind, existing only in the mounting, all-consuming pleasure...until she felt she would surely shatter if Hunter didn't ease himself into her that very instant.

Sarah begged him to take her, but Hunter continued to use his mouth to drive her on, holding her wrists to the bed gently when she would have tried to pull him over her. A flash from his mind caught her, an image of herself tied down and helpless to stop him while Hunter pleasured her like this, sating both of them in the process.

She shattered at the thought, bowing up from the bed and screaming her release, feeling wave after wave of mindless pleasure wash over her. Still, the images in his head drove her on, all the forms of ecstasy he wanted to introduce her to.

Hunter was suddenly over her, lifting her hips and easing into her, moving gently and building a friction that made Sarah ache for more. She pushed back toward him, stilling for a moment when she felt a burning sensation deep inside. Just as quickly, the burning was gone, and the ache returned.

He paused, searching her face as her eyes widened. Sarah smiled, letting him know that her reaction was more one of surprise than pain. Hunter kissed her as he started moving again, deeper this time now that the barrier had been taken. His movements became more urgent as he tested and found her body receptive to his faster, deeper thrusts.

Sarah opened her mind to him again. His mind was a riot of sensations and thoughts. He was relieved that he had taken her maidenhead so effortlessly. His

252

mind formed images of other sexual encounters he'd like to have with her. They stole her breath away—so many ways to enjoy each other. Hunter was convinced that he couldn't possibly endure the pleasure he was feeling for a moment longer even as it continued to engulf him.

She found herself experiencing Hunter's pleasure, his feeding hers until Sarah teetered at the edge of the abyss with him. Hunter tensed inside her, sending a warm explosion that shocked her with its heat and intimacy, touching places she never thought to reach in her body and her soul.

Her ragged cry was overpowered by Hunter's roar of release. Still miraculously connected to him, Sarah felt a shift in him that brought a sense of peace and purpose.

"Printing," she breathed. So that was printing.

He kissed her hand, gathering Sarah into his arms and laying feathery kisses on her face and neck.

Sarah wiped away a single tear from his cheek and looked at him in concern. "What's wrong?" she asked.

Hunter laughed and shook his head. "So beautiful." His lips skimmed her pulse point then down to the top of her breast. "You. Printing. Everything is beautiful."

"I think you're drugged," she accused.

Hunter pushed into her, anchoring her hips to him as he panted in pleasure. "On you, love. I'm drunk on you." He relaxed his arms, laying his weight on her and rocking his hips in a gentle exploration with his softening member.

"You know," she teased, "your mind has been making a lot of promises to me."

"Good. Let me know which ones you want to cash in on. We have the rest of our lives."

"Promise me the rest of the day, for a starter. I want you all to myself for the rest of the day."

His smile widened. "As you wish. What would you like to start with?"

"That shower we never took followed by that little fantasy you had while you were holding my wrists to the bed. I think I can find stockings or scarves or something that will do nicely."

He hardened within her again and groaned in pleasure. "Oh yes. Say the word, Sarah."

"We have all day, Hunter. What's in your mind right now sounds particularly appealing, actually. I'd like to try that." She could read his belief that she wasn't really reading his mind but rather teasing him that anything he was thinking would be erotic.

Hunter chuckled. "But, what I have in mind right now is feeling my son growing inside you," he teased, confirming what she already knew he was thinking.

Sarah smiled wickedly and wrapped her legs around his hips. "And I've heard that there is absolutely nothing like giving a Warrior carte blanche to start a baby growing to make him insatiable."

Hunter's hand traced down the flat plane of her stomach. "Are you giving me carte blanche?" he asked seriously.

"I'm making a request of my husband. I want you to love me, to play out every fantasy either one of us has until we have to take a few weeks off post-partum. I want to feel you rubbing your hands over my pregnant belly while you take me and know you love every second of it. Does that agree with you, husband?"

Hunter groaned and started moving inside her fast and hard, as if he was desperate to spill his seed in her again. "Yes. Now. Today. I'm going to do it today, Sarah."

She sank into the sensations of him claiming her all over again. When his climax came, she could almost imagine that he had really impregnated her. Sarah gasped at the sensation of a brilliant static discharge that passed between them.

Hunter smoothed her hair and furrowed his brow. "Did I hurt you?" he asked anxiously.

Sarah shook her head. "Just an aftershock of some sort," she decided.

He laughed lightly. "Maybe we did it."

"You're not getting off that easily," she informed him.

Hunter smiled a secretive smile.

"What is it?" she asked suspiciously.

"I'm not letting you out of my bed for any length of time for a few days. I hope you have no pressing plans elsewhere."

"It sounds good, but why?"

"You asked for a baby. I intend to make sure I grant that wish immediately. You wanted me insatiable for you," he reminded her.

"And?" There was more to it. There had to be.

"I know you said not to check, but I couldn't resist when you told me how much you wanted my son in you."

"I'm high cycle?" she asked in awe.

Hunter chuckled. "I guess it's too late to ask if you're absolutely sure."

Sarah eyed him suspiciously. "Why does it seem that Warriors have this unerring ability to claim women that are fertile? Unless they are actively avoiding a child, they have a young Warrior right away."

He flipped to place her over him, his thumbs playing at her breasts while he pushed up into her. Sarah gasped at the new sensations. Hunter's eyes darkened in hunger that made her go liquid for him.

"Tell me," she breathed, moving against him, grinding herself over him while he pressed her in with the flats of his hands.

"Corwyn had a theory about that. He believed that, even without sensing her, a Warrior knows when the woman he desires is approaching high cycle. He believed the urge to complete printing—even if you are actively avoiding pregnancy, becomes almost insurmountable as she approaches high cycle. In fact, he believed *Endspiel* could be directly correlated to a woman's release of pheromones announcing her ready or near-ready state."

Sarah stilled and met his eyes. "Perpetuation of the species," she mused. "A simple animal instinct."

Hunter shook his head with a serious look. "No. Never that. I would have married you, even if you'd decided never to grant me children. I love the idea of having children with you, but you would have been enough alone.

"Warriors have waited months, even years to reproduce with their mates. Warriors print on women who are using hormonal preventatives that suppress high cycle...women who can't produce children for them or that they believe can't carry a child.

"I'll admit the charge when you asked for a baby thrilled me unbearably, but I would have taken you with proper precautions against pregnancy as often as I could, without that enticement. I still will, if you wish it. It's probably already too late for that, but I will...if you have any doubts at all that you want this."

Sarah smiled an impish little grin. "In that case, let's get that shower," she offered. "I hope it's too late, Hunter. I want to make sure it's too late."

* * * *

Erin started chuckling.

"What's the joke this time?" Talon demanded, still bristling at how effectively she took him down—or maybe at losing his chance to spy on her again.

She wasn't sure about that. It was really too bad that Erin couldn't read his mind or see his shimmers by herself. It could come in handy, when Sarah stayed behind with Hunter.

Erin shrugged as she drained the last of her glass of milk and closed her connection to Sarah slowly, painfully. She knew it was the right thing to do. If the situation were reversed, Erin would want privacy with Curt.

She pushed up from the table and straightened her weapons over her hips. "Time for training," she mused, heading for the training room despite her loathing for indoor training, most likely because of her encounter with Lorian. "Who's up?" she asked over her shoulder.

"Hunter. You know that," her father replied in confusion.

Erin shook her head. "Scratched. I need another

partner."

"Scratched? Why is he scratched?"

"His business," she replied simply. "Trust me."

"Are you reading your brother's mind?" Jayde accused.

Erin shook her head as she unsheathed her weapons. "No. Sarah just let me know he's busy, and I shouldn't wait for him. That's all."

"With what?" she persisted.

"That's his business. You are not his house lords anymore, and he's had autonomy for a long time. Who's up?"

Jayde stepped forward. "I am."

Erin smiled. "Good. I haven't faced you in a few days. It will keep me on my toes."

Her mother's fighting style was significantly different than Talon's or even Hunter's. Her center of balance was more aligned with Erin's: dead body center and to the balls of the feet, as if they were dancing. Jayde had handled much of Erin's early training, teaching Erin the flowing movements that were so different than those of the men. Once she had mastered the basic movements and balance, her mother had turned most of the intensive training over to her father and brother.

She'd soon learned that Jayde's style kept her on her toes, watching for hidden attacks while the men were ultimately the harder, more aggressive fighters. Their attacks were fast, forceful, and could not be hidden. Even after Erin had trained in every North American range, with almost every Warrior in the world—something predictably not done for Hunter and that she was sure would continue for her, in an attempt to match her to a Warrior in the future—Erin found that her mother offered a fresh challenge that no man could. It was easy to see how Jayde had defeated Veriel. Still, now that Erin was training at full steam, not even her mother was much of a challenge anymore.

Jayde shook her head. "Aren't we supposed to be testing your ability to team with Sarah?" she asked suddenly.

Erin raised an eyebrow at her parents in disbelief. How dense could they be? "Sarah told me Hunter is busy," she repeated patiently. She bit back a sarcastic footnote.

"Oh," her mother said with a tight smile. "Are they—"

"Hunter's business," she growled.

"Did they ask you to close your mind?" Talon asked with his own raised eyebrow.

Erin tried unsuccessfully to stifle an impish grin. "No, but I did it anyway. Being able to spy on someone doesn't mean you should," she noted with a meaningful look at him.

Talon cast her a warning look. "Get moving," he ordered gruffly.

Erin set about training, alternating between her parents until Kohl strolled in.

"Maybe you should fight them together," he joked.

"Not a bad plan," Erin called over her shoulder. "Better yet, how about all three of you?" she teased in return.

"I'd be honored."

Talon considered the other lord carefully. "What's so funny, Kohl?"

"Erin hasn't told you?" he asked.

"It's none of Erin's business," she snapped at him, "or anyone else's for that matter. Erin does not go telling details of other people's lives."

"Well, considering Hunter told me, I'd suppose it's no secret."

"So, tell them already." She sent Jayde ducking with a well-aimed arc to the chest.

"They're sealing his printing. Sarah has agreed to marry him."

"Good," Erin decided. "That frees me to do what I want."

"And what is that?" Talon demanded.

Erin shrugged as she blocked one of Jayde's blades. "Hunter will provide the *König* heirs and the Crossbearers. I'm not going to be a brood mare. I will never willingly print. This—unwillingness you've seen me display is not a temporary thing."

Jayde stopped fighting abruptly, looking at her in shock and dismay. "What? When did you decide this?"

"Months ago. Now that I have autonomy, I can exercise my rights, in this case, my right not to print and not to have children."

Kohl blustered. "You can't," he exploded.

"Why not? My mother was given that freedom."

"I never intended to exercise it," she countered hotly.

"No. You wanted to choose your mate, but that is immaterial. You could have exercised it. I intend to."

Talon glared at her. "The Stone expects," he began angrily.

"Talked to it lately?" she interrupted him. "Corwyn had. He told me that no one could force me into anything I didn't truly want to do."

Kohl snorted. "He believed that. It cost him his wife and child. Take a lesson from that, young lady."

Talon's eyes narrowed. "The house lords expect that you will start touring and meeting all the young Warriors soon—at least within a few years. You will do that. If there is a match for you in our houses, the Stone will not allow you to ignore it."

"Fine. Tour me. It's your right to direct me to whatever range you see fit to strand me in. But, I will not be pressured. I am not willing, and any Warrior that doesn't show the proper respect for that will face me. Not you. Me!"

"On that point, I will defer. It's your right to exact your own punishment for offenses against you, unless it falls under a capital offense. We'll give you two years to come to your senses before we tour in earnest, but you will tour after you turn eighteen."

"As you wish."

"Where do we start?" Jayde asked.

"I would guess Europe would be a good place to start. Erin knows the North American Warriors pretty well, and she's already related to two houses. We may find a match over there."

Erin laughed harshly. "Don't hold your breath."

Chapter Fifteen

February 2, 2025

Sarah snuggled further into Hunter's arms and watched Erin worriedly. The young Warrior had been exceedingly withdrawn over the weeks since her announcement, brightening only when Hunter announced that they'd succeeded in conceiving a *König* baby.

Worse, Sarah had given her word not to reveal Erin's secrets. That had been torture, watching Erin hurting—and Hunter with her, with no way to soothe either of them.

Erin was good at what she was doing. She had invented a plausible excuse to avoid Maher range. It was pure genius, really. She'd begged for her two years of freedom to be spent in Hunter and Crossbearer ranges, where she would face no pressure. After that, Erin had agreed to a slow tour of the continent, where she knew few Warriors, effectively shutting herself off from Curt for three years...or more.

Still, Erin was unhappy with her plan, and Sarah couldn't help but feel it with her. She had to wonder if Curt was really as unaffected as he'd seemed. Hunter went on and on about the solicitous care the young man took with Erin, when Sarah made discrete inquiries about Adam's family. She had to wonder, based on that information, if there was more to the situation than Erin was seeing.

Still, Sarah had given her word. She couldn't find a way to clue Curt in. She couldn't even discuss the situation with Hunter, which was her first choice.

Anything she did, aside from discussing it with Erin, which was futile, would be breaking her oath. Even with no secrets of her own from her husband, she couldn't excuse breaking her oath to reveal Erin's.

She was so caught up in her own thoughts that she didn't see Hunter's comment coming until it was too late to stop him.

"So, you really do like driving everyone crazy, don't you?" he prodded Erin.

The younger woman groaned. "*Et tu, Jäger Kreuzträger-König?* What difference does it make? You and Sarah are already working on the next elder killer."

"You were born," he countered. "There's a reason for that."

"Strangely enough, the Stone gifted me with fighting abilities beyond the norm. Maybe I'm supposed to be a Night Warrior, and you—with your tremendous capacity for nurturing and protecting hellbent children—are meant to provide the babies. Has anyone but me considered that possibility? You know, you guys have a damned sexist view of this situation."

"You'll never be a Night Warrior. It's too dangerous," Hunter reiterated patiently.

"I'm dangerous," she countered just as patiently. "In case you slept through training today, I can hold my own against three Warriors without Sarah feeding me information. Even Corwyn could only take on two together."

"Don't get too cocky," he admonished.

"About what?" she complained. "It's not like I ever get to put all this training to any practical use."

"Count yourself lucky," he grumbled.

"Count me bored. I refuse to believe that there is

nothing more to life than having sex with and children to some self-important Warrior who's out for the notoriety of banging the *König* princess."

"You don't know what printing is like. I'd give just about anything to spend every moment of every day with Sarah."

"But, you wanted to print. I want to be a Warrior. I imagine it makes a big difference."

"Not according to Colin and Stephen. Neither one of them wanted to print."

Erin shook her head adamantly. "Stephen had a duty to print. He knew it and accepted it. Since Corwyn lost Anna and had no sons, and Colin had that lousy brush with printing, he was next to provide them." She smiled a lazy smile. "And, Corwyn and Stephen both ordered Colin to print. He would have been hurting if he had refused, so he accepted it. Not that Jan would have let him escape... But, I'm not accepting anything."

"Fine. I'll add my orders to Talon's, Jayde's, and every other house lord's. You have a duty."

"I do not accept those orders. Stephen and Colin didn't accept it until Anna was lost and they had no choice. Face it. You've got one hell of a bodyguard, Sarah. Nothing will touch you, if I can help it. As long as you're alive and capable of bearing children, I don't have to submit to what they're demanding of me."

Sarah groaned. "I'm not sure I'm comfortable with being your convenient excuse. After all—"

"You know my reasons," Erin cut her off cleanly.

"That doesn't mean I agree with them. You didn't agree with mine."

"And you're very happy. I know. I'm very happy for

you both. You know I won't be, if I change my mind. There's no happily ever after for me. There never was."

"No, I don't know that. I have only your opinion to go on. Your reasons could be as baseless as... Well, we'll see if mine are in time, but I'm taking the chance. I'm starting to think maybe yours are a little bit baseless, too."

Hunter leaned over her shoulder. "Maybe you should tell me what her reasons are and let me decide if they're baseless," he suggested.

Erin gave him a bland look. "If Sarah's vow means anything to her, she can't tell you. Don't hold it against her, though. It doesn't mean anything, as far as you're concerned."

"You seem awfully sure that Sarah will side with you."

"See, that's the problem. Don't lay that on her. Don't give Sarah a guilt trip on this. It's not choosing sides, if she decides to keep her vow. She gave her word in blood oath, and a blood oath is between the two parties alone. I'll keep my end, regardless. I gave my word.

"You have what you want, Hunter. Sarah can tell you that I'm a big part of that. All I'm asking is that you back off and let me have what I want, too. In return, if you want to look at it that way."

Hunter hesitated. His hands tightened around Sarah as he considered Erin's plea. His mind was working furiously. Hunter hadn't considered that Erin might have gone to bat for him. He hadn't considered that Sarah's change of heart had been anything but simply coming to her senses.

He cleared his throat. "Sarah, I won't ask you

specifics. Is Erin honest in her belief that she couldn't be happy with another course?"

Erin turned away, and she blanked her mind, steadfastly refusing to sway Sarah in any way, even unintentionally. That made keeping her vow even more imperative. Overall, Erin was one of the best manipulators Sarah had ever met, but she seemed to only be hurting herself with it, so Sarah had to wonder if it was within her rights to do anything about it. If Erin was listening, she gave no sign of it. She was listening. She had to be.

Sarah sighed. "Yes. Yes, she believes what she says. I don't know if she's right or wrong, but she believes she's right."

Hunter nodded against her shoulder. "All right, Erin. I don't like it, but I'll back off. I would like to make one observation, if I may."

"Sure," she answered without expression.

"You don't seem very happy with this course, either," he noted.

Erin smiled wryly. "Yeah. Life sucks all the way around, Hunter. Better this way than the other, but it still sucks. What I was born to, right?"

"You're sure about that? You're sure you have no other options?"

She nodded slowly. "I'm sure."

"You can't do anything the easy way, can you?"

"I suppose not," she admitted. "I wish life was simple. I really do, but it's not."

Sarah grimaced at the ring of truth in that. "I know you do. I wish it was simple for you, too. You know..."

Erin shook her head, pulling the rest of the thought from Sarah's mind as she knew she would. "I could never do that," she decided.

Chapter Sixteen

April 12, 2029

"The *Königs* are coming here?" Curt asked with a broad smile.

"Yeah, it's been awhile," Bryant noted. "It's been..."

"More than four years," he supplied. "They haven't been in our range for more than a day or two at a time since Erin got her autonomy."

"Can't imagine why," Bryant drawled. "Every Warrior deserves proper consideration."

"For what?" he demanded.

His brother smiled a predatory smile that set Curt's teeth on edge.

"That would be why she's stayed away," he grumbled.

"What?" he asked in an innocence that annoyed Curt all the more, because Bryant really didn't understand it.

"Erin's not trolling for a mate, Bryant. Her parents may be, but she's not. When she is, she'll be obvious about it. Erin doesn't believe in baiting. Until she, if she ever, decides she wants a mate, any pressure you put on her will only make her more determined than ever not to choose."

"How could you possibly know that?" Bryant demanded.

"Because, while you have been sniffing after her for the last eight years, I've been talking to her."

"So, you've been getting a foot in the door," he grumbled.

Curt sighed. Bryant really was clueless when it

came to women. Only he would think talking to a woman could have the solitary purpose of getting her into bed.

"No. You really are an idiot, aren't you? Get this... I became her friend, you dolt! I may be closer to her than Hunter or her father sometimes, but you know how friend is spelled in romance language? D-E-A-T-H. Got it?"

Bryant raised an eyebrow dubiously. "I've heard that. So, you're saying you have no interest?"

"Get real. I *am* male, but I only pursue willing women."

"How can you be so sure she wouldn't be willing, if a man showed a little interest?"

"Talked to the other young Warriors lately?"

Bryant shook his head. "Only Adam. Why?"

"Adam is a printed man. He's not making passes at Erin. The point is, Warriors who come on to Erin don't last long. From what I hear, she makes a habit of a brutal smack down followed by a sub-zero freeze out. That is a woman who does not appreciate unwelcome attention."

His brother's smile spread. "Got any personal experience going for you?" he inquired.

"No. She didn't have autonomy yet when I saw her last. Think I wanted to face Talon?"

"Guess not. Anyway, I'll let you get back to work. I have a beast I'm tracking."

Curt waved and watched him go. No, he hadn't wanted to face Talon, but that hadn't been what stopped him from kissing her. By the time Erin left Maher range, Curt would have taken on Talon, Jayde, Hunter, and Kord together for a single kiss. Her proclamation had stopped him.

He could still feel the cool grass beneath his cheek and her warm body lying next to his, resting after taking the rowboat out on the lake. They had come to their spot on the other side, the one where they would lay and talk about life as they dried off from swimming, but it was late November then, and there had been a chill in the air.

Curt moved his eyes over her body, feeling his instant reaction and suddenly glad for the jacket he wore that was now hiding his arousal. That body hadn't changed much in the years since they took on Adam together. It was slightly more lush, her arms stronger, her hair a mass of curls that hugged her scalp, but it was still Erin.

The problem was, every time he lay with her on the grass or leaned close to whisper to her or took her out driving on the back roads to get her practice in, it was harder to remind himself that Erin was anything but a girl he desired.

Worse, she made so many innocent moves— Erin didn't realize the danger she posed to herself. She was unschooled, so she couldn't realize that Curt's raging hormones interpreted everything sexually, even her movements when she curled into his chest or ran a finger over his arm. She didn't know the shear control involved in seeming unaffected by her.

He hadn't been printing, he decided. After all, Curt hadn't gone insane in four years without her. Even withdrawal from early printing was supposedly painful. He just—missed her. So, they were only friends after all, and anything else had just been his over-active nineteen-year-old hormones raising hell.

No, while Curt was trying to convince himself yet again that he could not be so bold as to tempt Talon's ire by kissing his daughter, Erin was coming to the decision that he found hurt far more than it should have.

"Know what I want?" she asked in a wistful voice.

"What's that?" he replied in neutral tones, running his fingers absently over her amulet through the bracer that was damp from the splashing they'd done with the oars.

"Freedom."

"You'll have your autonomy in a few months." *And, oh how he lived for that day!*

Curt blushed at the thought that he was far too much like Bryant, but could he help it if his dreams seemed to revolve around Erin seeking him out the night she had her autonomy for a tryst? Or something more permanent? It seemed that knowing she was sleeping just down the hall from him wrecked havoc with his mind and body.

"Not autonomy. Freedom."

He sobered at that. "If it were possible—" Curt sighed and tapped her blood mark above the collar of her jean jacket.

"I know, but I'm tired of the Stone ordering my life."

"So, what can we do about it?" he asked honestly. They'd discussed this subject many times.

"You? Not a thing. Me? I'll have my freedom—at least from the Stone. I may have to be a Warrior, but that's all I have to be."

"What does that mean?" he asked in concern.

"That means I'm not producing children. Ever. Let Hunter produce them. He's first born anyway."

"But, when you print, your body will want to, won't it?"

"Not if I never print. I won't. I simply won't ever let a man inside striking distance."

"Gee, thanks," he commented acidly.

Erin elbowed him in the ribs. "I don't mean you. After all, you're my friend."

Curt felt as if she had ripped out his heart, but he managed to laugh lightly. "Okay. What will you do for release?" he questioned.

Some irrational part of him needed to put a stop to this before he lost any chance he might salvage of making his own dreams come true. He was so very close. Just a few more months, and she'd be free to seek out any man she wanted, and Curt would be free to try to get her to see him as more than a friend.

"The same thing I do now, of course."

He couldn't help it. He choked on that one.

Erin turned to look at him curiously. "What? Don't you? When you don't pick up someone for release at a bar or something?" she asked.

"Of course I do," he shot back. Curt had been indulging in quite a bit of self-release of late. For some reason, picking up a woman for release while Erin was visiting felt like being unfaithful, though it had never bothered him when she'd visited before.

"Then, what's the problem? I have urges the same as you do," she explained patiently.

The problem was Curt didn't want to imagine her urges...or satisfying those urges at that moment. If he considered that too closely, Talon would have major issues with him. Followed by Kord, if he lived that long.

"It's not the same with a partner. It's more satisfying. I'm not sure self-gratification will be viable in the long run," he managed.

She gave him a teasing grin. "As if you'd ever shown the self-control to know? Since you never did, you can't possibly know if it was enough without a partner for comparison."

"You're right," he admitted grudgingly. "I can't know, can I?"

"Well, I will. I'm not a rutting animal, and I refuse to be one just because the Stone wants it. No printing. No husband. No babies. Not ever."

"The house lords will blow their stacks," Curt reminded her.

"There are male Warriors who never mate. My mother was given the choice never to print. If she had a choice, so do I. Unless I'm willing, no Warrior would dare touch me. I'm not willing, and I never will be."

"What if you're wrong? What if self-gratification isn't enough?" he asked quietly.

Erin blushed deeply and looked uncertain for the first time. "I—don't know. The same as you, I suppose. I'd have to find a willing man for simple release, a one-night stand, but it would have to be a human who can't print." She shook her head sadly at the thought. Okay, she hadn't thought that part through.

"I hope it doesn't come to that," he answered honestly. The last thing Curt wanted to think about was Erin in someone else's bed...or a series of other beds.

Erin snuggled her cheek to his shoulder. "I hope it doesn't either. I'd rather keep it simple."

Curt shook himself mentally. A week later, she'd left Maher range. Erin hadn't been back since then, except for brief visits while he was off chasing beasts.

He wondered if her self-gratification had lasted then decided that it was none of his business and less than conducive to his mental health. After all, he was her friend. Or was he? If he was just her friend, the idea of Erin in a succession of human beds wouldn't bother him as it did.

Erin had cut him off when she'd left, just like she had every other Warrior. She'd labeled him as a Warrior in an entire world of Warriors. Did that mean she saw him as a man and not a friend? She would have no reason to run from a friend she didn't see as a sexual being.

Curt wasn't sure which would be worse. If he was still her friend, could he get close to her and hint at more when he felt she was receptive? If he wasn't her friend, did that mean Erin saw him as a man? More important, when she came back in a week, would she see him as a man? And, could Curt see her as anything but a woman he desired?

* * * *

April 20, 2029

Curt took a deep breath then strode across the yard and plucked the sea bag from Erin's grip. She turned suddenly—warily, glaring at him. He locked on her face, deciding that drifting his gaze over the cut-offs and t-shirt would be dangerous business.

"Relax," he joked. "It's no reflection on you. Grab

the other bag, and I'll show you to your room."

"Same one as last time?" she asked brusquely.

"That's what I've heard."

Erin jumped down from the back of Talon's truck and reached for the bag in his hand. "I can find my way," she assured him.

"Kord sent me to help," he informed her.

"Then send him my thanks after you hand me my bag," she replied calmly. "I don't need any help."

Curt furrowed his brow. "Your choice, of course." He handed her the bag and walked to the door. He continued through, not stopping for her. Whatever Erin's problem was, Curt knew better than to crowd her.

He leaned against the far doorframe and watched as Erin trudged in with the sea bag strapped to her shoulder and her duffel in her other hand. The padded bracer on her left wrist was the only sign of Warrior wear. She wore jean cut-offs with a lavender v-neck t-shirt and white Keds with no socks. Even her bracer had been decorated with a bright, eye-catching design in jewel tones that made it appear more like a piece of jewelry than a piece of equipment.

Erin narrowed her eyes at him as she kicked the door shut behind her. "Problem?" she asked.

"No. Admiring the art on your bracer. I'll just make sure you make it up the stairs. Then I'll be on my way."

"Fine." She climbed the stairs, stopping to re-position her sea bag halfway up.

"It would be much easier if you'd just let me help," he noted.

"I'll bet," she replied sarcastically. "Look, Curt... I'm pretty sure you're honestly just trying to help, but don't."

"Friends, remember?" Okay, Curt was reaching now, but he had to talk to her. He couldn't live with Erin giving him the cold shoulder for the entire stay, even if it meant she saw him as a man.

She glanced at him uncertainly. "That's not a good idea. There have been a lot of changes in my life."

"You don't have to use your patented smack down on me. I know you better than that."

"I'm not the same person I was then. I can't be."

"Neither am I, but I'd still like to talk to you like I used to."

"I can't, Curt. It doesn't work like that anymore."

"Okay. I'll be around, if you change your mind. Can you make it up all right?"

"Yes. I'll be fine on my own."

That hurt. Curt didn't want her to be all right on her own. He wanted Erin to need him, to want him. "Then I'll go now." He turned and walked away.

It was several heartbeats before he heard Erin start up the stairs again. A slow smile spread over his lips. Maybe he'd confused her. Confused was better than any of the other Warriors ever managed with her.

* * * *

Erin stared at the empty doorway in surprise. Curt really walked away. She almost laughed in relief. Maybe, they could still be friends, after all. She sobered again. No, that was impossible. Erin knew it was impossible the last time she saw Curt, and the four years away had done nothing to change that fact. He might be able to be friends, but it wasn't enough for her.

It seemed almost funny that the one man who wasn't chasing her was the one she found most attractive, the only one she found sexually stimulating. Even at fifteen, Erin's fantasies for self-release had centered around Curt Maher, especially an immediate exercise of her autonomy with him when she was granted it. The fact that he saw her as a Warrior and a friend was appealing in its novelty and frustrating as far as her grand fantasy went.

Coming here now was a type of madness. Her madness!

Yes, Talon had ordered them back to Maher range, but the need in her to see Curt... Erin sighed. She'd debated the issue of touching him for days, not release but a kiss or exploration that could feed her fantasies for self-release before it lost effectiveness entirely.

He'd have to know that's all it was, but this was Curt. Curt was safe, in more ways than one. He wasn't looking to print on anyone, especially not her. He was well-schooled in taking meaningless release. Most of all, he would respect that someone else was only out for the same.

If Erin needed another reason, it would be all the secrets of hers he already kept. No, Curt wouldn't be out to brag about banging the *König* princess.

If she ever rescinded her vow and took a Warrior, Erin couldn't think of a Warrior she'd rather take release with than Curt, but she wasn't sure she could stop at once with Curt. That was the danger of him. She could picture more than release with him, and Erin wouldn't allow herself—*or Curt!*—to fall into that trap.

Not that it mattered. *Friends, remember?* The thought of it was like pouring alcohol in an open cut. Curt had always seen her as a friend and always would.

Erin still remembered the day she'd decided she had to leave Maher range. He'd made his feelings pretty clear. She'd been a kid...sisterly. It was Curt's duty to protect her, and he'd liked her company. Other than that, Erin had been out of luck.

Okay, maybe she had fumbled her attempts to gain his other attentions. Erin had no practice at it, after all; but if Curt ever had any hopes, her announcement of her 'plan' should have had some effect. He'd taken it in stride, laughed at it, even talked about her having sex with other men. The thought of Curt taking release with other women had been like a blade in her. Erin had decided she had to leave that day. Her joke of the grand plan had become a reality. If she couldn't have Curt, she didn't want anyone.

Erin sighed as she pushed the door to her room open. She stared in shock at the sight of the man stretched out on her bed, his upper body reclined against pillows stacked against the headboard.

Okay, this is a new approach. Stupid—but new. "What do you want, Bryant?" she demanded, dropping her bags on the floor unceremoniously and contemplating fishing her weapons out of the duffel.

"I just wanted to welcome you back to Maher range and make sure you get settled in."

She clenched her jaw shut, stopping short of grinding her teeth in irritation. "Kord already welcomed me, and I'm capable of unpacking on my own. Kindly leave my room."

"Are you sure? It would take half the time with help."

"Leave. I'm sure my belongings don't need your assistance. In other words, my unmentionables will remain as such with you, Warrior."

Bryant laughed in amusement and pushed from the bed, crossing to her. "If you need anything, I am at your service, Erin," he assured her, the unspoken invitation to return to bed with him stressed in the drawn out 'anything.'

"Thanks but no thanks. I don't recall you ever being particularly...helpful when I needed it before."

His smile dimmed. "That was eight years ago, and I paid a heavy price for it. Haven't you forgiven me yet, Erin?"

"Forgiven, yes. You were still young and stupid." *Still are stupid.* Erin pushed that thought away. "Forgotten, no. You make a mistake like that once, you could make it again. Only people who prove themselves to me have my back."

"After the beating I took? I don't think I'm capable of even considering a mistake like that again."

"That's nothing compared to the beating you'll get if you don't leave my room."

"As you wish." He smiled a predatory smile and bowed a little too low and close to her cleavage for Erin's comfort.

"Do I have to kill you, Bryant?" she warned.

"I'm going," he replied in renewed amusement, making his way to the door.

She watched the doorway for several seconds after he walked away then sighed and hoisted her sea bag onto the bed. "Keep going, Bryant. You're gonna keep going, because you won't be coming. Not with me anyway," she muttered.

"What was that?"

Erin jumped and threw a pillow at the doorway behind her. "Dammit, Dad! Don't ghost around me. I hate it when you do that." She flopped down on the bed and curled her arms around her legs.

Talon's smile was wide and teasing. "You're just mad that Sarah's not here. Sorry, honey. I couldn't resist. I saw a man leaving my daughter's room." He smiled that infuriating smile she always wanted to smack off his face.

"And it's such an unheard of event, you decided to snoop around a little. Don't get your hopes up. I didn't invite him in."

"So, I heard." He shook his head. "You'll never know unless you at least talk to them."

"Give it up. I've talked to them. I've trained with them. I'm less than impressed with the lot of them."

"So, no one strikes your fancy?"

"Should someone? So far as I've been able to tell, they all just want to be the newest *König*, to screw the *König* princess, or some variation on that theme. The fact that I have a nice body is pretty much icing on the cake to them. I'm tired of it, Dad."

"Not every Warrior is like that," he countered.

"Most of them. The rest are even more annoying or printed already and have found their real brain again. You know, the one not nestled conveniently in their jeans?"

"What about Curtis? You two used to get along well."

"Yeah, we were friends," Erin admitted, "but that

was a long time ago."

"Maybe you need a friend."

"I have friends. Hunter and Sarah, Alex and Peg—"

"All married couples," he noted.

"Stephen, Kord—"

"And old men." That smile settled on his face again.

"We've been through this, Dad. Mom was given the choice. I have autonomy. I have a choice."

"Yes, you do. I won't deny that, but—"

"Yeah. I know. The Stone tends to get what it wants. Corwyn warned me." *He also told me I had a choice.*

"That, too, but I was going to tell you that passing up something you know will make you happy is never a good idea, whether the Stone is in its corner or not."

"What am I passing up, Dad? Sex with some guy I don't even like well enough to have a conversation with?"

"I don't know. All I know is that the Stone told Lewis to bring you here, and you've been avoiding Maher range since you got your autonomy." Talon crossed his arms over his chest, stroking his chin with the fingers of one hand. "You know, I never realized that, until Lewis pointed it out to me. Why is that?"

Her mind locked as a sick certainty sank in. Her four years of freedom were more than over, and the Stone was trying to reel her in. With Adam mated and Curt unwilling, that left Bryant. "That's it. I'm leaving," she decided. *The sooner, the better. I will not be tied to Bryant!*

"Why?"

"Either the Stone is running my life again, or Lewis is trying to bait me to his boys. I don't like either reason, personally."

"So, you'll run away? I didn't raise a coward."

"There is a difference between running away and walking out," she reasoned.

"Not a big one. Why avoid Maher range?"

Erin shrugged, buying time to think of anything passable. Nothing came to mind. "Dunno," she managed. "I just didn't want to be around Bryant and Adam anymore, I guess."

"Where do you plan on going?"

"Hunter will take me in. He'll give me a cabin, if I ask."

"So, you'll become a hermit?" Talon raised an eyebrow dubiously.

"You know, you wouldn't believe how good that sounds. What difference does it make? I can't trust anyone this way, especially not you. Ghosting around and spying on me."

"Make me a deal."

"What deal?" she asked suspiciously.

"A month. Give me a month here in Maher range, and we'll go anywhere you want for the next six months. For that month, I won't spy on you or interfere in your life in any way."

"Bryant will be dead in a week." It was only fair to warn him, she supposed.

"So, he dies. You can't convince me you'd miss him."

"If we used that as a basis, we'd thin our ranks overnight," Erin countered acidly.

"Do we have a deal?" He put out his hand for her to clasp in agreement.

"You won't spy on me and ghost around?"

"You have my word."

"Can I get a blood oath on that?"

"Do I need to prove it that way?"

Erin clasped her father's wrist and met his eyes as his hand closed around her own, completely circling it. "You break your word, and all bets are off," she warned him. "House lord or no, I will not stand for it."

Chapter Seventeen

April 23, 2029

Curt knew his brother's days were numbered. For three days, Bryant had hovered over Erin, annoying her to threats of violence. A need to see him taught a lesson and a bristling look from Erin the one time he'd tried to intervene had convinced Curt to let her handle her own fight.

Curt's warnings to Bryant fell on deaf ears. The older man firmly believed that he was wearing her down. He optimistically theorized that he would have her bedded in less than two weeks. Curt was laying odds that Erin would drop the civil houseguest routine and deck him in less than half that. Three days was her absolute limit.

When the crash and masculine grunt of pain came from the front porch, Curt smiled and checked his watch. "Fifty-seven hours," he mused. "Idiot! This has to be a new record."

Kord looked at him curiously as Curt pushed to his feet and brushed the front of his jeans, smoothing the wrinkles leisurely.

"What was that?" he demanded.

"Nothing, Grandfather. Bryant is simply sampling Erin's patented smack down. I warned him, but you know Bryant." He shrugged and stretched his back as he turned toward the door.

His grandfather darkened in fury and took to his feet. "If Bryant has been hounding her, he'll answer to me," Kord fumed on his way to the door.

Curt fell in beside him. "I imagine Erin fights her

own battles, and I'll lay odds she doesn't lose."

"You knew about this and let Bryant at her?" His eyes narrowed dangerously.

Curt smiled widely. "Erin made it clear that she didn't want my interference. So, I told her to call if she changed her mind. Notice, I am not rushing to her aid."

"Then, what are you doing?"

"Going to laugh at Bryant, of course."

Kord scowled at him, but he didn't protest Curt accompanying him to the front porch.

Curt got his chance to laugh in spades. Bryant was pulling himself out of a puddle of mud over the side porch rail, while Erin sat with her bare feet curled under her on the porch swing, looking unruffled in her jeans and a peasant shirt, a Maher history open on her lap. She would change to Warrior wear for the evening soon. She always did for practice or the evening when she might have to battle, but she looked fresh and pretty in bright colors and indulged that love whenever she could.

"I warned you," Curt commented through his laughter.

"I warned him, too," Erin noted evenly. "Your brother doesn't heed very well."

Kord grunted. "A failing I thought I had cured." There was malice inherent in that simple statement.

"With your permission, I'll cure him of it. At least as far as I'm concerned."

Kord looked at her in concern. "Has he injured or offended you, Erin?"

"More of an affront, Kord. A woman can only say she's not interested so many times before it becomes a rather tedious situation."

Kord offered a snap of his head as a bow to her. "I'll inform Talon for you," he decided.

"That's not necessary. I'm not a freed female. I'm a Warrior. Unless it's a capital offense, I fight my own battles."

Bryant froze on the top riser. "You want me to battle you?"

"What's the matter?" she shot back. "Afraid of hurting the poor little Warrior girl?"

"After you tossed me over the railing like a rag doll?"

"Then, what's the problem?" Erin waited for his answer patiently.

"It's just not—"

"I know what you had planned, Bryant. You're a little more original in your approach to the whole thing, but you made it clear enough. I'm through playing nice. I tried nice, and you didn't respect it." She shook her head. "You should have left it at nice. I'm much easier to get along with that way."

"Okay. If a battle is what you really want, I'm game," he decided. A smile curved his lips.

Erin sighed and rubbed her forehead. "I don't suggest you try it, Bryant. The last Warrior who did couldn't leave his bed for three days."

* * * *

April 25, 2029

After the beating Erin gave Bryant, Curt should have been steering clear of her as he had been for the five days since her arrival, but some indefinable part of

286

him needed to talk to her. He waited until she curled into the porch swing for a little evening down time before approaching her. She stiffened before he was halfway across the porch to her.

Curt leaned against the railing where he was. "I just want to talk to you, Erin. I'm not coming on to you. Honest."

"Why?"

"I'm curious. I haven't seen you in over four years. Talk to me for a few minutes, and I'll walk away. I've given you complete privacy so far. I'll continue that practice after we talk, if that's what you want. My word of honor as a Warrior. Unlike some members of my family, I have always been honorable toward you."

She considered that. "What could you possibly want to know? It's not like my every move hasn't been watched intently by every Warrior in perdition, Curt. I don't have any secrets."

"You're talking places you've been and Warriors you've smacked down. That's legendary."

Erin blushed and looked away. "It's not like I'm not provoked. You know why I do it. I always strive for an amicable resolution first. I don't like beating them to a pulp, but dishonorable treatment needs stopped any way it takes."

"That's what I'm talking about. That is the type of information I want. Not where and who but why. I want to know the person you are now."

"Why?" she repeated.

"You left with hopes and dreams. I just want to know if you still have them. I want to know how they've worked out for you. Whether you still want to cash in on it or not, I see you as a friend." Curt paused as a pained look crossed her face for just an instant and was gone, replaced by skepticism. "I just want to know what happened to my friend. After that, if you don't want to be my friend, I'll walk away."

"I have your word of honor?"

"You do."

"All right then."

"Do you still intend never to do the Stone's will?" he asked.

Erin smiled tightly. "No mate, no husband, no children. I think my father is getting desperate. It's funny to watch, but it's annoying when he spies on me. If I could find some way of detecting his ghosting without Sarah, I'd teach him another lesson and leave scars this time." She grinned at the thought, and Curt decided it must be some private joke between her and her father. "At least I have a month free of it."

"Why's that?"

"One of our patented deals. I agree not to cause trouble for a month in Maher and he agrees to act like I'm an adult with autonomy. A whole month of no speeches, no spying, no nagging, and no interference. Heaven!" Her smile widened, and she leaned her head back to the cushion behind her while her foot rocked the swing lightly.

Gods, she was tempting! "What type of trouble does he think you'll cause?"

"I've threatened to take off for Cross when I get annoyed enough. I figure, if I don't really have autonomy, he shouldn't really be able to order me to stay with him. If he's going to break the rules of sanction, why shouldn't I?"

"Is it that simple?"

Erin chuckled. "Don't I wish. You know it's not, but every once in awhile, he realizes that I have a point, and it's a whole new ballgame for a little while."

"Like this deal you made?"

"Yeah, like that," she agreed.

"Will he last the month?"

"I hope so. I could use the break."

"So," he began slowly, "how's the rest of the plan? It working out all right?"

She looked at him in confusion. "What are you talking about?"

"Release," Curt said simply.

His heart was pounding, and he had no idea why. It wasn't any of his business, and even if she was taking simple release with humans, it wasn't like he wasn't doing the same. It wasn't like every unprinted Warrior over the age of fifteen wasn't doing the same. But, he knew it made some indefinable difference to him.

Erin darkened, and her jaw tightened in warning. "Why do you want to know that?" she challenged quietly.

"Academic interest," he lied. "So tell me. Is self-release enough, when you have no comparison?"

She bit her lower lip and looked away miserably. "Not exactly. No, it's not," she decided.

His heart sank. If it wasn't enough, she had undertaken her alternate plan. Curt dug his fingers into the upright until they ached. "I'm sorry it's not working out the way you planned," he managed in a voice that he wanted to sound compassionate but that was strangely wooden.

"Well, I guess there has to be a price for balking

the Stone."

Erin stared at the red semi-circle of the sun intently. If she was at least happy about what she was doing, Curt didn't think it would hurt so much to see.

He found himself wondering how often she found it necessary to seek out a man. Erin hadn't done it since she'd arrived, but many male Warriors could exist on self-release for weeks at a time before requiring a woman.

How does she do it? Did Erin go to bars and pick someone up? Curt wasn't sure what his reaction would be, if she left this miserably to accomplish it.

"I guess so," he agreed evenly. "But, I guess if it's working for you—"

"Well enough," she supplied quickly. "Nothing's perfect."

"Yeah." Curt couldn't respond reasonably to that statement. "I have to go into town now. Do me a favor and go in before I go. I just want to know you're safe first."

She headed for the door, her gaze still locked on the setting sun. "Sure." Erin stopped and met his eyes with a shy smile. "Still friends?" she asked.

Curt managed to paste on a smile that felt halfway believable. "Always. We'll always be friends, Erin." Saying it hurt, but it was all she would give him. He had to live with that somehow.

Erin nodded, but something indefinable flashed in her eyes. "Thanks, Curt."

"My pleasure." He watched Erin until the door closed behind her then stormed to the garage, a converted barn on the property, and pulled his car out.

It was too much! He still wanted her, and Erin still

saw him as a friend. She was taking other men, safe human men who couldn't print on her. All Curt wanted was the chance to love her, thoroughly and completely, just once. He wanted to see if release was enough and convince her if it wasn't. He wanted Erin to want him in her bed, and Curt was the last man on Earth she'd allow in her bed. A world full of convenient one-night stands, and he was unacceptable material.

Curt screamed in frustration as he drove. Erin had her autonomy, and she wasn't of his household. Even if she was as desperately unhappy as she seemed, there wasn't a damned thing he could do about it. His hands were tied as far as solving her problem or his own.

He went hunting with a vengeance. Some irrational part of his brain argued that no beasts meant no curse and no elder killers and no *Blutjagdfrau*. No beasts meant the freedom to pursue Erin, because there would be no need to do the Stone's bidding for her to be running from.

The pod of two low-levels and their high-level master that Curt found never stood a chance. He rationalized that they were only sniffing around after Erin anyway. They were simply too cowardly to bring the fight to him, so he took it to them. The battle was over far too soon, and the hive mind went into action. There were suddenly no beasts close who were foolish enough to tangle with a Warrior.

Curt returned to the house exhausted and found Kord waiting for him in the garage.

"What was that all about?" the Lord Maher demanded.

"I just needed to blow off some *Blutjagd*. It's been a

while since I've killed," he explained.

"It's been a week, and you train every day. What is it?"

"I need to be hunting. I'm a Night Warrior. This inaction is maddening." Okay, lack of action was maddening, but it wasn't the lack of battle that he meant. Still, Curt wasn't lying. "Maybe I should go out on trail for awhile," he suggested. Going out would remove him from the temptation of Erin and give him a way to blow off tension.

"No. Our duty to *König* is to provide our best Warriors for their protection. As long as they're in Maher range, you will be with them—just as the beasts will eventually congregate. Hunt when you feel the need, but let me know first next time."

He nodded stiffly. "Of course."

"Three tonight, huh?"

Curt grinned. "I got lucky and caught them together."

"No injuries, I trust."

"None."

"Good. We should get back to the house then."

Chapter Eighteen

April 27, 2029

Erin smiled across the table at Kord. "Still not coming down?" she asked in a gleeful tone. "I beat my personal best on this one. Four days now."

He raised an eyebrow and scowled at her. "I think you take far too much pleasure in this, young lady."

"I apologize, Lord Maher. I've left you one Warrior short. I would gladly offer my services in Bryant's stead."

"As what?" he scoffed.

"I don't suppose any of you would allow me to hunt like a normal Warrior," she teased.

"Erin," Talon warned.

"Didn't think so. Ah, well. Name your price. What will it be? Reordering the library? Washing the vehicles? Laying in firewood? I'm dangerous with the axe, but I can carry logs. Your choice. I am at your disposal."

"You mean that?" Kord asked.

Erin raised her right hand. "On my honor," she promised. "I've left you short-handed, and I am not afraid of a little hard work."

"All right then. Lewis is in Houston for the day, and your father and I have business to attend to. I need you to attend to Curtis's daily workout, since his brother is incapacitated. After that, we'll see what else you can do."

She looked at Curt suspiciously, but he seemed as surprised as she was. Erin met Kord's eyes and smiled. "I said I was at your service, and so I am. I promise not to leave you another Warrior short."

"You'll find Curtis much more a challenge than Bryant," he informed her.

"Good. I could use a challenge," she decided.

"Are you saying I'm not a challenge," Talon asked archly.

"No, and I don't need a trial to prove it. Besides, I promised my services to Kord. If I'm going to give Curt a proper workout, I can't be winded from you." Erin hid her amusement as well as her father hid his. He had ceased to be a challenge to her years ago, and they both knew it.

Curt smiled. "An hour?" he asked.

"Sure. That will give me time to suit up and finish breakfast."

An hour was actually about forty minutes longer than she needed—and more than her nerves needed. Erin spent most of the extra time pacing her room, debating the situation.

She surveyed her appearance in the full-length mirror. It was her typical workout/Warrior wear: a tight black t-shirt, relaxed-fit jeans, and steel-toed Timberland Pro Hikers. Other than the boots, it was what the men wore, less the overshirt she saved for cold nights. Erin had never been able to get comfortable in the high shin-armored boots the men preferred.

Typical workout clothes. Then, why was she so damned critical of it today? Curt saw her go out to train every day. Was facing him rather than one of her parents really so different?

"Of course it is, you dolt," she snapped at her reflection. Erin didn't have to practice in Warrior wear.

She could wear a shirt that was bright colors or low-cut— She growled in frustration. "Sure. Why not invite him to bed openly and be done with it?"

Erin sobered. *Kissing and petting. That's okay. No sex!*

She practically hummed in anticipation. She'd get a kiss from Curt today if it killed her. And it might, she realized, but Erin had a plan and the balls to carry it out—she hoped. This request of Kord's had played right into her hands, so why did she feel so out of control?

She went down to the porch fifteen minutes early and was surprised to see Curt waiting for her. "Ready?" Erin asked, hoping she was ready.

"Sure." He started leading the way to the training area.

No. That was the first thing she had to change about the normal plan. The training area was too close and too easily happened upon. "I'd rather get some close quarters training in, if you don't mind."

"Okay, we'll go into the training room."

"No, I hate indoor practice," she reminded him.

"Well, what do you want?" he asked patiently.

"Remember the little clearing on the other side of the lake?"

Curt's eyes narrowed. "Where we used to rest after a swim?"

Erin felt her cheeks heat. "Yeah, I guess it was. If it's a problem..." Okay, so she had crashed and burned there last time, but it was secluded and flat enough for training.

"No, that sounds fine to me." Curt turned and headed away.

Erin kicked herself mentally as she followed him. She was tempting fate, but she wanted to know what kissing him felt like. She wanted to know what his body would feel like pressed to hers, and she couldn't think of anywhere that she'd rather do it.

* * * *

Curt smiled, as Erin sidestepped his blow and regrouped next to a tree. She may not realize it, but he was about to bait her into a figuratively fatal mistake.

If she falls for it, he reminded himself. *If she doesn't unleash that legendary Blutjagd on me.* It was unlikely, but it *could* work. If it didn't, Curt could always claim it was a ploy to slip her up. He couldn't be any worse off than he was now, he theorized.

"What are you smiling about?" Erin asked suspiciously.

"You're very beautiful."

She scowled at him. Her gaze panned down Curt's body and climbed back up, her seeming confusion belying her irritation with that comment. Then an edge of *Blutjagd* lit in her skin. "Great," she growled, "another Warrior looking to bait me into printing."

Good. She was angry at that.

"Not me. I know better," he informed her.

"Meaning what?" Erin demanded. Her eyes glittered dangerously.

Curt hadn't realized how easy it would be to get past her calm and goad her into attacking in anger. "Only that I've heard you've chosen not to mate from your own lips. I can respect that." He scanned her body boldly, unsurprised that she evoked an immediate response in him.

Her eyes flicked to the half-erect bulge in his jeans then away. She shifted foot to foot, her hands fisting on the hilts of her weapons, her brow furrowed, meeting his eyes as if questioning that move. Had no man ever looked at her before? He knew Bryant had.

"That is truly a shame," he managed smoothly, adding a predatory leer that was not for show. Curt was playing with fire, and he knew it. Wanting Erin was a mistake. Telling her he wanted her might be an even bigger mistake.

Her face turned an angry red. He shifted as she lunged at him, grabbing Erin's left wrist in his empty left hand. Curt used her forward motion against her, swinging Erin around and locking her left arm behind her. Erin cried out as he swept her feet back from under her, falling with her with his knees around her legs and pitching his weapon away to wrap his right hand around the hilt of her right weapon, over her hand. Curt wrenched her right blade up to her throat, feeling Erin sink her head back into his shoulder in an attempt to escape the blade. In the end, she was immobilized in his grasp.

"Yield," he breathed next to her ear.

Erin didn't answer. She tested his hold, trying to yank her left arm back and causing him to tighten his grip slightly to compensate. She cursed him solidly in three separate languages. "Let me go, Curt."

Feeling the thrill of his victory, Curt nestled his face into her hair. "I don't think so. Am I the first man to best you, Erin?" he asked pointedly.

"Of course not," she snapped at him.

"Besides your father, your brother, and Corwyn?"

Erin hesitated. "Yes, you're the first," she admitted. "I guess that makes you feel pretty important," she ground out.

"No. It makes me worry. You shouldn't let someone goad you into attacking in anger. It's not hard to learn how to spin you, and it takes very little effort to make it believable. If it was a beast you made that mistake with—" He realized the thought was painful.

"I don't make mistakes with beasts," she grumbled.

"Only with me," he mused. "Why is that, Erin?" Curt nuzzled his face into her hair, hardening further at the scent of her, something herbal with a hint of mint and sweat.

"I don't know. Let me go, Curt," she pleaded with him, testing his grip again.

Curt closed his eyes. "In a minute. I want you to remember this mistake and never repeat it." And, he wanted to feel her body pressed to his for just another minute before she walked away from him again or tried to take his head.

"I will. Let me go," she demanded.

"You better," he growled. Was touching him that horrible for her? He pushed the thought away. Curt had no right to be angry about that.

She stilled, her breathing harsh, no doubt noting the change in him. "Why?"

Good. Erin realizes the position she's in. She won't repeat the mistake now. "Because, I'll let you go— eventually. If a beast captures you like this..." He bucked his hips against her, knowing she could feel his erection but needing to touch her.

Erin gasped, and her arms relaxed in his grip. "Is that what you want, Curt?"

"What? To bait you into printing? I don't believe in baiting. It's despicable."

"Release, Curt. Do you want to take release with me?"

His erection was suddenly pulsing and pinched in his jeans, spread tight with his legs around hers as they were. His blood boiled for release. Gods, how he wanted to! "I thought—" he stammered. *No printing. No husband. No babies.*

"I've had autonomy for four years. I never said I wouldn't take release. I'm not asking you to print. I'm offering you release. I'm sure you've taken release before," she commented acidly.

"That's what you want?" he asked, pushing his hips against her rounded bottom again.

Suddenly, her release with other men wasn't so painful to Curt. It would mean Erin didn't need him to be gentle, when he wanted to push her beneath him and take her in hard, hot strokes. Was he really so shallow that her having other men was only acceptable if Erin had him, too? That was a subject for another time. For now, Curt simply wanted her to want him. The rest could wait.

Erin dropped her left blade to the ground and groaned, pushing herself back to brush by him. "Curt," she breathed.

"Is it what you want?" he repeated, needing to hear that Erin wanted him as much as he wanted her.

"I don't believe in baiting, Curt. Let me go, one way or the other. Please, don't bait me."

He loosened his grip on her hands and moved his leg to release hers and bring relief to his aching cock. Curt expected her to retaliate for his treatment.

Wanting him was simply too good to be true, and he knew it. He closed his eyes and braced himself for the blow she would strike.

Erin spun around, and he felt her blade at his throat.

So, she'll leave a scar to remind me. He had seen that treatment before. Adam and Bryant learned from Calvin, and they believed in the old ways of training. When they trained Curt in Lewis's place, he got the same. He accepted that he never should have released Erin while she still held her weapon, but he'd wanted so much to believe that she wasn't baiting him.

"Look at me," she rasped.

Curt opened his eyes. Her face was hard, and she shook in anger. Erin wanted him to see the attack, to know that his mistake could have been fatal.

"Why?" she demanded.

"Why what?" he managed, no longer sure what she was doing. Erin should have pointed out his mistake and made it painful. Why was she asking him questions?

"Why did you make that mistake?"

"I don't know," Curt admitted sheepishly, leaning his throat to her blade for the cold comfort of the familiar surface. "I knew you'd retaliate."

Erin smoothed her free hand over the rigid length of him, and he shuddered in response. Errant visions of her unbuttoning his jeans and stroking him directly prompted a second.

"Is this why?" she asked. "Did wanting me make you that sloppy?"

"Yes. I hoped..."

"What? What did you hope?"

"That you weren't baiting me. That you really wanted to have sex with me."

She nodded and sheathed her blade. "Good. Then, let's get release, so we'll both stop making stupid mistakes," she decided.

Curt stared at her in shock, his breathing strangled. "You want— You made— Because of me?" he asked in awe, his blood heating at the prospect that he affected her that way.

Erin shrugged as she sheathed her other weapon and then his. Her hands moved to the buttons on his jeans. "You appeal to me."

"Why?" he managed.

She looked at his face with wide eyes then blushed deeply, her face softening. "Your eyes," she breathed. "They're beautiful."

Curt blushed. The midnight blue eyes that marked a Maher were always a source of ridicule. "My eyes? You like that?" he spat. His anger was forgotten immediately as her fingers, still undoing buttons patiently, brushed by the head of his erection.

Erin smiled. "You're a good fighter. I like the way you move—and you don't treat me like a woman or a child." She opened the last button and wrapped her fingers around him, never taking her eyes from his. "Do you want me, Curt?" she offered.

"Is it—" He groaned and bucked into her hand as she stroked him, unable even to sense her in his scattered state.

"I'm not high cycle," she assured him. "Tell me what you want."

Curt wrapped his arms around her, dragging Erin into a fierce kiss. Her initial hesitation disappeared, and she deepened the kiss, pulling lightly at his length while her tongue explored his mouth, sparring with his own. Erin unbuckled his weapons belt and tossed it a few feet away, and he did the same for her. Curt dragged her t-shirt from her jeans and went to work on her zipper frantically.

Release! His body was screaming for release. Erin had him in a state unlike any he had experienced before, even when he'd been a trainee with shaky control of his drives. Curt felt as if he had to lose himself in her or he would expire, as if the last five years were endless foreplay leading to this moment.

He plundered her mouth while he stripped Erin's clothing from her, breaking contact long enough to pull her shirt over her head and recapturing her before it had even cleared the crop of black curls around her ears. Erin pulled his shirt off his shoulders as Curt tossed her bra on the growing pile of clothing. She pressed her breasts, her nipples hard in her arousal, to his chest and breathed his name next to his ear.

Curt groaned and bent to suck at her hard nipples greedily. She cried out into his hair, trying unsuccessfully to muffle her reaction in his body. Her hands ran trails in his hair as she cradled his head to her breast.

"Say it again," he pleaded as he moved to her other breast, teasing it as she arched it into his mouth. "Say my name again."

Erin pulled him over her, lying back on the new grass. "Now, Curt," she pleaded in return. "Take me now."

He smiled wickedly and peeled her jeans down, dragging her boots off and uncovering Erin's body until only her ever-present bracer graced her delectable form. "Perfect," he decided. Curt ran his fingertips up the cleft between her thighs, finding her wet for him; Erin spread further for him and arched to his touch. It was better than any daydream he'd ever had of her.

"Now, Curt," she demanded.

His smile disappeared. Erin was ordering sex? He wasn't sure he was comfortable with that. Then, he met her eyes. The longing there made him shiver in anticipation.

Curt nodded and covered her with his body, dragging his jeans down his legs as he settled between her thighs. If Erin let him take her again, he would be slow with her. This time, they each wanted something very different. "Now," he agreed as he surged into her.

He stilled deep inside her, unsure of the sensation of claiming her. It hadn't been right. Erin's inner muscles clenched around him, not a gentle embrace as he would have expected. There had been an almost audible pop as he—*crossed a barrier?*

Curt cursed soundly as the truth hit him. He pushed up on his hands to stare at her. Erin's teeth were gritted in pain, and her hands were locked around his hips roughly. She unclenched her jaw and panted as she relaxed her muscles around him and under him. Erin smiled as she lowered her head back to the grass.

"You're untouched," he ground out dangerously. How dare she let him think— He could have taken Erin gently. Curt should have taken her gently. He swore again.

"Not anymore," she teased, trying to lighten his mood. She ran her hands over his buttocks and thighs slowly, licking her lip, a sensuous move that had his cock bucking against her virgin sheath.

Unswayed—at least his mind was—he glared at her. "Why didn't you tell me you'd never taken release?" he demanded.

"I have," she insisted.

His *Blutjagd* flared slightly at the lie, and his arm muscles notched down in warning.

Erin blushed. "I just hadn't taken...a man before."

"You pleasured yourself to release?"

She nodded slowly.

"Why didn't you *tell* me?"

"Would you have agreed?" she countered.

Curt wrestled with that one. He wanted her. He wanted her desperately. But knowing she was untouched?

He wouldn't have taken her this way, certainly. Here and now? He couldn't answer that. When Erin taunted him and offered it so freely, Curt had assumed she was experienced at tawdry little affairs. Knowing she was untouched, would he have set out to claim her like this?

"You wouldn't. You know you wouldn't. I want you, Curt. That hasn't changed."

He shifted uncomfortably. Curt's body still pulsed in his need, but his mind screamed at him to walk away—or to take her away to some situation that was appropriate for taking her the first time. Taking her like this was wrong somehow, irreverent. He shook his head in frustration. Curt started to push away, intent on talking this out, on learning why she'd felt it necessary—

Erin locked her arms around his shoulders.

"Please, Curt. I want you. I wouldn't be here if I didn't. Doesn't that count for anything?" Tears welled in her eyes, and she tried to blink them away.

"Have you ever tried to get a Warrior to bed you before?" he asked weakly, praying he wasn't just a means to an end.

Erin looked at him in shock. "No, I haven't."

"Why?"

She smiled wryly. "No one ever appealed to me before."

Curt tightened at the thought. Erin had saved herself for him. Not only was there no one else, but she hadn't even considered anyone else.

He captured her mouth in a searing kiss and lunged into her again, muting both their cries. Curt released her as the fire in his blood drove him on, taking her with a desperate need. In the end, he found he couldn't wait for her. He groaned his climax, feeling his seed pour into her. Erin cried out sharply at the sensation, and he felt her inner muscles contracting rhythmically, drawing every drop of him out until he lay stunned over her.

Curt curled his face to her shoulder, kissing the blood mark at her throat. "Do I still appeal to you?" he asked in exhaustion. Never had he been so spent after sex, but it felt wonderful.

Erin chuckled and threaded her fingers through his hair. "I think it's safe to say I'd spar with you again."

"With blades or in your bed?" he inquired.

"I have to choose?" she teased. "Maybe we should arrange a few more private training sessions, just to be sure."

That was a promising thought. If she was willing to take him again, he had a chance to convince Erin to more, but there were more pressing issues to be dealt with now.

Curt eased out of her and grimaced at the blood on Erin's thighs and along his length. "This could be a slight problem," he mused. If they went back stained in blood, someone was sure to object, autonomy or no.

Erin sighed dramatically. "There's a stream that feeds the lake twenty yards away, if you're not afraid of cold water."

He nodded. It was spring run-off. Cold wouldn't begin to describe the cold that water was, but it was fresh water.

"Will you continue to bleed?" he asked. Curt cringed inwardly at that. The first chance he'd ever had to deflower a virgin, and he'd botched it. He wasn't even sure what to expect now. Every Warrior who talked about the experience had different recollections. Every woman was different, he supposed.

He pulled his jeans back up, cursing his lack of control. He shouldn't have taken her this way, especially not once he knew it was her first time. The rules of sanction stated his course. Curt should have been gentle with her. Why hadn't he been gentle with her? He'd rutted like an animal, hard, fast, heedless of her innocence. There'd been nothing soft and gentle in what he'd done with her.

She shrugged. "I'm barely bleeding now. If I do, it will only be a little. I can take care of it when we get back." Erin looked up at him and smiled. "I've already bled much less than my mother did, and she claims my father was as gentle as a man can be. Stop looking like you've wounded me."

I might have wounded her. I could have...easily.

Curt helped her to her feet and followed her to the stream, smiling at the comfortable sway of her hips and her nude backside. Part of him, definite parts of him, wanted to drag Erin back to the soft grass for another go.

He shook himself mentally. *Erin just lost her maidenhead...and roughly to boot.* She was sure to be sore, and Curt had already argued that it was inappropriate to take her this way for a first time. The next would be unforgettable for her. Once could not possibly be enough. He knew that now.

She waded right out into the cold, mountain water and sank to her knees. Erin scrubbed herself clean without even a shiver. Curt winced as he rubbed handfuls of the icy water over his thighs, balls, and cock, removing her blood and the remnants of his seed. He watched as she ran a handful of water over the back of her hair and neck, aching to chase the droplets over her skin.

"How can you do that?" he asked.

"New England mountains." Erin smiled at him, and his breath caught at the glitter in her eyes.

He nodded grimly. Erin and her family rarely spent any length of time in one place. With the Cross family in New England, he was sure she had become acclimated to the area long ago.

They dressed in silence, and Erin returned to the stream to splash more water over her head and face, wetting her shirt slightly in the process.

"What are you doing?" he asked.

"Wet hair. It had to look like I did it this way

originally, didn't it?"

"In other words, this goes no further than us," he guessed. So much for taking Erin in a bed next time, unless he wanted to sneak off to a hotel with her.

Erin smiled crookedly. "Do you make a habit of discussing it when you take release?" she asked.

Curt furrowed his brow. "Of course not."

"Then you have your answer."

He nodded and followed her back to the house.

Talon and Kord were stretched out on the porch with a stack of research on the table between them, discussing whatever they were working on.

"How did you find my grandson, Erin?" Kord asked.

Curt straightened his back as she eyed him critically. For some reason, the fact that Erin had to consider it offended him.

What did you expect? A gushing comment that you were the best she's ever had? This is Erin.

"He has style, Lord Maher. Curt is the first worthy opponent outside my own family that I've encountered in a long time. You've trained him well."

Kord beamed at the compliment. "I thought he'd be a challenge for you. He is for me."

Talon raised an eyebrow at her. "So, you've found someone worthy of your practice hours. That's good. It looks as if you've had a workout," he noted, brushing dirt from the curls over her ear.

Erin smiled a predatory smile at her father. "No man but you has ever swept me off my feet, Dad—until today. My bruised knees alone are worth a rematch."

Kord laughed. "Really, Curtis. Is that any way to treat a lady?"

Curt smiled ruefully. "She's no lady, Grandfather. Erin might have presented you with my head today if she had a mind to. All for those bruised knees, I might add. Learning to avoid that particular trick is worth a rematch."

Talon smiled a secretive smile. "It sounds as if you have a lot to teach each other. I approve of this training time. Kord and I have a lot to work on anyway. It will be good to get a break."

Curt nodded stiffly. "Thank you, Lord *König*. I'll endeavor to teach Erin anything I can, but I doubt there's much I can."

That was a lie, he reminded himself. Erin was an innocent sexually, and Curt wanted to teach her everything he knew before she left again...if she left again. At least Erin saw him as a man, though Curt doubted he could ever see her as anything but a desirable woman who could take his head at a moment's notice.

Chapter Nineteen

Talon felt the beasts coming only a split-second after Erin did. Almost in unison, the rest of the Warriors launched to their feet and formed a fight ring in the living room. Three beasts lighted close to the door.

"There's more," Erin breathed. "They're hiding but not ghosted."

Talon nodded his agreement. He could sense at least six more. There were probably more ghosted. How the hell did the beasts track them here so quickly? More importantly, what would drive them to make so outward an attack? Why in these numbers when they knew who they faced?

"Name yourselves," he required.

"Ruiz," the Latino beast in the center said. He motioned right and left. "Minor and Fowler."

"What do you want, beasts?"

Minor smiled a twisted parody of a smile, showing his extended fangs. "We've come for your *Blutjagdfrau, König.*"

Jayde laughed harshly. "I'm right here. Come for me if you dare."

Ruiz joined in her laughter. "Not you, woman. We've come for your little one."

Talon barely registered Curtis pushing Erin into the center of the group and closing her in with his muscular back.

"Curt, don't do this to me," she growled at him, her voice obviously intended for his ears only.

"Stay where you are, Erin," Talon ordered.

She nodded quietly, but her *Blutjagd* stepped up another notch.

"What do you want with my daughter, beast?" he challenged.

"She's a blood Warrior." Ruiz shrugged, as if the answer should have been obvious.

"You have no use for her. You can't reproduce. Or has your master decided to try and claim her again?"

Fowler took a step up to Ruiz and glanced over Talon's shoulder. "I have a use for her," he leered. "Taking the blood Warrior before we kill her could be a welcome distraction."

"Why, beast?" Jayde demanded. "What has she done to injure you?"

Ruiz motioned as if his hands were tied. "We cannot allow more elder killers. She mates. She dies."

Erin groaned and shook her head.

"Anything you want to share with the room, Erin?" Talon asked pointedly.

"I haven't printed," she complained. "You said if I felt myself print— Dammit! You never said release."

Talon nodded in understanding. "I should have been more specific," he grumbled, annoyed at himself for so simple an oversight more than at Erin for exercising her rights.

"Guess that settled that argument," Jayde sighed. "Curtis, you cover her back."

"Yes, Lady *König*," he replied confidently, his face a vivid crimson.

Fowler laughed heartily. "How was she, Curtis of Maher? Will she amuse us?"

Talon was heartened that Curtis didn't so much as shift to look at the beast, holding position stalwartly while his jaw tightened. He was well trained, at least.

Talon shook his head at the phrase his daughter had used. *Swept me off my feet.* At least, Erin really had bruised and brush-burned knees to back up part of that story.

"Try it and die," Erin warned.

"That is a challenge I would gladly accept."

Fowler dematerialized and appeared with his claws already in mid-swing toward Curtis. The killing blow wasn't even difficult for the young Warrior.

Erin laughed and clapped him on the shoulder. "Smooth," she commented. "You were always smooth."

He smiled crookedly. "Wait until training tomorrow. I'll teach you that move."

A new beast appeared, and Erin flicked one of her blades off, landing a blow square in his heart. "I'll teach you that one. Oh, get my blade, will you?"

Curtis handed it back as the beast fell. "Smooth," he complimented her.

Jayde chuckled. "You two are a good team," she noted.

Erin sobered. "He's a good Warrior," she replied evenly.

* * * *

April 28, 2029

There were twenty-two beasts. It took most of the night to flush them all out and defeat them. By the time the sun came up, everyone was exhausted.

Talon looked around at the destruction, blearily thanking a few gods that it wasn't his mess to clean up. That was one of the saving graces of being a *König*. When the dance was over, getting far away always took precedence over the mop-up work.

Lewis and Bryant wandered away to grab food or sleep before they tackled the odious task of incinerating or otherwise disposing of twenty-two beasts. Kord leaned against the wall, no doubt waiting to see what would come of this fiasco before seeing to his own comforts.

Bryant glared at Curtis as he limped by him. "Death, huh?" he commented acidly.

"Shut up, Bryant. The lake is that way. You know what to do with it," Curt grumbled in response.

Erin started to trudge to her room.

"Where are you going?" Talon asked through a yawn.

"Packing. I assume we're not staying."

"Get back here and sit down," he commanded.

She leaned her head back against the doorframe and growled in frustration. "Do we have to discuss this, Dad? I mean, we've pretty well covered it, right? I didn't understand the ground rules. Is there anything else you forgot to tell me?" she asked miserably.

"Sit," he ordered.

Erin nodded and crossed to flop on the couch. "What do you need, Dad?"

Talon searched out Curtis, standing against the far wall looking very uncomfortable. "You too, Curtis. Get over here."

The young Warrior nodded and pushed off the wall, crossing the room with his fists shoved deep in his pockets and his jaw clenched. He sank down on the opposite end of the couch from Erin, studiously

313

avoiding looking at her. "This is awkward," he noted.

"Got that one right," she grumbled.

Jayde sat on a chair across from them. "You're not the first Warriors that have been stuck discussing your love lives with your house lords and parents."

Erin darkened. "It's not a love life. I took release. I'm not the first Warrior who's felt the need to do that, Mother. I thought it was a fairly straightforward kind of thing until I found out I didn't have all the information available."

Curtis rubbed his eyes. "Look, blame me, okay? I started it. I egged her on, and I should have stopped when I realized..." He groaned and stared at his hands.

"It was a little too late by then, don't you think?" Erin snapped at him. "I mean, lost it is lost it the world around, no matter what came next."

"I should have asked. I just assumed, and that was my fault."

"Knock it off, Curt. You knew who to blame right away, and it wasn't yourself."

"I'm sorry about that, as well. I was wrong to snap at you."

"No, you weren't. We've been through this, remember? I didn't tell you. I admitted that, and as I recall, you were a little upset about that fact. It was underhanded. Drop it. It's old news."

"Stop," Jayde demanded.

Talon shook himself mentally. He'd been immersed in the interaction between the young lovers to the exclusion of all else.

Erin nodded and took a deep breath. Curtis put up his hand in apology. They glanced at each other then away.

"Now," Jayde began, "let me get this straight. Curtis came on to you, and you went for it without telling him you were a virgin."

Erin covered Curtis's mouth with her hand before he could speak. "Actually, I led him to believe I wasn't...kind of specifically," she informed them.

Curtis pulled her hand away and darkened, shaking his head at her. He leaned back on the couch and stared at the ceiling, his hands folded over his stomach, apparently giving up on the discussion.

"Why?" Talon asked, too curious to let Jayde take this one.

"I wanted it," Erin admitted with a shrug. "Obviously, everyone else here has experienced that. I was sexually frustrated."

Curtis jerked his head forward and looked at her in disbelief, all his large muscles clamping down tight, his fists closing then opening again.

"What's on your mind, boy?" Kord demanded.

"Nothing, my lord. I'm simply...evaluating something."

"Do not go there," Erin warned.

"Just tell me if you were being honest," he asked, staring at her intently.

"I was." Erin met his eyes dead on in challenge.

"Okay, then." He nodded and looked away again, gritting his teeth.

"What does it matter now?" she demanded.

Curtis shrugged. "Not a damn thing, I suppose."

"Good. Keep it that way."

"Agreed," he replied, barely masking his annoyance with her.

"Damn right," she muttered at his back. Erin

looked at her parents in annoyance. "Anything else?" She started to stand, anticipating her dismissal.

"Sit," Talon ordered again.

Erin sighed and dropped to the couch.

"Now, did you two finish what you started out there or not?"

"I'm nowhere near high cycle," Erin assured him.

"I've already checked that. I asked if you two finished."

"Yes. I did," Curtis shot back at him.

"Why?" Jayde asked in amusement.

Curtis moved his mouth as if to speak then shut it with an audible snap. Erin swallowed painfully, and both stayed silent for several heartbeats.

"I asked him to," Erin admitted.

"I wanted to," Curtis chimed in almost in unison with her.

Erin turned on him. "Then, why did you initially push away?" she countered, clearly stung.

"Damned if I remember. It seemed to make sense at the time."

"I'll tell you why. You thought I was playing you," she shouted.

"No," he denied hotly. "I didn't."

"Remember what you asked me before you finished?" she demanded.

Curtis closed his eyes as if he was in pain.

"Is that your final answer, Warrior?"

He dropped his chin to his chest in defeat. "Would apologizing help?"

"Now? Not a chance, but thanks for the thought."

He covered his face with his hands and grumbled what Talon could only assume was either a string of curses or disparaging comments about his partner in crime.

Jayde smiled crookedly. "Can you two get along better than this?" she inquired.

Curtis looked up slowly. "Probably not," he admitted.

"That's too bad, because you're stuck with us for now. Pack your stuff. When we leave, you go with us."

Erin launched to her feet. "No," she protested. "You can't push us together. I'm not printing, and I'm not going to. You can't drag Curt along with us, hoping you can force this. I admire his fighting style. He's good looking. I needed release. That's it. You can't make it more, no matter how much you try."

"Sit," Talon demanded.

She looked at him warily and sat with her arms crossed over her chest.

"Are you going to argue with our decision too, Curtis?"

The young man looked at Erin in exasperation. He flinched as he met Kord's gaze. Finally, Curtis looked back at Talon and sighed. "No, Lord *König*. You know I am bound to obey your wishes."

"Good," Jayde broke in. "Because we don't know if this will make you a target. The safest place for you is with us."

"Safe?" he asked in disbelief. "I do not need a babysitter, especially not Erin. If that's your reason—"

"Competitive, aren't they?" Jayde confided in her husband. "Again, that's too damned bad. You and Erin pulled this stunt. Now you'll have to pay the piper."

Erin glared at her parents. "You promised me you wouldn't interfere in my life," she reminded them.

Talon shook his head at her. "You promised me a month in Maher range," he replied evenly.

Her face darkened in fury and her hands fisted. She reigned in her *Blutjagd*. "Anything else, Mom?" Erin asked, clearly irritated with the turn of events.

"No, that's all for now. I want both of you packed before breakfast. We hit the road after we eat, and it's going to be a long day in the car."

Erin and Curtis looked at each other angrily before pushing off to head in different directions. Talon sank to the empty couch and kicked his feet up onto the coffee table. He listened to the two doors slam and smiled at his wife as he knit his fingers behind his head.

"What are you up to, Jayde? You're not worried about Curtis."

She grinned widely. "I think our young lady protests too much."

"You think she's printing, too?"

"Not yet," Jayde admitted, "but I think she will."

"They battle well together, but they fight like cats and dogs otherwise."

"Yes, they do. It's going to be an interesting courtship. Do you approve, Kord?"

The old man shrugged and clapped a hand on Jayde's shoulder. "Not my place to disapprove. I just hope they both survive."

Chapter Twenty

May 12, 2029

Curt watched, as Erin slipped out of the cabin, pretending to be asleep as she snuck through the main room and out into the darkness outside. He slid his boots on, grabbed his weapons, and pulled a t-shirt over his shoulders before slipping out after her.

He followed her away from the cabin as if he was on a stalk and she was his bait. Curt needed the release of *Blutjagd*—or release with Erin. Chasing a woman this way was something a first night would do, but he contented himself with the knowledge that Talon and Jayde wouldn't be pleased with Erin's late-night activities. Warrior or not, she was *Blutjagdfrau*, and she shouldn't be prowling the night alone.

Erin stopped at the lake and peeled off her clothing. He watched in stunned disbelief, knowing he'd drag her back nude if she dared leave her weapons behind for a midnight swim. The thought of her firm, smooth bottom locked under his hand as he threw her over his shoulder made him instantly hard. Curt cursed his lack of control where Erin was concerned, ground his teeth, and tried to force back his arousal.

To his surprise, Erin picked up her belt and waded into the water until she was covered to her hips. Lying back, she kicked her way to the floating platform with the belt held to her chest. Curt sighed in relief. At least Erin was keeping her weapons with her on this mindless foray.

She hauled herself onto the platform and lay back

with her hands clasped behind her head and her face turned to the crescent moon peeking through the thick clouds. Erin raised her knee in the typical sprawl she adopted after a swim, and his mind was made up. She was just too tempting!

Curt pulled off his clothes and made his way to her quietly. She hadn't been teasing about the frigid water, but he pushed away the cold with the idea that he'd do his level best to convince Erin to let him warm up with her. It had been two weeks since he'd had her, and Curt was at the edges of endurance. He couldn't watch her without touching her anymore.

Erin sighed as he reached the edge of the platform. "Come on up, Curt. You might as well. You'll freeze otherwise."

"Is that an invitation?" he teased.

"Can I get rid of you?"

"No, you can't."

"Then, come up here before I have to explain the Warrior-sicle at the bottom of the lake."

Curt smiled as he hoisted himself over the top. He lay next to her, shivering slightly. "Invigorating," he commented. Being this close to her was invigorating.

Erin pushed up on her elbows and surveyed the length of him critically in the almost non-existent light. "I don't know. It seems to have made portions of you less vigorous," she noted.

He hardened at her appraising look. "Has it?"

"It will if I push you in again," she answered simply, lying back down.

"Now why would you do that?" he asked innocently. "Are you fond of Warrior-sicles?" He was certainly fond of the idea of her treating him like one—

or him treating her like one. *Maybe both at the same time. Gods! Oh, yes.*

Erin scowled at him. "You know what my parents are up to. We may not be baiting each other, but they are. I have no more intention of printing than you do, Curt."

Gods! If only that were true. "Do you intend to let them drive us both crazy needing release?" he countered.

She moved her gaze back to the sliver of the moon. "I can find my own release."

Curt pushed himself up on his elbow to return the favor of her appraisal. Even in the dim light, he could see her cheeks darken and smell her arousal clearly.

"So can I, but it's so much more gratifying with a woman," he commented. Curt knew he was lying. Self-release had ceased to be gratifying days ago. He needed more. He needed Erin.

She avoided his eyes. "I'll take your word for it," Erin countered smoothly. "I've never been fond of women."

Curt rolled next to her, wrapping a hand around her hip and drawing himself to her until his erection brushed over her thigh. He smiled his determination as her breathing hitched. "What about men? Do I still appeal?"

Erin licked her lips as if she was considering it, and she didn't push him away. "This is a bad idea," she finally breathed.

He ran his fingers over her nipple, mesmerized by her body's response to him. Both nipples hardened in invitation, and resisting them was nearly impossible. "I don't still appeal? Your body says otherwise." He rubbed the pad of his thumb over one taut nipple to make his point.

"You're playing with fire, Curt."

"Why? How?"

"What if one of us prints and the other doesn't? Are you willing to take that chance?"

"I won't print," he answered her confidently, knowing it was the reassurance Erin needed from him. "I guess that means we're safe."

She glared at him. "Other Warriors have been that blind," she informed him.

Curt wrapped his arms around her and dragged Erin into his hips possessively. "With you?" he growled. His blood burned. He ached to lose himself in her again, and the idea of any other man wanting that sparked fury in him.

Erin panted in restraint, and her breasts hardened against the wall of his chest. She closed her eyes and planted her palms against his shoulders in mute protest.

"With you?" he demanded again.

"No," she replied in a shaky voice. "Not with me. Please, let me go, Curt."

"Because no man has ever gotten this close," he prodded. Curt ran his lips up her jaw to her ear, nipping at her earlobe.

"Yes," she pleaded, whether to his attention or his question, he couldn't be sure.

Curt ran a hand up between her thighs, groaning at how ready she was. "You can't convince me that you don't want me, Erin. I'm not printing, but I do want you. Take release with me," he implored.

"I can't."

"Why?" he asked, rolling to press his erection firmly to her damp curls. "I know you're not printing."

Erin nestled her forehead to his shoulder. "No, I'm not," she whispered. "B-but it's too dangerous."

"To who?" He pulled her hips to him, encouraged to hear her stifled moan. Curt had to wear her down. Nothing but completion would satisfy now. "If neither of us is printing, who is it dangerous to?"

She didn't answer him. Instead, Erin rolled her hips against him in invitation. "Please, Curt," she breathed.

"Please what?" he asked innocently. "Tell me what you want."

Erin met his eyes with a desperation that moved him. "Take me. For the love of all that's holy, take me." She shook lightly in his arms.

That made him think, something Curt had been sorely lacking a few moments before. Was he enticing an unwilling woman into some semblance of willingness or was she willing?

"No," he decided. Curt rolled to his back, releasing her abruptly.

She leaned over him, seemingly furious at the sudden change in him. "You—you baiting bastard," Erin shot at him. She started to push to her feet.

He dragged her back to his chest and captured her mouth in a fierce, demanding kiss. "Take me," he ordered in a hoarse voice. "If you really want release, take it."

Erin nodded resolutely. She fell to him, nipping at his body and soothing away the exquisite pain with her soft mouth and tongue. She straddled his thighs and drew her hands down the length of his abdomen to his cock, arching to brush the wet heat of her center against his legs.

Curt groaned and stamped down the urge to pull her up and impale her on himself. Erin would have to be the aggressor this time. In addition to establishing her willingness, there was the matter of this circling that was required to get close to her. Curt didn't intend to have to seduce her next time, and he was determined that there would be a next time, as many next times as he could convince her of.

Erin met his eyes as she sank to take him into her mouth, drawing Curt to the brink of release. After the first few awkward moments, she moved as if it were really a dream he had concocted of the perfect pleasure she could be giving at that moment. Erin let him sink into a mindless pleasure until he was moving his hips, thrusting into her mouth and groaning hopelessly at the feeling of her tongue flicking over the thick veins along the bottom of his shaft. He cried out harshly in his restraint, wanting to take her but unwilling to end what she was doing to him.

She pulled back abruptly, breathing heavily but her eyes strangely hard. "No," she informed him. Erin planted her hands on the planking on either side of his chest and started to push to her feet.

Curt gave in to the urge that time. He clamped his hands around her hips and pulled Erin down around him, filling her with a sharp cry at how close he was to losing all self-control. Erin tried to pull out of his grip, but he held her to him. Curt slid one hand down over her thigh and drew his thumb in maddening circles over the sensitive nub nestled above his cock. Her struggling ceased abruptly, and she looked at him with heavy-lidded eyes.

"No?" he soothed her. "Are you unwilling? Will you scream for your father and have me face his blade? He'll kill me without question, if you cry rape. You know that. What do you want, Erin?"

Curt was walking a line he shouldn't have gone near now. If she said 'no,' he had to let Erin leave. Even now, he could forfeit his life, but if she made him stop now, he might as well.

She pushed up on her hands and knees again, and he released her. Anything less would definitely mean his life. Curt had lost his chance. He'd gone too far in trying to convince her. Erin would walk away, and he had to let her go. He braced himself for that moment when he would slide from her body, knowing he couldn't react when his printing would demand it.

Curt roared in shock and pleasure mixed as she drove herself onto him fully, throwing her head back with a growl of satisfaction. Erin moved over him, sending explosive sparks of arousal through Curt's mind and body. Never, not in all his life, had he imagined her like this.

Erin drew his hands to her pebbled nipples in invitation. Curt fondled her, growing rougher than he imagined possible as she quickened her pace with every touch. He watched her expressions breathlessly, pinching one nipple and then the other. Her sheath tightened in response, and her breathing hitched.

"Your mouth," she pleaded, leaning further over him to offer them to him. "I want your mouth again."

He sucked at her, biting and soothing as she had him until Erin arched back and cried out wildly. Her muscles contracted around him, and Curt bowed up into her, impaling her on his length and lifting Erin off the platform fully, his seed pouring into her in jerky spasms. She stilled, as he sank to the smooth wood, her hands splayed over his ribs and her chin dropped to her chest, eyes closed, panting.

She gasped, as his erection pulsed in aftershocks, sending a last draining spurt of Curt's seed into her. Erin opened her eyes and looked at him wearily. She pushed his hands from her hips and dragged herself off of him.

"Where are you going?" he asked evenly, uncertain of what her silence meant.

"Back to bed—alone." Erin's voice confused him even more than her silence had. It held a hard edge that was completely at odds with the passion she was lost in a moment before.

"Did I hurt you?" he asked.

"No. You can't hurt me. You can never hurt me," she informed him, a bite of something sarcastic or ironic in her tone. "This was the last time, Curt. I'm not doing this anymore."

Curt rolled to his feet in a panic and placed his hands on her shoulders. "Erin, talk to me. What have I done?" *I went too far, and she sees it now that I'm not leading the action.*

She pulled out of his hands and backed to the edge of the platform with her belt held to her chest. "Don't touch me," she demanded. "Don't ever touch me again. Listen to yourself, Curt. You don't want to print, but you're acting like you're going to. Don't do that to me. Don't do it to yourself. Please, don't touch me again—ever."

"I'm not," he began, but he knew Erin was right.

Curt wanted her again and again. He wanted to take her to her bed and claim Erin there with the *Königs* in the room below, listening to their passion. Curt wanted her to choose him, and she wasn't going to do that.

"You are...unless I stop you. I won't have it. You don't want it. Not really. Not in your rational mind, where it counts. I won't be a mindless, rutting animal, mating for life because I have no more control than that. I do have control, and I will exercise it.

"I'm going back to bed now. Don't accompany me to the cabin. I'll find my own way," she ordered.

Curt bowed his head stiffly, his jaw tense. "As you wish, Erin."

She nodded and slid into the water. Curt watched until she was at the shore and dressing before he followed, letting the icy water solidify his dark mood. He dressed, dragging his clothes on roughly.

Erin's words taunted him. *"What if one of us prints and the other doesn't?"* Curt took the chance, and he knew the end results would drive him insane.

* * * *

Erin bolted to the cabin, shaking in fury. She hated her parents for starting this game. She hated herself for allowing herself to be drawn into the game...and for her appalling lack of control. Erin hated Curt—

She stifled a sob. She didn't hate Curt. Erin couldn't hate him, dammit!

But, she couldn't allow him to print either. Curt didn't want to print, and she wouldn't trap an unwilling man, even if the printing made him think he was happy. That made it worse. He would be trapped in the spell of printing, denied even the awareness that he was an unwilling prisoner. Erin couldn't allow that. She wouldn't allow it. The first chance she got, she'd settle it.

She opened the door and started across the dark room to the loft ladder. A lamp clicked on, and her hands flew to her weapons while she blinked her eyes in the harsh light. Erin relaxed her hold on the hilts as her eyes focused on and her mind identified her father.

Her jaw tightened reflexively. *This is his fault.* His and her mother's—and the Stone's. "Waiting up for me?" she challenged. "I'm not a first night. I do have autonomy."

"Where is Curtis?" he asked, ignoring her jab at him.

"I don't know, and I don't care." She did care, and that was worse. "Probably tracking me for you. He seems to think you want that. I wonder where he would get an idea like that," she added wryly.

Talon smiled widely. "So, you haven't seen him?" he asked. "I thought you two were friends?"

"You know what they say, Dad. Sex only ruins it. Guess I should have considered that."

"You still battle well together. You train well together."

"Not any more. Send him home."

"Why?"

"He's a friend, but I'm afraid he could print."

"But not you?" Talon asked with a raised eyebrow.

Erin scowled at him. "You know me better than that. All you're doing is hurting him. Quit playing matchmaker before he ends up at the end of your blade."

"You think it will come to that?" he asked in surprise.

"I know it will. I'm not going to print. Deal with it." She turned to the ladder again.

"Erin?"

She stopped but didn't look back at him. "What?"

"I'm not sending Curtis away yet."

"Why? This is hopeless. You'll only hurt him."

"There's been unusual beast activity in Maher range. A high-level named Karelen demanded Curtis's whereabouts, before Adam defeated him. He's safer here."

"No, he's not. Curt's a good Warrior. He can survive the beasts. He won't survive if he stays." *And, neither will I.*

"We'll see," he mused.

Erin retreated to the loft and dropped to her bed miserably. Curt had to go. There had to be some way to arrange it. She couldn't let him print.

She curled into her pillow and held her breath as the door downstairs opened and closed. Erin could hear her father talking to Curt, but she couldn't make out the words. She prayed he was being discreet. Talon would insist Curt stay if he knew she took release with him again. Her father would know he was winning.

Her cheeks flamed at the memory of the two of them on the floating dock, her riding him like a wanton in clear view of anyone who wandered close. How damned discreet was that? Erin fumed at how his touch affected her. She had no self-control and no common sense when Curt was close to her.

Erin swallowed a sob, tears pooling in her eyes,

pressing her hands to her abdomen. *No common sense.* She had to get rid of Curt quickly—and he absolutely could not touch her now. Already, she was on the cusp of high cycle. Already, it might be too late. It had been too dangerous tonight, and she'd let him. *No common sense.*

Stupid for a woman...for a man, in my case. Hadn't she heard Kord use that line with his grandsons? The way Adam had printed on Jo was his usual target, and Adam hadn't been as stupid as she was being.

Erin only prayed he hadn't sensed her, that his madness wasn't so far ingrained that he would try to possess her that way. Curt still had a chance for escape, if it wasn't. It was still early enough for Erin to break printing, and it should still be early enough for him to. She prayed it was early enough for Curt to break the cycle.

It seemed unlikely that Curt had sensed her. He would have been more protective if he realized the possibility. Even if Curt said nothing, hoping for another chance to bank the odds in favor of a baby, he wouldn't have let Erin walk away into the night. He would have insisted on seeing her back to the cabin.

To my bed, if he could. Visions of that were detrimental to her remaining sanity.

She couldn't allow that. If Curt would have taken her to bed—even as far as the ladder, Erin would have taken him again and kept him there as long as she could. Then, there would have been a baby. Warrior genetics being what they were, there would have definitely been a baby in just a few days, and a baby would be a constant reminder of him.

Erin had to drive Curt away quickly, and she

couldn't let him touch her. If he decided to sense her, he'd see her cycle. If she conceived, he'd see that. Surely, that would drive him over the edge, making Curt think he craved her all the more when what he really craved was his son. He would insist on sealing printing then, a printing he didn't want. That would be worse than anything she could imagine.

But what if I send him away and it's already too late?

Erin clenched her jaw angrily. Her parents started this. It would be their turn to pay the piper. She'd give them a choice, a simple choice. Either they allow her to have and raise her child alone—lying and hiding the truth from Curt at all costs to protect him from the Warrior nature in him—or she'd threaten to abort. Erin knew she couldn't follow through with that threat, but they wouldn't.

They'd have to play it her way. Erin would not have Curt come to her out of duty, and she was capable of raising a child alone. If Corwyn had found Jayde right away, he would have raised her without Anna. Warriors had raised babies when their human wives were lost at or shortly after childbirth, the health of the baby not protecting the frail human mother. If they could manage, so could Erin.

She let a single tear roll down her cheek as the light disappeared from around the closed trap door. Erin cursed that part of herself that demanded she go to Curt and bring him back to her bed. She couldn't and she wouldn't. It was that simple.

* * * *

Talon surrendered the living room to Curtis and returned to bed. He peeled off his jeans and slid in next to Jayde. His wife turned into his body and ran her fingers through the silver shot black curls on his chest.

"Where have you been?" she asked sleepily.

"Waiting up for our daughter."

She startled, and he wrapped his arms around her to draw Jayde back to his chest, smoothing her hair in an attempt to quiet her upset.

"Where did she go?" she demanded quietly.

"Just for a walk to clear her head. Curtis followed her. She was well protected."

"But, she left alone," Jayde argued. "She takes too many chances."

"Leave her alone on this one. Please, Jayde."

"Why? You want her to continue giving us heart attacks?"

"I know you still fear the open night, but Erin has been raised a Warrior."

"You know what could happen," she argued. "Ten-megaton *Blutjagd* or no, she could still be killed or taken."

"Curtis would never allow that. They'd kill to protect each other, and together they're almost as unbeatable as Erin and Sarah with less weakness. Trust me on this. Erin needs to believe she's escaping, but she's perfectly safe."

"Promise me."

"I guarantee it. They're not printed yet, but there are only so many times they can come in contact and fight this. It would take a fool to miss the looks they give each other. If only they weren't so stubborn."

"That's Erin's doing. You know it is."

He sighed raggedly. "I know it is. Let Curtis protect her. He needs it as much as she needs escape."

Jayde nodded and settled into his chest. Talon kissed her hair as she let sleep reclaim her. His Warrior woman still had so many fears. It was a sign of her explosive introduction to her existence as a Warrior after living apart from them since birth. Still, Jayde let it affect their daughter far too much for Talon's tastes.

Secretly, he had been pleased that Hunter had first nighted Erin. Talon had been hard pressed to find a way to reason Jayde into the decision himself. His initial reaction had been borne out of shock that they had done something so underhanded, fear when he felt her light and knew for sure that she was battling, and Jayde's barely controlled panic.

Talon's decision to punish them had grown entirely out of their blatant lies. Had they told the truth, they would have faced nothing more than a word of censure from him. Hunter would never have made the mistake Erin described. Her brother took her out purposely, and anything beyond that was a lie.

The lie had to be punished. It was dishonorable and disrespectful. Erin was the most powerful Warrior Talon had ever met, but she required a sense of responsibility and obedience that he seemed at a loss to impart to her.

He sighed and shook his head. Erin had lied to him again tonight. There'd been no question in his mind about it, even before Curtis told a different story than she had.

Erin knew where the young Warrior was...or where he'd been shortly before their discussion. Only a run-in with Curtis could have put her in such a foul mood, and only an intimate encounter of some sort could have left the lingering smell of arousal on her that mixed with the smell of the lake water dampening her curls and belt and soaking her bracer.

Under the circumstances, Talon had decided a little fib was in order. The beasts in Maher range were restless, though they had never reached the frenzy that Jayde had caused when the 'supposedly dead' *Blutjagdfrau* lost her virginity. The beasts knew Erin existed, after all.

Karelen did make a comment about Curtis's relationship with Erin to Adam before he was killed, but to Talon's knowledge, none of them were hunting Curtis. Erin, as always, was their target. Few beasts saw the mate of a *Blutjagdfrau* as a threat.

Erin could lie to him and even to herself, if she chose, but she wasn't balking what she so desperately needed, while her father was alive to prevent it. Corwyn had once argued that Jayde had ignored a world full of men waiting for Talon, giving her innocence only to her chosen mate. The moment Talon learned his little cold fish had set out to seduce Curtis, he'd suspected Corwyn had the right idea. Only Erin's chosen mate would evoke such a heated response in her.

But while Jayde had thrown herself into that response, having patience only to save Talon's life, Erin seemed dead-set against a repeat performance of her passion for Curtis, even though they were both free to pursue it. Erin could deny her attraction to Curtis, but she wasn't fooling Talon.

While Jayde had never perfected ghosting and still left a faint trail that Erin could detect, without Sarah, neither Erin nor Curtis could see through Talon's. For well over a week, he had watched them avidly. Their eyes found each other often and lingered sadly. They grumbled to themselves and moped around. Neither of them was very happy, and the reason why was fairly obvious despite their denials.

It didn't surprise Talon that Curtis told a different story than Erin had. From her attitude, he guessed the two young Warriors hadn't planned this little outing or its outcome, whatever that outcome was precisely.

Talon shivered in the realization that he had no idea how far that outcome extended. He would have to keep an eye on things and make sure the pair didn't screw up what should be a sure thing. He should have tracked them when he found them both missing. Now, all Talon had were the lies he had been told and what little he could see and smell.

Curtis admitted seeing her, talking to her while they walked after he followed her out. His version was that they'd argued and she'd stormed back to the cabin ahead of him.

Overall, Talon was sure that story was closer to the truth than Erin's version, but even that wasn't the whole truth. Both of them had gone wading or swimming in the lake. Their clothing was dry, and he doubted that either of them was wearing a swimsuit beneath the clothing he could see. Barring the very remote possibility that they did so separately, the obvious conclusion was that the two were nude or near-nude in the water together at night. Only the fact that their weapons belts were damp made Talon relax about the chance they took. Whatever they did, they'd stayed armed for it.

Curtis came back in one piece, and Erin didn't

light. That meant, whatever transpired, Erin hadn't balked at it. *At first.* Talon sighed. The two of them made no sense. How could a pair of printing Warriors spend so much time arguing after—or even during sex? Erin never did anything the easy way or the expected way.

Talon stilled as his mind worked at something just out of reach. They had been in Cross range for about two weeks. They'd arrived two days after Erin's first intimate encounter with Curtis. Based on where she was in her cycle then, she should be nearing high cycle.

He smiled in the dark room. Maybe Corwyn was right about yet another thing. Erin's initial encounter with Curtis had been nowhere near high cycle, but it was an experiment. An experiment, he was sure, that they both thought they could walk away from. As her cycle peaked, ignoring the urge to print should become nearly impossible for them.

Nearly. Talon sobered. Erin was fully the most stubborn person Talon had ever encountered. He would have to keep a very close eye on the situation, after all. It would be exactly what he would expect of Erin. No Warrior took the chance of a child before printing. For that reason alone, Erin would, and knowing his daughter, she would succeed admirably.

Chapter Twenty-one

May 24, 2029

Curt speared a piece of sausage from his plate and popped it into his mouth, grinding it between his teeth in frustration. Twelve days! He hadn't touched Erin in twelve nerve-wracking days.

At first, he'd agreed out of a sense of putting her at ease with him. Taking Erin the way he had had been presumptuous and... Beastly. It was no wonder she was pushing him away. Was his madness so severe that he had all but forced himself on her?

Well, 'forced' was a little strong a word. Curt had definitely convinced her in a stronger-than-prudent manner, which in itself could be construed as a capital offense, if Erin had chosen to make a complaint of it. Considering who and what she was, it would have been a capital offense, he was sure. But, she hadn't.

Erin hadn't been unwilling.

Well, Curt couldn't have defended that. She did try to push away, but he'd convinced her to stay. He shuddered to consider that. Coaxing a woman into willingness was definitely an offense.

She hadn't been unready, and he'd given her every opportunity to walk away...except for that single moment when he'd held her locked to him—

Okay, several instances like that. Curt could have groaned at how bad it all sounded, even to himself. A judge would see him dead for it halfway through the recitation of events.

Still, he'd released her and given Erin leave to walk away. She hadn't. Erin had taken him, and she'd begged for him. She'd given herself to Curt freely and passionately.

Then, she'd pushed him away, demanding that he never touch her again. Even now, Curt had no idea what caused her to turn on him so suddenly, but having Erin again—having her beg for him again—became an obsession of sorts.

After the first four days, the idea of putting her at ease had evaporated, overpowered by his printing. Curt craved her, but Erin made it clear that her prohibition stood. He couldn't make love to her, couldn't kiss her, and couldn't touch her. Trying to lay a hand on her shoulder had landed him painfully on the kitchen floor with a bruise so deep that it was still tender three days later.

Erin had progressed from indifferent to hostile to psychotic over the previous four or five days. Even her parents couldn't get within a room's length of her except for meals and training now. After Curt's attempt to touch her, she'd snapped. Erin had started spending all her free time locked in her room. She appeared for training, and she picked at her meals. Other than that, she was very much a ghost.

Her parents had noticed the change in her. How could anyone not? To Curt's surprise, they seemed to be ignoring it. The entire thing was a powder keg and dynamite with a lit match setting by, and Curt was waiting to see whether Erin or Talon would blow first.

If it wasn't for Erin's stubborn refusal to touch him over the last twelve days, Curt might have thought she had been driven mad by printing, but no one could have that much self-control. Curt knew better than anyone in the cabin did what the urge to touch someone you were printing on was like. If he didn't touch her soon, Talon's blade would find a ready home.

As it was, Curt could only assume that Erin was angered or frightened by his actions at the lake. He ground his teeth on a soft bite of egg as he considered the irony that his mounting madness would put the nails in his coffin, as far as Erin was concerned. Printing had always been her greatest fear.

Talon looked back and forth between the two of them, something he had been doing more and more often lately. Curt focused his attention on his plate, pushing it away.

"Feeling all right, Curtis?" he asked pointedly.

"Fine," he lied. "Just fine, Talon."

"That's good, because I'm feeling a little under the weather today. You'll have to handle Erin's training."

Curt snapped a startled look at Talon then shifted his gaze to Erin. She was pale, and her eyes were wide. He closed his eyes, cursing himself for the reaction he was seeing.

"Are you all right?" Curt growled, desperate to give her an out despite the urge to spend time with her.

"I... Actually, I think whatever it is may be catching, Dad. I think I'll skip training today."

Curt noted the relief on her face, though she avoided his eyes. *Caching?* He wanted to snort in disbelief. Erin wasn't thinking. Since Warriors didn't get sick, if Talon was under the weather, he hadn't slept well enough to function with a clear head. That wasn't a catching sort of thing.

"Oh?" Talon said. "Maybe I should call Sylvia out."

"I'm sure a doctor isn't necessary. I'll be fine in a day or two," she replied evenly.

"Maybe you should tell me what's ailing you. After all, it might not be the same thing."

"I..." Erin met Curt's eyes, clenched her teeth, then looked back to her father. "I'm just a little achy and my stomach is a little upset. It's nothing serious...probably something I ate. I'm sure it will pass."

Curt had never heard of a case of food poisoning affecting a Warrior, either. *She'll say anything to get out of training with me.* He fumed at that.

"Hmm. Malaise and stomach? Maybe I should contact Sylvia after all."

"I said 'no.' For pities sake, I am an adult not a two-year-old."

Jayde glanced at her husband and picked up the ball in the strange way they seemed to have, even when one was completely in the dark about what the other was doing. They always took the other's lead when they were unsure. "If you're too sick to train, Sylvia might be a good idea, Erin," her mother chimed in innocently.

Erin launched to her feet. "Fine. I'll train. Dammit! You people are impossible." She stormed toward the ladder and swung up the first two rungs.

"Where are you going, honey?" Jayde called out brightly, knowing she was spinning Erin beautifully, Curt was sure.

"To get my weapons. Have Maher outside. Looks like he's done eating anyway."

Curt shook his head angrily and crossed to the couch. He pulled on his boots and weapons, uttering curses under his breath. Maher? How damned impersonal did Erin intend to get with him? He shuddered internally to consider it.

Talon came to sit next to him as Curt worked the buckles on his boots. "Don't take it easy on her," he instructed. "Take whatever you see, and take it well."

"Believe me, I won't take it easy on her. She's sure's hell done playing on my sympathy. The mighty Erin of *König,* elder hunter and *Blutjagdfrau,* thinks she can snap her fingers for the lowly Maher. I'll give her a workout she won't soon forget."

Talon clapped a hand on his shoulder. "That's the right attitude. Keep it in mind."

Curt stalked toward the door with Talon at his heels. "Playing sick to avoid working out with me," he fumed. "If it was you, she wouldn't have balked at sparring."

"Wrong and right," he replied evenly.

Curt looked over his shoulder, stilling just a stride onto the grass and staring in confusion at the man on the steps. Somehow, that comment made no sense. "What are you talking about?"

"She would have trained with me without a word. You're right about that."

He took another step then forced himself onward toward the center of the field, still trying to piece it together and failing. "What did I say wrong?"

"Erin really is sick. She's not lying about that. I'm pretty sure she feels like crap about now," he confided in profound amusement.

Curt stopped abruptly, feeling as if the air had been knocked out of him with a sledge. "If she's sick, call the doctor."

"She said 'no,' and she's fought in worse shape. She will again, no doubt."

"You're telling me that Erin really is sick. *Very*

sick...and you want me to beat her to a pulp, if I can manage it?" *Okay, Talon snapped first. It's official.*

"That's the general idea."

He looked over Talon's shoulder at Jayde, still on the porch. Did she know this plan? Did she even know Erin was really sick? Probably not. Jayde would have had Sylvia out if she knew. "Why?"

Talon smiled. "When I took Jayde into my custody... When I found her, she had to learn what nonsense I would not deal with. Sometimes, that meant wrestling her to the ground bodily and making the rules of engagement clear to her. Erin still thinks she can snap her fingers. That's nonsense. Teach her that you're her equal."

Curt furrowed his brow and watched Talon walk back to join Jayde on the porch. He threw an arm comfortably around his wife. The Lord and Lady *König* settled in to watch the fireworks, and it was going to be one hell of a show.

He turned from them in confusion. Curt was never going to understand this household. While he couldn't deny that he had stifled the urge several times to wrestle the hellcat—*his* hellcat to the ground and make her see reason, the fact that her family was encouraging it floored him.

They were not only encouraging it, they'd ordered Curt to teach Erin limits he wasn't sure he had any right to set for her. *König* was the house above all houses, and Erin was Stone-Chosen. She was one of the true elder hunters. Curt was nowhere near her league. Yet, Talon was proclaiming that Curt was Erin's equal and demanding he prove it.

"Are we training or not?" Erin asked acidly,

appearing beside him with due *König* stealth.

"Would you rather not? We could call the doctor and skip it," he replied evenly.

Her eyes narrowed. "You know that was bullshit. I'm not sick. Warriors don't get sick, remember?"

"Do I?" Curt asked pointedly. "Do I know it?" Talon said she was sick. If she really felt like shit, she had to know it.

And how does a Warrior get sick, in the first place? Was this like the illness she'd faced when she found her link to Sarah? If so, what was it this time?

Erin swallowed slowly and ducked her head, straightening her bracers.

Bingo! Talon knows his stuff.

"It's bullshit, Curt," she assured him.

At least she wasn't a good liar, he decided. "If you say so. At least I have a name again." He smiled crookedly. "Are you ready or not? I mean, if we're going to do this, let's do it."

"Fine." She unsheathed her weapons and stepped back several yards to prepare.

"I'll try not to touch you too much," Curt ground out, reminding himself that he was teaching Erin a lesson she desperately needed.

"Good. You do that."

"As you wish, Erin."

She scowled at him and rolled her eyes in response. Erin attacked first, fast and hard. Curt realized that she would draw blood if he faltered in the least.

Her fighting style was a shade different than the last time he'd battled with her. It wasn't just that she was fighting Curt like he was an enemy. He had seen her fight beasts before. It was something less definable than that. Her balance was different, not off but different. Her stance—had changed slightly.

He fought on pure instinct while his mind performed a critical analysis of what she was doing. Realization came slowly. Erin was leaving a hole. Curt watched it in disbelief. Since when did Erin ever leave a hole? She was an expert at finding and closing holes, both her own and those of opponents. She didn't make mistakes like that.

Curt shuddered inwardly. Talon had told him not to take it easy on her. He had to call her on the hole. Gently, he decided. Talon believed in gentle reminders. Curt landed his punch carefully.

Erin's cry of pain rattled him. He'd seen her take much harder hits without batting an eye. She staggered back from him, dropping her left blade to wrap that arm around her aching chest while she kept the right up at defensive. Her breathing was rough, and she ground her teeth. Erin was in pain—much more pain than his blow warranted, and she wasn't faking it.

He muttered several harsh curses as he sheathed his blade. How sick was Erin that she was in this much pain? What game was she playing by refusing medical aid?

Well, whatever game it was, it was over. Sylvia was coming out to the cabin, whether Erin liked it or not.

Curt stalked to her, trying to help her back to the cabin. Erin wrenched away from him before he could take her arm. He threw up his hands and growled in frustration.

"Dammit, Erin! I'm taking you back to the cabin

and calling the doctor. Quit fighting me."

"You do not touch me," she reminded him, her voice just a hair off of hysterical. "You never touch me. I'm not seeing a doctor. Give me a minute, and I'll be fine."

"My ass you will. What is the matter with you?" Curt moved for her again.

She sliced her remaining blade at him with a snarl, but it was a sloppy, half-hearted effort. He captured her wrist and snatched the blade from her hand, tossing it away. That was proof positive that she was in bad shape.

Curt started to rail at her, but the look on Erin's face stopped him cold. Her eyes were locked on the hand circling her wrist. She wasn't angry. She was terrified. A sudden certainty that Erin was afraid of a simple touch angered him again.

"Erin," he grumbled, "I'm not going to take you in front of your parents. I'm not going to take you when you're sick and hurt, anyway."

She met his eyes warily and tried to remove her wrist from his grasp. "Please, let me go," she whispered.

He looked at her in confusion. She wasn't being sexually excited by his touch. Why else would his touch—

Touch? It wasn't a prohibition on kissing or sex, but on touch in any form. Curt was never allowed to lay a hand on her. But, the only thing special touch did for him—

He tightened his grip slightly and sensed her, his *Blutjagd* spiking at the fact that she was off cycle. *And she knew it!* Curt didn't question that she did.

345

Her face drained of color. "Curt, please—"

"Walk," he ordered her, barely containing the urge to physically hurt someone...not Erin, but someone. *Someone around here deserves it.* Curt had to admit he was first on the list for a decent thrashing, but he wasn't alone in his need of one.

Erin shook her head and backed away as far as his grip would allow. She was shaking. Curt never thought he'd see Erin shake in fear, and it was him that she was afraid of.

"Walk or I'll carry you," he assured her, consciously gentling his voice.

"You wouldn't," she replied in shock.

Curt swung her so that his right arm was wrapped around her back, still grasping her right wrist. Erin stumbled into position and started beating ineffectually at his chest with her left hand. The angle was awkward for her since her hand was already wedged against him, and it worked to his advantage. Had Erin gone for his balls, it would have been more difficult for Curt to grab her left wrist in his free hand and transfer it into the vice grip of his right with the other.

He tried to draw her along, but Erin planted her feet like a stubborn mule. He looked at her in exasperation. "Are you going to kick? I will completely immobilize you if I have to. Do I have to resort to that?"

She shook her head slowly, but her shaking intensified. "Please, don't do this," she pleaded with him.

"Carry you? Okay, walk."

"No." Her voice cracked. "Don't do this." Erin was controlling her tears—barely.

Curt sighed and swung her legs up onto his left

arm. He stalked to the cabin, fuming. Talon knew, and he let Curt strike her. *He urged me to strike her.*

Curt's jaw tightened as he saw Talon holding Jayde back. *Damn them both!* Teaching Erin a lesson was one thing. This was madness. In a moment of crystal clarity, Curt knew that Talon was the one he wanted to hurt, but he had more important things to worry about at the moment.

Jayde lunged for her daughter as Curt mounted the steps. He sidestepped her, snarling at the interference.

Talon wrapped his arms around his wife, restraining her in a bear hug. "No. This is between them," he soothed her.

"She's hurt," Jayde argued.

"I'm fine," Erin answered miserably.

"Leave," Curt ordered. "Both of you, get out. I want a few hours of peace to talk."

Erin looked at him in shock and started fighting his grip. Curt shifted his hold to keep her from kicking him, and she stopped, realizing it was futile.

"Dad, you can't allow this," she begged him.

Curt pulled Erin further into his chest in mute warning to her father, and she wiggled in his grip. "Quit squirming, or I will tie you hand and foot," he warned. It was yet another mental video he didn't need to indulge in.

"You wouldn't dare."

"Wanna bet?" he replied dangerously. Curt glared at Talon. "I said 'leave'."

The older man nodded. "Do you want me to call Sylvia?" he offered.

"You know what Erin needs. Why don't you go to

town and get it?" he replied, not bothering to stifle his sarcasm.

Erin looked at her parents in shock. "Dad?"

Talon smiled and patted her cheek, pulling his hand back at a warning grumble from Curt. "See you in a few hours, honey. Believe me, your mother and I learned that secrets like this can be fatal."

"Oh...oh no. Dad, please don't leave me here like this."

"Talon," Jayde demanded.

"Later," he assured her. Talon smiled and gave his wife a nudge down the stairs. "Never try to hide anything from us, Erin." He nodded to Curt and stepped down to Jayde. "We'll give you four hours or so. Oh, and we're switching rooms around. If you want to get Erin settled in—"

Curt glared at him. "Just leave!"

Talon nodded and dragged Jayde along toward their truck.

"Talon," she warned. "You *are* going to explain everything to me."

"On the way," he promised.

Erin didn't watch them leave. She turned her face away from all of them, and Curt could feel the hitching breaths that announced her tears.

His heart softened. "Relax. We need to talk."

He pushed the door open and crossed to the master bedroom. Curt groaned as he realized that the bed was freshly made up and Jayde and Talon's bags were packed to move. "Can't they be just a little subtle?" he complained.

"Why should they? They think they've got all the aces. They can afford to be cocky."

Curt settled her on the bed carefully, and Erin skittered away as soon as she was free of him.

"Calm down. I just want to talk to you," he soothed her.

She shook her head. "Nothing to talk about," she mumbled.

"That," he started to storm. He bit it off as she flinched. Curt took a deep breath and stuffed his hands in his pockets to keep from shaking her. He dropped his voice to a strained whisper. "That is my baby—*our*—baby."

Erin curled onto the pillow facing away from him and wrapped her arms around her chest. "I don't...want you...to do your duty," she replied in a halting voice. "I'm a Warrior, too. I'm perfect...perfectly capable of doing this alone."

Curt felt his jaw drop. Of everything he'd expected to hear, this wasn't even in the running. "Duty? Damn you! That is my baby you're carrying. Do you think I give a damn about duty right now?"

She shook her head. "I don't—"

"Then, let me explain it," he interrupted her.

"Don't."

"You are the most frustrating woman I have ever met. Don't you get it? I want this baby, and I want you."

"You can't. You don't," she managed.

"Why?" he demanded.

"Because it's not real." She sat up abruptly and stared at him with red-rimmed eyes. "You don't want me. Not really, in the happily-ever-after type of way complete with beasts. You're just printing. Don't you get it?"

"Why in the world would you think I don't want you? I can't keep my hands off of you. I'm miserable without you. I know you better than anyone in the world. What do I have to do to prove that I want you?"

"You said it over and over. You don't want to print. Just release. If you don't want it, you don't want it. Anything else is a trick, a trap that you don't even have the common sense to try and escape, because that's part of the trap. You actually think you want to be there."

Curt laughed harshly at that. "I lied," he admitted. "Do you have any idea how confusing that is? Human men tell women they love them to get them into bed. I had to assure you that I didn't want more than gratuitous sex, because admitting what I really wanted would have sent you running. I was lying to you when you were fifteen, and I've been lying ever since. Do you know how ridiculous this is? How ironic? How fucking insane?"

Erin looked at him in shock. "No. Why should I believe you?"

"Because it's true. You have to be able to feel it when I touch you."

She shook her head. "Release. Simple release," she denied.

"You don't have the comparison to know." Curt sobered at that. He was glad she didn't, on some level. "Why didn't you tell me?" he whispered.

"I won't allow you to be trapped into staying with me. Not by printing and not by this baby. I don't bait."

"You're baiting right now," he countered. "You're dangling every wonderful thing I ever wanted in front of me and denying me it."

She shook her head mutely, and a pained expression crossed her face.

"Were you ever going to tell me?"

"Not if I could avoid it," she managed weakly. "I thought... If I could swear certain key people to secrecy, lie if I had to—dates and facts, avoid Maher range... My only pressing problem would have been the telltale blue eyes, if the baby had them. If he did, I'd be screwed."

"Do you realize how utterly impossible that would be? Avoiding Maher range is easy enough for you, but hiding a Warrior child? The security for the birth alone would have been paramount."

"You mean hiding *my* child," Erin replied miserably. "No one else needs a small army for childbirth."

"Our child," he snapped at her. She couldn't forget that. Curt wouldn't let Erin forget it. "Did you want this? Did you just want a child with no strings attached? Was that the plan, Erin?" He fumed at the thought. It was too bad if she did want that, because she wasn't getting it.

"No. I didn't plan this. I told you my plan long ago."

"No printing, no husband, no babies," he replied woodenly. "You're not thinking..." His heart pounded at the unwelcome possibility, and he held his breath for her answer.

"No," she protested, seemingly horrified by the suggestion. "You know I couldn't do that. You know me better than that."

Curt could nearly feel the steam rising in him, seeking a vent he wasn't capable of. He'd thought he knew Erin—until she hid his baby from him, until she planned on never telling him he had a son.

Plan. I didn't plan— "I know why I didn't sense you. I was too caught up to consider the practical side. Did you even check? I know you did the first time. Did you check at the lake?"

She met his eyes and paled, color draining from her lips. "Yes, I did. When you were so ready—"

"If you didn't want this, why would you go through with it high cycle? You had to know. Warriors are damned easy babies to start."

"I wasn't. I was on the cusp."

"But you knew it was too close," he prodded.

"Yes, I knew there was a chance."

"Then why did you do it?"

"It was a mistake. I wanted release with you again. I...should have stopped it. I started to several times, but..."

"But what? Why make that mistake?"

Erin settled her forehead into her hand, looking very tired. "I don't know," she whispered. "Everything got—confused."

"That happens when you're printing," he suggested. "I know."

Her jaw tensed. "I am not printing. I will never print."

"Why? Because the Stone has already won a child from you, and it's the only thing left to fight? This isn't a challenge match. So, you're having a child? Stone-Chosen or not, it was your choice."

"Was it?" she demanded. Her eyes widened and she darkened.

He sat beside her, and Erin pushed herself against the headboard firmly.

"If you didn't have a choice, you're printing. If you did have a choice, you wanted to have my baby. Which is it?"

"I don't," she began uncertainly. "I'm not printing."

"Good. Then, you wanted to have my baby."

"No. I made a simple mistake. I'm sure you've made a few miscalculations in your life."

"Are you sure? Maybe we should test it to be sure," he suggested, his blood already heating at the prospect of touching her again.

"No, I don't think that would be a good idea," Erin whispered, drawing her knees up to her chest like a shield.

"When you started to push off of me at the lake, I let you go. It felt like I'd die if I didn't finish, but I let you go. Why did you stay? Why did you make love to me, Erin?"

"It was sex, Curt. I wanted release. I was too close to stop." There was a hint of panic in that.

Curt shook his head in amusement. "I could."

She glared at him. "So, you're better than me at something. You've had more practice," she shot at him.

"Not at stopping. I found a willing woman, had her, and walked away. I never considered stopping before. It never hurt when they walked away—or I did. What do you feel when I touch you?" he crooned.

Erin averted her eyes, her cheeks crimson points in her still-pale face. "Pleasure. You're very good, very experienced."

"That's all?" He raised an eyebrow at her. "I don't believe you."

She stammered the beginnings of a protest. "I'm not willing this time," she warned.

"A kiss, Erin? Surely, after everything we've done together, you're not afraid of a kiss."

"I'm not afraid. I'm just not willing."

The urge to trap her in a mindless, searing embrace was tempting, but if Curt was right, she would submit willingly with little provocation. He leaned his face close to Erin's, and she braced her hands on his chest. Her eyes fluttered closed as he brushed his lips in soft trails over her cheek, her chin, her lower lip... Erin trembled, but she didn't protest. Curt could smell her arousal now. He nibbled at her ear and felt her shudder in response.

"Are you willing, Erin?"

"No," she moaned. "Please, stop this, Curt."

"Why?" He trailed his lips to the corner of her mouth. "One kiss," he tempted.

"I can't."

"Tell me why, and I'll stop," he promised, tasting her lips, tracing them with the tip of his tongue.

"You won't."

Curt watched her lips as they parted to speak, aching to drive his tongue into her mouth and end this torture. "I can stop," he assured her, nipping at her jaw lightly.

She opened her eyes and looked down at him with a truly miserable expression. "I can't," she admitted. "I never could."

"Never?" he asked, moving his lips to her throat and pausing on the rapid beat of her pulse.

Erin turned her head to offer her neck to him. Her hands softened against his chest, and she traced the muscles. Her fingers pulled at the buttons on his shirt.

Curt covered her hands to still her progress,

nipping at her neck again. "I promised to stop," he chided her. "Don't push that promise too far."

"What if I don't want you to stop?" she breathed.

"Then we'll finish...after our discussion."

She groaned. "The kiss you wanted?" Erin offered, moving her legs to lean her body closer to his in invitation.

"Explain the 'never' first." He moved his lips to the pale skin of her chest above her button-down shirt.

Erin had given off so many signs that he should have seen. She wasn't wearing her usual t-shirts. She walked more to her heels. Curt groaned in need as he realized she wasn't wearing a bra either, most likely too sore for the constricting material—or it was too tight. Her breasts were definitely fuller now.

"For the love of all that's holy, explain please," Curt breathed, pulling open another button and running his lips along the lower neckline of her shirt.

"Can you still stop?" she asked. There was no taunt in that; there was little question she was seeking a negative response from him.

"Do you want me to?" he countered.

"No, I don't." The admission wasn't an unhappy one that time. Her voice was wanting, needing.

"Good." Curt ran his tongue inside her shirt, teasing at the creamy skin, nearing the areola. He was glad Erin hadn't demanded to know if he could stop. He wasn't sure he could anymore.

"The mistake I made training in Maher range was no mistake. I wanted you to fell me. I wanted to know what your body would feel like pressed to mine, what...your kiss would feel like," she admitted slowly. "I didn't set out to have sex with you. That wasn't the plan."

"You certainly snarled at me for calling you on the opening," he noted, pressing a kiss to the hollow between her breasts on his way to explore the other side.

"Before you released me, you mean?"

"Yes."

"It wasn't what I wanted. There was almost no contact, except for our arms and the back of my head."

"You wanted to feel me over you?"

Erin groaned and arched her breast against his lips.

"You wanted me pressed into you intimately?" Curt wanted to feel that himself—now, but he had to know first.

"More than anything. When I felt that you were hard, I had to have you. I knew you'd be willing, and I couldn't have stopped. Not for anything."

"Why the blade to my throat?"

"I was afraid."

"Of me?"

He released her hand and brushed his fingers over her nipple through the shirt. Curt froze as Erin cried out harshly, but he realized that it was a cry of pleasure when she moved further into his hand. It wasn't that her breasts were in pain as much as it was that the increased blood flow made them ultra-sensitive to each touch, good and bad.

She met his eyes and blushed. "You made a mistake you'd never make. I was afraid you were printing."

"That frightened you. Was it because you didn't want to print?"

"Partly." She looked away and worried her lower lip.

Curt turned her chin until she met his eyes again then laid another kiss on her chest. "Tell me."

"I was afraid of printing in general. I was always afraid a Warrior would print and end up on my father's blade, because I didn't feel the same way."

"Why? What made you fear that?"

Erin shot him a look of pure misery. "Warriors have made overtures, since I started my training...long before I was old enough to... Like Bryant. I know a Warrior can print on a woman with very little encouragement then pay the price. The men all seemed to want to bait me into printing so they could have the mighty *Blutjagdfrau*." She laughed harshly.

"Mighty? It was tiring. I had to be cold. I could never joke or flirt. I even had to be careful smiling at someone or laughing at his jokes. Gods forbid a Warrior would get the wrong idea. I'd be the death of him—literally. It got to the point that the first sign of interest meant a warning. If that didn't work, I had to crush him in battle and refuse him as a training partner. I guess habits are hard to break."

"I never realized. You must have felt like the prize in a grope." *A world full of Bryants?* That was a scary concept. If every man treated her that way— If even a large percentage did, it was no wonder Erin shut herself off from all the men.

Erin nodded, pulling back the tears in her eyes. "I don't want to be a prize. That's why I chose you."

"I don't understand. Why me?"

"You've never treated me that way. You treat me like any other Warrior, like a friend. You talk to me and care what I feel. That means more to me than you could ever understand."

"So, giving me your maidenhead was a reward?" he asked in confusion.

"No." She blushed deeply. "I didn't intend to print. I didn't really intend to let it go that far, until I was trapped in your arms and knew you wanted it as badly as I did. I thought you were safe. You kept saying you wanted to be friends. I thought you wouldn't print, but I still wanted you. I think I've wanted you since the day we took on Adam together. If I was going to give it to anyone, it certainly wouldn't have been one of those..." She waved her hand in frustration.

"Baiting bastards?" he guessed.

Erin winced and laid her forehead against his shoulder. "I am sorry, Curt. Lumping you with the rest of them was unkind."

He worked his fingers along the tense muscles in the back of her neck, cradling her face to him. "As long as you know the truth now. Did you know I was following you the night at the lake?"

She raised her face, seemingly confused. "Of course. You weren't hiding yourself from me. I swam out to the dock because I thought you wouldn't follow."

"The cold water?" Curt guessed.

Erin nodded. "I couldn't very well send you away. You wouldn't have left me out there at night—naked. So, I tried to turn you down in my usual style."

"Which didn't work," he teased.

"You kept touching me," she complained. "I had all these reasons why I shouldn't—why I couldn't let you take release with me again, and you kept touching me."

"Being close to high cycle?" he asked.

"Yes. And, I knew I was starting to print. If I kept taking release with you, wanting what I was wanting, I'd be the one insane. What a joke that would have been. Not to mention, you kept reiterating that you wouldn't print."

Curt groaned in understanding. "You were printing, and I was assuring you I wouldn't and vice versa. It's amazing we weren't both insane."

"I think I was. Why else would I let you touch me after all my arguments not to?" she noted miserably.

"Was that why you couldn't let me touch you again after that night on the lake? Because you'd finish printing with a man who said he didn't love you?"

"That was part of it."

"And the rest?"

"I'm almost ashamed to admit this."

"Go on," he urged her. Curt had to hear it all. He had to understand what was driving Erin away, so there would be no more barriers.

"I knew you'd see I was high cycle—or pregnant."

"And I'd stay out of duty, because I wouldn't print," he guessed.

"Or worse. If what you saw was the high cycle, I was afraid you'd use it as an opportunity."

"Opportunity for what?"

Erin closed her eyes and turned her face away again. "I can't believe I even considered this," she growled. "Old habits die hard, and I was lumping you in again. I was afraid you'd use your rather convincing manner on me a few more times before I passed high cycle to ensure a baby and trap me."

"I don't understand. You were printing. Wouldn't

you want me to stay?"

"Out of duty or as your possession?" she asked in disbelief.

"I'm sorry. That should have made sense to me without asking you to spell it out." He paused. "Okay, let's cover the basics. We *are* each printing on the other, and we have been for a long damned time. No one feels trapped by the idea of printing—I hope."

Erin shook her head slowly. "I'm still adjusting to the idea of a baby, but I want this child very badly."

"Good," he breathed in relief. "You know I want you, not a prize. You know I'm not baiting you, and I'm not here for duty or to possess you. And—" He ran his hand over her abdomen lightly. "I want this baby nearly as much as I want you."

She smiled shyly. "Can we add that I know you're the only Warrior I'd have a baby with?"

"I'd be honored if you would." He took her hands. "I'll give you forever, Erin. Say you want that, and we'll end this torture."

She smiled crookedly. "If I agree, is the discussion over?"

"Are you feeling ill?" He panned his gaze over her in concern. Erin was more than a little pale, and she hadn't been eating well. That would have to change.

"No. You promised we'd finish what we started after our discussion," she reminded him.

Curt smiled a predatory smile, which made Erin gasp in delight, and dragged her to him to capture her mouth. He set out to possess her utterly and found Erin possessing him with equal intensity. He lay her beneath him, scooping her legs around his hips as he followed her down onto the bed. A groan escaped from deep in Curt's chest as she arched to meet him.

"This is what I'm offering, Erin. Myself. You know me. Will you accept this forever?"

"I can't imagine another minute without you. What about you? You're willing to accept a neurotic Warrior woman who's likely to take your head when the cravings and morning sickness act up?"

"Can I hide your weapons?"

"No. My mother trained through both of her pregnancies. I want to do the same unless I'm feeling really lousy."

"How did she do that without risking her baby?" he asked in confusion.

"Ask Dad later. They figured out some way."

Curt growled at the mention of her father, wrapping his arms closer around her, pulling Erin to him protectively. "You ask him. I haven't forgiven him yet." For Talon's sake, the lord might want to keep his distance until Curt adjusted to the idea of being a father.

"For what?"

"He demanded I land a blow on you. He knew you were carrying my child, and he still ordered me to strike you. I want to kill him right now, Erin. Forgive me for this lack of control, but he shouldn't have done that to you."

My mate! His blood boiled for vengeance. Erin was his, and Talon had posed a threat to her. Talon had pitted Curt against his own helpless child. The idea of what Curt might have done, ignorant of the possible outcomes, shook him and deepened his anger. *If I had struck a more sensitive spot...* The thought was chilling. Erin would have survived a blow to her abdomen, even a much harder blow, but their baby—

Erin smoothed her hands over him, soothing his uncontrolled *Blutjagd* back into a manageable range and igniting another flame despite Curt's sick grief at what he might have done.

"Let me explain. You could only take a blow open to you, right?" Erin reasoned.

"Obviously." Curt met her eyes, drowning in their depths and lost in a need to have her forgive his trespass. "Erin, please—"

She covered his mouth with her fingers to still him. "Did I leave holes near my abdomen?"

He furrowed his brow. "No, that was tight," he admitted.

"Dad trains with me every day. He knew I was loosening up my chest defense because crowding it hurt, and he knew I'd tightened my abdominal defense. There was only one hole to find. He knew it would be hell on me when you did, but he also knew you wouldn't do either of us permanent harm with the blow."

"And he knew I couldn't bear to hurt you like that more than once."

"That would be my guess. So, if it comes to blows, don't hit him too hard." The impish grin on her face lightened his mood remarkably.

"Me? Land a punch on Talon?" Daydreams of killing the Lord *König* aside, they were simply dreams. He had a better chance of pounding his grandfather, father, and Adam together into the ground than besting Talon Elder Killer.

Erin chuckled. "I'll teach you how later. I'll teach you how to take him down." She ran a hand up his thigh in invitation. "Much later."

Curt groaned, leaning to kiss her.

Erin held him back with one hand braced to his chest. "Not so fast, Warrior. You skipped a step."

"What step?" he asked urgently, his blood burning to complete his printing nearly as hot and pressing as his burn to kill Talon had been moments earlier.

"I posed you a question that you haven't answered. Are you willing to accept the neurotic, hot-tempered woman I am forever? I have to print too, you know."

"I loved you five years ago. I love you now. I will love you forever," he promised.

Chapter Twenty-two

Erin slid her hand away and lunged up to kiss him. It was a fierce, demanding kiss that swept him away. She started to undress him, but Curt captured her hands and guided them to the bed. If he didn't stop her, this time would be as rushed as the others, and that was unacceptable. She stared at him, begging under her breath for the seal they both needed.

"I have to have you, Curt. Please, don't bait me. Not now."

"I won't. I just want to explore you. I want to take the time to give you pleasure this time. Don't make me rush."

She nodded slowly. "Teach me." It was the invitation he'd hoped for since she was too young to make such an offer.

Curt removed her clothing, wanting to see and feel her immediately. Erin was glorious.

He bent to run his tongue over her nipple. Her breasts were fuller than he'd imagined when he saw the cleavage in her shirt. They were harder now, her formerly-pink nipples a deeper hue close to rose.

They were more sensitive. His guess had been right on that. They were much more sensitive. He couldn't dream now of being how rough he was the night...

He smiled as he continued running his tongue in swirling circles around her darkened nipples. She threw her head back and cradled him to her. Erin wound her fingers in his hair, groaning in delight at the exquisite care he was showing her.

Curt ran his hand down her stomach lightly. *The*

night our son was conceived. I was so rough with her. I had no patience. He would show Erin infinite patience now. He left her chest to lay feathery kisses down her abdomen. *My son.*

Erin arched her hips to him, and he moved lower, aching to taste her. He hadn't taken the time to taste her yet. He spread her legs, and she looked at him with heavy eyes.

"Your clothes. Take them off for me, Curt. I want to feel you, not your clothes."

Curt nodded and dragged his shirt off over his shoulders. Erin lay back to watch him and licked her lips. Encouraged by her response, he unbuttoned his jeans and peeled them down to free himself.

Her eyes widened, and her breath caught. Curt ran his hand along his length, and she followed the movement with hungry eyes. He stood from the bed and removed his boots and his jeans.

As he kicked his socks away, her fingers glided along his length. Erin sat at the edge of the bed, her mouth leaving hot trails along his length as she tested the feel of him in her hand.

Curt smiled as he caught her look of amazement. He had to remind himself that his responsive little bride was still practically virginal. Despite the fact that she carried his child, Erin's experience was almost non-existent. One rushed, groping affair and one equally-rushed romp on an almost pitch black night were the sum total of her experience. Where Curt had taken the time to look at her their first time, Erin hadn't taken the time to do more than react to the rush of feelings, a fact that was both exciting and lamentable in hindsight.

Erin met his eyes and blushed. "Are you— Have you always been this big?" she asked in embarrassment.

Her shy inquiry made him want her all the more. How could a woman be so much a vixen and an innocent at the same time? It was intoxicating.

He chuckled darkly. "Do you know how perfect that is? A man can't ask for more, you know."

"Have you?" she asked again, honestly interested in the answer to her question.

"Only for you."

She furrowed her brow.

"What's wrong?"

"I'm..." Her blush deepened, bringing a touch of color to her entire face. "It's silly to wonder how it fits comfortably. I know that a woman stretches for it as she does to deliver a baby, but..." She shrugged.

Curt threw his head back and laughed that time. "Well, we know it does fit. I suggest we do research into the subject and come to our own conclusions."

Erin smiled widely and stroked him again, watching as he ground his teeth in the shock of it. At the moment he was regaining his control, she sank to capture him in her mouth. Curt wound his hands in her curls and groaned as her head moved in her intimate assault on his plan of a long, slow seduction.

"How the hell did you learn this?" he pleaded. "Have you experimented? If you have, I don't know whether to thank the man or kill him."

She released him, giggling wildly, and ran her tongue over the sensitive underside. "No. I simply snuck some videos that belonged to Hunter." Her eyes glittered.

His smile widened. "Did you enjoy them?" If so, how had she enjoyed them?

"Not particularly, but they were very informative."

"Ah. Well, since this is a learning experience, I'm going to show you what it does to me."

"How?" Her voice was a mere whisper, but he read her hunger at the suggestion.

Curt climbed back on the bed and spread her legs, kneeling between her thighs. Erin was so trusting. She simply waited patiently...eagerly for his next move. He cupped her chin in his hands and kissed her gently.

"I'm going to show you how it would have been our first time, if I had known you were still untouched."

She nodded slowly. "I'd like that."

He pleasured her slowly, tasting her mouth until they were both mindless. When Curt moved to her breasts, she moaned beneath his gentle ministrations. His fingers stroked at her sensitive folds, and Erin lay back and arched to him. Curt played his fingers in her, driving her toward release.

"Curt, please," she pleaded with him.

"We're not done," he soothed her. "You don't know what you make me feel yet."

Erin groaned. "I need you, Curt. I won't survive much more."

"I love it when you beg for me. I thought it the most erotic thing in the world when you ordered me into you while your eyes pleaded, until the first time you begged me to take you. I love to hear my name as a plea on your lips."

"I'll beg, Curt. Please, take me."

"All right."

She sighed in relief then bowed up, as his fingers

spread her to the first caress of his tongue inside her. Erin cried out as Curt swirled within her, cupping her taste into his mouth and finding himself drunk on her essence. When he felt she was at the limits of her endurance, he moved to her clit, sucking gently.

Erin screamed in pure need. "Please, Curt," she sobbed.

Curt responded by flicking his tongue over the sensitive hood.

"I understand now. Please."

He eased his fingers into her, smiling as she shuddered. "So close, Erin. Will you come for me?"

"Always. Take me, please."

"Soon," he crooned, dipping his fingers in and out of her. He sucked in his breath as she moved against him, reaching for a climax that was very close to her now. "Come for me, Erin. Come for me, and I'll show you how painlessly your maidenhead should have been taken."

Curt returned his mouth to her, driving Erin onward until she shattered around him. He buried his cock in her smoothly as the first contractions gripped her. His groan was lost in her scream of pure pleasure. Curt moved against the continuing contractions, her cries gripping his heart as her hands and her internal muscles gripped his body to her. His climax took him before Erin's had a chance to abate, and her body drew in his seed greedily, taking all of him as if starving for his touch.

She opened her eyes in shock as he filled her. The backwash of his release sealed his printing, and he guessed that she felt it too. The tension that had been building for the last month seemed to flow out with his seed. Curt sank over her shoulder, feeling as if a portion of his soul would remain in her forever but feeling Erin's answering presence in him. He kissed her neck lovingly, feeling her skin tingle beneath his lips.

"Do you see how you make me feel?" he breathed.

"I wish I had told you that I was untouched." Her voice was light but laced with a longing that touched him, making Curt wish he had asked for her choice the first time—or the second.

He chuckled as her words set off a new train of thought in him. "That may have been a problem."

"Because you wouldn't have taken me at all," Erin guessed, looking lost and forlorn.

"No," he teased, "because your screams would have drawn a crowd." Curt nuzzled her breast then glanced up at her with a hungry look. "Let me make you scream like that to drive your father mad," he begged.

Erin laughed hysterically, nodding her head as she wrapped her leg over his thigh in a strangely comfortable manner.

Curt joined her laughter as his cell phone started ringing. "Perfect timing, at least," he muttered as he fished for his jeans.

"If it's my parents, tell them to bring back orange juice, strawberries, and chocolate ice cream. Oh, and banana cream pie. Really good stuff from Rose's."

He looked at her in shock, ignoring the second ring. "Are you craving already?"

"No. I want you again and again. Give them as many errands as you can arrange. It would serve them right." A crooked smile curved her full lips, and she raised an eyebrow. "You can make me scream tonight or tomorrow. You can make me scream every time," she invited.

Curt flipped his phone open. "Hello," he laughed into it.

"Well, Curtis. You're in a fine mood today," Kord commented.

"Yes I am, my Lord. What can I do for you?"

"It's nothing important. I was just wondering if you have a time frame for returning to our range."

"Hold on, Grandfather."

"Certainly."

Curt pressed the phone solidly to his shoulder. "You said Jeremy is your favorite doctor in all the ranges, right?"

"Yes, but why?" she asked in confusion.

He drew Erin to her side and ran a hand over the damp curls above their still-loosely-locked bodies, shivering at the knowledge that his son slept safe inside her.

Erin nodded in understanding. "Yes. Please, I want Jeremy to deliver me."

Curt kissed her and returned the phone to his ear. "Checking the schedule, Grandfather."

"And the schedule says?"

"We'll be there for a short visit within the month. Our long visit will be in January."

"We? Our?"

"At least my wife and I," he countered smoothly. "The rest of the family is optional, but they'll probably tag along for the ride."

"Wife? When did this happen? I only spoke to Talon last week," Kord demanded.

"Recently."

Erin stifled a blast of laughter at that one.

"Who is she?"

Curt chuckled, grimacing and sighing inwardly as he softened enough to slide from her warm body. Obviously, Talon had been filling Kord in on the disastrous state of affairs, and Kord assumed Curt went off half-cocked and took another woman to mate, screwing up the Stone's plan for them all.

Kord caught on quickly. "You've got to be kidding. Don't you know that you should have informed the houses immediately?"

"Spread the word to those baiting bucks that my wife—that Erin is off the market permanently. Any man who dares molest her will answer to me, and I will make it a most painful affair." He looked at his wife sternly. The days of Erin fighting her own battles were at an end, at least until his son was safely delivered of her.

She nodded her agreement without argument.

"Is there anything else I should know? Or they should know?" he asked pointedly.

"You'll need to contact Jeremy for me."

"Is there a problem?" Kord's voice was abruptly urgent.

"Not a problem at all. Let him know he'll be delivering the newest *König* in January. I want the initial work-up within a month. Set it up, and we'll work around that."

"I don't suppose you mean Hunter's wife," he replied acidly.

"No, I do not. I mean a *König* with blue eyes...or so my wife wishes."

"She'd love it," Erin interjected.

Kord groaned. "I thought Erin wasn't high cycle

when you took her."

"She wasn't the first time I took her. Since then... Let's just say that printing does interesting things to a person, Grandfather."

"Yes, it does," he agreed. "You know, I printed at twenty-two. I always knew you'd go early."

"Not so early. I would have taken Erin to my bed happily at nineteen, had she been inclined to let me."

"Take care of her, Curtis. I'll spread the news."

"Thank you. Now, if you'll excuse us, we were just celebrating our baby."

"Of course. Celebrate. This is definite cause for celebration," he replied in weary amusement.

Curt disconnected and dropped the phone behind Erin as his hand circled her hip, hungry for her again already. "I think Kord is in shock, but he'll get the ball rolling. Now about that celebration..." He lowered his face toward her impish grin and sealed his mouth to hers. "I want you on top of me like I took you at the lake," he informed her.

"You want to do that right, too," she teased.

"Mmm...Yes, just the way you deserve to be treated. Think you'll scream for me again?"

Erin leaned forward to kiss him, molding her body to Curt's as she traced her hands over his arms and shoulders.

Their kiss dissolved into laughter as the cell phone at her back rang again.

She scooped it up before he could. "Lousy timing. It's either my parents or your brothers. Either way, it's my turn for fun," she teased, opening the connection. "Hello."

Erin smiled at him and rolled her eyes. "Just fine,

Mom. We'll move our belongings later. We're still discussing things. You *did* promise us three or four hours, you know.

"You're right. Dad promised us that long.

"Okay. No ladders for me. I'm sure Curt will hand things down for me."

He nodded his agreement, fighting the tension in his jaw. No ladders for her, indeed. Erin had been climbing into that damned loft on that rickety old ladder for more than a week with his son inside her. The urge to have a long talk with her about her irresponsibility was growing. *Training, climbing, not eating properly. What else do I need to add to it? Might as well make a list.*

Erin ran a finger down his chest, scattering his thoughts with her hungry look. "Yes, actually there are. We have no orange juice, which Curt reminded me is necessary for the folic acid. We could use some fruits and vegetables. Strawberries, plums, bananas and the makings of a big salad sound particularly good. I'd also like something sweet—chocolate ice cream and banana cream pie. Add some 'Double Stuf' Oreos to that. Oh, and whiting or cod," she added excitedly.

Curt wrinkled his nose at the sound of all of them in her mind together, let alone her belly. She had to be craving to come up with such a list.

Erin stifled a giggle as she met his eyes. "Well, you asked," she countered what was undoubtedly a similar complaint from her mother.

Her brow furrowed. "No. That won't be necessary. Curt and I have decided to use Jeremy in Maher range. Sylvia won't have to do more than write a few prescriptions and do a few check-ups the months we're in this range."

Her smile returned, and she ran her fingertips down Curt's chest to the nest of curls around his cock. He stirred to life, even before she cupped him. Biting her lip lightly, Erin teased him. He lengthened and thickened in her hand, aching to delve into the heat of her body again.

The look of invitation in Erin's eyes drove him on. Hard and ready, Curt drew her leg over his hip and scooted lower on the bed to plant the tip of his cock in her, relishing it as she closed her eyes to the sensations washing over her. He rocked gently, working just the tip in and out of her while she arched to him, seeking fulfillment.

She met his eyes with a fierce determination. "Mom, I have to go now. My husband and I have more decisions to make." Erin didn't wait for an answer before disconnecting and groaning in her need.

Curt continued his play. She strained against him, trying to force him deeper inside her, but he pulled back, teasing her.

Erin bit her lip lightly. "Please, Curt," she breathed.

"I love it when you say that," he reminded her as he dragged her hips to him and lunged into her fully. Her sharp cry of longing was music to his ears.

Chapter Twenty-three

May 27, 2029

Erin opened the door and threw herself into her brother's arms.

Hunter laughed, a joyous sound deep in his chest. "I missed you," he crowed. "I'm glad you're back in my range. I promise to visit you more often now that you're here again."

"You better," she warned. "You haven't come to see me the whole time we've been here."

"I was on trail," he apologized.

"Uh huh. Sure." She glanced over his shoulder then dropped to the porch. "Sarah! You brought Sarah and Mikel and didn't tell me."

Sarah's eyes glittered. "Hello, Erin. May we come in?"

"Of course. It's your house, after all." She smiled at Mikel and put out her hands to him. "I bet I know where there are some milk and cookies hiding," she tempted him.

Her three-year-old nephew charged up the stairs into her waiting arms. Erin laughed, as he planted a wet kiss on her cheek, then turned to cart him into the kitchen. She settled Mikel at the table with a pile of Oreos between them and two glasses of milk.

The Oreos were heavenly, and that was saying a lot. Despite how great food sounded to her, Erin found that she could barely stomach it most of the time. She admitted to Curt that her father's assessment of her feeling awful was correct.

Hiding in her room had served two useful

purposes. The first was hiding from him and her family, but the second had been direr.

Erin had been battling almost constant nausea and exhaustion for days. She'd been required to show her face for meals and training, and it was all she could do to keep her stomach under control for that long. At times, the very sight and smell of the food on her plate made her long to curl up around a toilet bowl, but Erin had managed to push it around her plate and swallow at least a few mouthfuls before escaping back to her room. The half-bath off of her loft bedroom had been a lifesaver. The few times she absolutely could not contain herself, Erin had given up the fight as quietly as possible before retreating to her bed.

Curt was worried about her. She knew that. More than once, he'd smoothed Erin's hair and brought a cool cloth for her during a particularly bad bout only to carry her back to bed to rest in the aftermath.

He'd cursed Talon more than once for not telling him. Only once did he chide Erin that she should have told him, that she shouldn't have suffered it alone, and that she shouldn't have continued to train and act as if there was nothing wrong. Curt blamed himself, on some level, for not caring for Erin when she needed him, even though her own secrecy had caused it. She had finally forced him back to training after two days constantly at her side, though he'd left her resting in bed with her cell phone and orders to call him immediately if she felt worse again.

Hunter sank into a chair across from them with a mug of coffee. "You spoil him, you know," he accused good-naturedly, trying to affect mock annoyance and failing utterly. "It's not even nine thirty, and you're feeding him sweets."

"Too early for a snack?" Erin asked in surprise.

"A little," Sarah admitted.

She smiled through a mouthful of cookie and ruffled Mikel's hair. "That's all right, little man. Tell your Daddy it will be his turn soon enough. Turnabout is fair play in this family."

Hunter's mug stopped a few inches from his mouth. His smile disappeared as he lowered it to the table. "Meaning what?" he asked suspiciously.

Erin grinned. No one told him. Everyone assumed that Hunter would already know, since she was in his range. "Meaning you're going to be an uncle," she replied happily, glad to be able to break the news to someone.

"You're pregnant?" he thundered.

Mikel startled at his father's outburst.

Erin soothed him and handed him another cookie, suddenly not hungry for them herself. She shot her brother a scathing look. "Boy, you kill a mood pretty quickly," she spat, angry at herself for being on the edge of tears in the face of Hunter's reaction. He was supposed to be happy for her, dammit!

He pulled back the *Blutjagd* burning in his skin. "Who's the father, Erin?" he demanded. "You're not printed." His eyes suddenly filled with a mixture of uncertainty and hope. "Are you?"

"Of course I am. Why else would I do something so insanely reckless?" Erin bit back tears again and pushed her milk away, sure that she would lose it if she attempted more.

His tension released, and he looked at her sadly,

probably regretful now that he'd reacted so intensely.

Sarah wrapped her arms around him. "You love torturing him, don't you?" she asked, trying to lighten Erin's mood.

"Of course. Don't you?" She managed a weak smile to back it up.

Sarah laughed her tinkling laugh. "Endlessly," she admitted.

Hunter sulked, Erin guessed more from his inability to cheer her again than from actual upset over their teasing. "So—it's Curt, isn't it?"

Erin smiled as Sarah laughed again.

"Who else would it be?" she asked her husband. "It was Curt when she was fifteen, and it's been Curt ever since."

"I think it was Curt when I was twelve," Erin grumbled. "But girls do mature faster than boys do."

Hunter scrubbed a hand over the back of his neck. "I should have known. I've been expecting this since before you had autonomy, and after what happened in Maher range..." He scowled at her. "I thought you weren't high cycle," he accused.

"I wasn't—in Maher range." Erin quirked a smile up and raised an eyebrow at his shocked expression.

"You conceived here? In my range?"

"Wanna know where? It's quite a story."

"That's probably more information than I need." Hunter blushed and downed a mouthful of his coffee.

"Too bad. Maybe I'll tell Sarah and let her torture you," she suggested.

Sarah's rich laughter washed over Erin, warming her. "Oh, I already know. You let a very vivid image fill your mind when you teased him. I should be shocked, but somehow it seems fitting for you. I trust you two have learned to use a bed now?"

Erin joined in her laughter, nodding furiously. Oh, yes. She and Curt had been making use of the bed as often as her tender stomach allowed.

"Oh...my." Sarah blushed. "You two are energetic, aren't you?"

Erin laughed harder. "I should have known. You know, I closed my mind when you two consummated. You could give me a little privacy." As a human sensitive and a powerful telepath linked to her sister-in-law, Erin knew on some level that Sarah wouldn't be able to resist the urge to look.

"I'd have to shield you completely. You have a bit of a one-track mind."

"Look who's talking," she grumbled, darkening in embarrassment.

Hunter shifted nervously, finding his feet and refilling his coffee mug. "Where is everyone?"

"Training. Sit down, and I'll stop teasing. I promise. When Mikel's done eating, we'll all go together."

He nodded and headed for the door. "I'll meet you outside when you're ready."

"So untrusting."

"You're as devious as Mom. What's to trust?" Hunter made his way outside to the chorus of snickers from his wife and sister.

Erin shook her head at his retreating back. She raised a cookie to her lips then put it down with a grimace as she realized her brief respite was at an end yet again. "He hasn't changed much," she commented.

"Actually, Hunter has calmed down a lot, except where you're concerned. You should have seen him when news of your—deflowering came back to him."

* * * *

Curt looked up and smiled at the approaching group. He glanced at Jayde and Talon, as they sparred together. The three of them had been partnering off in a circular fashion, switching opponents at the end of each round.

Curt found Erin's description of her father's tactics, style, and weaknesses flawless. She really was an expert at what she did. He reveled in Talon's surprise when he'd landed blow after blow. Even changing tactics hadn't helped him. Erin had been thorough in her descriptions of alternate forms Talon switched to when he needed to throw someone off.

His *Blutjagd* had been appeased after the first match they'd fought. His father-in-law had nodded to Curt in understanding as he'd left the field. Talon knew what Curt was fighting for and had no problems taking his punishment for the danger he'd posed to Curt's family by encouraging him to strike his pregnant bride. That settled between them privately, the rest of the blows Curt had rained on the lord were pure joy of training.

He moved to Erin, lifting the child she carried to his own hip gently. Curt smiled at Mikel. He had never met Hunter's wife and son, but the boy could be no one else.

The child looked at him as if in serious consideration, and Curt nodded his approval. Erin had told him about Mikel. The boy had a dazzling intellect, but he rarely spoke. He watched people, made determinations that he filed away for future use. It was unclear whether Mikel had inherited his mother's gifts. It was unclear if he was creating his own personal catalog of information he would use to lead. Mikel nodded quietly, letting Curt know his interview was over.

Curt planted a playful kiss on Erin's cheek and pulled her closer to himself. "What are you doing carrying this big boy?" he teased. "You have enough to carry."

Her smile spread. "I should warn you that I've been torturing Hunter with that fact."

Curt glanced at the rather uncomfortable-looking Lord Crossbearer and nodded to him. "Should I be worricd?" he whispered to his wife.

"No. You're almost as good as he is."

"Almost?" Curt raised a teasing eyebrow at her.

"Oh, I forgot to tell you." Erin leaned close to his ear and bit at it lightly. "He leaves a hole if you lead him left suddenly. His right knee."

"You are a wicked woman," he decided.

"Uh-uh. I am a woman who wants you desperately and will reward you handsomely for knocking my brother on his ass, just this once."

His smile widened at the idea of her handsome reward, even as his mind tried to decipher what Hunter had done to land himself on Erin's bad side. Curt cradled her head with his free hand and drew Erin into a passionate kiss. He felt Mikel being lifted from his arms and glanced at the woman taking him.

"You must be Sarah," he stated in a hoarse voice.

"Kiss your wife, Curt." Her smile was almost mocking as she made her way back to her husband.

His smile returned. "Yes, Lady Crossbearer," he drawled, returning to his gentle plunder of Erin's mouth and noting the faint taste of chocolate. Lords, but her diet was horrible for supporting a baby! It seemed sweet things were all Erin could keep down on a regular basis. Curt wrapped his now-free arm around her hips as she snuggled into his body. When she finally took a step back, he held onto her hips playfully.

"Good morning," she greeted him huskily.

"Feeling better?" She was pale, and the purple circles still stained beneath her eyes. Curt resolved to make sure she got a nap that afternoon.

Erin nodded. "Much, actually."

"Did you eat? Chocolate does not count as food," he reminded her.

She darkened slightly, just a touch of red high in her pale cheeks.

Hunter cleared his throat. "Don't tell me the few cookies you shared with Mikel were all you ate," he warned.

"Not quite. I had some of the breadsticks Curt left with me to settle my stomach."

Curt raised an eyebrow, demanding details.

"Two—well...nearly two," she qualified.

Sarah placed a hand on her husband's chest to calm him. "Come back to the house, Erin. We should get some real food into you," she soothed them both, obviously trying to head off an argument.

Erin swallowed slowly and shook her head. Her face paled again, and she started shaking lightly. Curt knew this reaction. He tightened his arms slightly, waiting to see how severe her nausea was this time.

"I'm not sure I can," she admitted.

When she swallowed a second time, he swung her up into his arms and headed for the cabin. "I told you to stay put until you felt better and to call me if you felt worse," he chided her as Erin sank her cheek to his chest. "I knew I should have stayed with you."

"It comes and goes," she complained.

"Then stay in bed."

A weak smile curved her mouth. "Is that a proposition?"

Curt's scowl softened, and he laughed. "You are a wicked, tempting vixen," he decided.

"You love it," she accused, closing her eyes in exhaustion. Erin was obviously holding back her urge to throw up again, and that only tired her more.

Curt didn't answer. He suddenly realized that Sarah and Hunter were matching his pace with Mikel close behind. Curt started as he realized that Mikel had a presence he could feel clearly already. The child was a powerhouse, but what sort of powerhouse was still undetermined.

"How far along is she?" Sarah asked quietly.

"She was on the forward cusp of high cycle two weeks ago. I can't say for sure what day she conceived."

"Probably three days later or so," she mused. Sarah chewed on her lower lip. "That makes her twenty-five days into the pregnancy by the doctor's timetable. Erin must be having a lot of trouble adjusting to this baby. It's early for this."

Hunter grunted his agreement. "Have you considered consulting a doctor?" he asked.

Curt arched an eyebrow at his new brother-in-law.

"You do know this woman, right?" he countered.

"There's nothing a doctor can do yet," Erin added in exhaustion.

"See? We have an appointment with Jeremy in Maher range in two weeks. Erin is convinced that she's just sensitive to the change in body chemistry. She's been sick for almost a week now."

"Even if it's not that, it's too early to change anything," she continued miserably.

Curt kissed the top of her head gently, though his gut clenched at the thought. Warrior babies didn't have problems like miscarriage, but a Warrior baby had never been conceived before printing like this—at least not that anyone knew of.

"Don't even think such a thing," he breathed, as much to himself as to her. "Young Warriors are strong. I've never heard of a case of one being lost."

"Unless the mother was, too," she reminded him in a morose, little voice.

"Only if the mother was the one in trouble in the first place," he soothed her.

Erin was a Warrior. She would be physically incapable of such weakness in childbearing. It was a given. Curt wouldn't contemplate that reality could vary from that solemn trust and truth.

"There's a first time for everything." She seemed on the verge of tears again. Her moods were raw and unpredictable lately. "Like my blood mark."

Curt sighed. Erin carried the mark of Zel, death or an ending. There had never been a Zel before, even in the first war with the beasts. Only Zel and Jee, the mark of Justice, were completely unheard of. Now, Erin had been born Zel, and Mikel carried the mark of

Jee.

Since her birth, Warriors had argued what the mark meant. Some argued that she was destined to destroy the final elder. Some argued that she would see the final days of the war in her lifetime. Some even argued that she herself would kill the last of the beasts on Earth and free them all.

Erin had come up with a more disturbing thought in one of her depressed moods. She feared she wouldn't be able to carry a child, and the mark of Zel meant she had always been intended to be a Warrior only and not a mother, just as she'd once argued she was more suited.

"Not with my wife and my child," he decided. "I will not allow any outcome but the one every Warrior has been gifted so far."

"Maybe you're carrying twins," Sarah offered brightly.

Hunter tried to warn her off, but Erin had already opened her eyes. She regarded the older woman sadly.

"Warriors never have twins," she informed Sarah.

"There's a first time for everything," she countered smoothly.

Chapter Twenty-four

June 11, 2029

Erin shifted nervously. She had never been a fan of doctors, so saying Jeremy was her favorite doctor was akin to saying that a simple beheading you never saw coming was the best way to die a violent death. Erin jumped, as he entered the room, wishing yet again that she could simply take some mail order tests and be done with the whole thing.

The doctor smiled warmly. He was one of the younger doctors, only a resident when he was saved by Kord ten years earlier.

His eyes crinkled in amusement at her typical attack of nerves as he approached her. "There's no need to fear me, Erin," Jeremy soothed her.

She always wondered if his attempts to put her at ease stemmed from his bedside manner or from his fear that she would snap and kill him.

"News to me," Erin muttered in her typical response to his soothing. She clasped Curt's hand tightly in her own and managed a wan smile.

"Curt explained your concerns. I'm sure it's nothing to worry about, but I promise to be thorough. It will mean a few extra vials of blood and a few extra minutes of examination, but I will be thorough."

She nodded. "I understand. You know that stuff doesn't bother me."

"Yeah. It's just doctors that bother you, not what we do. Is there anyone else you want in here?"

Erin shook her head. "No. Curt is all I need. Anyone else would make me nuts."

"Good. Then, we'll get this rolling. I brought Jacquie in to give me a hand. She'll take some quick blood tests."

"What for?"

"Make sure you're not anemic. You are pale," he noted, adding the information to her chart. "Check blood sugar and hCG levels. In the meantime, you're far enough along to have a transvaginal ultrasound to check for twins. If there is anything out of the ordinary, that's the most likely thing."

"Warriors don't have twins," she mumbled.

"So Curt assures me. We'll still check."

Erin nodded her agreement and allowed Jacquie to draw the blood: eight vials of it. "Worse than a damn beast," she muttered to everyone's amusement but her own.

Jeremy asked a seemingly endless array of questions about her health and symptoms, whether she was taking her vitamins and eating well, and any medical history that might have been missing from her patchwork records. Since Erin didn't get sick and she avoided doctors like the plague, there wasn't much that could be missing.

Finally, he accepted the lab reports back from Jacquie and smiled. "Looks good. We may opt for some extra vitamins until you can hold down more food, but overall it looks pretty good. We'll get you into the ultrasound room in a minute." Jeremy handed Erin a long robe. "Undress from the waist down. Weapons, too." He smiled at that. "Jacquie will lead you over when you're ready. I'll meet you there."

Jacquie smiled and shook her head. "I'll be in the hall. Let me know when you're ready." She handed them a large plastic bag. "Drop everything in here so you can dress in the bathroom on that side. Better than dragging back here for no good reason."

Erin watched the door close behind them and sighed. She started to undress, but Curt took her hands away from the button on her jeans and pulled her to his chest.

"You're shaking," he whispered next to her ear. "I never thought I'd see you shaking again."

"Only when my heart is on the line, someone I care about," she managed.

"I promise you it will be all right. Even if there's something wrong..." He took a ragged breath.

"You haven't mentioned that possibility to your family, have you?"

"Only the *Königs* know. Gods willing, no one else will ever have to know." His hands moved to the button of her jeans. Curt undressed her, pushing Erin's clothing down her body and lifting her to the table to strip her as Jeremy had asked. He wrapped the robe around her reverently and slid her back to his side, hoisting the bag of clothing and equipment.

"Why is this so nerve wracking?" she asked hopelessly, seeing the matching torture in her husband's midnight blue eyes.

"This is just the beginning. We have decades of this. Training, amulets, childhood accidents, first night—"

"I hope," she whispered.

"We will." He guided her to the door and out to Jacquie.

The espresso-skinned woman smiled a motherly smile at her, and Erin couldn't help but return it.

Having Jacquie here was a stroke of genius for Jeremy. Erin remembered the first time she'd met the nurse. It had been the night she'd driven Lorian to ground, and the older woman's compassion had been the only thing keeping her sane while Jeremy stitched Hunter and they checked for broken bones on her.

Erin took a deep breath. "What can they really see on an ultrasound, Jacquie? I mean, the baby is so little..."

Jacquie wrapped an arm around her shoulders, dwarfing the younger woman with her five foot nine and hundred and eighty build. "You'd be surprised, honey. The technology has come a long way since your mother's day. The imaging alone will allow us to zoom in and see the baby or babies in there like we had a microscope on them. It will show us blood flow in the cord and through the rudimentary heart chamber. At this stage, a healthy cord, well-formed baby, and rushing blood through that chamber is as good as it gets. We'll be able to check all of that."

Erin wound her hand through Curt's, praying it was 'as good as it gets.'

"It will be," he assured her.

She smiled up at him. "I thought only Sarah read minds."

"She's been giving me pointers," he managed with a straight face.

Erin punched him in the ribs playfully. "No one gives you pointers but me," she scolded him.

* * * *

Talon paced the floor of the waiting room like a

caged tiger.

"Sit down," Jayde ordered him. "You're making me nervous."

He dropped into a chair, feeling his entire nervous system jumping uncontrollably. "What is taking them so long in there?" he growled.

"Patience," she hissed back at him. "Jeremy is just being thorough. Remember how nerve wracking my first visit to Laura was? Even our protected humans understand how important *König* babies are. He won't leave anything to chance."

Talon grunted his agreement, bristling lightly at his wife's gentle barb. He remembered Jayde's first ultrasound all too well, and it was far too much like the current situation for his tastes. Talon remembered his terror, carefully hidden from Jayde, that the test would reveal their child killed in her womb, assassinated by Veriel while the beast had her unprotected in his grasp. He knew very well that Erin and Curtis would either emerge devastated or as the happiest couple in the world.

"What is wrong with you two?" Kord asked suspiciously.

Jayde sighed. "Our baby is having a baby," she lied smoothly. "It's not an easy thing to face the circus we experienced when my children were born, Kord. I wouldn't wish beast attacks and elders on her for anything."

The old man's eyes narrowed. "It's more than that," he decided. "You love Sarah like a daughter, and she's hunted too. You were never nervous about her pregnancy. Not like this, anyway."

Talon raised his head breathlessly, ignoring

Jayde's response. He could see the quartet of people through the glass, and his heart sank. Erin looked shell-shocked. She nodded grimly at something Jeremy said and wound her arm around Curtis's, laying her cheek on his bicep. Curtis regarded the doctor seriously as he shook his hand. He guided Erin out into the waiting room with a gentle kiss on the top of her head. Her weapons belt was looped around his shoulder.

Talon stood, feeling Jayde and Kord tense behind him. "What's wrong?" he asked, reining in his natural response to a threat to his child.

Jeremy waved him back. "There are just a few extra ground rules for this pregnancy," he assured them. "Limit her stress and her travel. More tests. We'll see her more often."

Curtis met his eyes wearily. "No training allowed. If we can avoid it, no battles either," he added.

"What's wrong?" Kord echoed before Talon could repeat himself.

The old man was firmly holding back a strong *Blutjagd*. If this was serious news, Talon knew he might find himself acting against his old friend.

Jeremy smiled. "Erin has just decided to exercise her unique nature, as usual."

Her eyes lit in annoyance. "I hardly managed this alone," she protested.

Curtis grinned wickedly. "This is your body's part of the arrangement," he stated in a teasing voice.

Erin smacked his arm, and her husband recoiled, chuckling at her anger.

"Well, who the hell invited you to fertilize both eggs?" she demanded. "You had a little something to do with it. As I recall, you were pursuing me at the time."

Talon bit back a laugh of pure relief. *Twins! Gods alive, she's having twins.*

Curtis laughed harder and pulled her to his chest. "And what a pursuit it was," he crooned tenderly.

"Obviously. As if this isn't proof enough of that." Erin wound her arms around his chest. "You better be up for helping—diapers and all," she warned.

"What happened to you being 'perfectly capable of doing this alone'?" he mused.

"That was before I knew there were two. Two of you? Gods help me! Not to mention, you were the one who insisted that we seal our printing," she reasoned. "You're stuck, Curt. Deal with it."

"I'll do more than deal with it. I'll get Adam and Jo to give me Baby Care one-oh-one with their new little one," he promised.

"You better," she grumbled into his chest.

The older Warriors watched the exchange in a mixture of shock and amusement.

"Twins?" Kord finally demanded.

Curtis smiled widely. "We made the Warriors' records book."

"I'll say. Fifteen hundred years and seven families without a single set of twins," he replied in awe. "You're sure about this?"

"We have the pictures to prove it." Curtis beamed.

Talon laughed, remembering the lure of those first pictures.

Erin scowled. "The Stone is just punishing me for wasted time," she decided.

"You're only twenty," Jayde protested.

Erin darkened and buried her face in her

husband's chest.

Curtis smirked. "Didn't you know? There was a reason Erin left Maher range before she got her autonomy. There was a reason she stayed away until Lewis ordered her back. She was busy hiding out...from me."

Erin punched him ineffectually. "You are entirely too full of yourself. What am I saying? I'm entirely too full of you."

"Not yet," he teased. "And before you say it, since you're not allowed to train and battle, I am hiding your weapons."

"Keep this up and that's the only way you'll live to see our children born."

Curtis held her to him, nuzzling his face to hers, looking very pleased with himself. "I can't wait to feel them moving inside you. You're beautiful. You know that?"

"I'll be fat," she complained.

"Not fat. Just wonderfully pregnant."

Chapter Twenty-five

December 24, 2029

The assembled Warriors' heads shot up as Erin rushed into the room. Her eyes were wide, and her hands were cupped under the swell of her womb. Curt went to her, pulling her into his embrace, his heart hammering.

"What's wrong? Is it the babies?" he asked urgently.

She was less than thirty-five weeks, and Jeremy warned that she could go early, but they were afraid of the consequences of that. Full-term, they could trust that the healthy nature of Warrior babies would suffice and deliver at home. More than a month early, they would have to brave a hospital birth, complete with the attendant problems of security, for the sake of possible problems.

"He's coming," she whispered. "He's close. We have to get out of here."

Curt backed off and met her eyes in confusion. "Who, Erin? What's wrong?"

Hunter vaulted over the back of the couch and made it to them in two long strides. "Lorian? He's coming here?"

She nodded, shivering in the knowledge. "Yes. He's almost here."

"Sarah?" Jayde asked.

The sensitive shook her head. "I don't sense anything."

Erin ground out a curse. "Hook in. Use my senses like I use yours— Please, Sarah. Trust me."

Sarah's eyes widened almost immediately and she scrambled to her feet. "You have range. She's right." She scooped up Mikel from the floor, though he stood at almost her chest height at four years old. "Five minutes at the most. Christ! They can move, can't they?"

"Three," Erin corrected her, looking weary. "Can you use my range with your definition? I know we've never—"

"Dunno. Let's try it."

They sucked in their breath in unison.

"Dammit!" Sarah exploded.

"Oh, Sarah. I taught you better language than that. It's a fucking war," Erin breathed. "I'm not good at separating the mists. How many is that?"

"We'll discuss it in the Stone room." Sarah jogged from the room with Mikel on her hip, staring back at Erin expectantly.

"How many, Sarah?" she demanded, walking as quickly as she could manage after her friend.

"I stopped counting at forty. Does that tell you anything?"

Erin froze in shock.

Curt wrapped an arm around her, guiding Erin toward the training room and the safety of the Stone. "Come on, Erin. He's not getting anywhere near you. I promise."

He could see the terror in her eyes. "Stay with me," she pleaded.

"I can't. You know I can't."

"For some moldy code of honor? The hell with it!" Erin pulled his hand over the mound of their babies. "I need you, Curt. I need you alive and with us. Protect us. Stay with us and protect us."

"I won't die. Do you honestly think the rest of these guys would let that happen?"

"This is Lorian. You don't understand what he'll do. I can't lose you."

"You're right. You can't. You won't, but I have to do this," he explained patiently.

Erin pushed him away violently, pulling back tears. "You don't have to. You'd leave me to raise our children alone for this crap. Go away, Curt. I'm going in there so I'll at least have—" Her eyes widened. She turned without finishing her thought and stormed away from him.

"Erin!" Curt's mind whirled at her reaction, and his heart hurt at her anger with him, her dismissal.

"It's okay," Hunter told him. "Let's go."

"I don't get it. Explain it to me," he pleaded with his brother-in-law as they headed back to the living room. "Is it just that she can't battle?" They hadn't had to since Erin was banned from it, but Curt had seen her shunted out of a battle before and not seen this reaction.

Hunter shook his head. "The last time Lorian came for her, she used that parting line on me. Erin loves you. Of everyone here, she's afraid Lorian wants to take you out to hurt her. She'll get over it. After all, if you can down me..." He smiled.

"Erin told me your holes," Curt admitted.

Hunter laughed nervously. "Yeah. We'll discuss that later. Right now, we have a war brewing." He shook his head. "I knew it was bad news when Lewis ordered us all here, but I didn't think it was this bad. He ordered me to bring my whole family, after all. If your father survives this, I'm going to beat him unconscious for dragging my wife and son into this."

Talon looked up as they came back in. "All settled?" he asked.

Hunter nodded. "Erin knows what to do."

"I hope she follows orders this time," her father grumbled.

Jayde loped into the room, passing out spare blades. "Okay. We have this room. Kord, Lewis, Adam, Terrin Kaufmann, and Alex Armen have the library. Garrett and Joel Hunter, William Farmer, and Patrick Smith have the kitchen."

"No," Adam replied from the doorway as he made his way to them. "I've moved William to the library. I'm with you."

"Why?" Curt asked in confusion.

"Because she needs you to survive. Erin may not accept my protection, but she'll let me keep your butt alive. I owe her this one. Whether she likes it or not, I'm repaying my debt."

Curt stiffened and met his eyes evenly. "I don't need you as a babysitter, Adam. Take a hike."

"Uh-uh. Stone orders, I march. I keep your shoulder."

Talon chuckled heartily. "Boy, does this sound familiar. Take my advice, guys. Adam, stay out of his way. Curt's protecting his wife and children. Curt, let him help. Quit arguing and get ready to battle."

Jayde straightened and pulled her blades. "Like right now, gentlemen. Here they come."

Curt watched in shock as the high-levels started materializing. There seemed an endless army of them arriving. He cursed soundly. Sarah had stopped counting at forty. There were more than forty crowded in the room and hallway with more fanned out around the other groups of Warriors.

Was it too much to hope that a higher than average concentration was sent here because it was the *Königs* they would be fighting? Curt shuddered in the realization that it probably wasn't that simple. Only the fact that Sarah, Mikel, Erin, and his babies were safe from harm calmed him for what was coming. Surely, no one else would survive this night.

There were more than ten to one. Ten humans or even low-levels to one Warrior of caliber at a shot—even ten highs spread out over hours wouldn't be unthinkable. But, more than ten highs at once to each Warrior was a death sentence. Perhaps, if all the Warriors were in one place, they could form a fight ring and hold off a few survivors until morning. Possibly, but they weren't.

For what seemed an endless period of time, beast and Warrior faced off without moving a muscle. The beasts held their ground patiently, as if waiting for a signal to move.

"Why aren't they attacking," Curt whispered to Hunter.

The older man shrugged. "I don't like this. They're up to something."

"What? Sarah and Erin are protected. The children are protected. They know they're safe with the Stone, and they won't come out. Will they?"

"I think Erin has learned her lesson about that. I hope she has." Hunter grimaced. "Okay, this is Erin. Let us protect you. If they hurt you, they may have a chance of snaring her somehow."

Talon moved forward until he was even with Adam. "Name yourself and tell us where your master is," he demanded.

A blonde, green-eyed beast laughed, showing his fangs. "I am Gruber. I'd introduce my friends, but that would take far too much time. You don't really need to know our names, do you?"

"Considering the circumstances, I think the name of the spokesman is sufficient. Where's your master? What is this madness?"

"Lorian is close. We have no plan. We are here to defend ourselves only. If you don't attack, we don't harm you. If we stand here until the dawn breaks and we are forced to ground in pain, that's what we do."

"What's the point?" Curt asked in annoyance. "This doesn't bode well," he added to Hunter under his breath.

"Lorian has personal business with your women. You are to stay out of the way. That's why we are here." He shrugged as if in disinterest.

"That's impossible," Adam decided. "The Stone protects them. Even an elder can't approach them now."

"With malice, that is true," Gruber agreed. "It amazes me how little you understand about the Stone when you've had it all these years."

An ear-splitting scream ripped through the house.

"Sarah," Hunter breathed. "Please, let it just be a face at the window or door." The last was said so softly, Curt almost didn't hear it.

"Don't touch her," Erin's voice demanded. "Stand down!"

Adam turned and pulled Curt to the floor, as he

launched for the beast army.

The younger man suddenly found himself buried in Warriors. "It's Erin. I have to get to her," he reasoned. "You have to let me go."

Curt roared out his frustration as one of the amulets repelled an attack. Which amulet was an uncertain thing. It could be Sarah's or Mikel's as easily as Erin's. Sarah screamed again, not in pain but in terror. He struggled against the hands holding him with increasing desperation.

Jayde cradled his head. "You have to release it, Curt. Listen to me. We're going to lead you to her. You go unarmed and guarded. Hunter will give you an amulet. If you don't fight, they won't. Their plan depends on you attacking. If you love her, you won't attack. Do you understand me?"

Curt nodded slowly, releasing his bloodlust despite the sound of battling from other areas of the house. *Please. Not Erin. It's too early for her to go into labor.* "If I do this, Hunter does it, too. We both get to our wives alive. Agreed?"

"I can't. I'm a true elder hunter," the Lord Crossbearer whispered fiercely, his jaw tight. Still, his gaze flicked toward the hallway and the Stone room beyond.

Adam reached into his pocket. "Actually, you can and you will. My father sent a Maher lord's amulet with me. He sent me here to fight—or I suppose not to fight, and he said I would know what he gave me this for. It's for you, Hunter. Put it on."

Hunter looked at him in shock. "The Stone ordered him to do this?"

"Must have."

Hunter nodded and dropped the offered amulet over his head, tucking it beneath his shirts. He settled Curt's over his head. "Now yours," he ordered. "Tuck it so it can't be severed."

Hands released him, and Curt did as he was ordered.

Adam dragged him to his feet and nodded slowly. "We'll get you there," he promised.

"Your weapons," Talon ordered. "Both of you."

The pair flashed each other pained expressions as they handed over their belts.

Hunter squared his shoulders as the other Warriors surrounded them. "I feel like an idiot," he growled. "Twelve years of training for what? When the chips are down, I have to act like a child before first night."

Curt grinned. "At least I'm not forced into this as a *König* born." He sobered slightly. "I'll swallow my pride, if it gets us our wives and children."

Hunter nodded his agreement. "Let's go."

* * * *

Erin found the largest belt she could and loaded it with three training blades, then strapped it low over her hips and under her babies. The training weights were essential for the grip size, but she cringed at the loss of mass compared to her own weapons.

Sarah watched her nervously. "You're not really going to use those, are you? In your condition?"

"Only if I have to," Erin assured her.

"You can't leave this room. You know that."

"I'm well aware of that fact. I have no intentions of

making that mistake again."

"Then, why would you need them?" Sarah persisted.

"I never trust beasts. Lorian is up to something. Attacking now with so many? He knows we'll be in this room. He'd have to. He knows my condition and the fact that you have Mikel here. No, he has a plan."

"Maybe, he thought we wouldn't see him coming. Maybe, he thought we'd be out in the house somewhere," she suggested hopefully.

Erin shook her head. "Not a chance. Between the two of us, he knew we'd be secluded in here. So, what is he up to?"

Sarah shrugged. "Beasts can't enter here. Not even elders. I can't see what plan he could possibly have."

"He's got something up his sleeve. I don't know what, but I have a feeling we're not going to enjoy it."

Sarah's eyes widened. "Christ! They're here. They're everywhere, and they're still arriving."

"How many?"

"If they ever stop coming, I'll let you know." Sarah sounded slightly panicked.

"Where's Lorian?"

"He's still floating around out there, waiting for his troops to get in place."

"How many? Give me an idea, here," Erin demanded.

"We have thirteen plus the three of us."

"I know that! What about them?"

Sarah swallowed hard and shook her head. "Call it ten to one. It would be close enough to the truth."

Erin couldn't tell if the sick swirl she was experiencing was her own or Sarah's. From the moment she hooked in to see it for herself, Erin knew Lorian had outdone himself. She closed off the connection with a sob. She couldn't watch it.

"It will be all right," Sarah whispered. "I know Hunter can handle ten."

Erin crossed to her and hugged her, though whether she was seeking comfort or giving it, she wasn't sure. She furrowed her brow. There was no battle. What were the Warriors doing? Taking every name out there in preparation?

Sarah sucked in her breath and pointed a shaky finger at the Stone pedestal. Erin followed her line of sight, turning with a hand on the hilt of her right blade. Standing next to the Stone, large as life, was Lorian.

The beast smiled his rows of perfect, white teeth, his fangs retracted. "Good evening, ladies," he crooned. "Both of my mates in the same place. How convenient for me."

Sarah let out a squeak of protest, but Erin only narrowed her eyes.

"It's an illusion," she decided. "He can't come here." To prove her point, Erin threw one of her blades.

Lorian caught it. The stench of beast blood filled the air. The elder threw the blade aside and raised his hand to show the deep, flowing cut on his palm.

Sarah took an unsteady step back. "I tried to tell you. That is not an illusion," she breathed.

"I can see that. Don't scream. He wants us to scream to cause turmoil."

Lorian reached his cut hand toward the Stone, and Erin held her breath, her eyes widening in shock.

The beast laughed. "You think I can't touch the

Stone?" he taunted. "The Stone and I are old acquaintances. It stole my soul and made me what I am today."

Erin laughed harshly. "You gave your life. You offered it in fair trade for practical immortality and invulnerability. You lasted the longest. I think it was a fair trade."

Lorian's eyes narrowed. "It wasn't remotely," he informed her coolly. "Promises were made and broken. I thought I would still have my property, my freedom, and the right to choose a woman. I thought I was giving up so little: the sun, food, and children."

"Emotions, your soul..." Erin drawled. "Cut the act, Lorian."

Lorian laid his hand on the Stone, and Erin shuddered at the sight of it.

"Now the promises can be made right. I can have everything I was promised and more." He smiled at them, a smile that seemed open and honest. "You remember what I showed you, Erin? Despite your belief, it's all I've ever lived for."

His hand slid off the Stone, leaving a smear of his foul blood that she ached to wipe away. As if the Stone agreed, blue fire lit it momentarily. When the fire receded, the smudge was gone with it, and she thanked the god Dobler for that gift.

Erin met his eyes again, letting his speech sink in. "I'm printed now. Nothing you do can change that. We print for life. You know that."

"I'm capable of more than you can imagine. I can take you in a way that your body and mind, even your soul won't recognize the difference."

Erin shuddered at the concept. "Impossible," she

decided.

"Very possible. Nothing is beyond me."

"Except love and caring, watching the sun rise, enjoying a meal lovingly prepared for you—"

"You think I can't express love? You think I can't touch another in tenderness?" He moved toward them smoothly, silently. "Such things are not beyond me. I am capable of differentiating between things that cause you pleasure and those that cause you pain. I can live forever causing you pleasure."

Sarah clamped her free hand on Erin's shoulder, tugging gently to remind her to back away from the elder as he came for them. Sarah's voice was sure and strong. "I concede that you can. Why would you want to?"

Lorian shook his head sadly. "No emotions. Erin accused me of having no emotion, but you're wrong."

"No kind emotion, then," Erin qualified quietly, trying not to panic the cornered Warriors. "You feel no kind emotions, so why would you want to evoke them?"

Lorian moved suddenly. His hand reached for Sarah's cheek. She ducked further behind Erin with Mikel in her arms, screaming in terror, knowing what shattering pain his touch would bring.

Erin lunged her blades at him, forcing the elder back. "Don't touch her. Stand down," she ordered.

The beast nodded grimly. "That hurts, Erin. Your mistrust wounds me. Your blades cause me pain. I feel loneliness and grief. I want! I crave! I long for companionship and touch, a simple kind eye. Is that so hard to understand?"

"Why? What happiness can it possibly give you?" she inquired, still shaking lightly from the close call with Sarah.

"None," he admitted. "Not in the way you feel it, but it would give me respite from the emptiness and hurt. Even that would be bliss of a sort after these long centuries."

"Why us? Choose a human woman we don't expect. It would be easy enough for you," she reasoned.

"I want," he repeated. "I want children. The two of you are the only women that can provide children for me."

Erin ran a hand over her squirming babies nervously. "Why now?" she breathed. He was going to use her babies against her somehow. She could feel it.

"You're close to term. It will be easy now. I have only to take you into my custody with no fears of you losing that which you carry."

"What difference would it make? You can't possibly want another man's children."

"Not in the way you believe. I want my own, but I can be kind because of your feelings, and you are mortal. I can't change that fact. If I'm right..."

Lorian lunged suddenly. Erin held her ground to shield Sarah. His hand barely brushed her cheek, the merest whisper of a touch, but the force sent her staggering back into Sarah and Mikel before she could regain her balance. Sarah's scream of fear echoed in Erin's ears, as the beast smiled widely and backed away from Erin's flashing blades again.

He laughed. "You carry my next mate within you, just as I'd hoped you would. I heard musings that you carried twins, but I thought the information at fault."

Erin backed further into Sarah for comfort, her hand splayed over her babies, her mind in a riot. There had been ultrasounds. Of course, there were. They knew that at least one of the babies was a boy. In four attempts, they had only seen equipment on one baby. By the last time, Jeremy had theorized that both of them were boys, and they were simply seeing whichever baby felt like being social that day.

She groaned at the thought that Lorian might be right as much as the completely ridiculous thought that if they made it out of this, girl clothing would have to be purchased. Everything they'd bought had been for little boys.

The mental riot intensified as impressions of the battle outside the door reached her mind via Sarah's shimmers. Kord and Lewis were both dead. Garret, Colin Hunter's youngest son, was dead. Patrick was gravely wounded. Miraculously, the rest were still alive.

She looked at Sarah. *How many? What's the score?*

Sarah shook her head. *{They've only lost twenty-five so far. The sheer numbers we're facing make this impossible.}*

Erin furrowed her brow. *That makes no sense. With the Königs wading in, the body count should be much higher. What is going on out there?*

[They know the secret of winning. They are making their way to you with no violence.]

Erin's eyes widened, and she snapped a look at Sarah, but the voice wasn't hers. She knew it wasn't.

The older woman looked at her in confusion. *{What is it?}*

Are you hooked in to me fully?

{Are you kidding? Of course I am!}

You didn't hear that? You didn't sense it?

{Sense what?}

Who are you?

{Fear. Erin, don't crack on me.}

Shush! There's someone else in my mind.

{Who?}

Shut up and let me find out!

{Sheepish apologetic agreement...}

Who are you?

Only silence met her.

Why are they using no violence?

[To approach the Stone, the beasts must intend no violence. They cannot attack, though they may defend themselves.]

Who are you?

Silence again.

Where are you?

[In you. Lewis of Maher is gone, now. You are the new chosen one, the holder of all I am, all the power I possess.] The voice said it simply, a serene statement of fact.

The Stone!

A faint sense of amusement flavored the link, but it was strained and somewhat brittle around the edges. *[Yes, young one.]*

But my mark... It's not Syth.

Erin's mind seized on the truth. There was no Syth. Another hadn't been born. They'd assumed Lewis would live a long life, because his replacement hadn't been born. Had anyone realized that? There was no Syth, and the Stone lord was dead.

[You are correct. There is no need of a Syth, now.]

"What are you up to?" Lorian demanded.

"Watching the battle," Sarah informed him. *{Whatever you're doing, do it fast. He's getting edgy on* *us.}*

"And you?" he asked Erin pointedly.

"The same." *What must I do?*

[Come to me to claim your power. Cross your blades and touch them to the surface of the Stone. I will instruct you.]

Erin nodded and backed Sarah away at an angle toward the Stone.

Lorian followed, cocking his head and narrowing his eyes suspiciously. "What are you doing?"

"Getting breathing room," Erin snapped. "Your breath smells like centuries of death."

"A small fault that is easily remedied." He shrugged, allowing them a bit more distance since they were headed away from the door.

Erin placed the pedestal between them, and Lorian smiled a predatory smile.

"You think that small barrier means anything to me?"

"Probably not. What's your plan?" she countered. Erin needed to get him off balance, unready for her move. "For the sake of our children, you cannot force us to give up our amulets. What will you do when the sun rises or when our family reaches us? You cannot resort to violence, or you lose."

His smile disappeared, and his eyes glinted dangerously. "How can you know that?"

"Sarah is a telepath. She read it from Lewis's mind and told me," Erin lied smoothly.

Sarah's hand tightened on the back of her shirt. *{Who really told you?}*

Don't ask what you don't want to know. Reassurance.

{Him? You're connected to that beast? Panic and disbelief.}

Don't be ridiculous!

Lorian's fangs extended, wavered, and retreated, peeking into then out of his sneer. "If Lewis of Maher knew it, why didn't he heed it?"

Sarah laughed weakly. "He didn't ask the Stone, until it was too late," she lied. "Leave it to a man not to stop and get directions." *{What are you doing? You're tensing.}*

Break off, now.

{What? Confusion and unease.}

I don't want backwash on you. I don't think it's possible, but I can't take that chance. You need to break off before I do this.

{I'm leaving. Don't get us killed.}

Erin waited a long moment before meeting Lorian's eyes again. "What's your plan, Lorian? You can't win this one. There can be no battle in this room. You know that. All we have to do is wait you out."

"You don't have the time." His smile returned and widened. "You give birth tonight. Already, you feel discomfort. You know you do. If they try to remove you from this room, the rules of engagement change. It will be a standoff. The question is...who will yield the battle first?"

Erin searched her memories. She ached, but she had attributed it to stress and exhaustion. There was nothing that she would have labeled as labor pains.

She raised her chin in challenge. "I never yield." Without warning, she crossed her blades before her face and laid them over the Stone.

Somewhere in the distance, Erin could hear her

mother's voice.

"No," Lorian bellowed.

He surged for her as the flash of blue fire enveloped Erin's whole world. As her eyes fluttered closed, she saw the elder tossed away from them, his outstretched hand blackened and smoking.

He intended harm, her mind supplied numbly.

[Welcome, daughter.] The Stone's voice was more natural this way, with the contact. *[I have waited countless centuries for you. So many times, the plan has gone awry, because I tire. With you, I find true rest. There will be no more wars, no more beasts, no more pact to defend. All will be freed this time.]*

How? What must I do?

[Learn.] Information, boundless and pure, poured through the blue mist and into Erin. Time lost all meaning. The Stone's history flowed through her, countless battles reaching back to pre-first cursed history. This wasn't the second beast war or even the third, though it was the longest. So many plans which had been foiled over the years— The Stone had been thwarted again and again, Her plans disrupted so that the end was long in coming.

How? You are all powerful!

[No. I tire. I am weary and in need of rest. Man shall lose my protection, but he shall also lose the threat I pose. I die.]

It's not over, yet! Panic.

[Calm. You and yours shall be the end, once my threat is gone.]

How?

[Learn.] The stream of information started again. The Stone's power and limitations flowed into her.

Even in Her weakened state, the depth of that power was almost unfathomable. A plan took shape, a frightening plan.

I can't!

[Then, all is lost.] The voice was weary, sad. *[I cannot force your compliance.]*

What will happen to me? To my babies, if I do this?

[See what will be. You are my peace.]

An ocean of light washed over Erin, bringing images of the future the Stone would write, if she agreed.

[Will you be my salvation?] The voice was a mere whisper, full of desperate longing.

I thought no one could do what you're showing me.

[Unless I wish it. Only to grant me death. Will you grant me the death I seek? You know I am incapable of lying to you. Will you?]

The timeless, powerful stone was begging favors of Erin? The thought shook her. *I am ever your servant.*

A light caress touched her mind. *[Laughter. Love. Then, do what you must, my child. I have given you the power you will need to complete your task—with my deepest gratitude.]*

The blue light faded away, and Erin collapsed to her knees, fighting for an end to the flat spin her senses were in. She dragged air into her lungs painfully, seeking for the way back to her current reality.

Sarah's hand rubbed her back. "Erin, snap out of it," she pleaded. "Erin, come back to me. He's pissed."

She raised her head, staring at the enflamed elder.

Enflamed. Flames were dancing in his black eyes, and his fangs were bared in a look of pure fury.

"What have you done?" he raged at her. His voice seemed to vibrate the walls.

"My duty," she whispered as she pushed to her feet. "The duty I was born to." Her amulet burned on her wrist.

[You know your course.]

I am your servant. Erin prayed that the Stone wouldn't fail this time.

[We are one, a force unto ourselves. With your strength and my aid and knowledge, we cannot fail. Balk me in nothing, and we will prevail.]

How strange her life had become. Erin was agreeing to follow the Stone with unquestioning loyalty when little more than a half a year ago, her only wish had been to balk Her in any way she could. The irony was almost too much to bear without laughing out loud.

Erin met Lorian's eyes and nodded in challenge. She handed the right training blade to Mikel. As always, the child took the strange turn of events in stride, unnaturally calm and collected about anything life threw at him. It occurred to Erin that he hadn't made a sound since Lorian's approach, even while his mother had been screaming and dodging the elder.

She nodded to him. "You know what to do," Erin said in complete confidence.

He raised his jaw proudly and gave a slight nod that lifted her lips in a smile.

Sarah tightened her grip on her son. "He's a child," she pleaded.

Erin touched his face fondly. "He's more than that, and you know it. Put him down, Sarah. Trust me on this one. Would I ever hurt him?"

Mikel smiled at his mother's obvious distress and kissed her cheek. "It's all right," he assured her. "Trust Aunt Erin."

Sarah released her son to the floor with a groan. "I'm going to regret this," she decided.

Mikel took her hand and smiled. "No, you won't," he promised solemnly.

Erin laughed lightly as she turned back to Lorian. Her smile widened, as the elder looked at all of them suspiciously.

"What's the matter, Lorian? Not so sure anymore, are you?" Her free hand moved to unbuckle her bracer.

Sarah gripped her arm. "Are you insane?" she screeched.

Erin peeled her hand away easily. "Trust me. I know what I'm doing."

Sarah shook her head in disbelief and horror. "No! You can't do this. Hunter!"

Erin covered her mouth. *The Stone is directing me. She won't let any of us come to harm. Trust me.*

Sarah nodded and stepped away. *{You better be right, or both of our husbands will skin me alive for letting you do this.}*

How would you stop me? Amusement. I am right. Relax.

{Yeah, right!} Her inner voice was miserable.

Erin finished removing her bracer and pulled her amulet off. It glowed vivid blue as she tied it around the hilt of the weapon Mikel held. She touched the blade fondly, feeling the power beating in the metal already. "Wielded by mine, swing always true," Erin breathed the simple blessing and prayer combined.

"It will," Mikel replied calmly.

She turned to face Lorian again.

The elder's face was steeped in his perceived victory. "You're mine," he gloated.

Erin laughed in amusement. "You think the Stone will ever let you touch me, now?"

"Being Stone lord didn't save Corwyn Lord Hunter or Lewis of Maher," he noted confidently.

"You were drawn by my blood mark, Lorian," she crooned. "Distinctive, is it not?"

He faltered. His smile disappeared. "It is," he admitted.

Erin glided toward him, still graceful despite the formidable mound of her pregnant belly that jutted out before her. "You remember the ancient language, of course. My mother's symbol was that of Ani. She's the mother of the true elder slayers. Do you remember what my mark is?"

Lorian took a step back, his pale skin turning ashen. "Zel," he breathed.

"Zel," she agreed. "Do you remember what Zel denotes, Lorian?"

"An ending," he supplied.

"Death," she corrected him. "Only in death are you freed. I am death, Lorian. You wish an end to your suffering and want. I am that freedom, as my mother was Veriel's."

She advanced on him smoothly, her eyes narrowing as he started to retreat. His eyes widened in shock, and she knew the source of his dismay immediately.

"No tricks here, Lorian. None of your powers will work now."

Erin threw her remaining blade away as she closed

on him, smiling at Sarah's squeak of fear. She had no need of the weapon for this fight and she knew it. "You are unarmed. I am unarmed. I am Zel, Lorian. It is my duty and honor to deliver you to justice."

The killing blow, when it came, came from behind him...silently. Lorian sank to his knees and looked at the Warrior who'd taken his heart in detached understanding.

Erin circled him silently and took Mikel's hand, her chin raised proudly. She knelt next to her nephew and used the blood coating the weapon ripped from Lorian's heart to paint the blood seals on Mikel. The child stood soberly, the vision of a proud young Warrior, while she accomplished her task.

She met Lorian's dying eyes and smiled sadly. "I free you, brother. I am Zel, and I deliver you into the hands of Jee." She uncovered the blood mark on Mikel's ribcage. "Meet Jee, Lorian Dado. As you recall, he is called Justice."

A single tear wound down the elder's face, as she led Mikel back to his mother. Erin felt the life leave Lorian's body. The Stone glowed a brilliant blue, and all hell broke loose beyond the door.

Chapter Twenty-six

Curt held his breath as the group surged forth into the waiting beasts. Gruber bared his teeth in annoyance, but as Jayde surmised, he could do nothing as long as the Warriors didn't attack. The beasts paced them, pressing in shoulder to shoulder and seething barely controlled fury at Curt and Hunter as they moved within the group.

"It's working," Adam stated in disbelief as he brushed past another beast.

"Of course," Jayde replied in a smug, rather amused tone.

"Oh, doesn't Hans look happy," Hunter taunted Gruber.

Curt nodded, a jerky motion in his restraint. "Just get me to my wife," he growled.

He felt the deaths of the other Warriors, and the remaining voices identified the dead. *My father. Kord.* They were both gone. "Adam, you better damned well stay alive," he breathed.

His brother shook his head slowly. "I didn't want this."

Hunter sighed. "I was younger. So was Corwyn. You'll do fine."

"Better than Bryant," Curt added. His heart started to pound, as the beasts closed in behind their group. "I refuse to offer up allegiance to him."

"You don't have to, *König*-Maher," Adam drawled.

Curt's heart sank. *Only if Erin survives this.* He was only *König* with his wife and children. If he didn't have them, Curt would be only a Maher—one hell-bent on his own death, at that!

Jayde screamed directions over the sound of fighting, and the house fell quiet, as the other Warriors lowered their weapons and started moving slowly through the throng of beasts.

"No," Lorian bellowed.

A clap of thunder shook the house, followed by a string of curses from Sarah. Then there was dead silence from the direction of the Stone room.

Hunter restrained Curt bodily. "He's not happy, but he can't hurt her. Stay cool," he breathed. "With no malice, remember?"

Curt nodded shakily and started moving forward again. "He's hurt," he realized. It wasn't the minor injury Lorian had sustained the first time around. This one was deeper. It was something that wouldn't heal unless he went to ground, but it wasn't a mortal wound either.

"Not badly," Adam qualified, coming to the same conclusion he had.

They were into the hallway, and the Warriors left alive in the library had crowded around them to close in the two young husbands, when the next outburst came from the back.

Sarah's voice was high-pitched and panicked. "Erin, snap out of it. Erin, come back to me. He's pissed."

Curt glared at Gruber as the beast laughed at the outburst, no doubt believing that Lorian had the upper hand and Erin was unable to fight him. He cursed inwardly, praying it wasn't another mind-fuck like the one Lorian had laid on her the first time. She wouldn't deal well with it, if it was.

Their positions reversed, as Lorian responded.

"What have you done?" he stormed.

"Something he hates," Curt decided. "What else would she do?"

Sarah's next outburst chilled him. She was beyond panic into terror. "Are you insane?"

"Erin," Curt groaned. "What are you doing?"

"You married her," Hunter dismissed his complaint.

"And you didn't warn me," he shot back in annoyance. Erin may be stuck improvising, but Curt didn't have to like it.

Sarah's voice was frantic now. "No! You can't do this. Hunter!"

Terrin and William immobilized the two Warriors, while Gruber took up his mocking laughter again.

"Relax," Talon growled at them. "We'll be there in just a few minutes."

Joel and Patrick slid into the procession and nodded to the other Warriors.

Joel laughed nervously. "If only my father was alive to see this. He wouldn't believe it was possible," he decided.

They inched toward the door to the training room and the Stone. The beasts got increasingly restless as the silence from the room deepened. Erin struck a blow—a bad one, but the beast still lived.

"I don't like this," Curt breathed. "They're getting antsy."

Hunter nodded. "It's coming apart," he agreed. "Why is it coming apart?"

Several of the beasts roared, as Lorian died.

"Ah, shit," Adam breathed. "She killed him."

"Uh, that's good news, right?" Joel asked. "I mean, turneds can't turn new beasts. It will take a while, but it's essentially over."

"Good for the women and children. Bad for us," Terrin grumbled, summing up the problem perfectly.

While most of the beasts surged toward the Warriors, Gruber faded back toward the closed door.

"Come on," Curt ordered Hunter. "We have to get to him."

"How?" he asked in frustration, bracing Patrick up, as a beast tried to force him back.

Curt laughed and punched a beast over Talon's shoulder. It launched back into the two behind it as Curt skidded into Hunter. "Just like a battering ram," he mused as he pushed past Talon and started striking blows with a vicious smile. "Didn't your sister teach you anything useful?" he teased. He barely registered that Hunter was following him into the throng, until they bumped together several times.

"This is insane," Hunter complained. "Why am I doing this? Remind me, please!"

"No sense of adventure," Curt joked as he plowed another two beasts away with a right jab.

"You have to have a sense of adventure to put up with my sister—and a sense of humor. She would find this hysterical."

The remaining beasts parted before them, as the door opened. Curt surged into the room, breathing hard...and stopped short.

Erin leaned against the Stone pedestal, looking cool and unruffled for all the squawking from the room. A few feet away, Lorian lay crumpled on the floor.

"Mikel," Hunter breathed.

Curt trailed his gaze over the four-year-old child in shock. Mikel had a training weapon clenched in his tiny fists, and his eyes were locked on the motionless beast taking in the scene. The blade was fouled with Lorian's blood, and the blood seals were painted on him carefully. An amulet was wrapped around the hilt of the weapon.

He diverted his attention back to his wife. Her bracer was gone. Her amulet was gone. The cold look of battle was in her eyes as she stared at Gruber.

"Sarah?" Hunter asked quietly, at a loss to make sense of any of it, Curt was sure.

"Uh...l-long story. Whatever Erin does, follow her lead. Trust me." Sarah looked slightly shell-shocked.

"Mikel killed Lorian?" he asked in confusion.

"We've raised an elder killer, honey." She shrugged and continued in a shaky voice. "He's a little young for first night, I guess—"

Mikel motioned his weapon toward Lorian slowly. "Gramma would say Aunt Erin had the assist on this one," he offered the family joke lightly. He motioned his weapon back to Gruber. "You should leave, beast. You don't know what you face. Lorian ran from Aunt Erin." He lifted the corner of his mouth in amusement. "It didn't do him any good, but you might win yourself a few more minutes of life."

Erin chuckled at Mikel's speech, fully more than Curt had heard him say in the six months they'd spent in Cross earlier in the pregnancy combined, and Sarah visited with the *Königs* often.

"Now, Mikel," she chided him. "Don't tease the poor beast. He actually believes he has a chance. Touch the

Stone and become the new Veriel, right?"

"Erin, don't get too cocky," Hunter reminded her. He glanced from his son to his sister warily, still trying to piece together the strange events.

"Actually," Sarah offered, "you have no idea just how much right she has to be superior right now."

"What's your name, beast?" Erin asked.

"Gruber," he growled. "You think to stop me? An unarmed, unprotected," he cast a sneer at Mikel, "pregnant woman?" He laughed as he stepped toward her.

Curt started to throw himself toward her, but she motioned Hunter to stop him, and Curt found himself pinned to the older man's chest.

Erin sighed. "You forgot *König*-Crossbearer born, elder hunter, *Blutjagdfrau*, Stone lord, and Zel personified."

Curt sucked in his breath and stopped fighting in his shock. "Stone lord?"

Sarah nodded her head in a jerky motion.

"Zel? How is Zel personified?"

"Uh, part of that long story. Death personified was a little too scary for Lorian." Sarah flicked an uneasy glance at Erin then at her son. "By the way, honey... You never explained what Jee personified would be like. We need to have a talk."

Hunter shot a startled look from Erin to Mikel, as if the idea that both of them bore the unique symbols hadn't occurred to him before. "Jee and Zel as a team in battle? Gruber, you may want to back off."

He said it laughing hysterically, and Curtis was uncertain whether or not Hunter had cracked at the implication of the destructive force or even at who was wielding it in battle. Surely, no one could guess that a pregnant woman and a child could be frightening, until you considered what they represented.

"Is that it, Gruber?" Erin asked him in a singsong voice. "Do you want to be the new Veriel? Do you want to touch the Stone?"

Erin traced her fingers over the pedestal again and again. What seemed an aimless movement took form with repetition. The mark of Zel, Erin's symbol, was traced in a visual mantra, while Gruber stared at the motion, spellbound.

He seemed to find his voice abruptly, shaking his head as if coming out of a trance. "You know I do."

She nodded. "Okay. Mikel, go see your mother. Let me handle this." Erin smiled indulgently as the child scowled at her and stormed back to his mother's arms.

Sarah backed toward the far corner, shielding her son in her arms, as if she expected a bolt of lightening to strike.

Erin ambled to the back of the pedestal and waved an arm in welcome. "Touch it, Gruber—if you dare."

Curt shook his head, trying to clear the situation for himself. The elders were trapped. Why set them free again? "Uh—Erin, is this a good idea?" he asked urgently.

"Trust me. This is the best idea I've had all day."

Sarah erupted in a sound between a snort and a sob. "One more of your great ideas and I may die of fright."

"Relax. I promised not to get us killed," Erin argued.

"Actually, you never promised it, as I recall."

"I promise, then. Back off! This isn't as easy as it

looks."

"You think?" Sarah quipped.

Erin rolled her eyes and scowled at Gruber. "Yes or no, Gruber? Carte blanche. Touch it."

The beast hissed at her in warning, his fangs extended. He moved forward, locking his eyes on the Stone and relinquishing his attention on Erin for the first time since she'd made the offer. She snapped her eyes to Curt's and motioned with her head for him to move. Without question, he grabbed Hunter by the shoulder and dragged him halfway across the room.

Gruber smiled triumphantly and reached for the Stone. The blue flash and the thunderclap seemed to fill the room. The beast flew backward into the wall Hunter and Curt had vacated with a sickening crunch that announced major injury. His hands were burned, blistered, and smoking. He screamed and stretched his hands out to her wordlessly, confused and frightened.

Erin smiled. "Did you think it was so simple? You are already damned, and you weren't damned by the Stone. It amazes me how little you know about the Stone when you seek to possess it."

She moved to the pedestal, bowing her head reverently. "As your servant, I stand. Find peace, old friend." Erin pulled the Stone from its base and cradled it in her hands.

Curt screamed her name in shock and dismay and tried to bolt for her.

Hunter tackled him. "It's too late. Whatever she's done, we can't stop it now. Just pray she knows what she's doing," Hunter breathed close to his ear.

"She can't," Curt managed, pulling back sobs. "No one can touch the Stone, not even the Stone lord. Even he can only use the clamps."

"Let's hope you're wrong."

The blue glow from the Stone enveloped Erin's body, and she closed her eyes and seemed to drink it in. Curt gave up trying to count the seconds she stood motionless. Time lost all meaning. He watched her, terrified that he and her family would be forced to destroy Erin when it was over.

The glow sank into her skin, and Erin dropped her chin to her chest. Her hands clenched around the Stone, now dull and lifeless, and it disintegrated into dust and sifted through her fingers to the floor.

She raised her eyes to her husband and brother, and Curt drew in his breath sharply. Her eyes glowed the same icy blue as the glow that had surrounded the Stone moments—minutes—hours before.

"Everything's fine," she soothed him. "The Stone is at peace. The elders are destroyed. They can never be freed again. When it's over, it's over for good this time. Zel, the end of an era and death personified, has come. When the last beast dies, there will never be another Cursed Warrior or beast."

Gruber barreled at her in a rage, screaming his frustration. Erin held up her hand, and the beast found himself held a little more than two yards from her, beating at an invisible wall.

"Do you know why the sacred weapons kill?" she asked sadly. "Why you can't use your powers when one is planted in you?"

Gruber hissed and beat at the wall harder, declining to answer her and desperate to get to her. His mutterings gave an indication of a portion of his frustration. He couldn't dematerialize. He was well and truly trapped where she wanted him.

"It's not the metal we use. It's a simple iron tainted with carbon. The difference is in the blade. Every blade is touched by the Stone's glow after it's shaped, forged in the blue fire."

Erin scooped a training blade off of the floor awkwardly and ran her palm over the flat of the blade. It glowed with the Stone's fire just as she had. She set it on the pedestal reverently.

"The blade does damage, but it's the Stone's power that kills and that renders the powers stolen from it originally useless. That's why another blade will bleed you to ground when your heart is taken, but a sacred weapon kills."

"The Stone is dead," Gruber growled. "The Warriors are powerless to stop us now."

Erin opened her hand, palm up, and a ball of blue energy crackled in the center. "The fire is what kills. The power lives on." She blew across her palm, a sensuous move, and the ball shot toward the beast, passing easily through the barrier and burning a hole where his heart once was.

Gruber looked at the hole in shock, a move Curt had seen many beasts make after their heart was taken. He crumpled to the floor, reaching his hand to her in an unspoken question.

"I free you," Erin whispered.

Her head snapped around, at the rising sound of battle in the hall. She raised both hands and threw her head back. A shock wave of blue light exploded out from her position. Curt flinched as it passed by him, but it merely tingled a warm trail over his skin that was entirely too enjoyable for something he would assume was deadly. Erin sank to her knees with her hands over the swell of their children and dropped her chin to her chest, panting in exhaustion, sweat coating her body.

In the hall, Jayde screamed in shock. A riot of other voices tumbled over each other. Curt heard them dimly, some clearer than others.

"What the hell was that?" Terrin demanded.

"Who cares?" Adam decided. "They're dead. Are you complaining?"

"No way," Joel asserted.

"Did you feel that?" Talon asked. "It was like a warm wave."

"Not to them," Jayde answered.

Hunter pulled Curt back to his feet, as the confused shouting disintegrated and footsteps thundered toward the room. Jayde gasped at the scene inside and bolted to Sarah and Mikel.

Curt ignored her chattering and the questions thrown at them about Mikel's condition. He wrestled himself free of Hunter's grip and started for Erin. His brother-in-law sighed and let him go, though he watched the exchange warily as he headed for his own family.

Curt shook in fear as he made his way to her. He had to make sure Erin was still herself. If Erin was a beast, he would have no choice but to kill her. Curt knew that just as he knew that if he lost her, his next blow would be to follow her.

Erin raised her face to him as he knelt beside her. Her eyes had returned to their normal color. For that, he was grateful.

She shook, and her face was pale. "Say

something," she breathed. "Please, Curt."

He ran a hand along her cheek and sighed as she brushed her face into it to kiss his palm. "What did you do?" he asked quietly.

"The Stone asked me to carry Her power. She needed to rest. She was tired of wars." She looked at him hopelessly.

"You're not..."

"I'm not a beast. They can't rise again. They're dust, just as they should have been centuries ago."

He hesitated, wanting so much to believe her unconditionally. Still, no one could touch the Stone.

Erin sighed, grabbing a sacred weapon from the floor and wiping it carefully on her maternity jeans before slicing her palm with it. "Wanna make a blood oath on it?" she joked weakly as her blood welled up red in her hand.

Curt took the blade from her hand and pulled her to his chest, afraid to let her go. "I thought I'd lost you," he breathed into her hair.

Erin pushed back and ran her uninjured hand over his cheek. She sealed her mouth to his urgently, drawing him into a mindless, searing kiss. She pulled back again, her breathing ragged. "What do you think? Am I still me?" she asked seriously.

Curt chuckled as he drew her to her feet. "It's a safe bet, but I'm testing that theory when we get relocated," he warned.

"Gladly." Her smile was warm and playful despite her pallor.

He wrapped his arm around Erin's shoulder and led her to the group of people crowded around Mikel and Sarah.

"Don't tell me what I saw," Sarah objected hotly.

Adam shook his head. "I don't know what really happened, but there is no way a human four-year-old, even one *König* born, took out an elder that easily and neatly."

Erin pushed into the circle with Curt snuggled to her back. "Like an untrained twelve-year-old little girl *König* born couldn't drive one to ground?" she asked pointedly. "If it makes you feel better, I drove Lorian into Mikel's blade. The kill was his own and beautifully done, my little Jee, elder killer."

Mikel beamed and tipped his head in a bow. "You deserve a special title, Aunt Erin. What do you call someone elders run from in fear when she pursues unarmed?"

She smiled and shrugged. "Scary?" she suggested.

"The smack down queen of the Warriors," Curt amended in a teasing tone.

Mikel giggled. "Zel, the wonder babe?" he offered, covering his mouth with his little hand.

"Wonder babe?" Sarah thundered. "Who taught you that one?" She snapped a seething look at her husband.

"Not me," Hunter denied.

"I bet! We'll discuss that one," she warned.

"Where's the Stone?" Joel asked abruptly, breaking the mood. "And what's with the weapon?" His hand reached toward the pedestal.

"No," Erin thundered, whirling out of Curt's arms and reaching out for the blade before the older Warrior could connect with it. She nestled it to her chest. "This one is mine."

"It's just a training blade," he argued.

Sarah snorted. "Trust me, Joel. You do not want that blade," she assured him.

"Where's the Stone?" he demanded again.

Sarah sighed. "Oh, show them already and stop this damned internal argument about it."

Erin nodded and placed the weapon in her hand back on the pedestal. She put her hand out to Curt. "Give me the other one. I might as well have a matched set."

He nodded and placed it in her hand, kissing her cheek and backing away. "Be careful," he requested.

Erin smiled grimly. "Piece of cake," she assured him. She closed her eyes, balancing the weapon on its hilt in the center of her palm.

Curt held his breath as the other Warriors crowded in around him.

"What is she doing?" Talon asked.

"You wouldn't believe him, if he told you," Hunter commented. "Just watch."

"She's too tired for this," Curt breathed. "She should have waited."

"She's fine," Sarah assured him.

Erin's eyes opened, glowing their blue fire, and William backed off in shock, coming up against Patrick as he tried to flee. The glow started as a spot on her hand and moved up the weapon, bathing its length in crackling power. She closed her eyes as the light faded, sucking in a deep breath.

When her eyes opened again, their normal color had returned. Without a word, Erin flipped the blade and buried it in Gruber's body. The blue fire seemed to engulf the entire beast at once, charring him instantly to something resembling dying embers.

Erin crossed to him and wrenched the blade free, nodding as the dark form collapsed into dust. She returned to the pedestal, wiped the dust of the beast onto her jeans and placed the blade carefully crossed over the other.

She curled into Curt's waiting arm and faced the silent Warriors. "Questions?" she asked lightly.

"Who was that?" Joel questioned, pointing at the pile of ashes next to the pedestal.

"The body of the Stone and the spirits of the elders." She shrugged.

"What happens if we touch those blades?" Terrin asked. "Will we end up like Mr. Crispy over there?"

"No, but did you get a good look at Mr. Crispy's deep-fried hands? You wouldn't like the experience. It would take a while to heal."

Curt furrowed his brow. "What about the children? I don't know a child that doesn't play with his parents' blades."

Erin sighed. "Hunter, try to hold Mikel's weapon," she ordered.

Her brother nodded uncertainly and took the blade from his son's out-stretched hand. He dropped it immediately, shaking his hand, and Mikel retrieved it with a shake of his head and a big grin.

"What did you do to it?" Hunter demanded.

"I charged my amulet, not the blade itself. Come here, Mikel."

She started to hoist him, but Curt took over. "Let me." He gave her the fierce look he reserved for times when he felt she was doing too much, and she nodded her agreement and backed off slightly as he lifted the child.

"Is this safe?" Sarah asked nervously.

Erin looked at her in disbelief. "This is Mikel! My own impetuous nature aside, Sarah—"

"I know. I apologize. It's just—"

"He's your son. You're allowed to worry, but I would never allow him to be hurt. I know his limitations. You saw that tonight."

She smiled warmly. "Your turn soon enough." Sarah sobered and seemed to grow agitated. "If what Lorian said is true... How do you feel?"

"I think he was bluffing. If I'm having babies before the sun rises, I better be going into labor PDQ or not at all."

Curt startled and ran a hand over his children. "Labor?" he asked in a strangled voice. It was too early for that. If Erin was in labor, there was no time to waste with all this silly questioning and demonstrations.

Erin shook her head wearily. "Not a pain," she assured him. "He was trying to shake me. It was sweet revenge to see him running scared."

"The look on his face when the Stone took his powers away was pure poetry," Sarah added gleefully.

She nodded. "Back to this. Mikel, touch the blade for me."

The child's fingers caressed the metal, trusting that he would be safe. He giggled. "It tickles. It's warm."

Erin grinned. "I think your Daddy would have a vastly different experience with it."

"How does it work?" Jayde asked.

"The Stone was sentient. We always knew that. She liked puzzles. We said She amused Herself— Actually,

She was trying to get through one damned plan without someone on one side or the other screwing it up!

"We never chanced anyone touching the Stone, because we mistakenly believed that no one could touch the Stone without dire consequences. True innocents could always touch Her. The Stone's power possesses something of that intelligence. The children are safe. The adults know better—or will after trying it once."

For a long moment, no one spoke. Finally, Joel cleared his throat and asked the question no one else thought to dare. "What exactly are you now?"

"I am a vessel. I hold and harness the Stone's power. As Her servant, I could do no less. As Zel, it was what I was born to do. Everything from my ten-megaton *Blutjagd* to my telepathic link with Sarah has been training specific to becoming the vessel the Stone needed."

Curt nodded. "The elders were destroyed with the Stone," he explained. "When the last turned dies, we're free. All of us. Forever. There will be no more Cursed Warriors."

"When you die?" Talon asked her.

"If the beasts are all dead, the fire dies with me. If not..." Erin ran a hand over her pregnant womb slowly. "Katie will become the vessel."

Curt sent Mikel back to his mother and skated his hands over her with a broad smile. "You're giving me a girl," he breathed. "That shy little thing has been hiding all this time, after all."

Erin nodded happily. "And a boy," she reminded him. "Corwyn and Kaitlyn *König*-Maher...if that's acceptable to you."

He nodded without taking his hands off of his children. Her grandfather and his mother commemorated? It was a beautiful thing. "Oh, it is," he decided. "I wouldn't have it any other way."

* * * *

December 25, 2029

Curt lay in the bed, staring at the ceiling of the room Adam had sent them to while the others burned the bodies and moved possessions from the training house. In a room down the hall, Sarah and Mikel slept as Erin slept beside him. All of them were doubtless exhausted from the events of the evening.

He'd been in this house many times. It was the manor house of his home range, after all, but he'd never slept in this room before. This was the lord's suite. Though it was Adam's place now, Curt had no doubts that whatever range they roamed would extend this same courtesy to them—and to Katie and her mate after them. Zel, the Stone vessels, were the new true elite, with good reason.

Erin's explanations had gone on for another half an hour. As stunned as Curt had been to see her kill the turneds, he wished he had been there to see Lorian backing down as she stalked him, bare-handed and unprotected, his fondest wish become his worst nightmare intent on his destruction.

Finally, Erin had seemed to sway on her feet, drained. Curt had demanded arrangements for her to rest immediately. He'd swept her into his arms even as he faced down the other Warriors with a fierce look unlike any they had seen from him in the past, amazed that Erin still seemed an insignificant weight while carrying both of his children.

Adam hadn't batted an eye. He'd simply directed them away to the manor house with a promise that Bryant would be along to guard their backs shortly. He'd ordered Sarah along—with Mikel sleeping on her shoulder, his prized blade still clasped in his hand.

Erin had slept against his shoulder for most of the drive, and Curt would have been content to simply settle his wife in bed, but she had other ideas.

Her arms wrapped around his neck and drew his face down to seal her mouth to his. For a few glorious moments, Curt lost himself in that kiss. Erin. She was his Erin. Whatever surprises the Stone had in store for them, she was still Erin.

He groaned and eased her away. "You need to sleep," he decided. "The babies—"

Erin silenced him with another kiss, a playful one, the one she used when she was about to do something that was mind-numbing to him in bed. "The babies are fine." She kissed him slower and deeper, dragging his shirt up his chest. "I want you, Curt. You said you'd test to see if I was still me." She tossed his shirt away and started unbuttoning his jeans. "I need you."

Curt undressed her, kissing and caressing as he went, heedless of whatever objections he had been expressing moments earlier. Erin. He had almost lost her. He suddenly realized that he needed this as much as she did. He needed to lose himself in her and prove to himself that they were both alive.

All alive. *He kissed the swell of her belly and ran his tongue over the squirming baby assaulting the heat of his touch. Which one was it? Was it his son or his shy daughter who would undoubtedly have a ten-megaton* Blutjagd *and a fiery temper just like her mother?*

Erin groaned and curled her hands in his hair, cradling his head to her for his intimate exploration. Curt moved lower, lifting her hips to drink in her sweet musk as he tasted her readiness for him and found her beyond simply ready. She cried out under his ministrations, begging him to take her.

Curt turned her in his hands so that she settled on her hands and knees. "I can't wait," he breathed in apology, though he knew she didn't want a lazy joining either. He eased into her, feeling the hot, slick tightness enveloping him, surrounding him in pure bliss. He sank to his heels with his hands locked on her hips, pulling Erin into his lap so that she settled over him with her head nestled into his shoulder.

He moved slowly, savoring her internal muscles gripping his pulsing length as he played follow the leader with a baby through her stomach. Their passion skyrocketed, and Curt found himself thrusting into her, hopelessly lost in the sensation. He nuzzled and nipped at her shoulder, neck and up to her jaw. Erin reached a hand back around his head and turned her face to kiss him with a fierce need.

Time seemed to stand still as he tensed inside her, filling Erin with his seed. His senses faded out momentarily, and the sensation of her orgasm pulling at him as her muscles contracted blocked out all else.

Sated, Curt cradled her to him and pulled Erin to the bed, spooned protectively in his arms and still locked deep inside her. He trailed his lips over her neck and shoulder lazily. "You're still you," he promised.

"Is that good or bad?" Erin asked, already half asleep.

"Good for us. Bad for beasts."

Erin had fallen into a fitful sleep in his arms. It was the unsettled nature of her rest that kept Curt awake and watchful. He smiled at the knowledge that he was being so protective of a woman with the power to slay almost a hundred high-levels in a single shot, but he was printed to her, and that was not a rational state.

Curt ran his lips over her temple, as Erin sighed and fidgeted restlessly yet again. He crooned to her; unsure, as he had been unsure for some time, whether or not she was actually asleep. She punched her pillow and uttered several harsh curses, settling that issue.

"What can I do?" Curt asked. "What do you need?" Whatever it was, he'd provide it.

"Call Adam and Hunter...right now...please." She was slightly breathless and extremely weary.

"Why? Are there beasts coming?" he asked urgently.

"Not yet, but soon," she decided. "Or maybe not. They know...what I can do to them...now."

"How do you know? The Stone's power or Sarah?"

"Neither. Deductive reasoning. Lorian...was right." She groaned. "We're having babies tonight, Daddy."

Curt launched off the bed, kissing Erin as he punched in Hunter's number from memory and fished for his clothes. Hope for the future or not, it was more than a month early, and he was fighting panic.

For the first time in history, a *Blutjagdfrau* was about to be born in a hospital. After all, what beast would be stupid enough to come now that word of Erin's abilities had circulated the hive mind? But, just in case, he'd have half the Warriors in the North American ranges in place as their private security crew by morning...

Autonomy

NOTE: This short is a small sequence that didn't quite fit in the timeline of Hunter's story in *König Cursebreakers*. But it needs to be told.

Chapter Twenty-seven

Erin grinned and blew out the candles on her cake, and the assembled Warriors cheered. She flicked a glance at Curt then away, unsheathing her sacred weapon and irreverently using it to slice the cake.

Warriors took plates and offered their congratulations on her adulthood, milling away again, but not Curt. He stood back, watching the procession with an unreadable expression etched onto his gorgeous face. Erin filled another plate with cake and set her blade down.

Bryant reached for the plate in her hand, murmuring his thanks, but Erin sidestepped him, skating the plate past his fingertips. Bryant could fend for himself. This slice wasn't intended for him. His younger brother would be the recipient.

Curt didn't move. He stood his ground, letting her come to him: confident, male, perfect. At nineteen, he was more than a head taller than most human men and had been since about her age. His midnight blue eyes met hers, not inviting her to him intimately but more...she hoped.

Erin stopped before him, not quite touching Curt. "Hungry?" she asked, hoping her voice sounded seductive to him.

His gaze flicked to the plate then to her mouth. "Yes." His voice was dark, full of a dangerous emotion that she prayed was arousal.

He didn't move to take the plate. Erin faltered. How did one seduce a man? Inspiration struck. She dragged her finger through the icing and brought it to Curt's mouth.

His eyes darkened, and his nostrils flared slightly. His lips parted, and he took the tip of her finger into his mouth. At the first hint of suction, Erin's nipples hardened against her lavender t-shirt, painfully tight in the simple bra beneath. Curt flicked his tongue over her fingertip. He released her slowly, every muscle in his body taut as if he waged some inner battle.

The noise level in the room had dropped considerably. Neither of them turned to look, knowing that the other Warriors were watching this interaction carefully, possibly gauging how serious it might be.

Erin took a step closer and tilted her face up to his. "Sweet sixteen," she hinted, praying that Curt was as interested as he seemed.

For a long moment, he didn't move. She cursed her overactive imagination. For all these years, no man had dared touch her on fear of death. Now that one could, with her invitation to do so, the only one she wanted seemed unwilling to touch her.

Curt nodded, and her heart stuttered in response. He raised one hand, his fingers tangling in the short curls clipped close to her scalp as his face closed on hers slowly. The room went silent. Even her heart seemed to still. If it pounded in anticipation, Erin didn't note it. Her eyes fluttered shut, as his mouth touched hers, his tongue parting her lips neatly.

The mating of their mouths wasn't hesitant. Erin shook herself mentally at that. Why would she expect Curt to be hesitant? He was a Warrior, one of the finest alive outside of her own family, and he was experienced with women.

Rational thought deserted her as their mouths

mated fully. The kiss was hot, fevered in its intensity, addictive.

Her grip on the plate faltered. The stoneware was lifted up and away as it slipped from her fingertips. The clatter of it being deposited on a countertop registered in her shattered consciousness along with the realization that Curt was the only Warrior close enough to have saved the bit of dinnerware.

Curt's free hand wrapped around her hip and pulled Erin closer to his body. She gasped, her eyes opening in surprise and her mouth parting from his, as the ridge of his cock pressed into her stomach.

He stared into her eyes. There was no uncertainty in his expression. There was no unasked question. Curt intended to take her to bed and exercise her autonomy fully. He simply waited for her agreement, as the rules of sanction decreed.

"Get a room," Bryant grumbled.

Curt didn't bother to issue his typical response to his brother. He didn't smile. He didn't even question that she'd go to bed with him.

"Yours or mine?" he asked.

Erin smiled at that, a giddy laugh bubbling up inside her. "Yes." She didn't care where she exercised her autonomy as long as it was Curt she exercised it with.

He nodded and looked to the Warriors around the table as if questioning if any of them had some reason to try and interfere with their rights, perhaps challenging them to try it. Erin followed his line of sight, noting the various reactions of the individuals present.

Bryant was sour, no doubt angry that Erin hadn't

sought him out as her first.

Adam shot Curt a look of warning that annoyed her. Vow of protection or no, it wasn't Adam's place to remind his youngest brother that playing with Erin's heart would be dangerous business.

Lewis nodded his approval to his son, though Erin and Curt needed no one's permission to exercise their autonomy—or to mate formally. If he was expressing the Stone's permission, it was wasted. As long as Erin took a Warrior to mate, the Stone would be pleased with her choice.

Kord's reaction was the most striking of anyone in Curt's family. He was amused. Erin swallowed a nervous laugh. No doubt the old lord thanked his family god, *Len*, that his youngest grandson hadn't risked death as Kord had at not much older than Curt was now. Sharing the overactive urge to take release and print, Erin knew Kord worried that Curt would follow in his footsteps in other ways.

Her own family's reactions were no surprise to her. The look Hunter shot Curt was a near mirror of Adam's. Maybe that was what older brothers were best at, the look that promised death if you stepped out of line.

Her mother smiled sadly. Jayde's sadness wasn't clear. Maybe she grieved the loss of her youngest child to adulthood. Maybe she wished she'd prepared Erin better for this moment. Erin returned her smile, hoping to put her mother at ease. She couldn't be in safer hands than Curt's.

Talon stood straight and tall, the lord of all lords. Erin found herself holding her breath, though she knew that, by the rules of sanction, he couldn't stop them. If anyone could get away with breaking those rules, her father could...with nothing more than a decree that would have to go to the council of lords before her autonomy was secure. He met her eyes then Curt's, nodding his agreement, and Erin felt that same giddy joy rising in her.

Curt didn't hesitate. He turned Erin toward the doorway and urged her up the stairs. At the top, she hesitated. Erin hadn't specified which room they'd use, so she wasn't certain which way to turn.

As if reading her thoughts perfectly, Curt turned her left, away from her room and toward his. Her heart hammered at that, at the idea of him claiming her maidenhead in his bed, her blood staining his sheets. It seemed more intimate than them going to her bed, more possessive for him to want this.

Erin looked around his room, though she hardly needed to. She'd been here many times, but this time she was free to indulge in the wild fantasies she'd harbored for the last few years, fantasies of Curt's hands and mouth doing glorious things to her without fear of anyone protesting the exploration.

She turned to investigate a sound behind her. The sight of Curt toeing off his boots, already bare-chested, made her head swim. Erin eased her t-shirt from her jeans, numbly noting that having sex with him meant divesting herself of clothing as well.

Curt pulled her hands away, shaking his head. Before she found the words to question his reluctance, he slid his hands beneath her untucked shirt, his palms skating up her ribcage and pushing the lavender material toward her rapidly-beating heart. Erin bit her lip at the arousal that simple touch caused, at the knowledge that he wouldn't stop until they were both sated.

He paused at her chest, tracing the sensitive tips of her nipples with the pads of his thumbs. Erin closed her eyes, laying her head back and arching into his hands for more. Curt growled at that, reaching behind her to unhook her bra. He urged her arms up and pushed both articles of clothing up and off smoothly, letting them fall to the floor.

For several agonizing minutes, the only sense Erin had of him was Curt's ragged breathing, the heat bathing her already sensitized lips. She lowered her hands, touching the chest she knew so well, the chest she'd practically salivated to taste on their many swims in the lake. Curt didn't move, allowing her to glide her fingertips over his shoulders and arms, his chest and down the taut expanse of his belly, following the line of crisp curls toward his jeans.

Just when she would have opened her eyes, his body moved. The floor vibrated as he dropped to one knee, and he took her breast in his mouth, suckling at her. Like their kiss downstairs, there was nothing slow and hesitant about the way he touched her. Curt was ravenous, thorough in his attention.

Her womb exploded in sympathetic sensation. The phantom feeling of fingers exploring her core was nearly too much. Erin stifled a scream of pleasure in response, her hands curling into the short black hair on his head.

Curt's mouth retreated, and he laid a kiss on the tip of her quickly-cooling nipple. "Don't," he ordered. "Don't hold back."

She met his eyes, trying to make sense of that.

"You want me to scream?"

His eyes announced his decision clearly. That was precisely what he wanted her to do.

She nodded, though she didn't understand why he would want it. Maybe he wanted the other men to hear it. No. That wasn't like Curt. His reasons were more personal. She was sure of that.

Erin watched him unbuckle her weapons belt and drop it to the floor. She stared at it, a nervous knot in her stomach. She hadn't been more than two yards from her blades at night in the last four years. Curt knew that.

"I'm your protection tonight," he informed her. "Trust me."

She nodded again. Curt was the one person she did trust that much.

As if testing her agreement to everything he'd requested so far, his mouth closed on her other breast, his fingers urging her thighs apart to stroke at the spreading damp spot at the apex.

Erin shouted his name, a plea for more mixed with a plea for the end of this torture driving her to it. He looked up at her, a feral smile on his face. He stroked her again, and she rumbled in protest—or perhaps acceptance. Even Erin couldn't be sure which it was.

Curt returned to his suckling, his fingers seeking out the sensitive spot far to the front of her sex through her jeans. With every sound that escaped her lips, his play became more intense, until Erin made the connection she'd been searching for. He wanted her to scream, because hearing it excited him.

At last, he broke off. His hands cupped her hips, steadying her. "Your legs are shaking," he noted.

"You—" Erin faltered, as he nipped at her nipple then laid a long, slow lick over the spot, her trembling more pronounced—even to her.

"I think it's time to lie down." Curt stood, hoisting her over his shoulder as he rose.

Some rational kernel in her mind argued that Erin should protest being carried this way, but the realization that he was carrying her off to ravish her stilled that protest before she could utter it. Erin closed her eyes to the sound of the blankets being thrown back. Curt took her down to the cool sheets in a smooth motion that left him crouched over her, his lips pressed to her stomach, caressing, circling, his tongue darting out to taunt and taste.

Erin opened her eyes, meeting the midnight blue depths of his. Curt kissed lower, brushing his lips over her navel as his fingers went to work on her jeans.

It was sweet torture. He peeled back the faded denim, inch by inch, exploring the skin beneath it as it appeared. Erin groaned at that, lifting her buttocks off the bed to speed the process. Curt eased her jeans and underwear down her hips until her curls peeked from the top, pressing a kiss into them, a rumbling groan vibrating through to her womb.

"Curt, please," she whispered. If he didn't take her soon, she'd incinerate right here on his bed.

"A good start," he replied.

"I don't understand," she admitted. Gods, but she wanted to understand!

He peeled her jeans back further, his breath teasing at her engorged tissues, making them throb in a heartbeat of invitation she knew instinctively he could sense. As if confirming that belief, Curt inhaled

447

deeply.

The slow approach to undressing her was abandoned. Her Keds were pitched away, and her jeans and underwear soon followed.

Erin forced her breathing to continue, as Curt pulled his weapons belt off and placed it on the headboard as she usually did. He yanked his button fly open in a single tug and pushed his jeans down to his knees. Erin couldn't have recounted how he got his jeans the rest of the way off if asked. She was rapt on the length of his cock bobbing toward her.

Breathe, she admonished herself sternly. Surely, she was only this lightheaded because she'd stopped breathing when his jeans disappeared down his thighs. "Please," she managed again, her voice slightly strangled in the effort to force speech.

Curt chuckled. "I'm going to give you so much pleasure, you'll beg for it," he promised.

Erin shook her head in disbelief. She *was* begging for him. Her entire body was a live wire of sensation. What more could he want?

He lowered himself to the bed on his stomach, his cock disappearing beneath him as he spread her legs around his shoulders. Curt moved slowly as if challenging Erin not to stop him, daring her to allow him anything he wanted.

He couldn't— She screamed in pleasure, as his tongue stroked up her seam, a leisurely caress of heat against her. Erin bowed up, trying to close her legs to the overwhelming sensations.

Curt held them spread wide. His tongue darted to her clit. He explored slowly then more vigorously, his hands reducing her attempts to thrash away to a mere wriggling that only helped him pleasure her. His tongue traveled back to her slit again, taunting her with his knowledge of sex, promising to educate her properly.

Erin trembled, the vibrations intensifying the already mind-blowing sensations. She groaned, anticipating his next move but unwilling—perhaps unable—to form the words to stop him. She screamed again, as his tongue slid home between her labia, the slight sensation of stretching rocking her to her core. Erin licked her lips, imagining how full his much larger cock would make her feel. It was a sensation she couldn't wait to experience.

Curt didn't give her much time to consider it. His mouth stole her ability to reason with ease and precision. He was relentless. He nibbled at her, licked at her, thrust his tongue in again and again, until Erin felt like her whole body was primed for an explosion. Curt was holding off her climax, she was certain.

That knowledge drove her near mad. Erin panted out pleas for him to take her, to allow her to come, to change what he was doing to speed her there—anything but a plea for him to stop. When he let her slip over, she howled in ecstasy.

His tongue left her. Curt's body was abruptly over her, his mouth fevered against hers. Erin's mind reeled at the heavy musk in his mouth. Was that what she tasted like? Somehow, that thought seemed to step up her arousal another notch.

His cock brushed the skin of her inner thigh, and Erin tried to shift toward it. Had her mouth not been otherwise occupied, she would have cursed her inability to move beneath his bulk.

Curt eased back from the kiss, a taunting smile curving his lips. "You still want it now that you've come?"

If Erin could have reached his blades, she would have given him a scar for that. "Curt," she warned. "If you tease me for one more—"

"Not on your life." His expression was suddenly serious.

She gasped, as he shifted. Curt eased the head of his cock through her labia, stilling as she whimpered. The feeling was exquisite, but the longing to feel all of him was almost more than she could stand.

"Too much?" he asked.

Erin shook her head, praying he wouldn't stop. It wasn't too much. It wasn't nearly enough. He pushed deeper, and she closed her eyes, reining in her unruly heart rate.

Curt's hands cupped her face. "Look at me," he grumbled.

She complied. His eyes had turned nearly black in arousal, and his expression was fierce, possessive. Erin gulped down a breath at that. He was possessing her in the most intimate way a man could, and she loved it. He eased back then in again, slightly deeper. It wasn't enough, and that fact was maddening. Erin sobbed, needing more.

"Pain?" he asked.

"No."

"I'm going to—"

"Yes," she interrupted him, pleading silently for him to finish what he'd started.

His next stroke filled her. Erin cried out in a mixture of pleasure and pain. The throbbing inside her became an urgent drumbeat, a call for him to match that beat instead of lying nestled to her cervix.

Curt started to soothe her, offering apologies for the pain. Erin shook her head, shifting herself further onto him as Curt retreated.

He didn't question that. His body pistoned in and out of hers, his pleas and promises mixing with Erin's, whispers that bared more than their bodies to each other. She vaguely noted the things he was saying: a request for her not to leave his bed, promised pleasures he'd gift her while she was there, his love.

Erin answered all of them in the affirmative, the concept that Curt wanted more than one night of simple release like a heady drug. His profession of love propelled her toward another climax.

His final request came without warning. "Take me as your mate."

She stared at him, certain that she'd started hallucinating. She couldn't have heard him right. Erin started to ask him to repeat himself, but Curt beat her to the punch.

"I want you to be my mate. I don't want you to leave me—ever." He said it calmly, in a voice that sounded almost too rational. Only his eyes belied that outward calm, their turbulent blue expressing a mixture of fear and longing he wouldn't admit in words.

"Yes," she whispered.

As if her quiet admission was too much, Curt roared out his possession of her, his body filling hers with heat, the gentle pounding of that release sending her over again.

* * * *

And, he woke. Curt fisted his hands in his sheets, venting a growl of frustration into his pillow. His body ached, so close to release he could taste the sweet endorphin rush. Curt cursed softly, well aware that relieving himself now would do no good. After these dreams, it never did.

They hadn't been this bad in more than a month. Now, he'd suffered them for four straight days.

In addition to that, he woke every time with the maddening urge to go to her. At first, he'd considered jumping in his car and driving all the way to New Hampshire. Now he felt he'd die if he didn't get on a plane. Never mind that his own family, the Cross family, and the *Königs* would all kill him for that choice.

Not if the dreams are true, his mind argued. *If she does want you like that, they would all forgive you for jumping ship and showing up at her doorstep unannounced. You were wrong to let her leave.*

Curt shook his head in an attempt to dislodge that thought. *Right. I'm going to just show up and give Erin the lovestruck look, and she'll fall into my arms.*

He growled again. He hadn't been wrong to let her leave. Erin's choice could not be argued. The rules of sanction were clear on that point. Curt wasn't a rogue who convinced unwilling women...no matter how much he wanted this one.

Still, the urge to go to her ate at him until Curt felt he was going mad. He groaned at that. Was he suffering for breaking printing? Was that what was driving him? No. That would have come sooner, the moment Erin walked out of his life. This was simply torturing himself with the knowledge that Erin would soon have autonomy.

Curt glanced at the bedside clock, sighing deeply. It was eleven thirty—past midnight on the east coast where Erin was. "Happy birthday, Erin," he offered sadly. "I hope you enjoy your autonomy."

He curled to his side, fighting back the misery drowning him. Four years! For four long years he'd waited for Erin's right to choose a mate. Now she had it, and she'd used it to leave him. Now she was half a continent away, suffering from some mysterious ailment that Lewis had sent Adam to guard her through.

Adam! As if Erin wanted his oldest brother anywhere near her!

She wouldn't even talk to Curt. Erin had cut herself off from him completely when she'd left Maher range. And, it was within her rights to do it.

Curt closed his eyes, praying for sweeter dreams, burying the nagging calculation that he could be in Crossbearer before Erin cut her cake. He drifted off to sleep.

Erin grinned and blew out the candles on her cake, and the assembled Warriors cheered. She flicked a glance at Curt then away, unsheathing her sacred weapon and irreverently using it to slice the cake.

* * * *

Erin stared out the window, raising her wrist to check the time. *What difference did it make? Did she really think Curt was coming?*

He might. He would if you called him. You have autonomy now. You could offer—

She growled at that. Erin had all but thrown herself at her dear friend. For what? What had it gotten her? A pat on the head and a reminder that she was nothing more than a little sister to Curt.

It was pathetic. She was pathetic! If he drove up that road right now, she'd have him in bed in thirty seconds. Only, there was no way he would drive up that road.

Erin knew the whole Warrior world wanted her to choose a mate, but they were in for a very big surprise. If that mate wasn't Curt, there wouldn't be a mate. "Autonomy," she grumbled. "I have the right to choose."

She curled into bed, ignoring the nagging voice in the back of her mind. *Autonomy. You have the right to make your own mistakes like any other adult.*

Sleep claimed Erin, an unsettled sleep in which Curt stood across the room as she blew out her candles: wanting her, loving her, waiting for Erin to come claim him.

Claimed: König Mate

Chapter Twenty-eight

January 15, 2028

Mikel of *König*-Crossbearer stared at the lady's belly in surprise, watching the purple and blue sparkles dancing on the surface of her shirt in fascination. *She* was in there, the one who would come to him when he was a man.

He reached for her mind, desperate to know her before her parents took her far away from him. She'd be half a world away, across the ocean that he knew no one could see the end of.

She was comfortable, snug in her watery home on the plane of her mother's lush womb. She was strong, courageous, the perfect mate for a *König*.

He needed a name for her. Though Mikel knew her parents were of the Smith family, it wasn't enough information for him. It wasn't enough to think of her as *she*. Mikel searched the lady's mind frantically, locking on the name hidden there. *Perfect!*

He rushed to her and pressed a kiss to her belly, speaking with his mind to his young mate, telling her about the day she would join him in Cross range.

"How cute," the lady cried out in glee.

His mother started across the room, her shimmer flickering in concern. "Mikel?" she asked. "What is it?"

He met her eyes, patting the lady's belly, smiling. "Baby," he announced. "My Holly."

The lady gasped, covering his hand with her own. "Oh, Patrick," she breathed. Her joy sent shards of white light through the green of her shimmer.

"What is it?" his mother asked again.

"Patrick just told me a few days ago, and..." She stopped, tears pooled in her eyes.

Mikel looked at her curiously. Was she upset that she carried his mate? She was crying, but the tears were ones of happiness. He sighed in relief.

The Warrior took over for her, drawing his attention from the lady. "If the baby was a girl, we'd planned to name her Holly."

Mikel looked up at him in surprise. Not that he knew the baby's name but at the edge of *Blutjagd* burning in his skin, his braid of red shimmer expanding and being fought back again.

He sighed at a flash of insight. The Warrior thought he was protecting his daughter. Mikel's proclamation of her as 'my Holly' had been perceived as a threat.

He struggled for the words to explain himself then ground his teeth in frustration. Mikel was aware of so much, but he was limited in expression, his two-year-old body hampering his ability to communicate the things he knew to be true.

It doesn't matter, he assured himself. Even if he could explain the connection between himself and Holly, her parents wouldn't believe him. Even if they did believe him, he wouldn't be a sealed *Krieger der Nacht* for many years. Until then, it wasn't appropriate to ask permission to claim his mate.

He turned away, already missing her. Mikel took his mother's hand, casting one last look at Holly. It would be many years before he'd see her again. The Warrior's mind was full of plans, plans to keep her from him, but Mikel was a *König*. Nothing would deny him his proper mate. The Stone would see to that.

Chapter Twenty-nine

September 25, 2048

Patrick Smith slammed his hand down on the desk between himself and his uncle. "Being my house lord does not give you the right to demand this," he growled.

Vince rubbed his forehead. "I will forgive that outburst, but do not abuse my patience."

He nodded, fisting his hand in frustration.

"Sit down, Patrick."

He obeyed, abruptly wary. Something told him that *König* would get his way in the end, and he didn't like it.

"Now, need I remind you that you are required to obey the *Königs*?"

"Lord and Lady *König*," he grumbled.

Vince scowled at him. "You doubt that Talon and Jayde will issue the order, if you refuse this invitation? That Erin will back it? That Hunter..."

"Invitation?" he snapped. "I am being *ordered* to turn my daughter over to—"

"It is nothing of the sort," he shouted. "*König* or not, Mikel knows the rules of sanction. He won't be forcing himself on Holly or even convincing her to willingness. All he asks is that you bring her to Cross and consider a suit."

"And, if I do not choose to consider it?" he challenged.

Vince stared at him in seeming disbelief. "I really don't understand you, Patrick. Any other father would be glad to—"

"Would they? Would they, really? Why my daughter, Vince? Why Holly?"

"I can't say. They say Mikel sees inside of people's souls. They say he cannot be lied to. When he met you in Cross—"

"Do not remind me." Patrick managed a calm voice, though his heart pounded in near terror. The moment Mikel had pronounced Holly as his own had haunted him for two decades. Had he ever doubted this day would come? All of his careful plans were laid to rest by one order from the house above all houses, and he would lose his daughter in the end.

His uncle sighed. "Go, Patrick. Stay as short a time as you like, but let him meet Holly. She is under no obligation to accept a suit. At her word, you can refuse."

He nodded, more at ease. "We won't be staying long," he vowed. He started to stand.

"Patrick?" Vince seemed abruptly grave.

"Yes?" His stomach clenched in a manner not unlike the sick feeling a Warrior experienced when a beast was feeding nearby. His senses warned of approaching danger.

"If Holly agrees to be courted—"

"I don't—"

"Remote, I know, but if she agrees, consider carefully before you refuse her. And, I wouldn't dissuade her before she goes. It might be deemed as dishonorable."

* * * *

Holly smiled, reaching her hand back to clasp her

father's.

He chuckled, but it was a strained sound. "You always know," he murmured, stroking her fingers.

"I *am* a sensitive, Father. Now, why don't you sit down and tell me what's bothering you." There was no question of that. His usual pale yellow aura was ringed in muddy red and a touch of deep purple.

He stepped over the bench and sank down beside her, his posture stiff, seemingly discomfited by something.

"This isn't like you," she noted. Her father hadn't seemed so ill at ease since her mother died. *No. That's not true. The month following my eighteenth birthday, he was always on edge, much like this.*

"I know. I..." He rubbed a hand over his eyes, abruptly showing signs of fatigue.

She raised an eyebrow. Her father had never been this tongue-tied before.

"We received an invitation today," he informed her, sounding more like he was issuing an order than telling her about a social occasion.

"Really? Under any other circumstances, I'd say that was good news, but your reaction doesn't make that seem likely. Tell me about it."

He darkened, a flash of anger glowing in his aura. "It isn't my place to say whether this *invitation* is good news or not."

"Then, whose place is it?" she asked, honestly perplexed by that odd proclamation. It was obvious that her father wasn't happy about the situation, but he couldn't tell her why?

Patrick met her eyes, misery tearing through his expression of simple unease.

"Mine?" she guessed.

"Yes. It is."

She hesitated, momentarily at a loss. "I don't understand. Who issued this invitation? Where are we supposed to be going? For what reason?"

"The invitation is from Mikel of *König*-Crossbearer."

"To go to America? I've never been there." A swirl of excitement circulated in her belly at the idea of seeing someplace new. What could be wrong with that?

He ground his teeth, *Blutjagd* shining white hot around him. "No, you haven't," he agreed.

She swallowed a sudden knot of apprehension. He felt there was some threat in this, but did she dare ask why? "Why has he called for us?" she asked.

"It seems the young prince has decided to take a mate."

"Twenty-two is a bit young for that, I suppose, but what does it have to do with us?" A wild conjecture flirted at her mind, and she shoved it away in dogged disbelief.

"He wants to meet you."

Her head spun. "Meet me? Why does he want to meet me?" Surely, he didn't think she'd agree to marry a man she'd never met.

"You are under no obligation—"

"You gave him permission?" she demanded. "Without consulting me?"

"Of course not! I would never encourage a man you didn't want."

"Then tell him I have no intentions of coming," she asserted. "How dare he order me to come to him like some—like some mail-order bride!"

Her father stroked her cheek, smiling weakly. "I am

ordered to bring you—"

"I won't go."

"Shhh," he soothed her. "All you need do is walk in and tell him you have no interest. Then we can leave, and I will show you the sights of New York before we return home."

Her breath caught at that. How long had she dreamed of seeing New York City? "Broadway?" she requested. "Central Park?"

"Grand Central Station. The opera. The ballet. You have my vow that I will take you anywhere and everywhere you wish." His smile widened as it always did when he knew she would be pleased with a surprise.

"Very well," she decided. "I will give the *prince* his answer in person."

Chapter Thirty

October 2, 2048

Mikel sat in his office, trying desperately to calm his scattered nerves. Holly would arrive soon, and for the first time, he found himself doubting his perceptions. What if he'd been wrong all those years ago? What if Holly didn't want him?

He shook himself mentally. When had he ever been wrong? He wasn't wrong. Not about this. If his perceptions weren't proof enough, the maddening itch to see her was further evidence that there was more at work than a simple dream.

But, what if he'd called for her too soon? What if she wasn't prepared to accept him yet? No. If that was the case, he wouldn't be half-mad for the three months he'd already wasted before he'd issued the invitation to Patrick of Schmeidt and his daughter.

A car pulled up out front, and Mikel turned his chair toward the window, forcing himself not to rush to it. She'd come to him. He knew she would. He'd known it twenty years ago, and nothing had changed in all that time.

The sounds of conversation moved closer, and he strained to hear them better. His heart stuttered at a female voice then settled as he recognized it as his mother's.

A knock came at the door.

"Come in," Mikel called out. He didn't turn around immediately, waiting for them to enter instead.

"Mikel?" his mother called.

He took a deep breath and turned to them, his eyes

passing over the rigid Warrior he remembered and locking on Holly. She wasn't looking his direction. Her eyes roamed his private shelves of books in awe.

She was petite, easily as tiny as his aunt Erin was. She wore a floor-length flowing peach gown that accented her dark features. It hugged her breasts and hips, flaring out to hide the rest of her form. Her dark curls reached her upper thighs and were restrained only by a gold clip at the nape of her neck. Errant curls escaped the clip and framed her face.

Mikel opened himself to her shimmer, praying it was as he remembered it. It was the vibrant blue of a young human sensitive with flecks of red—and better—gold and purple that marked his mate. He hadn't been wrong after all. He noted the red again. Her annoyance was something he could handle. If the rest of her shimmer was right, and it was, her anger would be overcome in time.

He stared at her, unable to look away. She was utterly captivating, and he hoped she found him the same.

Holly ran her fingertips over a leather-bound copy of *Salem's Lot*, biting her lip lightly. Her shimmer swirled with flecks of peach the color of her dress. He smiled. She wanted to read the books. They intrigued her.

"Signed by the author," he noted. "You may borrow any book you like."

Her face darkened, and she pulled her hand back, fisting it at her side. "I don't think so," she replied in a crisp, slightly cool voice, renewed annoyance making her shimmer fairly crackle with sparks of red and gold. She turned to him. "You see, I'm not—"

Holly broke off as she met his eyes. She gasped in surprise, and the streaks of purple in her shimmer became dominant, drowning out every other color until it was nearly all Mikel could see.

"Staying," she whispered.

Mikel raised an eyebrow, biting back a laugh. "Are you saying you won't give me consideration?" he challenged.

* * * *

His aura was beautiful—nearly entirely lavender with a stunning halo of gold. But, it was more than that. The feeling that she knew him was unbelievably strong.

It's impossible, she reasoned. *I've never been to America.*

Still, she couldn't shake the feeling that she knew Mikel of *König*-Crossbearer. The surety was maddening in its intensity.

She panned her gaze over his upper body, her gaze settling on the dark hair peeking from the vee of his Hunter green button-down shirt. Not black like most Warriors wore, which made it new, interesting, and appealing.

She would have liked to have claimed that it was the only remarkable thing about him—aside from his aura, but it wasn't. His hair and eyes were, at first glance, the same as any Warrior-born possessed, the same as her own, but there was something deeper in Mikel, something that made her examine those features a second time, something she couldn't name.

"Holly?" her father asked, his voice laced in

concern. "Are you all right?"

"Yes." Her voice sounded strange to her.

"Are you leaving me, Holly?" Mikel asked, his voice soft and inviting. "Are you refusing to consider me?"

Yes! But, her mouth wouldn't form the word.

Her heart ached at the thought of leaving. Her father stood in the edges of her peripheral vision, his body taut in anger, waiting for her to refuse Mikel. She should refuse him after the way he summoned her.

Invited, some corner of her mind argued. *He invited you, and you were only upset because of your father's reaction. Remember your excitement when you learned you'd been invited to America by Mikel?*

No. They'd been ordered to come. Her father said— He'd never lied to her before. Why would he now?

She started to speak, but her mouth refused the order again. It was one little word. Why couldn't she say it?

"Holly?" Mikel asked. "Are you refusing—"

"No," she breathed.

His smile was stunning, and his aura brightened.

"Are you certain you want to do this?" her father demanded. "If, at any time, you change your mind—"

"Certain," she agreed, nodding slowly.

Mikel bowed his head to her. "Then, I ask you, Patrick of Schmeidt, Warrior to Warrior, for the right to court your daughter with the intention of mating—if she chooses to accept me."

Her father glowed in *Blutjagd*. For a moment, she was certain he'd refuse Mikel's bid, and a hopeless need to convince him gripped her.

He nodded, fisting his hand and speaking through the tension in his jaw. "If you truly wish this, I cannot stand in your way."

He could, and he wanted to, but he hadn't. Holly smiled her thanks, though some rational corner of her mind argued that she was mad to complicate her life this way. She had no intentions of mating with anyone, let alone a self-centered prince like Mikel.

It was his aura, she decided. There was something about his aura that she felt the need to examine.

"Perhaps we should leave them to talk," Lady Crossbearer suggested.

Her father shot a scathing look at Mikel then grumbled his agreement, touching her cheek before he stormed out the door.

An awkward silence fell in his wake. Holly clasped her hands and looked to the shelves again, seeking to escape Mikel's disconcerting gaze.

"Are you sure you don't want to read them?" he offered.

She scanned the titles, so many books her father didn't approve of. "You realize that some people may consider a *Krieger der Nacht* collecting vampire literature to be in poor taste," she informed him.

Holly peeked at him out of the corner of her eye, watching his smile widen and a swallowed laugh make his Adam's apple bob.

"You don't," he stated confidently.

She felt her face heat in embarrassment. *It is said he cannot be lied to.* She didn't answer him.

"If you wish to read them—"

"I do," she admitted. Her father had never permitted her to read vampire books, especially those that were horror.

She peeked at him again, wondering at his choice

not to approach her. He had permission to pursue her. Why didn't he?

"Good. Then, please do."

"Why?" she asked, pulling out a book and staring at the cover intently, a vampire standing behind a woman holding a dagger.

"Perhaps we can discuss them. I would like to discuss them with you."

"No. I mean... Why did you ask for me?"

He didn't answer. Mikel seemed to consider her carefully.

"You don't know me," she insisted, unnerved by his silence. Why didn't he say something?

"Do you believe that?" The question seemed to cause him pain.

She wanted to scream an outraged "yes" at him, but she couldn't—again. The feeling that she knew him was too strong to ignore. Did he feel the same thing?

"We've never been formally introduced," he admitted, "but we have met."

"Have you come to Schmeidt?" she asked, searching her memories of visiting Warriors frantically for Mikel and coming to a blank wall.

"Never. With so few Crossbearers, there was never an opportunity for me to visit Europe."

"I've never been to America," she informed him. "So, we have not met."

He scowled. "You've been here. Your father simply never chose to tell you that you have, of course," he grumbled.

"Are you saying my father lied to me?" she demanded, furious at the insinuation.

"No. It was a convenient omission, one he no doubt

felt would never be necessary to rectify."

"A lie! My father does not lie, Mikel."

He bowed his head to her, his eyes hard. He didn't even have the sense to apologize.

"I can see we have nothing to discuss," she snapped, storming into the hall and slamming the office door behind her.

Holly rushed down the hallway toward the rooms Lady Crossbearer had pointed out to her, her heart hammering, expecting Mikel to stop her at any second. She looked back as she reached the doorway to her assigned rooms then stared in disbelief. He hadn't followed her?

She pushed inside the room, her hands trembling. Nothing Mikel did made sense to her.

* * * *

"Holly?" Patrick asked. "What's wrong?"

His daughter's gaze shot to his. She stiffened then relaxed with a sigh, crossing the room to hug him, pressing a book to his spine.

"You're trembling," he noted, biting back fury. "What is it? Did Mikel—"

"He didn't touch me," she snapped at him, burying her face in his chest.

He took a calming breath. "Then what?"

"I shouldn't have agreed. We should leave," she whispered miserably.

His head spun at her sudden changes of mood and decision. "Why *did* you agree?"

Holly shrugged. "He— Mikel confuses me. I don't...understand why...how..."

"Why are you shaking?"

"In anger, I assure you."

"What has he done?" *Prince or no, I will gut him if he's harmed her, if he's broken the rules of sanction in any way.*

She pushed away and started pacing the room, her arms crossed under her chest, the book flat against her stomach.

"Holly?" he prompted her.

"I have never *been* to America before," she grumbled.

Patrick winced. So, it had come to that.

"And he dared! Do you know he dared insinuate—"

"That you had and I'd lied," he managed, sick in the realization that, from some point of view, Mikel was telling her the truth, and Patrick had lied to her for her entire life. He'd had to lie to her. Telling her the truth had been too dangerous.

She stopped pacing, staring into space. Just when he would have prompted her again, she spoke softly. "No. He— Mikel claimed it was an omission you felt you wouldn't have to correct."

"How gracious of him," Patrick noted in annoyance. Couldn't Mikel fight him fairly? Couldn't he just call Patrick a liar and be done with it? Hating Mikel would be easier if he wasn't making excuses for his adversaries.

"But, you would never..." Holly stopped speaking abruptly as she turned to him. Her expression melted into a look of horror. "Dear gods! You didn't!"

"It was before you were born," he justified. "You were conceived during a visit—"

"Here?" She darkened at the thought.

Patrick ran a hand through his hair, nodding. "In this room, actually," he admitted.

Holly ambled to the bed, seemingly stunned. She sank to it, pressing the book to her chest. "Mikel— He said we met, but if that was my only visit..."

He rubbed the ache building in the base of his skull, grimacing at more than the pain. Why had he never told her? Because he'd feared she'd seek Mikel out in fascination? Damn the man!

"I don't understand," she pleaded.

"He knew you existed almost before I did—without even touching your mother. He knew you were female. He told us you were."

"And?" Her voice was tiny and uncertain.

"He claimed you as his own." Patrick fought the tension in his jaw at the memory of that moment, at the wild urge to kill a toddler for daring such a thing. "He had no right!"

"And so, you refused every request I made to visit America," she accused.

He nodded. "Yes. I did. I was afraid he would find a way to steal you away from me."

Holly glared at him. "You hid the truth from me," she informed him. "You lied to me...about myself." She was abruptly miserable. "Just as Mikel said you had."

"Holly," he pleaded.

"Go away. I don't want to see you right now."

"Holly—"

"I'm not saying I've decided to become Mikel's mate, but it seems I've misjudged him. I've done him a disservice, and I owe him an apology—as soon as I decide how best to do that."

She looked to the book in her hand, touching the

cover reverently. Patrick wanted to inquire what it was, but he left instead, fearing she'd rebuff him again.

* * * *

Holly looked up from her dinner, staring at the empty space at the Lord Crossbearer's left. She pushed her food around her plate, her stomach churning far too much to consider eating any of it.

"Where is Mikel?" she asked, expecting a cool response from the lord and lady for her appalling behavior.

Lady Crossbearer smiled. "He took dinner in his office tonight. He says he has work, but I suspect Mikel felt he was overwhelming you."

She nodded, though she knew the real reason he'd taken his meal in his office. She'd offended him and not had the good grace to apologize yet.

"Are you all right, Holly?" the lord asked.

"Fine," she lied. "I'm just not very hungry tonight."

"Jet lag?" the Lady asked. "It is a six-hour difference for you."

Holly managed a weak smile. "I suppose so. I think I'll retire, if you don't mind."

"Of course. A good night's sleep should set you right."

She left the table, avoiding her father's eyes when she knew he wanted to catch her attention. She wandered up the stairs, pausing at the top. Her room beckoned, a safe haven from what she knew she *should* do. It would be so easy to go there and hide from her embarrassment.

Except, I'll feel guilty until I offer the apology Mikel is due. Holly sighed and turned right instead of left. She took a deep breath and knocked on his door.

"Come in, Holly."

She winced, opening the door and entering without meeting his eyes. He didn't speak. After a long moment of silence, she chanced a look at him.

Mikel stared at her, his expression unreadable. He twirled a pen between his fingers and leaned back in his chair. "Do we have something to discuss?" he asked evenly.

Holly felt her cheeks heat. He was taunting her with her own angry words. "I owe you an apology."

"You don't," he assured her.

She faltered. "I do. You were right. I asked my father directly. He never told me. I'm sorry that I—"

"You don't need to be."

"What?" Why did nothing about Mikel make sense?

He dropped the pen on the desk, laying his hands on the arms of his chair. "You defended what you'd always been told was true. There's nothing to be sorry for. Of course, you assumed I was the one who was lying. You had no reason to believe me.

"I learned long ago that knowing something doesn't mean you should say it. Sometimes, I forget myself and speak without considering the consequences on those around me."

"Like you did when you pronounced I was yours all those years ago?"

He scowled, his face pinking slightly. His aura muddied a bit but with an indeterminate color that told her nothing of his feelings. "I was a toddler," he explained. "I hadn't reasoned what your father would make of my pronouncement."

"But, you still believe it." She didn't question it.

"Yes. I do. More than ever."

"Why me?"

"Why did you stay when you came prepared to blast me out of the water and leave?"

She gasped. "How could you know that?"

"Do your shimmers—your auras tell you anything?" he countered.

"Sometimes." But not nearly as much as she'd like with Mikel. She ambled to the sofa and sat. "Little things. Mainly the emotional state of the subject." She met his eyes. "I have heard..."

He raised an eyebrow. "What have you heard?"

"I have heard your auras tell you much more."

Mikel smiled. "Yes. They do."

"I have heard you cannot be lied to."

"Also true."

"And...that you see inside people's souls?"

"Ahhh. An excellent story. Would that it were so, but there are limits. Ethics are situational. Even I cannot foresee what might come. I am not a precognitive, after all. Shimmers tell a moment in time and a general state of being. They cannot tell me more than that."

"What does my aura tell you?"

"The blue base tells me you are a human sensitive. Your identifiers tell me that you are headstrong, inquisitive, more relaxed than when you walked through the door..."

"And?"

"My mate," he offered simply. "If you choose to be."

Holly swallowed hard. "You don't know me," she protested. *I don't know you!*

"I intend to get to know you."

Her heart started pounding, the more carnal ways a Warrior could use to get to know a woman settling in her mind. Overall, it wasn't an unpleasant montage of images, though it was an exceedingly disconcerting experience.

"Not until you're ready for an intimate relationship," he vowed.

"And, if I never am?" Meeting his gaze suddenly seemed difficult.

He smiled, his eyes glittering in amusement that turned his aura a vivid rose.

She forced a breath, well aware that he knew precisely what she'd been thinking moments earlier. "Why did you skip dinner? Were you angry with me?" she asked, seeking to change the subject.

"No. I wasn't angry with you. I knew you weren't ready to spend time with me yet." He sighed. "Forcing my company on you won't win your trust, Holly. You have to want to get to know me."

That is why he doesn't approach. "I would like to get to know you, Mikel." At least, she might discover why she found it hard to refuse him.

"That is the truth," he said in something resembling amazement. "Very well. May I make a suggestion?"

She motioned for him to continue. "Please."

"Read the book you borrowed and join me for a picnic lunch tomorrow. We'll discuss vampire literature—and perhaps ourselves."

"Agreed."

"Perhaps you would care to read more of my books, and we can meet to discuss them, if you care for my company."

Holly nodded, her heart beating fast in anticipation. "Well...I suppose I should read the book." She stood, smoothing her skirt and preparing to return to her rooms.

His smile dimmed somewhat, making her wonder if he was saddened by her departure. That seemed unlikely. How could she affect him so markedly in so short a time?

"Sleep well, Holly." His tone implied that he wished she'd sleep well in his arms.

She turned abruptly, heading for the door in a mixture of desire and confusion. "Until tomorrow, Mikel."

* * * *

Holly paused in her reading, placing the book on the bed beside her. She took a calming breath, the vision of the last paragraph burned into her mind. If all vampire books were like this one, it was no wonder her father had never let her read them. The simmering sensuality left her in a marked state of arousal.

Her stomach grumbled, reminding her of another need she'd been denying. She should have eaten dinner. Now she was uncertain whether she should go hungry or risk appearing a poor houseguest by raiding the kitchen when she hadn't been given leave to do so.

A knock came at the door.

"Come in," she announced automatically, half-expecting her father, bearing some gift in apology for the argument they'd had earlier.

Whoever it was didn't comply. She furrowed her

brow, her senses telling her that someone stood outside the door but not who without a direct line of sight.

"Come in," she repeated.

Still, the person neither answered nor entered.

Holly pushed from the bed, straightening her robe and heading to the door. She hesitated as the person moved. He stopped in response, just after she did. She gasped.

Mikel! It had to be Mikel. The only other person capable of this was the Lady Crossbearer, and Holly felt certain she wouldn't play such games.

For a moment, neither of them moved. Holly took a step, and Mikel mirrored her move. She rushed toward the door, determined to learn what his game was, grumbling an oath as he loped away. She wrenched the door open and looked toward his office.

Mikel stood two doors further down the hall, leaning against the frame as if in repose. His aura told another tale. It was the lavender she'd noticed first but ringed with the muddy red halo that indicated uncertainty. She stared at that, trying to discern why he would feel this way.

He motioned toward his feet, and she looked down.

There was a tray of food set against the wall. Holly stared at it in disbelief then looked to Mikel, intent on questioning him. He was gone, most likely into the door he'd been leaning against moments before.

She picked up the tray and carried it inside, her mouth watering. Mikel had made her a sandwich with a side of sliced fresh fruit, a salad, and potato salad. Glasses of milk and apple juice rounded out the meal, and a single orchid, most likely from the greenhouse

out back, graced a vase, adding just a touch of beauty
to the arrangement.

Holly stilled as she set the tray on the desk against
the far wall, a flash of color beneath the white linen
napkin catching her eye. She pulled the folded piece of
paper free and opened it. She read it twice, finally
pressing it to her chest, the words circling in her mind
until she felt dizzy.

My home is yours. Mikel

Chapter Thirty-one

October 3, 2048

Mikel smiled, remembering the sweet torture of watching the arousal color Holly's shimmer as she'd read the night before. He could have closed himself off to the experience, but there was something addictive in seeing her responses to what she read.

He knew the book she chose intimately, of course. For a split-second, he'd almost suggested she choose another. He was glad that he hadn't.

"No, not every vampire book is so sensual," he assured her. "You simply chose one that was."

Her shimmer flickered with lights of forest green and peach, noting a hunger for more. He closed his eyes, the need to steer her toward more of the same beating at him.

How long could he stand it? Not touching her was likely to drive him insane, especially knowing she possessed a fiercely-sexual nature, but experiencing her pleasure, even in this vicarious manner, was too enjoyable to pass up.

She moved away slightly, shifting her legs under her, deep in thought, according to the Navy blue flecks in her shimmer. "With literature such as that, it's no wonder a few women have refused the amulet and allowed themselves to be used again."

He opened his eyes, raising an eyebrow in surprise. "I wouldn't blame the books. I'm certain some beasts are practiced at making the experience pleasurable."

She scrunched up her nose in disgust. "Still, the idea of a beast retaining his kind emotions," she scoffed.

"Yes. I agree." *Though Erin swears Veriel did, it is wholly unbelievable.* "Have you noticed how many other facts the author got right, though?" The book had always been one of his favorites for that reason, and more than once this afternoon, he'd wondered if she chose it, because Holly felt his energies in it more strongly than the others.

"Yes. I did notice that. It was rather disconcerting," she admitted. "Do you think she's met a protected?"

"It's possible but unlikely. Our protected don't typically compromise us; fear of losing protection is a powerful thing, after all. No. With that storyline, the beast with kind emotions, it's more likely that the author's information came either from a beast or a willing human donor."

"Yes. I suppose so." She looked to the stream, lost in thought.

Mikel studied her profile, aching to run his fingertip along her lips. She was beautiful, and she would be his—if he let her come to him and didn't pressure her for more than she was willing to give.

"Do you believe someone can know his soulmate immediately?" she asked.

He stared at her, stunned that Holly had chosen that plot point to discuss with him so soon. "Yes. I do." *I have.*

She turned to him, her expression earnest. "Is that what it's like for you?"

"Very much," he admitted. Much more than he'd like to admit sometimes, but he was not a beast, and he wouldn't resort to that. Though it might work as it had in the first story in the book, it could just as easily backfire as it had in the second. That was another reason he read that book often, as a cautionary tale to himself.

"Is it..."

He smiled at her hesitancy. "Yes?"

Her cheeks darkened to deep rose. "Is it difficult for you?"

He pretended not to understand what she was asking. "Difficult? Getting to know you is wonderful." At least, he hadn't lied.

"No. I mean... You never touch me. Is it difficult not to? If you are so certain—"

"Yes. It's hard not to, but I am not a beast. I vowed not to touch you until you were ready to be touched."

Holly lay back on the blanket and stared at the clouds. His gaze fastened on the lush lines of her chest beneath the Hunter green dress she'd worn for their picnic. Mikel dragged his gaze away, taking another calming breath.

"Is that what this is?" she asked suddenly.

"What would that be?" he asked.

"This strange reluctance I have to leaving you."

He stared at her, heartened that she admitted what she felt so easily.

"This sense of comfort in your company. This—" She met his eyes, running her fingertips over his knee.

Mikel shivered, his cock rising at her invitation. "You're asking me to touch you?" he managed.

Holly smiled smugly. "If what you believe is true, shouldn't I feel it if you do?" she challenged.

He stretched out beside her, leaning up on his elbow so that he looked down on her. "It's more than that," he informed her. "You want me to kiss you."

She nodded, her eyes locked with his, breathless. "Yes."

"Yes."

Mikel planted his hand beside her head, lowering his face until his lips were brushing hers, intent on a long, slow seduction. She sighed, closing her lips on his lower lip, then his upper.

"More?" he rasped, holding himself in rigid control.

"Yes," she pleaded in a whisper, her eyes closing.

He kissed her more purposefully, his tongue flicking at her lips then delving inside when she parted them. The fire of their mixed shimmers shot up around them, drowning out his sense of the world outside of its borders. All that existed was Holly: her sweet scent, her soft skin, the sighs and moans that escaped her lips from kiss to kiss, the curves of her body pressed hard to his—

Mikel stilled, forcing his mind to function when it had no intention of doing so. He was over her fully, his cock cradled at the apex of her thighs, his hands fisted in her curls.

Holly opened her eyes, slumberous eyes that begged for more, that begged for him to push her dress up and take her as the beast had taken his soulmate outside her father's gardens in the book she'd read.

I am not a beast.

He eased off of her, smoothing her hair and laying a solemn kiss on her swollen lips.

She grasped at his shirt, her eyes wide in confusion. "Mikel—"

"Not this way," he managed. "When we do this, I'll know you want it. You won't regret it, and I won't take advantage."

"I don't..."

"We should go back to the house."

Chapter Thirty-two

October 10, 2048

Holly tossed the book she was reading to the foot of the bed, moving restlessly. What was the point of reading when she couldn't even concentrate on the print?

It seemed Mikel was trying to drive her insane. In the week since their first picnic, they'd discussed a book a day—and shared heated loveplay. That very afternoon, she'd found herself laid over his desk, dragging her skirts up to facilitate his possession, his mouth ravenous against hers, his hand teasing at her breast through the bodice of her gown. And still he'd stopped, proclaiming that their first time wouldn't pass that way.

Every step seemed dependant on her to make the first move. She saw Mikel at meals, but after them, he would leave her with a bow of his head if she didn't follow and pursue more time with him. Other than that, he stayed to his private spaces almost exclusively—never approaching her own, only coming to her if he'd asked for her company previously and meeting her in a common area of the house. While she was always welcome to enter his domain, he never ventured to her, never approached her personal space without an invitation to do so.

She couldn't stand the waiting anymore. If he didn't make love to her tonight, she would leave and not look back.

Holly let herself out into the hall and strode to the door Mikel had disappeared through when he'd left the tray for her, hoping it was his bedroom. She hesitated long enough to assure herself that someone was inside the room and wished again that she could see her auras through obstacles as Lady Crossbearer and Mikel could.

Should she knock? Holly decided against it and pushed the door open, entering and closing herself in. She didn't look up immediately, half-afraid that she'd intruded on the lord and lady's rooms.

"You wish to see me, Holly?" Mikel asked calmly, as if he'd expected her to walk into his room.

She bit back a laugh. He probably had expected it. This was the same man who'd brought her a meal when she was hungry, when he'd been nowhere near her to see her discomfort with his own eyes.

She glanced up at him, her smile disappearing.

He sat up in bed, nude and semi-erect. Mikel made no move to cover himself. He seemed completely at ease with his nudity, completely comfortable with her bold perusal of him.

"Holly?" he reminded her.

She untied her robe and eased it off, letting it fall to the floor around her ankles. Mikel sucked in his breath and his muscles tensed, but he offered no comment. His cock hardened, coming to rest against the flat plane below his navel. Encouraged, Holly pushed the straps of her nightgown off of her shoulders and let the silky material slide to the floor, watching it pool around her feet. She'd chosen what to wear carefully, the most alluring gown she owned with no underclothes beneath.

There was no movement or sound from the bed. She stepped out of the nightgown, chancing a look at him, half-afraid he'd turn her away again.

His gaze followed the line of her body from feet to face, slowly, hungrily. "You're coming to me willingly?" he asked. "You're willing to—consider at least, being my mate?"

"Yes. I am." Holly didn't give him a chance to dismiss her simply. She walked to the bed, sinking to the edge of the mattress with her legs folded under her.

Mikel wrapped his hands around her waist and drew her across his body until her head lay pillowed on his opposite shoulder and his arm supported her back. His breathing hitched, and he closed his eyes as if seeking control—or praying.

His mouth closed on hers, not in the mindless passion they'd shared for the last week but in patient exploration. His hands roamed her body, mapping every curve until she felt faint in anticipation. When she arched to him for more, his movements became more purposeful though no more hurried, teasing her breasts to aching points then her clit. She was moaning into his mouth, wet and aching, before he eased her to the bed and rolled her to her side against his chest.

"You came to me," he breathed in something resembling awe, as if it was significant that she'd pursued this step with him. "You want me."

Holly nodded, tracing the blood mark over his ribs. How could he question that she'd want him? This was Mikel of Crossbearer, a *König* prince. He was powerful—both as a sensitive/psychic and as a *Krieger der Nacht*. He'd killed the final elder, Lorian, at only four years of age. He was handsome, intelligent, thoughtful, had a wonderful sense of humor—"

"And?" he asked, nearly begged of her.

"I love you," she breathed.

Mikel groaned. He recited a verse in the ancient language of the Stone.

She furrowed her brow in confusion at that.

"You are my life," he translated. "I would shed my blood or give my life for you without thought of my duty to do so."

Holly gasped in surprise. "The ancient joining ceremony."

There was no mistaking those words. She'd always thought they were beautiful, a wonderful testament to the commitment a Warrior had for his sealed mate. If Mikel made this vow to her, he must be very close to *Endspiel* and serious about printing. Considering that, it was amazing that he'd been able to refuse her this long.

He nodded. "Will you be mine?"

She leaned her head down, planting her lips over his blood mark. Mikel groaned again, his hands grasping handfuls of her hair lightly.

"Make me yours, Mikel. I will be bound." It was a huge step, one that could never be undone. Still, Holly didn't question that it was the right choice.

He guided her mouth back to his, his kiss less restrained. "You will never regret this," he promised.

"I know." If he sealed to her, he would be unable to cause her discomfort without reason to do so. Even then, her displeasure would be acutely uncomfortable for him.

They seemed to leave their slow exploration behind in a heartbeat. Her body ached and burned for him. She arched her back, laboring for breath as Mikel trailed his mouth from her lips, down her throat, and to her breasts, licking and sucking at her.

Holly moaned, awash in the intensity of the sensations. She'd felt his hands there several times, but his mouth was a thousand times better, much more so than she'd anticipated. Her core was more than ready, throbbing in a cadence she wanted him to match. Mikel would find that rhythm. She knew he would. She grasped at his shoulders, tugging him over her, begging silently for him to end the torment she'd been in for the previous week.

His body covered hers, turning her beneath him as he rose up over her and captured her mouth in a near bruising kiss. She spread for him, gasping as his cock brushed against her aching center.

Mikel pulled back slightly, panting, trembling, seemingly at the edges of restraint. "Are you sure? I can be slow."

She nodded frantically. If he made her wait much longer, she'd surely cry for wanting more.

He thrust into her, his ragged cry mixing with her scream of pleasure. There was discomfort, but it only seemed to give the pleasure a keener edge. He remained motionless, while her body adjusted to his length filling her, stretching her, and making the ache for him increase. The throbbing returned, more urgent and insistent.

"Oh, yes," he breathed, his eyes glazed in need.

His hips rolled smoothly, cycling faster and faster until they matched the cadence her body set. Holly rose to meet him, whimpering and panting in her rapid rise.

Mikel murmured endearments, oaths to several of

the ancient gods, and finally, "You are mine."

Her body was abruptly swamped in waves of delight that she suspected he'd seen coming before she had. Mikel thrust deep, his body pistoning in hers as his seed pulsed into her, caressing her with his heat. Her sharp cry of surprise was swallowed by his roar of climax, in the claiming of a mate.

His lavender aura blazed up around them, turning flame blue then settling on a bright gold. Holly raised her hand, looking at the precious metallic glow in awe. She sought out Mikel's eyes, struggling for words.

"You are a *König* now," he soothed her.

She nodded solemnly. She'd asked to be his, but she'd never expected so outward a sign of it.

He met her lips, a heated exchange that soon spiraled out of control. Holly smiled as his erection came to life within her again.

"What is it?" he asked, a lazy smile curving his lips.

"If we continue this way, my father won't have to be told that I've accepted you."

Mikel chuckled. "Your scream when I entered you has announced that clearly, and my cry at the seal alerted the entire household." He blushed, pressing deep into her and groaning in response. "I could apologize, but I refuse to apologize that our first time was so enjoyable."

She arched against him. "Hmmm... Perhaps, we should change rooms," she suggested.

He scowled, looking around at his room critically. "There's something wrong with my room?" he asked, seemingly concerned at the thought. "Granted, it needs your touch, but..."

Holly nipped at his chin, forcing his attention back

to her. "A silly wish," she whispered.

"What wish? I would give you almost anything. You know that." His fingers laced through hers, and his hips slid slowly against her, pushing them both toward another release.

"My father said I was conceived here—in the room you assigned me to." She felt her cheeks heat as he looked up with a purely male smile of satisfaction. "Yes. I figured out that must have been your doing nearly the moment he told me what the room's significance was."

Mikel chuckled. "If you wish to make love there, we will, but I know something your father overlooked."

"What's that?" she asked.

"You were conceived in that room, but you were conceived in this bed. I claimed it as my own long ago."

"As you claimed me." Somehow, that seemed appropriate.

He raised an eyebrow at that, and she nodded in understanding. She'd had the choice to be here or not.

"And I came to you," she finished aloud.

"Yes. You did."

The End

The Stone Alphabet

꒰ Ani (birth/the mother)- Regana first Lady Kreuzträger, Jayde Marie Albright

ρ Baroo (thunder)- Olbrecht first Lord Kaufmann

ʃ Dobler (twin peace-bringer)- Ditrich first Lord Jäger

ϱ Fih (twin war)- Geldric/the beast Cerran, Cody König-Armen

ᔆ Geil (iron)- Bryon König-Kaufmann

ᘏ Hir (the cool wood)- Gerhardus first Lord Landwirt

ჳ Iol (immovable ice)- Redulf/the beast Carstol

ʃ Jee (justice)- Mikel of Crossbearer-König and all descendants thereof

ρ Kor (the bear)- Corwyn of König-Maher

ᔨ Len (mountain)- Wilhelmus first Lord Maher

ᔔ Mul (flowing water)- Mitchell König-Farmer

ᓏ Nul (stealth of the night)- Bertolf/the beast Draden

ᔕ Ori (the sun)- Pauwel first Lord Kreuzträger, Hunter Lord Crossbearer-König

ᘺ Pol (the horse)- Dado/the beast Lorian

ᴓ Reg (intensity of the fire)- Jörg/the beast Veriel

Syth (the Stone lord)- Master Trainer Sibold, Gawen first Lord
Schwertträger, Etienne Lord Kaufmann, Joseph Lord Armen,
Carrick Lord Armen, Corwyn Lord Hunter, Lewis of Maher

Tes (stars and moon)- Kevin König-Smith

Vin (wind)- Cunczel first Lord Schmied

Wul (the wolf)- Tilbrand/the beast Resten

Zel (ending/death)- Erin of Crossbearer-König, Kaitlyn "Katie"
of König-Maher, Skye of König-Armen, Victorious Ellen
"Vick/Vicky" of König-Smith, Margaret Elizabeth "Maggie"
König-Farmer, Colette "Lettie" Kong-Kaufmann

About the Author

Brenna Lyons wears many hats, sometimes all on the same day: former president of EPIC, author of more than 100 published works, owner of Fireborn Publishing, columnist, special needs teacher, wife, mother...and member in good standing of more than 60 writing advocacy groups.

In her first ten years published in novel-length, she's won 3 EPIC e-Book Awards (out of 15 finalists) and finaled for 3 PEARLS (including one Honorable Mention, second to NY Times Bestseller Angela Knight), 2 CAPAS, and a Dream Realm Award. She's also taken Spinetingler's Book of the Year for 2007.

Brenna writes in 26 established worlds plus stand-alones, poetry, articles and essays. She's a bestseller in indie/e fantasy and horror, straight genre and cross-genres thereof. Brenna has been termed "one of the most deviant erotic minds in the publishing world...not for the weak." (Rachelle for Fallen Angels Reviews) Milieu-heavy dark work is practically Brenna's calling card, with or without the erotic content.

She teaches classes in everything from POV studies to advanced editing, networking to marketing. Brenna enjoys hearing from people who read her work and can be reached by e-mail.

Website: http://www.brennalyons.com/

Facebook: http://www.facebook.com/brenna.lyons

Email: brennalyons4168@live.com

Also by this Author

Available from *Fireborn Publishing*

KEIF'S DEN AND PACK
Keif's Pack
Mother of the Keif
Keif's Den (Coming Soon)

PROPHECY
Prophecy: Revelations
Prophecy: Rapture
The Prophet's Mate
Prophecy: Rampage - Meet Gavin
Prophecy: Rampage (Coming Soon)

THE FANTASY CLUB
The Consort

Beyond the Veil
Fairy Wishes (Coming Soon)
Mine for the Night
Once in a Blue Moon
Overtime Pay
Stay With Me
The Fire God's Woman
The Punishment of Phoebus Apollo
Werewolf U

Available from *Phaze Books*

ANGEL-WING SAGA
Sons of Heaven: Beldon
Daughters of Man: Prize Match
Sons of Heaven: Unexpected Mates
Daughters of Man: Claiming a Princess

STAR MAGES
The Master's Lover

XXAN WAR
Daahan Rising
Crossbred Son
Raashh Decisions

Enslaved
All I Want for Christmas is You
Fates Magic
All's Fair...
Black Sail
Mama's Tales
Dream Walk
Unexpected Daddy
Phaze in Verse
We Shall Live Again
May the Best Man Win
Nevermore
Marked
And It Was Good

Available from ***Mundania Press***

STAR MAGES
Written in the Stars

Fairy Dreams
Monsters of Myth Anthology

Available from ***Under the Moon***

RENEGADES SERIES
TYGERS
Renegade's Run
Max Sec

URBAN GRIMM
Catch Me, If You Can
Three Wishes
Temptation of Eve

With Great Power
Undead in Blue
Evil Overlords Union Issue #1 Anthology
Undead Embrace
"*Playing Games*" in *Forbidden Love: Bad Boys*
"*Marked*" in *Forbidden Love: Wicked Women*
"*The Master's Lover*" in *Forbidden Love: Sacred Bands*

Available from **Logical Lust**

"*Mine for the Night*" in *The Cougar Book* Anthology

Available from **Coming Together Charity Anthologies**

INSTINCT SERIES
"*Foundling*" in *Coming Together: Into the Light* Anthology

"*Claim Mate*" (available separately and as part of the *Coming Together: Against the Odds* Anthology)
"*The Fire God's Woman*" in *Coming Together: Under Fire* Anthology

Available **self-published**

KEGIN SERIES
Earth-Born Lord
Graham: Training the Earth-Born Lord

NIGHT WARRIORS
Claiming a Lady

Stone Lord
Mother's Son

COLOR OF LOVE
A Safe Heart

Snapshots from a Poet's Life

Award-Winning Books

EPPIE/EPIC eBOOK AWARDS WINNERS
Coming Together: Against the Odds- 2010
Time Currents- 2010
Coming Together: Into the Light- 2011

EPPIE/EPIC eBOOK AWARDS FINALISTS
Fion's Daughter- 2004
Collected Poems: Book One- 2005 (now titled *Snapshots of a Poet's Life*)
Renegade's Run- 2005
Rites of Mating- 2006
All I Want for Christmas- 2006
Phaze in Verse- 2008
"The Fire God's Woman" in *Coming Together: Under Fire*- 2009
Three Wishes- 2010
Matchmaker's Misery- 2010
The Cougar Book- 2011
The Master's Lover- 2011
Bride Ball- 2011

DREAM REALM AWARDS FINALIST
Last Chance for Love- 2003

PEARL HONORABLE MENTION
Night Warriors- 2004

PEARL FINALISTS
Schente Night- 2003 (now included in *The Last of Fion's Daughters*)
König Cursebreakers- 2004 (now titled *Will of the Stone*)

JOYFULLY REVIEWED BEST BOOKS OF 2010
Written in the Stars- 2010

SPINETINGLER'S BOOK OF THE YEAR 2007
NOBODY: An Anthology of Dark Fiction- 2007 (Brenna's pieces of the anthology can be found in *Beyond the Veil*)

TRS's CAPA FINALISTS
Ultimate Warriors- 2004 (Brenna's portion is now available as
With Great Power)
Written in the Stars

LOVE ROMANCE AND MORE CAFÉ BOOK OF THE YEAR
RUNNER UP
Last Chance for Love- 2008

ROAD TO ROMANCE REVIEWERS' CHOICE AWARD
Prophecy: Revelations- 2004

LOVE ROMANCES REVIEWERS' CHOICE AWARD
Black Sail- 2003

ROMANCE JUNKIES BOOK CLUB STAFF PICK
TYGERS- 2003

FALLEN ANGELS ROMANCE RECOMMENDED READ
Devon's Price-2005 (now available in *Bearing Armen*)

JOYFULLY RECOMMENDED READ
Fairy Dreams- 2008
The Last of Fion's Daughters- 2009

TREBLE HEART FINALIST
Prophecy: Revelations- 2003

www.ingramcontent.com/pod-product-compliance
Lightning Source LLC
Chambersburg PA
CBHW030923020726
47498CB00001B/93